The labor... provided everything needed by the technicians. Twenty armed men from Espinosa's Oaxaca drug organization provided security. They kept a careful watch for any strangers arriving at the fishing village or the larger village of Juchitan, twelve miles away. The foreign bomb experts grumbled about the isolation but methodically worked at their tasks, encouraged by the very large bonuses payable upon completion of the checkout and repackaging of the bombs. Unfortunately for them, it was a bonus they would not collect. The plan was too important to risk any leaks; they would never leave the hacienda.

The reconfiguration of the bombs was technically simple—coupling a small programmed digital timer and semtex explosive triggering device to the bomb. The more difficult problem was to size the bombs as small as possible to fit inside innocuous containers like briefcases and packages wrapped in brown paper, stamped, addressed, and ready to be mailed. A hydro-electric plant, the central terminal of an airport, two government buildings, and an open-air marketplace were the targets for five of the bombs. Navarro allowed only the most experienced bomb technician to work on the sixth bomb: it would be reconfigured to fit within the false bottom of a cylindrical steel container—a container with radioactive warning labels attached....

REVENGE IN EXILE

Scot McCauley

LEISURE BOOKS NEW YORK CITY

A LEISURE BOOK®

October 2005

Published by

Dorchester Publishing Co., Inc.
200 Madison Avenue
New York, NY 10016

ISBN 0-8439-5630-5

The name "Leisure Books" and the stylized "L" with design are trademarks of Dorchester Publishing Co., Inc.

Printed in the United States of America.

Visit us on the web at www.dorchesterpub.com.

*First and foremost, I cannot fully express
my gratitude to my agent, Cynthia Manson, who
refused to cast me adrift and encouraged me
with her unending support.*

*My gratitude also to the many shipmates,
in and out of uniform, who provided excellent
guidance and expertise.*

*And finally, my wife, Mary Ann,
and my family, who never wavered in their
inspiration and encouragement.*

REVENGE
IN EXILE

CHAPTER 1

Washington, D.C.

Darkness had given way to a hazy sunrise when the rented gray Ford sedan parked in one of the empty Treasury Department official visitor spaces. The large man behind the wheel sat motionless. Every few minutes he scanned the underground garage for anything unusual. He had repeated the same routine for the past four mornings and did not expect any surprises.

José Chapa Cordero had spent several hours each day walking around the long blocks surrounding the Treasury Building, looking like any other tourist. He had switched hotels three times during his six-day stay to minimize the risk that someone might remember him, using credit cards with different names to register at the Ritz-Carlton in Pentagon City, the L'Enfant Plaza, and the Jefferson.

Chapa squinted at his watch. He thought about lighting a cigarette, then decided that there wasn't enough time. During previous visits, he had confirmed that a single parking attendant was on duty at the parking entrance only between the hours of 7:00 A.M. and 7:00 P.M. It was now twelve minutes after six; the attendant was unlikely to arrive until at least 6:45. Chapa pushed the seat back, lowered the windows, and stared ahead, calmly waiting.

Within minutes, a 1994 white Volvo would park in the reserved P-2 parking slot directly across from the elevator. Retired Brigadier General Peter Swanson, the recently appointed U.S. Drug Czar, routinely arrived an hour or so before his staff. Chapa checked his watch again. It was time. He eased out of the car and walked to the garage elevator that connected the basement to the eight levels of the Treasury Building. He wore a dark raincoat over a suit and dark red tie, and carried a scuffed black attaché case. Other than the ever-present sunglasses, he looked the part of any government employee going to work early.

Chapa opened the elevator and stepped inside. The door automatically closed. He secured the HOLD button with a four-inch piece of duct tape. It was only a few minutes before he heard the distinctive sound of the worn muffler on Swanson's car. He opened his attaché case, withdrew an automatic pistol with a long silencer on it, and then removed his sunglasses. When the general pushed the elevator's call button, the door opened, and he stepped inside. In the fleeting moment before he fired, Chapa could see from Swanson's eyes that he knew he was going to die. A single round penetrated the general's forehead and smashed through his skull, spattering part of his brains over the now closed elevator doors. Swanson did not fall but slid down the side of the elevator car into a grotesque sitting position in one corner. Just to make sure, Chapa felt for a pulse in the man's neck; but it was clear that a second round was unnecessary.

Chapa removed the tape over the HOLD button, picked up the spent 9-mm shell casing, and punched the OPEN button.

He pressed the Ruger P-89 close to his side as the elevator doors opened. After quickly scanning the garage, he reached inside the elevator and hit the button for the sixth floor. The doors closed and the elevator started its ascent, carrying its gruesome burden.

Standing at an outdoor public phone directly across from the FBI Building, Chapa used a phone card to direct dial an Ensenada cellular number. Javier Navarro was expecting the call. He got up from the breakfast table, and walked outside.

"The business is completed."

"Thank you. Did the negotiations go smoothly?"

"There were no unexpected problems."

"I am pleased. When will I see you?"

"If you don't have anything more, I'll leave now."

"No, nothing else."

Navarro returned to the breakfast table and refilled his coffee cup before retracing his steps to the outside patio. He had no misgivings about killing the American who headed their so-called War on Drugs. It was a necessary signal that the drug cartel would not tolerate any interference, especially from the prying do-gooders across the border. Navarro understood what he needed to do to maintain his leadership of the drug cartel that he carefully put together in the early 1980s. He knew that some of the drug lords would question the action taken but he did not care. They were weak and spoiled from the fortune gained from his direction of the cartel. Over the past five years, he had doubled revenues and expected the drug lords to do what they were told.

Navarro did not like or need them. He thought of them as arrogant children who made stupid mistakes. Once again, they were making noise about the recent stepped-up government pressure on drug trafficking. They spent hundreds of millions of dollars at Navarro's direction to buy protection and political influence; they wanted the pressure to stop.

"The business with Swanson will shut them up," Navarro thought. "All I need to do is to keep the greedy bastards happy and rich until I finish expanding internationally. Then I will deal with them."

CHAPTER 2

Estoril, Portugal

The former president of Mexico spent most of each day on the patio even though his villa boasted a 9,000 square foot main house, several small detached guesthouses, and a three-room pool house. Standing on the rugged cliffs overhanging the Estoril Riviera, the villa was surrounded by a lushly landscaped garden with lemon and orange trees. The fronds of tall palms shaded the main house and rustled in the gentle morning breeze.

Long before its rental by Victor Hidalgo, the villa and adjacent properties had been summer retreats for Portuguese royalty. The rooms were large, airy, and comfortable, with dark maroon terra-cotta floors and green wood shutters that kept the interior shaded and cool.

It was a comfortable setting for someone who was an exile from his own country. He wasn't in some remote place, cut off from the rest of the world; Madrid, Nice, and Genoa were within easy reach. More important, the Portuguese government provided the former president both security and anonymity. But in the early part of his five years in Portugal, Hidalgo had derived little pleasure from his surroundings. His life had been turned upside down when he left Mexico City in disgrace—stripped of the coveted traditional party leadership accorded a former president. When his young wife died unexpectedly from what the doctors termed a cerebral hemorrhage a few months after they arrived in Portugal, he had actually considered committing suicide. Only his anger and his pride made him reject such thoughts—and begin planning his return to Mexico.

Hidalgo was just over six feet tall and, at fifty-six, looked considerably younger than his age, though his hair was beginning to turn gray. A large but not unattractive, hawk-like nose was complemented by pale blue-green eyes, eyes that missed little.

He was looking out over the sea when he heard footsteps behind him. Ramiro Chemor walked across the patio, smiling and carrying an airline duty-free bag. He was ten years younger than Hidalgo and considerably shorter. With his wavy black hair, soft brown eyes, and darker complexion he looked more typically Mexican—and more Indio than *blanco*. He had served in Hidalgo's cabinet, and remained one of his closest and most trusted friends.

"I figured that I would find you out here, sir."

"Ah, Ramiro I am so happy to see you." He hugged his colleague in a brief *abrazo*, and then motioned him to sit down in one of the wicker chairs arranged around a large table with a glass top.

"A small offering *por la casa*," Chemor announced, extracting a bottle of Delamain cognac from the bag and setting it on the table. It was Hidalgo's favorite and he appreciated the gesture.

"We will sample some of this tonight," Hidalgo said, then fell silent for several moments.

"On days like this, I remember how it used to be and how much we could have accomplished if . . ."

"And we can still do it. But, I apologize for being late. I flew in just when the sun was going down and decided not to face those hairpin turns on the road up here until morning."

"You made the right decision; no apologies necessary. I called the airlines and they informed me that your plane was late. Now tell me, what is happening?"

"The situation is deteriorating . . ."

"But of course! What can one expect? We could have dealt with the trade deficit—not yielded to U.S. and European devaluation pressures."

"That is all past. We need to . . ."

Hidalgo ignored Chemor, got out of his chair, and started pacing up and down the patio, waving his arms in a gesture of anger and frustration. "All Posadas had to do was to demonstrate leadership, support the peso. How could he be so weak . . . then act surprised when foreign investment collapsed? And I am the fool responsible for putting him in office."

Hidalgo turned away and looked down at the villas on the coastline with the azure Mediterranean below. When he successfully negotiated an equal partner status for Mexico in the North American Free Trade Agreement (NAFTA), he had been hailed at home and abroad as one of the great men of the twentieth century.

"How did it happen?" He stopped pacing and stared at Chemor with a baffled expression. He had negotiated a White House pledge to support the peso—and counted on it to reassure major investors and financial institutions abroad. *What made the White House renege and start the tragic downhill spiral for Mexico and him personally?* After years of anguish trying to understand what had happened, he knew the answer. He had been the victim of a conspiracy to drive him out of Mexico.

7

Everything had unraveled so quickly. Following the peso collapse, charges of corruption—particularly accusations of drug trafficking by his brother, Francisco—unleashed the fury of the nation against the formerly popular president. The final blow came when his anointed successor, Jorge Posadas, turned against him. He blamed Hidalgo for the devastating peso crisis and subsequent recession. Hidalgo had expected once his term was over, to play a leading role in the long ruling Institutional Revolutionary Party (PRI) and ensure that the many programs he had successfully implemented would continue. Instead he had been effectively driven from his native country and forced to watch his legacy discredited.

As Chemor listened to Hidalgo, he began to fear that the former president was going down the same road that triggered crushing bouts of depression.

"Sir, you and I know what happened. We can't control the past . . . but we can change things if we focus on the months ahead."

Hidalgo, deep in thought, frowned, and then suddenly smiled. "You are right of course. We need to forget the past and move forward."

Three weeks earlier Victor Hidalgo had surprised his fellow citizens, and those across the border, by announcing that he would return to Mexico City. The news—less than a year before national elections—caused an immediate tide of public opinion turning in his favor. In the rush for the story behind Hildalgo's decision, he was prepared for the expected hard questions.

"How do you intend to handle the constitutional restriction against a former president seeking office—if you decide to run for president?"

"You are jumping ahead," Hidalgo replied with a wide and friendly smile. "As I mentioned, I've made no decision to run for any office." He paused and observed the expressions on the faces of the reporters. "Now, concerning the constitution let me say something that everyone knows. Mexico needs a strong leader. In the coming elections, the people of Mexico—and not antiquated constitutional laws—will decide who that person will be."

Hidalgo moved to a seat next to Chemor and appeared relaxed. "Okay. What news did you bring from Mexico City?"

"Well sir, as you know, your announcement to return has stirred up a real hornet's nest, just as you expected. You would enjoy watching the TV talking heads scrambling around trying to cover how they failed to anticipate your decision. Before I left, I also heard that the White House had asked *Azteca Periferico* for a tape of the entire press conference. I find that very interesting indeed."

Chemor noticed a faint blush of anger on Hidalgo's face when he mentioned the White House. "Tomorrow's *Mediodia* will report that the ruling party's repeated failure to govern has opened the door for you and the opposition Party of the Democratic Revolution. That's quite a pointed statement from that government-controlled paper."

Hidalgo did not respond, but just stretched out his long legs and looked off into the distance. He was thinking about how everything had changed, speeded up, following his announcement to return. He was pleased with the initial, surprising positive response, but a large number of his countrymen still blamed him for the devastating economic downturn. Something they felt was the direct result of moving ahead too quickly with democratic reforms and embracing the United States. Nevertheless, Hidalgo knew that the majority of working people still believed in him. He had made the decision; there was no turning back. He turned toward Chemor and playfully poked him with his index finger.

"Come . . . enough of all this political stuff. I am forgetting my manners. Let's go to lunch," said a smiling Hidalgo, extending his hand.

* * *

They sipped dry greenish Portuguese wine and nibbled on marinated olives at a small restaurant near the villa before enjoying a *caldo verde* soup and sea bass with almonds. Chemor continued to review what was planned for Hidalgo's homecoming and his tentative schedule of appearances and speeches, but he sensed that his *jeffe*'s thoughts were elsewhere.

"Have I lost you somewhere, sir?"

"I'm sorry Ramiro . . . the food here is so good. You are such a dear friend to get me out of my confinement and make me see what I am missing in life. No more business. We will finish lunch and spend the afternoon in a new museum that just opened."

CHAPTER 3

The White House

Charles Washburn was having a difficult time accepting the shocking news of Pete Swanson. He felt deeply the loss of a close friend and even a sense of personal responsibility for the tragic killing. After all, it was his policy to directly confront and attack the insidious drug problem on both sides of the border. After years of watching the devastating impact from illicit drugs, he made it a major theme of his presidency to lash out at the whole corrupt system, especially those in the Mexican government who were on the cartel's payrolls. In the days following the assassination, he had disciplined himself to forego the anger and feelings inside him, and how he reacted in public. The Republicans would wait only a few days before portraying the assassination as another example of a failed program—his failed program. One member of the leadership already had spoken out on one of the network Sunday gasbag shows. Washburn knew that he had to find a way to shift the responsibility where it belonged, which was on Congress and its woefully insufficient funding for the war on drugs, both at home and abroad. It was a war that the United States had been waging for over a half century; one that the country was losing.

"Well, I'll be ready for them."

The president's sudden outburst made Sybil Washburn turn and frown at her husband. She watched him ignore his breakfast as he stopped restlessly pacing around and stood at a window of the family quarters, ignoring the bright, cloudless morning outside and impatiently paging through the daily press digest. He scowled when he saw the latest presidential poll numbers reported in the media.

"Will you please sit down? You're driving me crazy circling the table mumbling at everything."

Like Hidalgo, Washburn was quite tall, over six feet four. He had a large, leonine head with dark brown hair and extraordinarily large, powerful hands, a great asset for any politician working the rope line in a crowd eager for his handshake. His face was remarkably expressive, often reflecting his mood more openly than he liked, but the power of his smile had worked its magic on voters since his first run for office for the Missouri legislature many years before. This particular morning his countenance betrayed the anger boiling inside him; anger that his wife hoped would not spill over when he met with his cabinet at ten. Washburn dropped the press-briefing book on the table and leaned against the back of a chair, trying to calm down.

"I'm sorry, honey, but I am getting sick and tired of the same old self-serving blather of the *New York Times* and *Washington Post*. How everything wrong in the world is our fault. When are they going to get off that kick?"

Sybil shook her head and smiled sympathetically. "So when did you start believing everything you read in the papers?"

* * *

Washburn knew he was not a favorite of the press. His charm, unlike Jack Kennedy's, was lost on the Washington press corps as well as the permanent establishment that he acidly referred to as the "Georgetown Mafia." But with the voters in the last election, the charm had been outrageously successful, enabling him to make his way largely undamaged through the minefields of issues and special interests. He had great, natural political skills; perhaps the most important was his ability to convince a single individual or an entire audience that he heard and understood them, agreed with them, was on their side. He had decided early in his term that he would reach over the heads of the media, Congress, and even his own party, and go directly to the voters. And it was working. The economy was humming along, a record low level of unemployment had defused or at least put off the reckoning with many social problems, and America's ability to project its power was unchallenged. But the inevitable media snipping that even Ronald Reagan and Dwight Eisenhower had experienced (and handled with equanimity) at the height of their popularity was a constant, sometimes almost unbearable source of frustration and irritation. Washburn did his best not to show it, but his press secretary, for one, knew how severe the problem was and did his best to limit the number of press conferences. His highly photogenic boss liked photo ops—and loathed most reporters except for a handful, most of them from his native state. But Washburn knew that the murder of Swanson and its implications left him no choice but to give the media what is was baying for—a forceful response to a savage and unquestionably evil act. There was no way he could avoid a full-blown press conference—but not yet; he didn't want to be facing questions when he didn't have the answers the media was pressing for.

As the president entered the West Wing Cabinet Room for the Monday morning meeting, he had already built up a head of steam and cut off the usual exchange of pleasantries. He dropped the press-briefing book down on the highly polished mahogany table as the cabinet members quickly took their seats.

"What in the hell are we doing about General Swanson?"

The response to the president's outburst fell to the secretary of state, Richard Snyder. He made a striking contrast to Washburn. Small, patrician in his features and manner, with narrow shoulders and a somewhat scholarly air about him, he was in his mid-seventies and a respected old-school diplomat who had served two presidents. Snyder had worked as a junior aide to Dean Acheson in the old State Department and had seen more and learned more about how Washington functioned than anyone else did in the room, including the president. Snyder was responsible for the antidrug strategy that had distinguished Washburn from the other presidential candidates and contributed significantly to the wave of voter support in the critical last months of a close, historically low turnout election.

"Mr. President, we simply have no leads. No organization has come forward to claim responsibility." Although the president was about to break in, Snyder forged ahead. Snyder had recommended Swanson, a friend and protégé, while serving on the transition team after the election. It had been almost like losing a son but Snyder mourned privately, not letting the world know how devastated he was. "It doesn't mean we're not doing anything, sir. A special task force, headed by the FBI director with representatives from every law enforcement agency, is meeting at this very moment. In all fairness, they've only had forty-eight hours. Jeffery Boyd will give us an update tomorrow. Until then," continued Snyder, slowly looking from one cabinet member to another to make sure they would follow his lead, "we need to carefully measure our response. Congress would love to use this to challenge your post-NAFTA expansion and other bilateral initiatives. More importantly

Mr. President, your announcement concerning the creation of a Free Trade Area of the Americas has put the Republicans on the defensive. We need to exploit this and not allow them to shift the public focus to the assassination and its implications—certainly not what House Majority Leader has been telling the press he thinks they are. His remarks were irresponsible; I suggest we not dignify them with any response whatsoever."

The president continued to fiddle with the briefing book, opening and closing it. He was still angry and wanted to challenge Snyder's advice to ride out the storm until they had some reliable information to go on, but he thought better of it. He was aware that people remembered his predecessors as great leaders because people like Richard Snyder told them what they had to do and trained them to lead. When you have someone like that on your side, you listen, he reminded himself.

"Well, we need to do something—have you seen the latest polling numbers? And the *Post* just won't give up—they seem to be buying the Majority Leader's brilliant opinion that killing Swanson was no less than a declaration of war by the drug cartel. Damned disappointing."

"Those numbers from the *New York Times/CBS* poll don't mean anything, Mr. President," his press secretary, Jim Browning assured him, in a voice that was more confident than he actually felt. "They are almost a week old. Once your FTAA proposal hit the headlines, the flash polls show your numbers are up from seven to nine points."

"Goddamn! Now that's the first good news I've heard around here." The scowl on the president's face was transformed by a grin as he looked around the table to see the others' reactions.

"And there are other good things happening that—"

Here we go again, thought David Andrews, the president's national security adviser. More spin from the press secretary. The truth was that the Republicans were effectively using the problems in Mexico to discredit the administration's policies. Andrews was spending more and more of his time trying to convince the president to put some distance between the White House and the ruling party—especially with a second term election less than a year away. The problem was that the State Department was pushing the president to stay closely aligned with the ruling party even while things were going south in Mexico City. He simply could not understand Snyder's commitment to Posadas, who was presiding over a growing and obvious disaster. And he knew that the Republicans would resist offering a Bob Rubin type of rescue package. Posadas was a sinking ship; the administration could easily go down with him.

David Andrews had been on the fast track in various state department positions before Washburn pulled him into the national security adviser's position. After working tirelessly to keep the president apprised of security issues around the world, he had gotten the attention and coveted personal time with the president. Although the proposal for an ultimately successful renegotiation of NAFTA and the antidrug initiative had pushed Washburn over the top four years ago, the bloom was off the rose. David had already decided that he would take every opportunity to convince the president to backpedal from his personal commitment to the ruling party. It was a risky move to oppose the secretary of state but Andrews believed that the close ties with Posadas were bad for the administration—and more important, a fatal threat to his own political ambitions.

"I agree with the State Department's assessment," the director of Central Intelligence, Leslie Drummond said, ignoring the press secretary's cheerleading. "Pete Swanson and his DEA troops were pressing on both sides of the border and retaliatory threats are part of the package. Everything points toward the cartel on this one but we need a lot more collateral before we make a case that they ordered Pete Swanson's killing."

The director's comments led to a spirited, freewheeling discussion; even the secretary of agriculture, normally someone who kept a profile lower than a snake's, piped up with a suggestion that made Andrews groan inwardly. The president, who normally moved cabinet meetings along briskly, in part because they bored him, remained curiously detached and let the meeting ramble on.

"How do we know that it wasn't a politically motivated assassination?" The president broke in on the discussion and resumed control of the meeting. The question stopped everyone. Nobody, especially the DCI, was eager to respond.

Snyder shifted in his chair and took a deep breath. "What do you mean, Mr. President?"

"Well, the Mexican Mafia—La Eme or whatever they call themselves—or that revolutionary Zapatista Rebel Group. Who knows what is going on in that country . . . Hidalgo stirring things up again? After all, he just announced that he is returning to Mexico. Takes a hell of a nerve, if you ask me. We're being killed by what's happening down there. Now this. If it does turn out that the tail gets pinned to the Mexican donkey—even if it is just some lunatic who acted on his own, which I doubt—we are going to have a firestorm to put out. If we can."

"The president could be right," the vice president said thoughtfully. "Hidalgo is a smart, tough politician and what better way to put Posadas and his successor in a real bind before their elections next year. I bet he would love to get back into power again and use the drug cartel to finance his campaign." He glanced at Washburn quickly to see if he was singing from the right page in the hymnbook. "Hidalgo is poison. We had enough of him a few years back—we don't need that business again . . ."

"We will look into it, Mr. President. But we don't have anyone close to Hidalgo. We have no idea of what his game plan is," Snyder quickly responded, cutting off Michael Kerr. Snyder did not like the direction in which the vice president was going. He wondered who was feeding Kerr, as this was not the first time that the vice president had placed blame for persistent problems on the former popular Mexican president. When Hidalgo announced his intention to return to Mexico City earlier in the week, the chief of staff reported that President Washburn had been furious. Although Snyder had been out of government during the Hidalgo administration, he was aware of the bitter relations between the White House and Hidalgo during the last year of Hidalgo's term. The revelations about possible Hidalgo family ties to the drug cartel in addition to the inevitable corruption in his government in a country where corruption was endemic, had led to a crisis in U.S.-Mexican relations. Snyder had privately speculated that Washington had delivered a coup de grâce to the mortally wounded Hidalgo regime. Even though he was then merely an outsider watching the debacle unfold, what he gleamed from his many contacts in the government was that they were baffled as anyone by the situation that had arisen in Mexico in those few, frantic months. From what he knew about Hidalgo, this criminal involvement was difficult to reconcile with the man himself and all that he seemed to have stood for in his push for democratic reforms. Snyder also admired the way Hidalgo had handled the devastating public humiliation with grace and dignity. The whole business did not seem to add up. The corruption allegations came after Hidalgo's six years of market-oriented reforms that started to elevate Mexico out of the third world. Richard Snyder firmly believed that such fundamental and structural economic changes had to take place in Mexico before the United States could make any real progress with NAFTA, the FTAA, or drug trafficking. Whatever was going on, they were stuck with Posadas now and Snyder was determined not to waiver from his position that it was time for the United States to get it right with its southern neighbor.

The president nodded to Kerr and then looked at his watch. "We've run over the scheduled time, so let's all get back to work. I don't want anyone publicly—or even privately—speculating on who might be responsible for killing General Swanson. We can't go off half-cocked and just assume the obvious. Swanson had other enemies—this country has its own full share of drug lords who don't wish us well and who are making billions off poisoning our people. Who knows? We've been coming down on everyone from the Colombians to the Afghans, who are still moving a lot of heroin out of the poppy fields."

He looked around the table to make sure that his words had sunk in. "I know it is virtually impossible to stop leaks in this town, but on this one keep it tight."

The president was already out of his chair before he finished with his admonition. The cabinet members quickly rose and started gathering up the papers in front of them. As the president started to leave through the door, he suddenly turned and pointed a finger at the vice president.

"Mike, I want you to take the chair of that interagency task force. Get us out ahead of the curve on this thing. The report I got from the Justice Department tells me nothing. The killer wore latex gloves, apparently. There was little physical evidence to go on. No witnesses."

The president paused as another thought hit him and turned to the secretary of the Treasury Department. "And by the way, do something about your security next door. Every damn parking garage in Washington has surveillance cameras. I simply can't believe that anyone can drive in off the street and have access to your garage and elevator. You've got the whole Secret Service—get them to work on this and get the GSA to put some cameras in that garage pronto."

As the president left, an embarrassed secretary of the treasury was making notes on a yellow legal pad.

Before returning to his office at Foggy Bottom, Snyder stopped by his first-floor White House office still thinking about how strongly the president had reacted to the prospect of Hidalgo's imminent return to Mexico. He closed the door.

"What am I missing?" He asked himself. "Who is getting the president all riled up about Hidalgo?"

He did not think that it was the vice president, but at the same time he wondered what the vice president had meant about not wanting to deal in that Hidalgo business again. That seemed to imply some previous dealings. Snyder tried to recall some of the significant and contentious issues with Hidalgo from the previous administration as he shuffled some papers inside his briefcase. He abruptly stopped.

"Promontorio Mountain . . . could that be it?" The thought came out of nowhere. Promontorio had caused so much anxiety and disappointment for the president's predecessor. Although the White House had been successful keeping the issue buried, Snyder knew that it had the potential to become a national issue.

Snyder pushed back in his chair and thought about the Promontorio Mountain Repository. After years of research and hundreds of millions of dollars, President Hidalgo had abruptly halted the final phases of construction of the prototype nuclear waste repository deep in the mountains of Sonora Mexico. Years earlier, the U.S. Congress had supported their Republican governors' efforts to keep the waste repository out of their districts—much to the chagrin of the White House. When pressure increased from the powerful energy lobby for the White House to come up with a solution to the growing nuclear waste problem, the focus shifted to a possible site in Mexico. Hidalgo had initially agreed to locate the repository in Sonora as a means to kick-start the depressed northern border area economy. Part of the bargain was the use of Mexican labor and contractors to excavate and build the repository, something the Department of Energy fought— and lost. However, the issue of control remained the sticky wicket. When Congress would not agree to joint control of the repository, Hidalgo stopped construction and turned it into a nasty sovereignty issue. Once Hidalgo was gone, his successor, Jorge Fosadas, quietly resumed construction and put an end to complaints about infringement on Mexico's sovereign authority. Snyder had heard that the quid pro quo was a much-needed financial bailout of the tottering Mexican economy. Now after five years and millions of dollars, the prototype repository was finally ready to accept nuclear waste for permanent stowage. With elections less than a year away, Snyder knew that the White House could ill afford a national debate on locating a nuclear waste site in a foreign country that was now beginning to appear ungovernable.

Snyder got up and looked out the window. There has to be something else but what is it, he thought. The repository is probably only part of it. What is the president afraid of? He closed his briefcase and opened the door to leave. He was surprised to find a Secret Service agent waiting outside, who informed him that the president wanted to see him. *Maybe I will find out some answers to my questions. And maybe I will find out something I don't want to know,* he thought as he headed for the Oval Office.

CHAPTER 4

Washington, D.C.

United-290 was three hours into the five and a half-hour flight from San Francisco to Washington Dulles. Palmer had finally drifted off to a fitful sleep after a lunch of salmon salad with wilted lettuce salvaged by a decent Sonoma chardonnay. The *New York Times*, with its headlines about the assassination of the president's drug czar, was scattered on the empty seat next to him. He had been wondering, from the moment he got the invitation to spend the weekend in Washington with his best friend, David Andrews, and his wife, if the sudden invitation had anything to do with Swanson's murder. But he decided, just before he drifted off for a nap, that the National Security Adviser would have said something if there were more to the invitation. Palmer had already made it clear to Andrews that he did not intend to return to his former position on the National Security Council staff and Andrews had made only a token effort to persuade him to change his mind.

As it turned out, Palmer had welcomed the call. Since

leaving the NSC staff, his life during the past six months in San Francisco had been unremarkable. He had returned to San Francisco following the death of his father and unexpected following by his mother. He found himself going through the motions of settling his parents' estate—and drinking himself to sleep on far too many nights. It was as if he was steaming around in a dense fog and could not find a way to break out of it; perhaps he didn't really want to. Three years ago, Palmer had lost the only person he really loved in a senseless drug-fueled murder a few blocks from where they lived near the Presidio. The loss of his wife left him empty and full of rage—and guilt. Now, years later, he was still trying to find a way to free himself from that deep-seated feeling and thirst for revenge that had taken over his life.

The nap came quickly after the second glass of chardonnay. And the unwanted dream. A dream that was a variation of all the others but always started the same way: Palmer was watching a football game on television while his wife, Catherine, was putting dishes and glasses away in the kitchen.

"Cole, I'm going to run some errands and gas up the van so we can get an early start to Napa in the morning."

Palmer looked up at her. She was dressed casually in layers of shirts and slacks and looked like a college student. Even in the fall season, with its long stretches of gray, overcast skies, Catherine managed to retain a tan, which accentuated her green eyes and emphasized her superbly conditioned body, the body of a woman who loved to ski and swim and play tennis.

"Do you want me to come along?" Palmer asked half-heartedly, his eyes wandering back to the Navy–Notre Dame game.

"Um, well, would you like to?" Catherine responded with a wry grin knowing what the answer would be.

"Eh, I have, eh, you know, things I ought to do before Monday classes come around. I thought things would be a lot slower at the PG level."

Catherine rolled her eyes at her husband and reminded him in a firm voice that tomorrow was a non-football television day. As she started to go out the front door, she looked back at Palmer and grinned, warning him. "And don't even think of turning on the radio in the car or comments like, 'I just want to check the score or see if they get a touchdown.' Remember—we agreed. It's our time together—no interferences, OK?" She picked up her oversized handbag and said, "I should be back in an hour or so."

In the abandoned and desolate waterfront area off Hunters Point, a gang of young teenagers, all younger than sixteen, drifted into one of the rundown warehouses. They had seen and done things that made them far older than their years. Most of their families had given up on them; they were like feral dogs, slinking through the streets at night and by day holing up in a house in Daly City owned by a dealer everyone called Warthog because he was so damn big and so damned ugly. They did little jobs for him—selling on the street, some "bad debt collecting" and acting as sentries, keeping a sharp lookout for any sign that the narcs were going to pull a drug bust on Warthog. He, in turn, paid them by giving them a place to eat, plenty of junk food, and all the marijuana and coke they wanted. Warthog didn't do heroin—he knew that stone junkies screwed up sooner or later—so that meant his "employees" weren't allowed to do heroin either . . . unless they wanted to be terminated.

They called themselves the Lobos; their gang colors were displayed by the distinctive yellow and red bandanas tied over their foreheads. The cops were well aware of the Lobos. All but two of them had been in and out of the system; as juveniles, they usually got off with light sentences if they didn't get probation. They were street-smart, avoiding fights with other gangs and staying just beyond the reach of the law. But they did have a high-risk initiation ritual. A prospective member was expected to pull off an armed robbery using only a knife—and if the victim got hurt, then so much the better. They got extra credibility for that.

Zap Xiong was only fourteen when he set out that particular Saturday night to show that he had the right stuff. He caught a bus, got off at Van Ness, and started walking the Presidio perimeter. He knew that he should be thinking about some kind of plan but he could not concentrate. It was getting dark and he was edgy. He stopped and lit one of the two remaining marijuana joints hidden in his black windbreaker. Zap was not sure he was up to doing what they wanted. He thought about not ever coming back and doing something else. The problem was that he could not think of what he would do or where he could go. He started to cut through one of the tree-lined paths when he saw the lights of a mini shopping mall at the end of the block. He had to go to the bathroom and saw that the restroom door of the Atlas gas station was partly open so he slipped in. As Zap came back outside, a Mercedes SUV had just stopped at the pump line and a woman was halfway to the enclosed cashier's window. Zap pulled his head down toward his skinny chest and quickly covered the distance to the SUV, keeping himself out of the cashier's line of sight. He rolled his small frame under the car and tried to control his breathing. His hands were shaking but he managed to pull out a thin, razor sharp knife tied to his leg under his jeans. Moments later, he heard steps returning and then saw a woman's shoes approach the rear of the SUV. Zap was sweating and felt claustrophobic as he lurked in the darkness under the car. His head was close to the gas tank, and he could hear and smell the gas pouring into it. He had to move, so he started inching his way forward. He felt as if he could not breathe and imagined the car pressing down and crushing him. Just as he was ready to roll out the other side and run away, he heard the pump stop and the gas cap replaced. As the woman started to get back into the car, he shifted around toward the left front door. Something made him lash out at the woman's foot as it started moving upward. Catherine felt the knife dig into her left ankle and tried to pull her leg inside. When she saw the blood gushing from her ankle, waves of shock hit her. Zap was up instantly crouching alongside the open door, out of view of the cashier. For a few seconds he froze, unable to decide whether to run or finish the job. When he saw the woman struggling not to fall across the seat, he felt a new surge of energy. Catherine was aware that he was looming over her and realized she had to do something. She slammed her elbow into Zap's face, knocking him backward while she pushed her body up against the steering wheel to blow the horn. Alerted by the sound, the cashier locked in his booth behind bulletproof glass, asked over a loudspeaker if she was having a problem. Zap picked himself up and saw the cashier straining to see what was happening some forty feet away from his booth. The noise of the horn and cashier yelling over the loudspeaker were too much for Zap; he panicked and started frantically slashing at the woman slumped over the steering wheel until her body fell sideways onto the front seat and the blaring horn stopped. For a few moments, Zap just stared at his victim, who was covered with blood. He ran across the street, dropped the knife into a storm drain, and raced toward the darkened Presidio.

Catherine had been gone over two hours and Palmer started to worry. He walked outside and continued down the street, thinking that Catherine would be coming around the corner any minute. When he reached the end of the road, he saw the flashing lights of an ambulance and police cars at the gas station they used. When he saw the SUV, he stopped and felt a chill ripple down his spine. He started running.

"Let me through. What happened . . . oh, God . . . no . . . no . . . it can't be."

Palmer pushed past the police officers and medics. He knew without asking that the worst had happened.

The dream always ended the same way with Palmer trying to lift Catherine's limp body out of the bloodstained interior of the SUV. As he watched his young wife struggle for her last breaths, Palmer was almost blinded by his tears.

Palmer woke up shivering, wet with perspiration. He forced himself to get out of his seat and walked to the back of the airplane wondering if the nightmares would ever end. He leaned against the rear exit door staring through the small window at the fluffy clouds beneath the plane.

"Are you all right?"

David looked at the man standing across from him waiting for one of the lavatories. He took out his handkerchief and wiped his face.

"Thanks, I'm fine. I just needed to stretch out." Palmer nodded and returned to his seat.

But he wasn't going to be fine; he might never be fine again. He remembered that Hemingway said that sooner or later, life breaks all of us but some get strong in the broken places. He was determined to overcome the horror, to stop keeping the dreams at bay by drinking at night, pushing himself into a dreamless sleep.

The police had been able to tell him very little. A thorough search of the crime scene turned up the knife in the catch basin of the storm drain but there was not a match for the fingerprints found on it. The driver of a van delivering pizzas had caught a glimpse of someone running across the street but he was able to provide only a sketchy description, which included the colors of the bandana on the perp's head. But when the cops came down on the Lobos, they hit a stone wall. What they didn't know was that early in the morning following the murder, Warthog had put Zap on a bus to San Diego, with instructions to contact a man in Tijuana. Warthog also knew that Zap's body was now buried in a shallow grave somewhere in the Baja desert.

The inspector handling the case did not hold out any false hope.

"Mr. Palmer, we'll keep this case open as long as it takes. We're pretty sure that a member of that gang was responsible, but getting those little scumbags to talk is another matter. We tossed the house—I mean every damn inch of it—and came up with zilch. The place had been cleaned out. Traces of marijuana in one of the kitchen cabinets but not enough to bring a charge against the owner."

He put his hand on Palmer's arm and said, in a voice that conveyed his frustration and his compassion for the victim's husband, "But they will screw up. Count on it. One of them might even be stupid enough to boast about it and we'll hear about it from a snitch. We are going to stay on them, keep the pressure on."

Palmer tried to keep his anger under control; he knew the police would do their best. Based on the coroner's report, the police had concluded that the pattern of the wounds Catherine had sustained in a robbery gone wrong indicated that the assailant was probably on drugs—or else was a psychopath. Or both.

Palmer tried to immerge himself in his Navy postgraduate studies and find his way back to some semblance of a life. But the burning rage got the best of him and he resigned from the Navy and dropped out of school. As the days and then weeks passed and the police continued to report no progress, Palmer made contact with a group of people—parents, spouses, other family members—who had lost someone they loved through drugs, in various ways. In the face of official disapproval by the police department (but unofficial sympathy from some individuals on the force) they had taken action, exacted retribution. They mounted a variety of operations; burning down a crack house one day, assaulting dealers on the street and breaking up drug sales on another. Eventually, Palmer figured out that continuing down this path would not bring Catherine back to life. He needed to reclaim his life while he still could.

Palmer headed east and settled in an Annapolis cottage across the Severn from the Naval Academy. One of his former shipmates asked him to take care of his three-year-old J-35 during the period that he was away on duty in London. For the first time since the loss of Catherine, Palmer was doing something he loved. The change also freed him from his ties to the questionable vigilante anti-drug group on the West Coast. After almost a year of sailing, Palmer thought that he was breaking out of the grip of obsessive memories that had skewed his thinking and led to self-destructive behavior. Andrews's offer to join the NSC staff provided the opportunity to test his resolve. But the dreams refused to go away.

Palmer moved into the military liaison position on the NSC staff. The billet did not reveal his actual duties; he spent the majority of his time on special and sensitive CIA operations. Although he initially resisted assignments connected to drugs, it was not long before he was actively scheming to take part in the most violent and risky drug-interdiction operations in South America. Although Palmer seemed to have himself under control, rumors began to spread about his unyielding take-no-prisoner attitude, which began to provoke concern at the highest levels.

* * *

"Cole, what do you think about shifting over to the SI area for a while. You've been stuck in special ops for almost two years. SI could use some help."

"You're the boss, David, although I don't know squat about satellite imaging," Palmer answered hesitantly. "I also wouldn't believe everything you hear."

Andrews knew that Palmer was his own toughest critic and judge. At the same time, he had heard about Palmer's dark side manifesting itself during some recent operations. He knew that anger and a thirst for revenge partly accounted for Palmer's personal fearlessness, a fearlessness that could put him and others at risk.

Andrews did not want to get into what he had been hearing and decided to back off. "I am just asking Cole. The job is open when and if you want to move."

Palmer was embarrassed that his closest friend had to bring up the issue. On more than one occasion, he had been unable to understand some of his own behavior. Deep down, he knew what the problem was. He considered asking what Andrews had been hearing about him but decided to let it pass. He realized that Andrews was uncomfortable talking about it.

"Sorry. I didn't mean to sound as if I didn't care. I understand what you're saying and if I need to do something, I'll let you know . . . and thanks David." Palmer realized that he was on the ragged edge. He despised what a drug-crazed kid had done to Catherine; he wanted to exterminate them all—the addicts who robbed and killed, the dealers who killed in their own way, and the men in the shadows in Colombia and Mexico, Afghanistan, and the Golden Triangle who were making billions by poisoning his country.

A few months after their conversation, Palmer's father died from a stroke and his mother survived him by only a few days. With Andrews's support and sympathy, Palmer headed to San Francisco to handle the final arrangements.

Now, after almost six months, the business was finished. In many ways, it was a last gesture of love and respect for his parents and another opportunity to step back and put a new life together.

When he finally worked up the courage to return to the apartment that he and Catherine shared next to the Presidio, he sat on the grassy hill above it for hours recalling their times together. He knew that Catherine would have disapproved of his pent-up anger, fixation on revenge, and the unlawful things that he had done. With tears in his eyes, he silently promised to work it out—but he still felt bereft of the support he so desperately needed and that she could have given him.

Palmer snapped out of his thoughts as the plane started its approach to Dulles. Following landing, the Boeing 757 slowly taxied to the debarkation ramp at Gate C. As he followed the passengers for the short walk to the waiting shuttle buses huddled between Terminal C and the main terminal, he belatedly reminded himself to pick up something for David's wife. Brooke had been Catherine's best friend and Bryn Mawr roommate. She, more than anyone, understood just how devastating Catherine's death had been for him. At the same time, she had made it clear that Palmer could not let his grief and anger fill the void in his life. "It would not be fair to Catherine," she had told Cole firmly. "You know that your finest tribute, your most loving gift to her, is to continue to build the life you began together."

Palmer did not have to wait long. He saw the silver BMW flash its lights and swing toward where he was standing at the curb.

"Cole! Great to see you. Hard to believe that it's been almost seven months since you left the staff," Andrews yelled while leaping out of the half-parked car and embracing Palmer.

"Thanks for invite . . . great to be back. I'm really looking forward to spending some time with you and Brooke."

Within minutes, they headed off on the airport toll road for Andrews's home off N Street in Georgetown.

The two men were similar not only appearance but also in their quiet and reserved style, a style that complemented their forceful and resolute characters. Both men had the kind of aura that intimidated some people, but led the more perceptive, at first meeting, to take them seriously. They were not guys you could screw around with. Palmer was an athletic six-foot-three and had a half-inch on Andrews and a somewhat heavier build. Because of their service background, both men carried themselves confidently, their posture upright, their stride purposeful and energetic. Andrews had blond hair, dark blue eyes, and a face that gave him an almost movie star handsomeness, making a marked contrast to Palmer's more irregular features, thick black eyebrows over deep-set, dark eyes, which with a nose that gave his face a certain hawk-like aspect, made him look a bit more rugged.

Both had served in the Navy. Andrews was assigned duty on destroyers following a long pipeline of technical school. Palmer had gone directly in the Navy SEAL program following graduation and then crossdecked to destroyer duty, which is how they came to meet when both attended the Destroyer School in Newport. The school was a specialized training program for those who had completed three to four years of at-sea destroyer operations, received impeccable evaluations which documented outstanding performance, and had strong backing from their superiors.

Andrews had graduated magna cum laude from Yale with a BA before entering the Navy OCS program. His family was prominent in Greenwich going back several generations, and he had followed his grandfather and father to Yale. Palmer finished number seven in his class at "Canoe U," or more formally, the Naval Academy. When he graduated from high school, his father, who ran a struggling insurance agency, told him that he could either work his way through college or compete for a place at one of the service academies. The Navy had quickly identified both men as bright overachievers and potential fast-track officer material.

It did not take long for them to emerge as class leaders among their peers at destroyer school. Both of them were popular, but neither made many close friends at the school. Their friendship evolved, seasoned with a natural, healthy competitiveness, and tended to keep others at a distance. In the classroom, the differences between the two became evident. Andrews invariably defended the foreign policy of the United States and its use of military power, vigorously if needed, in defense of national interests. Palmer sometimes argued that there were other ways to accomplish the mission. He tended to take a more considered, nuanced view of things and resisted coming to hasty conclusions. But Andrews was a believer in absolutes. Things were black or white; there was no room for gray in his world. Palmer, for example, was willing to place a significant part of the responsibility for the Vietnam debacle on the senior military commanders. Andrews argued that it was the failures of America's political will that had made the war ultimately unwinnable. Neither would give ground. But in the years to follow, their views and attitudes would undergo profound changes.

During mid-year break at destroyer school, Andrews returned home to Greenwich and surprised everyone by becoming engaged to the girl that he had fallen in love with when he was a gangly fourteen-year-old high school freshman at Groton. They had dated off and on since their first encounter at a dance at Brooke's school and throughout their years at Yale and Bryn Mawr. Andrews had put a lot of miles on the car he was given after graduating from prep school, shuttling between New Haven and the Main Line.

Brooke was an only child. Her father, like many fathers, loved having a daughter but wanted a son. When David came along, he was the next best thing. A partner in one of the older and more conservative investment banks in New York, Dwight Lawson expected that, in the natural course of things, Andrews would go to work for the firm, maybe starting out on the bond trading desk.

"Now that the engagement is official, Brooke's mother and I are mighty pleased." Brooke's father had put an arm around Andrews and steered him to the library following dinner with the family. "I'd like you to think about taking a position in our shop to find out what the business is all about. It's a lot more exciting than you might think. We are one of the many engines powering this economy—and not in a small way, I hasten to add," he said with a chuckle.

Andrews had been aware of earlier subtle pressures on him to consider some line of work other than going to sea. Lawson didn't see his daughter leading the life of a Navy wife, moving from one base or town to another when her husband was reassigned.

"I really appreciate the confidence, sir, but I've decided to postpone any decision until my service is up."

"Well, yes . . . of course. However, there are ways to do that . . . you know, the reserves. The Navy has units in all the major cities. I'm sure something can be arranged, no fuss or anything."

"Again, I appreciate your offer but I really do want to finish what I started." Andrews had not only inherited his father's independent spirit but also his Scottish stubbornness and knew what he wanted.

Palmer had taken to Brooke the first moment he met her. She was another independent spirit, highly intelligent and a woman with an acerbic wit that could keep Andrews off balance. She also had a way of relating comfortably to people from backgrounds very different from and less privileged than her own—and she was totally, unreservedly in love with his best friend. Palmer was amazed how well-connected Andrews was—until he met Brooke. She came from old money and all the self-assurance that comes with it. And she was determined to use such access in her own creative fashion. Palmer figured that this did not include a Navy career for David Andrews.

Six months later, Andrews and Palmer shared the class prize for overall academics, performance, and leadership. It was only the second time in the history of the destroyer school that two officers shared the award. Graduation day was also special because of the announcement of follow-on assignments. Palmer's orders to postgraduate studies at the Navy Postgraduate School in Monterey were well received—not least by Palmer's parents, who lived only an hour or so away in Tiburon. Andrews was assigned to serve as one of the military aides to the secretary of defense, a most prestigious job for a lieutenant in any branch of the armed forces. The assignment surprised everyone including Andrews who expected to go to PG school with Palmer or return to sea as a destroyer department head. Two in attendance were not surprised. Brooke's parents were friends of the defense secretary—and generous contributors to the party then in power.

After the ceremony there were more cheers when Andrews announced that he was about to become a married man—and invited all hands to the June wedding in Greenwich.

The manicured lawns and large stone or brick houses on

tree-lined Round Hill Road made a fitting backdrop for one of the weddings of the year in Greenwich. Brooke Andrews, as she was soon to be, had deliberately arranged for Cole Palmer to sit at the same table at the reception with her best friend from school, Catherine Peters, who also worked with her at Citicorp in Manhattan. Catherine was a knockout—an eleven on a scale of ten according to Palmer's automatic rating system. She had, he quickly discovered, an enormous appetite for life and new experiences. She had a rare ability to live in the moment, to be fully alive and connected with whatever was going on around her. She was also incredibly sensual; Palmer could not keep his eyes off her. Only a few months after David and Brooke's wedding, few who knew Catherine and Cole were surprised when Citicorp reassigned Catherine to their bank in San Francisco—a bank only an hour or so from the Naval Postgraduate School in Monterey.

After a seven-month courtship, Cole and Catherine were married in Philadelphia where she had grown up. It was a large wedding, with the numerous family members and friends from Philadelphia and San Francisco attending. Andrews was Palmer's best man and Brooke was her best friend's bridesmaid. In the few quiet moments that Palmer and Andrews had together, Andrews informed his shipmate that he intended to resign his commission when his service was up at the end of the year. Palmer had guessed right. Brooke had no intentions of being a peripatetic Navy wife and Andrews was interested in playing a significant role in applying America's power—but not from the deck of a destroyer.

After a long weekend in Bermuda, Palmer and his radiant wife flew to San Francisco and moved into Catherine's apartment—a block away from the gates of the Presidio. Catherine had an instinctive flair for giving any room a distinctive yet simple, uncluttered, and cozy ambiance.

Palmer found that he could make the commute to PG school in Monterey in less than an hour and could use the open space of the Presidio for jogging and walking with Catherine after dinner. Whenever they did not have a social obligation at school, they spent misty San Francisco evenings exploring the seemingly endless restaurants and small shops in areas from North Beach to Fisherman's Wharf. Palmer, whose experience of fine cuisine had been limited, loved going to small but excellent restaurants with Catherine, who introduced him to sushi and all the pleasures of lemongrass in Thai cooking.

Catherine was everything Palmer had ever dreamed of— a natural athlete who enjoyed everything from tennis to sailing to hiking. She widened his intellectual and spiritual horizons while teaching him, by example, a form of serenity and life-affirming cheerfulness that encouraged him to escape from his usual reserved, even somewhat dour, self. Unlike Brooke, Catherine had no preconceived plans for their future together. Nor did she have any difficulty adapting to the unwritten rules for a Navy wife. She was, he thought, a woman for all seasons.

When David Andrews accompanied the secretary of defense on trips to the West Coast, they always found time to meet at one of Catherine's new restaurant discoveries.

"I'm glad that one of us is working and can get out to visit now and then," Andrews once said, kidding Palmer about the easy, good life that came with duty at the postgraduate school.

"I wouldn't call flying around with the SecDef arduous, pal. Anyway, when you come to see us, it's the only time you get a reality check!"

Although they lived on different coasts, Andrews and Palmer made efforts to meet as frequently as possible. In between meetings, they had long conversations over the phone or exchanged e-mail. Nevertheless, Palmer sensed a gradual change in their relationship. Andrews was increasingly drawn into the whirlpool of Washington parties where contacts were made, alliances tentatively forged, and status enhanced. While Palmer, at first, enjoyed listening to his friend's stories of political intrigue, he became increasingly concerned that Andrews was turning into a person he no longer really knew. Catherine had less patience: "You two go off and have some guy talk. I'm going to a yoga class."

"You don't really believe all that crap that Washington puts out, David?"

Andrews frowned and volleyed back at his friend. "The problem with you is that you have your head in the clouds. You always have. You spend too much time with those civilian eggheads out here. The world is not the uncomplicated place you like to think it is."

Palmer began to believe that Andrews saw himself as the city mouse visiting the country mouse, and it pissed him off. What really mattered, after all? His life with Catherine and his deepening commitment to the naval service was what it was really all about. It might be political at the command level and in the endless corridors of the Pentagon; but if he got back to sea duty, he would reconnect with the unambiguous and functional reality of the U.S. Navy.

Andrews, it seemed to him, lived in another country. One he could not begin to understand. And one in which he would never feel at home.

CHAPTER 5

Villa Rosselet

Victor Hidalgo sipped his morning coffee as he prepared for the meeting only minutes away—a meeting critical to his strategy to return to power and save his beloved country from chaos. In the end, it would come down to his ability to rally his guests to his cause—including guests he loathed.

Hidalgo had briefly greeted his visitors when they arrived at the villa during the previous evening. In a few moments, he would face a cross section of Mexico's political and business elite. Several of them had served in Hidalgo's administration; others were now with the current administration or held positions of great responsibility in financial institutions and the judiciary. The presence of two men from a very different background, however, had astounded all the others. Hidalgo had invited La Eme and one of the cartels' most powerful drug lords. Ramiro Chemor had vehemently argued against including them during his visit two weeks ago.

"Why do you want to take the risk of having any association with them? The ruling party will find out and the allegations will start again. It will be a disaster."

"Yes, yes. I understand what you are saying, Ramiro. I also understand the risk. However, before we involve others, we need a commitment that La Eme will not act against them or interfere with our plans. You and I know that this meeting is the only opportunity we will have. Bringing in Navarro and one of the drug lords is dangerous, but necessary." Because of what happened to his brother, Hidalgo knew how dangerous La Eme—Mexico's version of the Mafia—were.

"The guests are assembled, sir." Hidalgo's staff director announced.

"Thank you, Alejandro. Are they in a good mood?"

"Well . . . they . . . they appear to me to be still somewhat in a state of shock. Perhaps something that you expected with your two surprise guests."

"Oh, yes," Hidalgo said, grinning cheerfully. "Yes, I think that you are right."

Hidalgo followed his director and entered the large formal dinning room of the villa. The murmur of conversation between the invitees sitting around a long mahogany table ceased. All eyes were riveted on the man many of them had expected to return to Mexico within a year or so, not five, after his abrupt departure.

Hidalgo placed a set of notes on the table and addressed each of the men individually, adding some personal touches, and demonstrating how much he valued their friendship and commending them for their service to the nation. He could feel some of the tension in the room dissipating.

"Gentlemen, thank you for travelling so far to meet with me. Your presence honors me indeed. It is a very important day. As many of you already know, the time has come to act, to restore Mexico to its people, and—"

Applause broke out before he could continue with his opening remarks. Hidalgo stopped and saw that his two special guests had not joined in the applause. I cannot worry about them, Hidalgo thought. The others are ready to move forward. I need to find someway to convince them that they can openly support me without the fear or intimidation by La Eme. He cleared his throat and drew a deep breath.

"And our course will restore the dignity and sovereignty of our nation!"

Again those assembled broke into applause; this time it was a standing ovation. Hidalgo did not glance at La Eme leader, Javier Navarro, who did not stand. Nor did the portly man sitting next to him.

When the applause died down and his guests took their seats, Hidalgo continued. "The political action plan that we all worked so hard to develop is in the folder in front of you." He paused for several minutes to give them a chance to thumb through the pages. "As you already know, implementing the plan commenced when I announced my return to Mexico City a few weeks ago after consulting with you."

Hidalgo looked around the table, studying the faces of his guests, especially those of Navarro and Arturo Espinosa, a confidant of La Eme leader. He did not let Chemor know how surprised he had been when they accepted his invitation. He wondered how long it would take to find out if his gamble would work.

He put his copy of the plan down and continued. "I was heartened by the positive response to my announcement that I would return to Mexico. Perhaps I should take these long vacations more often," he said with a deadpan expression—and then broke into a wide grin. People around the table were laughing but stopped when Hidalgo's expression became somber.

"I wish everything could be as easy but we have a tough

road ahead and the media coverage will intensify on both sides of the border. From this day on, your commitment to this cause will become public." Hidalgo paused when he saw the expected concerned look in their eyes. He did not allow them to interrupt. "Yes, we must deal with our neighbors and openly present our program for reforming the government in Mexico to the Americans, especially those in the U.S. border cities. Whether we like it or not, what happens in the United States directly affects us. It is critical to our strategy. Mexico cannot ignore the interests of the United States—but it can't afford to subordinate its own to theirs. You need only consider what has happened in the last six months. Posadas has become—our country has become—a prisoner of politics that defer far too much to Washington. Meanwhile, everything we worked for— changes in the whole political system, shifting some of the excessive power of the executive branch to the legislature, reforming and strengthening the judiciary, restructuring an entrenched, stultifying bureaucracy—has been stalled or reversed."

He took a sip of water from the glass in front of him and squared his broad shoulders.

"What I was trying to do was elevate our country, which is, in far too many ways, a Third World nation, to the status it deserves. That will require not only massive economic changes but a reassertion of our sovereignty and some forceful realignment of our relationship with our neighbor to the north." What he could have added was that he would have to confront the lawlessness that was tearing the already strained fabric of his country's civil society to shreds. There had been hundreds of drug-related killings and kidnappings, pervasive corruption in the police, the military, and the courts. The gap between the upper and middle classes and the poor in his country, always wide, was getting even wider. Too many of his people had barely enough to eat, far too many could not read or write.

As in Colombia, the drug lords could openly defy the state and challenge its lawful authority; in Baja the cartel operated as a state within a state. And two of the men responsible were sitting in this very room.

But his greatest fear was that Mexico, thrown by its currency and economic crisis into the worst depression since the 1930s, was teetering on the edge of revolution. The ineffectual Posadas government, the ruling party, and their American supporters seemed to be oblivious. It would take little to trigger a social avalanche. But it was not yet the time to speak openly of all this.

"This will be an expensive campaign and I need your money as well as your commitment to challenge the ruling party." There was absolute silence in the room as those present began to consider just how difficult the road ahead would be. Hidalgo cleared his throat and went on, his voice loud and confident.

"Yes, our Independent Party will campaign from Sonora to the Yucatan. We will not exclude anyone—and that means our message has to reach beyond Mexico City to the small towns and rural areas. Each of you has responsibilities for these areas. The importance of organizing the reception and press coverage is critical. Make no mistake. Your work in these areas will determine our success."

"Pardon me. What is the message you are referring to?" Arturo Espinosa, the cartel drug lord, was the only one present dressed informally—a golf shirt open at the collar displaying a gold chain and crucifix. His belly spilled over the belt of his trousers and his massive biceps strained the knit fabric sleeves of his shirt. He surveyed the world with unblinking reptilian eyes set in a balding head that resembled the shape of a soccer ball. Sitting next to him could be quite unpleasant; his breath stank from the garlic cloves he chewed on constantly, regarding it as preventive medicine for everything from flu to impotence.

Hidalgo stopped. He had finally gotten some response

from one of his two special guests. Everyone became quiet and turned to look at them. The defiant, even hostile stares they got in return made the others quickly turn away. Hidalgo warned himself to proceed cautiously. Now was the time to pull off the most delicate part of what was, in effect, a deception operation.

"Thank you, Arturo, for coming so far and for the good question. Our message has to be simple so all Mexicans can be part of the movement. What I am talking about is something we all share and that is a commitment to social justice. A social justice that does not exclude the rural poor or the indigenous Indians of the South—a commitment to an expanded economy with a stable peso—a commitment to a higher standard of living and expanded education opportunities. And it is a message that our opposition will have a hard time challenging."

"Okay, but we've heard that stuff before," Espinosa said with unconcealed contempt, leaning back in his chair with his hands interlocked on top of his bulging stomach. Hidalgo did not immediately reply. Do they think I have not considered such things, he thought, suppressing his anger and retaining control of the meeting.

"I know what you mean, Arturo, and yes they are going to hear it again, and again. It is a fundamental part of our strategy. Listen carefully." He stopped and slapped his folder down on the table in front of him loudly enough to ensure he had everyone's attention. "We have what the world needs if only we can be smart enough to use it to our advantage. We have the natural resources and the hardworking cheap labor that the world competes for. Once we are back in power, the world will again beat a path to our door."

"But what about the United States? Do you actually believe they really want us to be successful and challenge them?" A member of the current administration asked; a man who had remained loyal to Hidalgo and refused to believe all the charges that had been thrown at him.

"Good question, José. The answer is that we will control our destiny—not the United States. We will play their game and announce that we support their political and economic initiatives to gain confidence. However, once in office and with our economy strengthened, everything will be contingent on how beneficial our cooperation with the Americans will be to Mexico. Again, let me make it clear. The greedy U.S. corporations that control the White House will not find business as usual in Mexico. As I said, we will control our own destiny and the United States will compete for our resources like every other country."

"Are you declaring yourself as a presidential candidate now, despite the constitutional barrier?"

"No Rafael. We must wait for public opinion to shift to our cause. In the interim, we will do our best to influence the outcome of the presidential and local elections. When pressed further, we will say that we hope a leader who understands the real needs of Mexico emerges."

"Yeah. I like that approach especially considering the constitutional ban of an ex-president seeking reelection," one of the guests said. He had been a judge during Hidalgo's administration and had become so bitter about the corruption of the judicial system that he had quit. "No sense in raising that issue too early."

"That's exactly the point I was just going to make, thank you. You are right. We need to create a bow wave of public support and help stimulate a demand for fundamental change before the national elections to keep the courts from interfering with their antiquated laws."

Everyone with the exception of the two special guests nodded in agreement. Their country faced a crisis as grave as the one that had shaken Mexico nearly a hundred years ago.

"I have one other announcement. I have asked Ramiro Chemor, who is already busy making preparations in Mexico City, to direct the campaign effort and he has accepted. I know that you agree that we are very fortunate to have someone of his stature and capability."

The announcement provoked vigorous applause. Chemor was regarded as smart, tough, and incorruptible. He was also admired for his ability to bring people together. His charm was of the sort quite different from Hidalgo's and his style more restrained and low key.

"There is one thing we need to clear up that has recently caused a setback." Hidalgo had lowered his voice and watched as all the heads turned toward him. "As you all know, the head of the U.S. antidrug program, General Swanson, was assassinated in Washington last month. This has caused a critical delay in my campaign timetable. I wanted to see what the fallout would be. We still haven't seen the full extent of it, so that is something we need to be aware of as we proceed."

Some people instinctively glanced toward Javier Navarro who had taken the seat at the opposite end of the table from Hidalgo. As the leader of La Eme and protector of the drug cartel, he was by far the most powerful of those present. Broad-shouldered and heavy-set, he had an impassive face, its skin pitted from a severe case of acne he suffered as a child. His thick black hair gleamed from the pomade he rubbed into it and his forearms were covered with a mat of hair that grew all over his body.

He heaved his bulky body frame out of his chair and stood up, then slowly looked around at the faces of those sitting at the table, his menacing stare sweeping from one to another like the beam from a lighthouse. The air in the room was suddenly filled with the smell of fear, and the acrid odor of his Cuban cigar. He removed the cigar from his mouth, exhaled a puff of smoke, and began to speak slowly, in a raspy voice.

"We have many problems today and Arturo and I did not come here to worry about some assassination of the meddling U.S. drug czar," he said without looking at anyone in particular. He stopped as if he was thinking about what to say next. No one moved. "We came to deliver a simple message. No government or individual can threaten our interests. That is our only concern. We don't care about your political parties—they are all the same. But they need to understand that we will do what is necessary to protect our interests."

The silence was overpowering as he stared with his dark, insomniac eyes at the faces around the table. Navarro shifted his stare to Hidalgo as he sat down, but Hidalgo refused to respond directly to his challenging words. What fools he thought to himself. No one knows for sure who killed Swanson, but La Eme and drug cartel has done plenty of damage with their own assassinations and kidnappings in Mexico. If he were to succeed, he would ultimately have to wipe these men off the face of the earth. He reminded himself again to control his anger. Navarro and the drug lords could jeopardize the support of his power base by intimidation and he needed to persuade them to remain on the sidelines until he got his campaign up and running. He had figured out a way that he could make that happen—if he could pull it off.

Hidalgo clasped his hands behind him. He waited before he spoke.

"Let me say that we understand the position of our compatriot. At the same time," he said firmly, returning Navarro's stare, "I know that Javier and Arturo understand how delicate our position is, how difficult it will be to consolidate public support—support that will cost the ruling party dearly. So we have a common interest."

Hidalgo watched to see Navarro's reaction. He knew that Navarro had already quietly committed the drug cartel's support to the radical PRD. But he was counting on

Navarro being shrewd enough to know that his fledgling Independent Party would draw loyal supporters from the ruling party as long as La Eme did not interfere. It was a trade-off and he needed to see if it would work.

Navarro raised his head abruptly, and silence again descended on the room following comments about Hidalgo's statement.

"You are right about that, Victor. Yes—the first priority is getting rid of the ruling party. But at some point, we need to know where you stand."

"But what are we going to do to protect our interests during the interim?" Espinosa broke in, ignoring a warning glance from Navarro.

Hidalgo was relieved by the interruption; it gave him an opportunity to answer the Eme leader in a less confrontational way. Hidalgo sat down.

"What we do is go on the offensive in a different way, Arturo. We use your ample resources to flood the media with charges that the U.S. drug policies represent a hypocritical double standard. In other words, we shift the blame to the United States as the largest consumer of illegal drugs. We turn it into a nationalistic cause—that Mexico resents being slandered and characterized as a drug-corrupted nation—all because of the U.S. appetite for drugs."

"Right! We need to make that clear," one of the guests, Alonzo Guerra, the president of one of the largest construction companies in Mexico, agreed. "They need to be told the truth."

Hidalgo did not respond to his supporter's statement, and plowed ahead, sensing that the meeting was headed in the desired direction. "We can work the U.S. Congress and demonstrate the real-life failures of the recent bilateral drug agreements. Consider the arrangement Posadas's regime had with Swanson's people, to allow joint interdiction operations. It started out with a big splash, but the results have been less than spectacular." Once more Hidalgo was refraining from saying what he really knew and what he suspected—that Swanson had been killed because he had started to wage war directly on the Mexican cartel by attacking their suppliers in Bolivia and Peru, and not confining his efforts to intercepting cocaine as it passed through Mexico on its way north.

"The U.S. president already has a serious credibility gap and we can widen it. With a concerted effort and your help, we can refocus the U.S. drug policies inside their own border where they belong. If they wish to solve their drug problem, they have to solve it on their own territory, not ours. Shifting the focus to the United States' failure to attack the real problem—drug consumption by its people—should help our mutual interests, Arturo."

When Espinosa started to respond, another glance from Navarro stopped him cold. He slid back in his chair, scowling but keeping his mouth shut. Another minute of silence passed before Navarro spoke, looking directly at Hidalgo.

"All right. We do it your way Victor—at least for now—and see what happens." As Hidalgo started to respond, he held his hand up, palm facing out, to indicate he was not finished. "But let me make one thing clear. We will not allow politicians to attack our organizations. If someone interferes, they will be dealt with."

Hidalgo knew that this was really Navarro's indirect response to his bringing up the recent assassination in Washington. He decided not to push it hoping that he made the point he wanted with the Mafia leader. He had bought some time; that was all he needed for now.

"Thank you, Javier. Yes, together we can make it work."

Hidalgo was quietly relieved. He had gambled that Navarro would not interfere with his Independent Party if he believed that it would cut a deal; leave his party alone while it split the ruling party and benefit the PRD. It appeared that his gamble had paid off. Hidalgo could see that his associates around the table were also relieved that this deal with the devil meant La Eme would not threaten his party supporters.

Hidalgo needed to get the group back on track and tapped his knuckles on the table.

"Let me quickly cover the various phases and responsibilities of our campaign strategy and designate those responsible for specific parts of it."

After an hour-long discussion, he decided that he had accomplished what he wanted and it was time to end the meeting. He reminded them that individual meetings would take place in the morning and he would see them at the banquet in the evening.

After all his guests had left the dining room, Hidalgo relaxed for the first time. It appeared that Navarro believed that he would be just like the others. Anyone could be bought; one just had to determine the price. There was the lingering warning from Navarro. Whatever happened, Hidalgo would not allow Navarro to take Mexico down the same path as Colombia. The Medellin and Cali drug cartels had actually challenged the government for control of that country and the power struggle continued to the present day. He swore to himself that he would die rather than let these monsters wreck his country.

As Hidalgo headed to his study, he saw that Navarro and Espinosa were sitting off by themselves, talking in a shaded area at the far end of the pool.

"What did you think of that nonsense, Arturo?"

"Well, it was just like you said it would be last night."

"That's because I understand how people like Hidalgo and the rest of those asshole politicians think. Look at them . . . like a bunch of fags around the pool. All they want is to get in power—and then feather their nests."

"You got that right, *jefe*. But Hidalgo—do you think he believes that he has any chance to get elected?"

"Who cares? What matters is that his loyalists will leave the ruling party."

"When Hidalgo was president, we didn't get much interference."

"Yeah. Those were the good days. Hidalgo was too busy with his stupid reforms. We actually got a shitload of help from his brother, Francisco, and others on our payroll," Navarro said and then laughed.

"Do you think Hidalgo knew what his brother and others were doing?"

"No. I really do not. Idealists like Hidalgo are so far removed from day-to-day reality with their grand plans that they lose track of what is really happening on the street. This is the reason we cannot trust them. The dangerous ones think they are on some mission to save everyone."

"Yeah, but can we beat the ruling party and Hildalgo and get the PRD in office?"

"If everything goes right we can. We will have to deal with Hildalgo if he starts getting too successful or the courts do not shut him down."

"And what about the United States?"

"We can deal with the United States," Navarro said confidently. "We are going to create some problems for them that will keep them busy and not worrying so much about the fucking 'drug problem' they have on their hands. Hay, let's enjoy ourselves and get a drink. We have accomplished what we needed to do. Hidalgo is just another dreamer. If he wakes up from his dream and gives us any trouble, we'll destroy him."

CHAPTER 6

Promontorio Mountain
Sonora, Mexico

The Gulfstream Two touched down at Tucson International and taxied to the commuter terminal. Clearances and other Mexican red tape made Tucson the favored jumping-off site for Promontorio Mountain although Hermosillo airport in Sonora was closer.

Mills glanced out the window before getting up to leave. There wasn't much to see except tarmac crews trying to stay out of the blistering sun. The pilot met him at the cockpit door.

"We had a nice tailwind; eighteen minutes before our ETA."

"Right. The sooner in, the sooner out," Mills muttered as he headed for the small exit hatch, fumbling for his sunglasses.

"Welcome back to the end of the world," he said glumly.

* * *

Dr. Hayden Mills was one of three assistant directors of the U.S. Department of Energy and point man for the controversial Promontorio Mountain Nuclear Waste Repository. He was in his late forties and still looked like the college professor he had been a decade earlier, with his baldpate that topped a face partially obscured by a well-trimmed beard and gold-rimmed spectacles. In deference to the climate, he was wearing an old seersucker suit. He made little effort to hide his dislike for his current surroundings—and the job he had been stuck with.

Promontorio Mountain was 140 miles southeast from the U.S.-Mexican border in the state of Sonora. The drive from the Tucson Airport to the Mexican border town of Nogalas was less than an hour on Interstate 19. After Nogalas, things got tougher. The desolate and only partially paved road to the mountain site—some 90 miles—was a test for any SUV. Mills hated every mile of the trip.

"Afternoon sir. How was the trip?"

"It was okay, Carl. Thanks for picking me up."

"Do you have any stops or shall we go direct?"

"No stops. The sooner we get there the better."

Once clear of the airport, Mills closed his eyes and reflected on his recent and unwelcomed notoriety following recent articles on Promontorio Mountain by both *Time* and *Newsweek*. The White House and DOE had tried in vain to determine who was responsible for the leak.

The mountain had a checkered history, ranging from early Indian sacred ground to scattered mines that never yielded any gold. More recently, after years of political bickering and millions of dollars spent on studies to find a permanent location in the United States for storage of the thousands of tons of radioactive waste generated by nuclear power plants, the focus shifted to Promontorio. The problem was not the technical challenge of storing the waste but rather the stubborn refusal of any local or state government in the United States to accept a repository. With tacit support from the Mexican government, the U.S. Congress gave up trying to gain consensus on a U.S. site and quietly approved moving ahead on Promontorio Mountain. Once the decision was made, hundreds of millions of additional engineering and construction dollars were spent to blast and drill out a series of caverns in the rock deep inside the mountain.

For years, the White House was successful in keeping the project in the desolate Sonora desert out of the national news. No one was sure how long the lid could be kept on things, given the failure of government-to-government negotiations over the issue of control. As President Hidalgo had approached the final year of his term, his demands for shared control of the repository played into the leadership of the Republican majority in Congress, who threatened to turn Promontorio Mountain into an election year issue. Exhaustive White House efforts failed and negotiations broke down, stalling the final phase of construction. The bitter conflict between the White House and President Hidalgo festered almost until the end of Hidalgo's term. Within a week of Hidalgo leaving Mexico in disgrace, both countries quietly signed an agreement to complete the repository construction. The contentious issues of shared control disappeared after a short-term U.S. bailout of the beleaguered peso and guarantees of abundant, cheap energy to the northern border manufacturing areas.

As the Grand Cherokee started to bounce around, Mills knew without opening his eyes that they had made the turn from Nogalas. By keeping his visits short and very low-key, he had been able to manage the project from his Washington office—until the *Time* and *Newsweek* articles screwed things up. The press and environmentalists had descended on the site, creating a major PR problem for Mills and his department. As another bump jostled him across the seat, he figured the politicians in Washington created and exacerbated more problems than they could keep up with or solve. And he was the one who had to duck questions he couldn't easily answer.

Although referred to as a mountain, Promontorio Mountain was actually more like a ridgeline that blended into the Sierra Madre mountain range. The DOE design plan called for a deep geologic repository large enough to hold 50,000 metric tons of nuclear waste. The highly radioactive waste from commercial power plants would take up 80 percent of the repository with the remaining 20 percent allocated to low-level hospital and research center radioactive waste. The thinking in Washington was that if the prototype proved successful, Congress could be persuaded to allocate sufficient funds to build follow-on sites in the United States.

"Carl, can you turn down the air? It's starting to get cold back here."

"I was just about to do that very thing. This time of year the bottom really drops out after the sun goes down."

"Yeah . . . right."

Mills looked out the window but paid no attention to the arid landscape. He had other things on his mind. He needed to ensure that he was not the fall guy if things turned sour during next month's House Energy Committee hearings on Promontorio Mountain. Ever since Congress scheduled the hearings, Mills had been worrying about his testimony and the potential impact on his career. He had turned down lucrative packages from General Electric and Baltimore Gas and Electric because he was given reason to believe that he might be appointed to the secretary's job when she retired. Now it was time to put up or shut up. During the past week in Washington, he had decided that he could use a recent declassified California Institute of Technology study that pointedly laid out the potential risks with a geological repository. Those in Congress who supported the White House decision could acknowledge and document the risks in the Congressional Record by citing the CalTech study as evidence that they had given careful thought to the downside and demonstrated their concern. Mills could dodge tough questions by falling back on what he hoped would be entered into the Congressional Record. He was doing what Congress directed—or seemed to direct—and, he told himself, it just might work.

As the SUV made the final turn into the repository site, Mills felt somewhat relieved. He had figured out what he needed to do.

"To hell with the political risks. I need to make those responsible in Congress go on record before I testify and put my ass on the line."

"What did you say, sir?"

"Nothing important, Carl. I'm glad we got here in one piece considering that poor excuse for a road."

CHAPTER 7

Georgetown

Andrews turned off the Dulles access road, crossed the Georgetown Bridge spanning the Potomac, and made the final turn on Foxhall Road. The three-story Georgian stood in contrast to some of the newer "MacMansions" built during the dot.com bubble and much despised by the members of the permanent Washington establishment who lived there.

Brooke Andrews was giving her final instructions to their housekeeper and cook, Rosario, when they arrived. Rosario had prepared a buffet of grilled swordfish, red-skin potatoes, and a salad. Cole, Brooke, and David served themselves from the side table in the dining room while Rosario retired to her quarters at the rear of the house.

They moved into the library after dinner for coffee and brandy. The hours passed quickly as they recounted what had been going on in their lives—and exchanged a fair amount of gossip. As Andrews reached for the decanter to refill Palmer's brandy snifter, Brooke interrupted.

"Hey, guys . . . I hate to be a wet blanket but I happen to know that David is fading fast. If he was lucky, he got two or three hours sleep last night after another one of those marathon meetings that you obviously don't miss, Cole."

Andrews grinned at his friend and said, with a Groucho Marx–like waggle of his eyebrows, "You know Brooke. She is always chasing me upstairs."

Brooke Andrews took a coaster off the gleaming Mission-style coffee table and tossed it at her husband. "See what I have to put up with?"

Cole Palmer laughed, but he could not help thinking about rumors he had heard of some stormy and difficult periods in their marriage. He discounted them, however, knowing that theirs was as much an alliance of power and influence as a love match.

"It might be three hours earlier for me but I'm beat. Have you got me in the same place?"

"Same room, Cole. Yell if you need anything. We'll probably be gone when you get up. I don't know if David told you that I accepted a great job at the World Bank— head of the currency exchange oversight committee. Someone at Citicorp put a good word in for me."

When Palmer found his way downstairs, Rosario greeted him cheerfully and offered him a cup of coffee. She informed him that dinner would be at seven and that Mrs. Andrews had driven in with Mr. Andrews and left her car keys for him. He sat down in a sunny breakfast nook off the kitchen and helped himself to some croissants and orange juice while glancing at the *Washington Post*. He skipped over the front-page news and saw that the annual sailboat show, squeezed along the Annapolis docks, was in its second day.

An hour later, Palmer finessed the impossible Annapolis parking by leaving the car inside the Naval Academy grounds and walking the four blocks to the city docks. He turned up the collar of his leather jacket as the cold winds came off the Chesapeake. Like Georgetown, the streets that ran down to the waterfront had an endless assortment of trendy shops and restaurants—but little parking. He was not in any hurry as he strolled along, eyeing the boats and imagining how they would handle and how many knots each one could make with every inch of sail deployed in a good, stiff breeze. After several hours of nautical daydreaming and twenty minutes spent admiring a Nautor Swan in beautiful condition and imagining himself sailing her single-handed across the Atlantic, he made his way over to Riordan's for its famous Chesapeake crab cakes before heading back, hoping to avoid the late afternoon traffic.

During dinner that evening, Palmer amused Andrews and Brooke with stories about the million-dollar boats and all the motley crowd of would-be sailors milling around the docks. Rosario had worked up a wonderful prime rib and Palmer's house gift, two bottles of California Preston merlot, complemented it perfectly. Andrews and Palmer soon started telling stories about some of the escapades while serving on destroyers, while Brooke listened patiently, having heard many of them more than once. After a pause in the yarn spinning, Cole raised his wineglass to Brooke and David.

"Before we get too far along with our creatively embellished sea stories, I want you to know how much your support and love have meant to me. I know that I haven't been good company, but I think I'm making some progress at last."

David Andrews nodded sympathetically; Brooke got up with tears in her eyes and embraced Palmer. As the evening went on, they laughed and talked about anything and everything since their happy days in Newport—but, by tacit consent, avoided mentioning events that had taken place during the years of Palmer's marriage.

Palmer had noticed Andrews falling into a moment of introspection while Rosario was clearing the table for desert and tried to guess, from the expression on his face, what was going on in his friend's mind. Despite the light-hearted tone of the evening's conversation, from time to time a somber expression had settled on Andrews's face. After dinner, Brooke led the two men into the large library and began fussing with the coffee service Rosario had left on the table. After pouring cups for the two men, she excused herself to powder her nose. Palmer and Andrews lapsed into an unaccustomed silence as they sipped their coffee.

"David, you haven't poured any brandy for Cole," Brooke chided him when she returned. Sweeping her long skirt to one side she settled on the sofa and then tucked her legs under her, leaning back against a large yellow cushion and staring at Palmer thoughtfully.

"Sorry, honey. I have been so interested in catching up with Cole that I forgot my duty as a host. I'm also trying to get Cole fully relaxed before I . . . I bring up a certain problem." Andrews had not meant to let it come out so abruptly and reproached himself for his clumsiness.

Before he could recover, Palmer seized the initiative.

"Ah! Could there be an ulterior motive behind your invitation?" Palmer said with a grin.

The quick comeback caught Andrews off balance. "Well . . . uh . . . no . . . nothing sinister . . . but—"

"But what?" Palmer pressed him. "Let's hear it.

Andrews shifted uneasily in his chair and fiddled with one of his cuff links. "Let me try and—"

Palmer could tell when his usually urbane and thoroughly composed friend was feeling both embarrassed and guilty about something. "You not going to try to talk me into taking some kind of job. You wouldn't do that to me, would you? Anyway, before you ask, the answer is no. I'm really not interested in all the games you folks play here in wonderland. I don't fit in. I found that out the last time."

Andrews remained seated shaking his head, smiling. "Well, I see you haven't changed any—still as bull-headed as usual."

"Maybe you're right. However, I really don't miss it."

The momentary silence that fell over the room was uncomfortable for all three of them. Palmer knew that something was really bugging his friend. Andrews's forced smile failed to conceal the conflict going on inside of him. In the short time he had been staying with them, Palmer had detected subtle changes in both Brooke and David. There was an edge of tension just below the surface of their easy charm and facile small talk. He looked over at Brooke for some indication of what was going on but her expression told him nothing. She sat on the couch like a big, alert cat, her luminous eyes gleaming, a faint and somewhat disconcerting smile on her face.

"Okay, Cole, I hear you. But give me a small break. It might even make me feel better talking about it. We can argue about it later."

Cole took a sip of cognac and nodded back to Andrews. "Okay, pal. Give it your best shot."

Andrews began to give Palmer a background briefing on the perilous situation in Mexico, obviously choosing his words with care. "As you probably know, the situation in Mexico is out of control. We are facing problems that have been ignored or dealt with by half-measures for years. Now we've run out of time. It's worse than Colombia; the stakes are higher. The combination of drug money undermining the authority of the government and the severity of the depression—well, Posadas has good intentions but not a clue as to a way out of the mess, so he's looking to us to survive. But there is no quick fix. We've done everything we can to squeeze the IMF and keep the peso from completely tanking. We've muscled the invest-ment banks and the big money movers to take a more op-timistic approach—"

"Why haven't we seen more about how bad it is in the press?" Palmer asked.

"Well, we've been working hard to keep it under the horizon and lucky at the same time. Fortunately, the net-works don't give much of a shit about covering Mexico; the cable outfits only want the scandal de jour and don't even know where Mexico is. The print media—ah, there's the problem. We know that the *New York Times* is going to run a four-parter in three weeks—in-depth coverage and all of it bad news. We have our own second-term elec-tions to contend with next year without being tarred with what is happening in Mexico. At the same time, if the rad-ical left PRD—controlled by the drug cartel—gets control of government, we'll have another Colombia on our hands."

Andrews's bringing up Colombia unleashed a flood of memories, most of them unpleasant, about sensitive opera-tions in which Palmer had been involved in Cali and Medellin—some of them black antidrug ops, ones that the U.S. government devoutly hoped neither the *New York Times* or anyone else would ever find out about. He had forced his way into several of them as a means of striking out against the Colombian cartel—trying to persuade him-self that his actions would somehow make up for his not being there with Catherine that night, for being unable to reach closure because her killer had never been found.

"Cole, are you with me?" Andrews saw that Palmer was mentally in some place far removed from Foxhall Road.

"Sorry about that . . . just thinking about that Cali oper-ation. It sounds like you are walking a tightrope, pal. I don't understand how they—PRD—think they can pull it off? Hasn't the ruling party been in office forever?"

"Yes, about seventy years. However, this time we are seeing a well-executed campaign of terror to discredit the Posadas regime."

Andrews pinched the bridge of his nose, beginning to show fatigue.

"The news gets worse. You probably heard that former president Hidalgo declared that he is returning to Mexico City. No one knows what his intentions are but this will stir things up even more with their national elections only a couple of months after ours. It's not a good picture. I don't know if you are aware that a series of killings has been carried out on our border—and even here in Washington."

Brooke turned and stared at her husband. "David, does the administration really believe that Swanson's assassination is part of this?"

Andrews shrugged his shoulders. "We don't know. It was a professional hit . . . in and out without anyone seeing anything. The Eme leader, a thug called Navarro, has made it clear that the drug cartel is the real power in Mexico and will not tolerate any interference in their lucrative drug business. In my thinking he sent us a message."

"I'm not sure I'm tracking the linkage of all this to Washburn's second term that you mentioned earlier." Palmer wondered where Andrews was headed—and what it had to do with him.

"Well, Washburn made a commitment in the campaign to help Mexico integrate itself into the global economy and make it a full democratic partner, somewhat like Canada. I personally think this was a fatal mistake. The secretary of state, however, has persuaded the president to stay the course—and that includes propping up a dying economy. We're just giving first aid to the mortally wounded. But we're stuck with Posadas, come what may—

and the chaos down there has handed the Republicans a major campaign issue."

"Wait a minute. What are we talking about here, David? How to get Mexico back on track or getting another four years in Washington?"

"The administration thinks it is one and the same," Andrews replied wearily. "Look, it comes down to this—we took Posadas to the dance, we have danced with him, and we have to take him home when the dance is over."

Palmer still had a problem with some of what Andrews had said.

"Isn't there another school of thought that says corporate America is driving our policies in Mexico?"

A faint blush of anger showed in Andrews's face.

"Oh God, let's not get into this business of blaming a country's problems on the multinationals. Big oil pissed off Mexico decades ago, so Mexico nationalized its oil resources. Sovereign nation, right? Take a hard look at how effectively Mexico has used its oil revenues for investment in infrastructure, for stimulating internal economic development. Mexico's biggest industry is manufacturing its own problems. And now it is choking on drug money—most of which doesn't do a damn thing for the economy but corrupt it. And people like Navarro have every interest in seeing Mexico get deeper in the shit. At the end of the day, he'll effectively own the country. The Colombians haven't managed to pull that off. Even the Russian oligarchs and their mafia co-conspirators aren't even in the same league as Navarro when it comes to sheer audacity."

Palmer knew where this argument was going. They had already played variations on the same theme repeatedly over the years.

"Shifting gears, you mentioned the former president—Hidalgo. How does he fit into this?"

"We're not sure. Yet. We know that Hidalgo maintains an effective network of loyal followers in and out of government. The people in Mexico still love him. He is a smart politician who feels the U.S. government betrayed him years ago. All of a sudden, we are seeing Mexico flooded with inflammatory nationalistic propaganda. You know—U.S. environmental standards are really a ploy to keep Mexico unable to compete . . . exploitation of cheap labor and resources . . . and so forth. The same kind of stuff Hidalgo was pushing when he was in office. And he sure would agree with you that American corporate interests have—how did you put it—'driven' American policy with respect to Mexico."

"There are some folks right here in Washington who support that thesis to some degree." Palmer noticed that Brooke was on the verge of saying something and then stopped short.

"Yeah, sure," Andrews snapped. "You sound like Sec-State. Snyder is on this kick that we owe Mexico. We need to make concessions. You know, an equal partner in everything. The problem is that it simply will not work until the government drives out the embedded corruption and lawlessness. The Republicans love this argument."

Palmer doggedly stuck to his line of reasoning.

"I understand that some people believe that the previous administration pulled the plug on Hidalgo, right?"

The question stopped David cold. After a quick exchange of glances with Brooke, he gave a dismissive shrug. "Don't believe everything that you hear, Cole. What the world knows is that the bottom dropped out of the peso shortly after Hidalgo's term ended—thanks to his blaming American corporate interference for too many of his country's problems—and because his idea of 'partnership' with the United States was colored by resentment. No, paranoia is a better word for it. We also know that there were Hidalgo administration and family members linked to the drug business. The recent conviction of his brother, Francisco, tells you something about the complicity of the former president. The ruling party ran Hidalgo out of town where he remained until last week's announcement."

Andrews and his wife looked at one another. While at the State Department, he had actively participated in the strategy to undermine Victor Hidalgo. And Brooke knew it; it was a strategy that her father and his friends approved of. Her husband's role had been a risky one, given his position in the State Department—but his quiet advocacy had paid off when Hidalgo was replaced by Posadas—and Andrews got the Cabinet appointment as the National Security Adviser.

"And where will Hidalgo get the money to finance his campaign if he decides to run?"

Andrews replied patiently, like a teacher responding to a student. "We're not sure that he is going to run—the Mexican Constitution doesn't allow him to—but I wouldn't bet the farm on it. It's a real mess."

Palmer remained skeptical about some of what Andrews was telling him. "I still don't understand how Hidalgo can have all this popular support if everyone believes he is so corrupt. I'm not privy to all the information you have but from what I do remember the charges against Hidalgo were possibly ah . . . trumped up?" Palmer glanced at Brooke, but she just sat there like an umpire watching a tennis match.

"You amaze me, Cole." Andrews grinned, but there was little humor in it. "I'm not sure who has been selling you this line of goods. Maybe those radicals you hang out with in California. But let's get back to the present."

"Okay, I hear you—but is all this really our business? During my couple of years in your office, it seemed that Mexico wasn't near number one on your outfit's agenda. I was tasked to focus in Colombia."

Andrews did not respond until Brooke suddenly got up from the couch and picked up the tray with the coffee service on it.

"That was then; this is now. Washburn's ace up the sleeve is the Free Trade Area of the Americas and an expanded NAFTA. In addition to Asia, and watching to see how China evolves, we see Europe moving toward a federal union characterized by favored-trading blocs, a common currency, and an independent defense force. We need to counter all that with the FTAA—and Mexico will be an important player."

Andrews called out to his wife as she was leaving the room, "Can you bring us some ice water? I've got a buzz going from all the brandy."

She glanced over her shoulder and replied, "Get your own water. I don't like the way you're headed—and by the way, it's getting late."

Andrews went on as if he had not heard her.

"During the past month, we've gotten pretty solid intel that the level of terrorism in Mexico is going to step up—and possibly spill over the border. It's pretty reliable; but we need to get a much better track on what is happening before we move."

"Why do I have the feeling that you're not finished telling me everything?"

"Have you heard about the Promontorio Mountain Repository?"

"No. Should I?"

"Well, you haven't been reading *Time* or *Newsweek* lately. You'll probably hear a lot more about it in the months ahead." Andrews went on to tell Palmer the whole story of the repository and the political issues surrounding it.

"But why would Posadas agree to stow nuclear waste in his country?"

"David, tell Cole what really got the project off dead center." Brooke had come back from the kitchen in time to overhear the exchange.

"Well . . . sure. We held up Posadas's request for financial support of the peso until he agreed to reopen Promontorio Mountain. It happened shortly after Hidalgo's six-year term ended—without any visibility or fanfare. We needed to get it done, Cole, and Mexico needed the financial support. It helped both countries."

Palmer was always amazed how his friend could make such elegantly simple equations. *Only interests, not friends,* he thought.

"What will keep Hidalgo from blowing the whistle?"

"The White House has arranged that the initial waste shipment will be from Mexico. That would blunt any immediate protests from environmentalists—at least the ones in Mexico. What we are really scared shitless about is the possibility of some terrorist action involving Promontorio—particularly because both countries have downplayed the whole deal. If the worst-case scenario plays out, the Congress will cut Washburn off at the knees—and then Posadas will be a dead duck."

Palmer was trying to sort out all this information—and still wondering what Andrews wanted from him.

"I still don't understand what the terrorists—whoever they are—hope to gain by a terrorist campaign."

Brooke Andrews suddenly broke in.

"David, why don't you tell Cole what this is really all about?"

Andrews looked relieved; his wife had given him his opening.

"We could lose everything if Posadas and Hidalgo start fighting—and the Mafia-backed PRD backs into power demonstrating that Mexico is ungovernable. If that happens, Washburn's second-term bets are off and as well as any hopes for a more democratic and open Mexico."

"And what about your own plans, David?" Brooke asked bluntly. She turned to Palmer and said, "I think you should know—Washburn has hinted to David that he could be the next secretary of state."

Palmer was stunned. Andrews, if he were indeed appointed and confirmed, would be one of the youngest men in history to fill that office.

Andrews abruptly got out of his chair and left the room.

"It is only fair you know what the stakes are," Brooke said quietly. "He needs you because he trusts you. I didn't want you to be involved in this. Let me come straight out. From what I know, you've gone off the reservation a number of times. I don't think David should have let you do it. But he knows how . . ."

She faltered for a moment and went on.

"Cole, you can't do anything about what has happened, I mean you can't make things right . . . look, I told David not to do this. I think he would be using you."

Before Palmer could respond she lifted her head defiantly and stared directly into his eyes. "This town is all about using people. Using, then being used, and then using—that is not you. David has decided to give up everything—in order to get the job. You don't have to play his game."

She broke off as Andrews came back into the library. "Well, what else have you laid on our guest?" he said brusquely.

"Nothing that he shouldn't know up front. Cole is as much my friend as yours . . . and I loved Cathy . . ."

She wrapped her arms around herself and addressed her husband as if Palmer were not in the room.

"Tell him what you really want him to do. Don't lie to him. For God's sake, he doesn't deserve it."

Andrews stared at her with open hostility. "Sure, I'll tell him. And I'll tell him I want him to serve his country, not me."

Palmer was aware of the tectonic plates of a marriage shifting in a way he could not fully understand.

"If he wants to have a piece of this, we've got two hours to pack and get to Dulles. I'll tell him what he needs to know on the way to the airport. If he doesn't like what he hears, then I'll turn the car around and he can go home. No harm done."

Brooke stood silently on the polished floor leading to the center hall, staring at the two men and continuing to wrap her arms around herself.

"Jesus, Brooke, what kind of monster do you think I am? Cole understands what we need to do sometimes to keep this world from flying apart."

Without responding to her husband, she walked toward the front stairs and then rested one slender hand on the railing.

"Don't do this, David."

As she went upstairs, Andrews leaned against the wall. Palmer could see that he was slightly drunk.

"Ask not, right, Cole? Well, go ahead and ask. If I give you the right answers you will get on the red-eye to Mexico City and be met by your contact from the U.S. Embassy—the commercial attaché. The bottom line is that I need someone who can cut through all this bullshit, someone I can trust to stop whatever is going down before a lot of people get killed. I hate asking you, Cole. Brooke is right. You've been through enough already. The problem is that I don't have any other options. If we don't get a handle on things quickly, we might not ever have the chance again."

CHAPTER 8

Guadalajara, Mexico

Navarro pulled alongside Espinosa's BMW at the deserted Neza soccer stadium. They routinely met and traveled alone secure in their own sense of power and invulnerability. It had been almost two months since their Portugal meeting with Hidalgo and Navarro wanted to hear if Espinosa had picked up anything from the other drug barons. He worked too hard to allow some stupid mistake by one of his esteemed colleagues who decided to cut a deal on the side or take some other action not authorized by Navarro. More than once Espinosa had provided a heads-up when trouble of this sort was brewing.

After years of hard and dangerous negotiation among the ruthless and competing drug barons, Navarro had established a cartel of the major drug lords to leverage the distribution and pricing of the increasing flow of elicit drugs. He then set out on an ambitious plan to recruit through either bribery or intimidation—or both—a network of high-level government and judicial officials, as well as one of the secretaries in the office of Posada's chief of staff, to further his plans for expansion of his market far beyond the United States. Europe was mostly wide open; even the Afghanistan and Pakistan wholesalers ran supply lines into the European Union. China was, for the moment, closed to him and Russia was too dangerous, given the ferocity of its *mafyia*. He did not intend to compete with them, even in the various nations that had broken away from the crumbling Soviet Union. At least not yet.

Navarro was generous with perks—country club memberships, lavish trips, access to real estate deals, and even access to prominent private secondary schools. It was money well spent; officials, particularly in the police and army, as well as judges and legislators, with large bank accounts quietly replenished with drug money, stalled legislation considered undesirable and kept government interference at bay. The cost to buy and maintain this network was not a problem with drug-related profits running into the billions of dollars. For those few who had a sudden attack of conscience, a visit from José Chapa or one of his compadres put them back on track.

Navarro joined Espinosa, pushing back the front passenger seat. Both were dressed casually in golf shirts and slacks. Espinosa cared little about the finer points of clothing and personal grooming. He was actually amused by the effect his appearance and coarse manners had on the young computer programmers, business school graduates, and other skilled professionals who staffed the many front companies set up by the cartel. Everything in his world was changing rapidly but Espinosa belonged to the old school, in which a readiness to do violence mattered more than subtlety and high tech. It did not matter to Navarro. He made an exception for his long-standing friend and kept him at his side. As with the quietly sinister Chapa, the only thing that mattered to Navarro was unquestioning loyalty.

"Did you listen to the news while driving down?"

"No," Espinosa replied, "I can't follow what those guys are saying. I switch to music."

"Well, Posadas was shooting off his mouth again . . . you know . . . the cartel represents the greatest threat to his administration and—get this—Mexico's national security."

"Well, he couldn't be more right about the first part," Espinosa said, and roared with laughter. "Posadas is a fool. How does he figure we are affecting national security? He should be worrying about all that *gringo* interference. He's letting the Americans call the shots—that's the threat to Mexico."

Despite the joint efforts of American and Mexican antidrug forces, the months following the Villa Rosselet meeting saw dramatically increased numbers of murders, kidnappings, and terrorist incidents, all part of the general lawlessness swamping Mexico. The deaths of two major political figures, a respected presidential candidate from the National Action Party (PAN) and the archbishop of Guadalajara, drew international attention and further damaged the government. The Mexico City daily newspaper, *Reforma*, reported the criminals were winning Mexico's war on crime, and that the Posadas administration seemed incapable of carrying the battle to the enemy.

"Our strategy is starting to work," Navarro said quietly, nodding his head, "and the PRD understands what we can do for them. Every now and then they start shooting off at the mouth and we have to set them right."

"I don't trust any of them, *jefe*. You would think the dumb sons of bitches would wake up after that accident to the PAN candidate, Gutierrez."

"Posadas will do his usual dance as long as he can," Navarro continued, without acknowledging Espinosa.

"He will try to turn things around and say it's all about a drug war over territory. The son of a bitch knows that I put a stop to that when I took over and formed the cartel."

"Now that the PAN candidate is out of the way, how long are you going to let Hidalgo play out his game? He made me nervous the way he talked in Portugal—like he was already president."

"I'm watching things develop. His independent party is doing just what I thought they would—pulling loyalists from the ruling party. The ruling party—and the follow-on president, Carlos Alverez—is in deep trouble. We'll let Hidalgo get a little further on before we pull the string. At this point, he can only make it worse for Posadas and Alverez."

They moved on to a discussion of other problems that had to be dealt with. The tone of the discussion was weirdly dispassionate.

"We need to make an example of the editor of *Diario de Juarez*. He had his warning and he ignored it," Navarro said firmly.

"Ayah!" Espinosa snorted through his flat nose. "Does the fool really think he's getting anywhere, cozying up to Posadas, claiming we are running the country? He's another dreamer; he doesn't understand that most of the ordinary people don't care what we do as long as they get their beans and rice."

Navarro took out a cigar and took his time lighting it carefully. When it was drawing to his satisfaction, he punched Espinosa in the shoulder playfully but with some force.

"Yeah. Let's make it a wake-up call for some of the other dreamers listening to him."

Navarro puffed on his cigar and remained silent for several minutes. Espinosa knew better than to interrupt the great man during his more meditative moments.

"It's time to step things up," Navarro suddenly announced. "What happened in Guerrero was just the tip of the iceberg," he said, referring to actions of the Zapatista Popular Revolutionary Army, a left-wing, ragtag group that had emerged after the rebellion in Guerrero three years earlier. "The Southern area is ripe for revolt and the poor bastards feel that they were better off during the Hidalgo administration. We've got something working that the government will not be able to recover from."

Espinosa was unaware of what Navarro was talking about and disappointed that he had not been consulted. But he was careful not to show it. Navarro told him what he needed to know; it was unhealthy to show excessive curiosity.

"Okay, I think we've covered everything," said Navarro as he threw his cigar out the window and started to get out of the car. "If things go as expected, we will soon hear the popular cry for the removal of Posadas. And once the momentum picks up," smiled Navarro, "the ruling party or anyone else will be powerless to stop it."

"The *gringos* still worry me. Everywhere we turn, they are interfering."

"Don't worry about them. It's been over three months since the Swanson business and they haven't done anything. We are going to give them reason to rethink their involvement in all this. It is up to them. If they are smart and dump the ruling party, our job will be easier."

CHAPTER 9

Minsk, Belarus
Formerly Belorusskaja of the Soviet Republic

Colonel Yuri Kaliniev was anxiously going through a new line item inventory in the frigid old warehouse that had once been a tractor factory and had been reconfigured to house the headquarters for the army's Minsk weapons storage facility. He pushed aside the report and rubbed his hands together trying to generate some warmth. It was early May but the long winter was still hanging around. If he was cold, the nine young men outside, draftees assigned to patrol the perimeter of the facility, were even colder; at least they were not in Chechnya.

Kaliniev pushed back from his desk; folders and reports haphazardly piled on top. He was tall—six-two with graying blond hair, a longish angular face with dark circles around his eyes. Out of personal pride, he retained an impressive military appearance with his short hair and carefully pressed uniform, although no one in the regional command really cared anymore.

He threw the inventory on the pile in front of him and looked at his watch. It was time to go home. But he had nothing to look forward to at his small apartment; and these days he found it difficult to get to sleep.

Seven weeks ago, Kaliniev had come across a canvas-covered pallet supporting six small bombs or mines during one of his routine inspections. He wasn't quite sure what sort of munitions they were. The pallet was in a remote underground stowage area of the arsenal—and these peculiar devices were not listed in the facility's latest master inventory of weapons. The dust-covered canvas attested to the fact that no one had tampered with or moved the pallet for some time.

"How in the hell did I miss checking that area out before?" Kaliniev had chided himself.

His initial reaction had been to report what he found—but something held him back. The weapons—whatever they were—intrigued him. Each of the six devices were contained in a gray metal box—less than half a meter long, about as thick as an attaché case, weighing only about 5 kilograms and with a recessed handle on each end. The only marking on them that he recognized was the familiar high-explosive warning and some special KGB markings that he did not understand. They had neither army markings nor serial numbers. What purpose were they for, he wondered.

"Enough punch to do a job on a tank or structure, maybe, if they contain something like Dynex," he said to himself. Dynex was the most powerful, highly concentrated explosive developed by the Russians. But it was so devastating that it was seldom used, especially by the military. There was a small access plate on the bottom of each device, probably covering the arming mechanism. No, these could not belong to the army, he thought. But he was the senior officer at the facility; its contents were his responsibility. After thinking it over carefully, he decided he would not report the devices. Instead of getting mired down in the endless paperwork he would have to file and the possible problems for him that might follow, he would find out where these devices came from and for what purpose.

When Kaliniev returned the next morning, he again started reviewing the old inventory records. He confirmed what he expected, that he would find nothing about the devices in the record. He decided to make a discreet call to an old friend in Moscow.

Long ago—it seemed like a century rather than two decades—Yuri Kaliniev had distinguished himself serving in Afghanistan. The country honored him as a Hero of the Soviet Union. It was a time that Kaliniev did not want to remember. Equipment was old and not properly maintained; logistical supply lines were nonexistent, leading not only to unnecessary battle casualities but also to widespread sickness from malnutrition and the lack of adequate winter clothing. The severe winter winds and snow that were pervasive in the Ghorband Valley Mountains added to the soldiers' misery. Under those conditions, most commanders were reluctant to lead and take those risks that win battles.

During one of these periods, the Afghans gathered in force and attacked the headquarters camp in the hours before sunrise. It was the first large-scale attack on a Soviet command camp in that sector. Within moments the rocket-propelled grenades blew away the headquarters' command post and the senior officer's quarters. Sheets of automatic-weapon fire rained down on the camp from the dark mountains and the accompanying mortar barrage was deafening. When the heavy fire abated, Afghan warriors emerged from the darkness to charge the barbed-wire perimeter. When it appeared that they were about to overrun the disorganized camp, Kaliniev and his well-disciplined troopers, who were returning from a night patrol, arrived at the Afghans' flank. The battle soon deteriorated into fierce close-in fighting. Kaliniev, wounded in the left shoulder, crawled from position to position; encouraging the stunned headquarters personnel to fight. Shrapnel had torn into his rotor cuff but Yuri would not let it slow him down. Someone had to lead. The battle finally ended when Yuri successfully deployed his armored vehicles with their superior firepower to force the enemy back into their mountain hideaways. Sixteen soldiers in his company were dead, along with 62 headquarters personnel and 139 Afghan warriors.

As the months of fighting continued, Kaliniev became increasingly discouraged, especially by the casualties chalked up to "accidents of war"—unnecessary losses of fine young Russian boys because of improper training and malfunctioning weapon systems. Yuri Kaliniev began to despise those in the Soviet Union who were destroying the army he loved. There was no welcome or reception when the demoralized Soviet army finally extracted itself from Afghanistan. Politicians now in charge of the army discharged the sick and sent them home without separation pay. The army dispersed the remaining tired and worn-out soldiers to army bases throughout Russia.

For the rest of his life, Kaliniev wished he had been killed—and not returned to his homeland. His entire family, wife and two boys, ten and fourteen, were killed in an aircraft accident while on their way to greet him on his return. An accident, he later found out, that was attributable to the lack of proper maintenance on the IL-18 military transport aircraft that they and other families were on. His faith in the leadership of Russia was shattered; all that meant the most to him was now gone forever. His family had been needlessly destroyed and the country that he had served so loyally betrayed and split into pieces.

And his persistent investigation into the cause of the crash had repercussions that put his career on a very slow track.

Kaliniev was trusted and admired still by a small number of friends who had served with him in Afghanistan. Anatoly Markovitch was one of them; but he was no longer in the army. While Vladimir Kryuchkov was heading what was still the KGB, Markovitch had managed to get himself recruited into the elite First Chief Directorate, which was responsible for foreign intelligence. After the coup attempt in August of 1991, the directorate became the SVR, doing the same business under a different name. Like many others, Markovitch had decided to make a change. He became a businessman—he owned a small and not particularly prosperous bar near the Arbat. And by necessity had made his peace with the people who offered him "protection"—a relationship to the *mafyia* that Kaliniev was not aware of when he placed a long-distance call to his old comrade in Moscow.

"Hay, Anatoly—how goes it?"

Markovitch did not have any happy news. "Things are terrible in Moscow, Yuri. I take the *elektrichka* out to the country and wander around with my memories before catching the last train back."

"Yes, I understand, Anatoly." The Russians have a passion for the countryside. It was the only way they could break away from the daily misery of life in a Russia where vodka consumption increased as life expectancy and public health declined. At least you could escape to the forests and pick mushrooms. If you were lucky, you might own a dacha, a wooden cottage out in the countryside.

Kaliniev took his time but gradually worked the conversation around to the point where he thought he could ask a guarded question.

"By the way, did you ever come across any small portable bombs or mines that were not part of the standard inventory when you were in the army?"

"Why do you want to know?" Markovitch asked cautiously.

"Better you don't ask, my friend."

There was a long silence on the line before Markovitch, now clearly nervous, said, "Tell me what these, ah . . . devices might look like."

After Kaliniev described what he had found, Markovitch said firmly. "I don't want to discuss such matters on the phone. The Interior Ministry still has ears. Do you come to Moscow?"

"Yes, there is a quarterly conference; the next one is two weeks from now."

Markovitch sighed and said reluctantly. "Come see me. Have a drink on the house. We will talk."

Kaliniev started to say good-bye when Markovitch interrupted him.

"I wouldn't discuss this with anyone if I were you. What we are talking about does not exist. Understand?"

CHAPTER 10

Mexico City

United 745 departed thirty-five minutes late for the 1900-mile run from Dulles to Mexico City. It was well after one in the morning by the time a minor mechanical problem was attended to and the flight attendants were able to do the cabin crosscheck to prepare for departure. Four and half-hours later, the hard touchdown at *Benito Juarez* International jolted Palmer awake.

When he stumbled off the plane in a fog of jet lag, he almost walked by the person waiting for him at the airport. Palmer had a dim mental image of Dr. Elizabeth Cramer as a somewhat desiccated former academic of a certain age. So he walked right by the strikingly attractive woman in her thirties who was standing near the gate.

Palmer felt someone tap him on his shoulder and wheeled around.

"You must be Cole Palmer. David Andrews faxed me your picture."

Palmer's suit was wrinkled, his shirt a bit grimy, and he

needed a shave. So he felt at a considerable disadvantage as he stared at her, unwittingly showing his surprise at seeing a woman with curly blond hair, wearing a dark blue dress that set off the lighter blue of her eyes and a striking figure.

She grinned at him and said, "*Bienvenida, estimado* Senor Palmer. Your hotel room isn't ready because the people currently in it won't be checking out until 11:00. So instead of letting them park you in another room and then move you, I'm going to take you home and feed you breakfast!" She was tempted to add, "and offer you a shower," but she thought that might be a bit forward considering that she had just met the man.

Without waiting for Palmer to respond, she continued. "Why don't you follow me and we'll weave our way to the parking lot. It isn't far."

Palmer followed her; garment bag draped over one shoulder and his rollaway obediently trailing behind. The huge banner hanging from the overhead did not ring any bells: COMO MEXICO NO HAY DOS—THERE IS NO PLACE LIKE MEXICO. He would soon come to savor the irony of that assertion.

They left the parking area in a nondescript Dodge van. Cramer confidently negotiated her way through the frantic morning rush of traffic and gave a running commentary on various landmarks as they drove toward the city.

"There are two basic seasons in Mexico City—wet and dry. November through April is the dry season and we average about seventy during the day but much colder in the evenings, sometimes dipping into the low forties."

Palmer wondered momentarily how his few winter clothes would look in such warm weather. He shrugged realizing he couldn't do anything about it. He closed his eyes for a few moments and recalled the many times that Catherine talked about the precolonial civilizations that made Mexico so fascinating and mysterious.

"We are coming up to the *Zocalo*, or center of the city. I never tire of taking in the sights around here."

The streets were full of colonial mansions wrapped around courtyards bursting with flowers and fountains. Passing the National Palace, Cramer pointed out that it now housed the offices of the president and covered two city blocks.

"Can you believe that is was built on the site of Montezuma's opulent palace?"

"It looks like a fun place to spend some time looking around."

"There are a million things to do—and all worthwhile. World-renowned museums, parks, the national opera and ballet, and tons of fantastic restaurants that you can only find by wandering around."

As Liz Cramer headed off the main boulevard, she abruptly changed the subject. "You're officially identified to the Foreign Ministry as being on TDY and attached to my office. Of course, the Interior Ministry knows who you are—more or less. I'll give you an update on things when we get to my place."

Palmer massaged a cramp in his neck and said, "Thanks for picking me up, Dr. Cramer."

She looked over at him. "Please drop the 'Doctor Cramer' bit. It makes me feel like I'm back at Ohio State pushing graduate students through their prelims. Liz will do."

Palmer smiled and said, "Right. Liz it is. And I'm Cole. Don't have a title right now."

She smiled back and said, "Don't worry. We made one up for you."

Twenty-five minutes later, they passed through a gated area guarded by two stone lions in the Polanco suburbs and went down a road lined with handsome two-story stone town houses bordering a vividly green golf course. Dr. Cramer pulled up and parked behind a white Volvo wagon parked in front of one of them.

"Wow! I'm impressed," Palmer said as he got out of the van. "Remind me never to play golf with you."

She looked puzzled by his remark and asked, "Why do you say that?"

"Well, you must get in a lot of rounds with this beautiful course right outside your front door."

As he took his two bags out of the van, she remarked crisply, "I'm not much for games—and I've never played a round of golf in my life."

Feeling like an idiot, Palmer followed her into the house and through a large formal living and dining area with high ceilings and plantation shutters on the windows to filter out some of the bright sunlight. The kitchen was huge and brightly tiled with wood-shuttered French doors opening to a tile-covered patio overlooking the seventh hole.

She waved him to a chair next to a long butcher-block table and started fixing bacon and eggs.

Trying to strike the right note, Palmer said hesitantly, "I never knew that they had such places just outside the city. Just like the states. It is really something."

"Thanks, and it's all mine. When my husband passed away two and a half years ago, I sold our Bethesda home and requested a billet overseas to help me get my life together. I was delighted when the State Department—with help from David Andrews—came up with Mexico City. You know . . . a new challenge might help me get over John's death. Anyway, it gave me some space and keeps me busy decorating the place. Now maybe I really should learn how to play golf," she said with a smile.

"I'm sorry about your husband, Liz, and I apologize for blundering into sensitive matters."

"Don't worry about it. At some point, I guess I was able to get on with life. I can finally talk about losing John. Now, let's see how these eggs turned out."

After finishing off a sizable plate of bacon, scrambled eggs, and wheat toast, Palmer pushed back from the table as Liz Cramer refilled his coffee.

"Great breakfast. I feel better already . . . thank you. I think I can handle that update now if that's okay with you?"

"Good." Liz took a chair at the kitchen table and poured herself a mug of coffee. She handed Palmer a two-page listing of embassy personnel and a schedule for the rest of the week. "Let's start with some of the folks you will be meeting and what your schedule looks like for the week. There are backup abstracts from the PFs of the important staff members in your office and you can read them when you get settled in. If we get a break between the staff introductions, the intel folks want to read you into some of the compartmented stuff." She glanced up at Palmer to see if he was following her.

"Okay, let's see. An office next to mine is available and you will meet your secretary tomorrow. Actually, she is my secretary and you are sharing her. She's been with the Foreign Service for fourteen years, so there's nothing she doesn't know about how the embassy functions." She started clearing away the dishes and putting them in the dishwasher, then turned to him. "Does this title sound OK to you—assistant to commercial attaché?" she asked.

"Yeah, right. How about attached to the attaché?" Palmer saw the startled look on Dr. Cramer's face and reminded himself that most people did not immediately appreciate his sense of humor. "Just kidding. I really don't care what I'm called," Palmer added with a grin.

Liz Cramer proceeded with the briefing, pausing occasionally to answer questions from Palmer. Several times during the briefing, Palmer found himself looking at Liz Cramer instead of concentrating on what she was saying. At the airport, he had not fully comprehended how beautiful she was. He guessed her to be about five feet eight and a well-distributed 125 pounds. She could easily pass for someone much younger. Her face was engagingly attractive with a slender nose above full lips. Her hair was pulled back, and there was a certain sparkle in her eyes as she got caught up in explaining what was going on inside her department in the embassy.

When she caught him covertly examining her, he shuffled his feet and smiled. "I'm paying attention. I just don't look like I am. Anyway, I was briefed on some of this by Andrews before he dumped me unceremoniously on the plane." Palmer forced himself to get back to the matter at hand. "Does La Eme really have the system so well wired that they can do pretty much what they want?"

"Unfortunately, yes. The corruption has been so pervasive for so long, so completely woven into the fabric of life in Mexico that people think that's the way things are—and always will be."

Palmer shook his head. "Okay, give me some insight into this new wave of terrorism that Andrews is so worried about. Have we picked up anything locally?"

"No. There is nothing coming through our intel and liaison channels in the embassy—and I would know. God knows we've had enough in the last six months. The first I heard about this new threat was from Andrews when he called to tell me you were on your way. I was as surprised as anyone."

"Well, that leads to another question. Why is the commerce attaché so well informed and what is the connection to the national security adviser?" Palmer asked with a wry smile.

Liz Cramer returned his smile and waited a few seconds before answering. "I'm an economist. I spend my time at the agency as an analyst. I specialize in Latin American economies—and I speak pretty good Spanish. David wanted someone on-site down here who could give him a picture of what was happening in all dimensions— economic, social, political."

"I sorta figured that out."

"David said to tell you that you're cleared for everything that comes through the embassy and that Richard Snyder would personally brief the ambassador about you. He um . . . also briefed me on your background, Cole. I was very sorry to hear about the loss of your wife."

"Well, I don't need to tell you it's tough. I don't suppose you ever get over the loss of a spouse. Things happen to you and you have no control over them. The only control you have is to make the best of every day with the people you love."

"Yes. I know exactly what you mean. But it also helps to have a demanding job to do. The toughest part of it, for you, will be getting the cooperation that the Posadas administration promised. We are in a very delicate position. Hidalgo is right about at least one thing that he is saying. We are going to have to step all over Mexico's sovereignty if we want to stop losing this war. And believe me, Cole, we are losing it."

CHAPTER 11

The White House

It was a little past seven on Monday morning when David Andrews arrived at the West Wing entrance to the White House. The gate guard recognized both the driver and the national security adviser, and gave Andrews a cheerful "Good morning, sir." He approached the car with a long pole that had a mirror fixed to one end. He carefully checked the underside of the vehicle, inspected the interior of the trunk, and waved the official driver on to his parking place in the lot between EOB and the White House. The agent's welcoming smile was a far cry from Brooke's early morning admonition concerning his weekend performance—as she put it—with Cole Palmer.

When he arrived for the Cabinet meeting, he nodded to secretary of state, Richard Snyder and the CIA director, Leslie Drummond, while proceeding to the small antique tables holding silver coffeepots and paper cups. He wondered if the White House was short on china as the room filled with principals, deputies, and other staffers for the meeting. Before he got to his seat, the vice president entered and took the chair normally occupied by the president at the head of the long and narrow twenty-foot mahogany table.

Michael Kerr was in his mid-sixties—small in stature, with a ruddy complexion and silvery white hair, and meticulously groomed. The tailored pinstripe suit came from Huntsman, his gleaming black shoes from Lobb, and his shirt, with French cuff and gold cuff links, from Thomas Pink. He was a bit of a dandy, in an old-fashioned southern way.

The purpose of the meeting was to review the latest results of the task force, headed by Kerr, which was investigating the assassination of Swanson. It took only fifteen minutes for all concerned to report that little progress had been made.

"The press is hammering the hell out of us," Kerr complained. "We have to throw them something. Don't we have any sort of theory . . ."

The director of Central Intelligence shook his head. "We have several more witnesses but what they've given us is not very helpful. Two think they saw a gray car entering the garage around 6:15 A.M. One of them thinks it was a Ford Taurus. We are using NCIC's computer—it's the fastest available—to collate information from every rental car agency, particularly the locations at the airports and Union Station. We are also examining the registration records of every hotel, B&B, motel, and rooming house in a radius of twenty miles from here."

Drummond shrugged and said, in an apologetic tone, "We can give some version of this to the media but when they press us we will have to admit that we don't have a clear lead, that we are just looking for match-ups that might take us somewhere. The best lead we have is that one of the witnesses is a pilot for American, sharp guy with good eyesight. He thinks the guy he saw in the car might have been Hispanic—but he wouldn't swear to it."

Kerr rambled on about ways to handle the media pressure. What really concerned him was that he was in command of a virtual army of law enforcement and intelligence officers; every day that passed without results only encouraged the conspiracy theorists and made him look ineffectual. His secret fear was that this process might go on for weeks, maybe months.

"Great," Andrews thought; as he listened to Kerr insist that more resources had to be committed. "Now we are really going to waste the morning." He had suffered through meetings involving the vice president on various national security and defense issues and was singularly unimpressed with the ex-senator from South Carolina.

Kerr finally recognized that he was just marching in place so he switched the discussion to topics that weren't on the agenda. Since the president was on a trip to three cities in the West and wouldn't be back for another day, Kerr took it upon himself to speak for POTUS.

"Let me remind you that the president intends to announce at the press conference on Friday that Mexico has been certified 'fully cooperating' in the antidrug campaign that Swanson initiated."

"Why can't we simply back off this flat-out support of the PRI?" Andrews asked himself. Congress was not going to sit still for the recertification, and certainly not fund additional aid. He closed his eyes and started thinking about how to get the president to stop blindly following the advice of his secretary of state and start worrying about his upcoming election.

The recertification announcement clearly caught Snyder by surprise. He had supported the initial certification last year but argued that insisting on annual recertification was an embarrassment to Mexico. Congress, unfortunately, did not see it that way. Still, he thought that the president could have found a way to compromise with Congress on the issue. Before Snyder could make a comment, the vice president continued.

"The president also wants to get moving on the fast-track trade authority. You know—fast-track Chile this year, set the stage for the FTAA. We do not have to stand back on this one. The voters like it. We need to make that point clear to certain members during the next few weeks before Congress breaks."

Kerr looked around, gauging the reactions of the members of the Cabinet.

"I should add that the president wants everyone to call their contacts and put the right spin on the drug certification announcement."

The vice president finished and turned to Snyder. "Richard, will you bring us up to date on what is going on in Mexico?"

Snyder, obviously uncomfortable about being the bearer of bad news, admitted that the revised NAFTA agreement had not produced the anticipated positive economic results.

The vice president looked surprised. "What I read indicates NAFTA is working."

"Here we go," Andrews thought. He hoped that Snyder wouldn't back off.

"Mr. Vice President, as the Council of Economic Advisors reported four days ago, the rural economy, especially in the southern states, is doing poorly and has unemployment rates as high as thirty to forty percent. Unfortunately, these conditions are not going to change quickly. Given the turbulent situation in Mexico, there is little hope of foreign investment coming in and stimulating the economy and the private sector down there is not significantly adding new plant and equipment. In fact, we are seeing a flight of capital from the country. Turning this around is going to take time and patience—and unfavorable trade balances—until the necessary infrastructure is in place. We need to be patient."

Snyder went on to describe the increasingly bleak situation Posadas was facing as his popularity declined in the face of the gathering strength of the PRD—and the uncertainty factor introduced by Hidalgo's imminent return.

At this point, the director of Central Intelligence broke in.

"Sir, there is something we can do. With the president's approval, Operation SKYHAWK is ready to roll." Drummond quickly glanced over at Snyder to determine if he agreed that it was the right moment to inject a positive note into an increasingly dispirited meeting.

"What the hell is Operation SKYHAWK? What does it have to do with what we're talking about?" The vice president glared at the CIA director.

Drummond saw Snyder nod so he decided to push ahead. "Mr. Vice President, the operation provides Posadas with specially trained law enforcement officers as well as paramilitary assets to go after the drug cartels' leadership. We've been training them for the past twelve weeks at a staging base near the border in Texas." Drummond realized that Kerr was not pleased at being left out of the loop on this one. He tried to smooth things over by adding; "I think you were out of town during the operation's brief, sir."

"You said the president approved this. What about the Mexican police and army? Where are they in all this?"

"Posadas feels that too many people at the command level are unreliable, so the police and the army have not been brought into the operation. Or, more precisely, a small number of Mexican personnel who are considered reliable are training with our people right now. President Posadas needs a strike force that he can deploy without the drug cartel knowing about it before it even gets under way."

"Let's be very clear," Snyder added, supporting Drummond. "We are well aware of the potential for this backfiring against us. We've carefully weighed the risks and decided we have no choice but to proceed. These elite units will have U.S. advisers with them. Well, frankly, more than advisers—we are taking the lead role in this and we already have a fair amount of personnel and material on the ground down there. Both Hidalgo and the PRD could exploit this. Nevertheless, I consider it a necessary risk, in view of the deteriorating situation and the need for some dramatic leadership by President Posadas."

"Is Posadas really fully committed on this? Is he going to hang in with us if things start going the wrong way?" The vice president slumped back into his chair.

"Yes, sir. He has the final approval. So he can't walk away from it."

"What kind of numbers are we talking about?" The attorney general asked.

"We have three hundred of the best young officers and non-coms from Army Special Forces as well as some Marine Combat Recon units—all with carefully vetted records. They are essentially ready to go but we will continue the training until we get the green light. Then they will be airlifted in, along with helicopter and fixed wing–supporting elements. By the way, Swanson thought that this was the only way to decapitate the cartel. We are going to bag as many of their top people as possible. It will make the Noriega extraction look like a minor operation in comparison."

Kerr looked directly at Snyder and said quietly, "We better know what we're doing here. If we don't, we'll get creamed on the Hill—of that I can assure you, knowing the disposition of my esteemed former colleagues in the Senate—and we, all of us, will be out of a job."

Without saying anything more, Kerr got up, indicating that the meeting was over. As the members of the Cabinet and others began to file out of the room, Andrews remained seated. He had reluctantly supported the operation. At least he had one person in Mexico he could trust; someone who could provide him with an effective back channel. If Palmer saw things turning sour, he would have no hesitation about recommending that the United States abort the operation.

If it were aborted in time, there was a possibility of damage control. If it were allowed to spin out of control, however, there would be no second term for Washburn. And David Spencer Andrews would probably lose whatever chance he had to occupy that office on the seventh floor of the sprawling building in Foggy Bottom, the nerve center of America's foreign policy.

CHAPTER 12

Cuidad Juarez, Mexico

Carpio Romero relaxed in the backseat of the twelve-year-old Ford—the faded paint and numerous dents attesting to its age. He was dressed in the only decent suit he owned with the coat jacket carefully folded next to him. His shirt—pressed but frayed at the cuffs—and tie were relics from a more prosperous era.

Although it had been a long day, Romero was pleased with his visit to Mexico City. As owner and editor of the *Diario de Juarez*, he and five other editors had spent two hours with President Posadas. They had stood in the background as Posadas announced his stepped-up antidrug strategy—a strategy pushed and funded by the United States and orchestrated by the late General Swanson. The moment to announce SKYHAWK had not come; for Posadas it was still more of an "if" than a "when," a sentiment that would have surprised those concerned in Washington.

Over national television, President Posadas stressed the critical need for an independent and free press.

"I want to applaud the six journalists standing behind me as the torchbearers of Mexico's pursuit of a new democracy. They are shining examples for our country—and for all who understand the importance of living in freedom."

Romero was particularly pleased when the president singled him out, praising his crusade against drug traffickers and corruption—a crusade that had led to almost daily threats to Romero, his newspaper, and his family. With seven journalists killed or kidnapped during the past three years, he was aware of the risk, yet despite his constant fear, something in Romero's character impelled him to take a stand.

Romero and his five colleagues were exceptions. With most newspapers struggling to stay alive in the plummeting economy, especially the small newspapers outside Mexico City, the majority of publishers and editors followed an unwritten rule to stay clear of anything to do with the drug cartel.

By the time the AeroMex 737 landed at Cuidad Juarez, it was almost ten o'clock. He told the driver that he wanted to stop off at the office and would find his own way home. When he entered the building, he was not surprised when his assistant editor and son, Amado, warmly greeted him. He figured that they would wait up to hear about his trip. Six months ago, Amado decided to forego the higher engineer's pay at a tile factory to help his father. As they warmly welcomed Romero and congratulated him, none of the three noticed the truck parked in the empty lot next to the newspaper building. Nor did they notice the two darkened vans discreetly parked around the corner from the building—streets normally vacant at this hour.

* * *

They sat for an hour in Romero's small office in the back of the cluttered one-story building and smoked while sipping the tequila that had been chilled in anticipation of his return.

Just as they were getting ready to leave for home, the truck exploded with such force that it blew in an entire side of the newspaper building. Dazed and bleeding from flying mortar and glass shrapnel, Romero was in a state of shock when armed men seized him as he stumbled from what was left of the building. He tried to clear his head and see if Amado and his associate made it out, but before he could turn around something struck the back of his head and he was bundled into one of the vans. As it accelerated down the empty street, Amado and the assistant editor stumbled from the blazing wreckage of the building. Two men were waiting; one shot Amado at close range, through the side of the face. The editor, dazed and bleeding from a deep cut in his arm, staggered down the street—until the second man shot him through the head.

While the president publicly deplored the murders, the failure of the police investigation to turn up any leads only confirmed the widespread impression that the regime was floundering.

Six days after the bombing of the newspaper building, the local police discovered the body of Romero dumped alongside the road outside the city. He had choked to death on his own blood after his assailants had cut out his tongue.

In a damage control effort, Jim Browning, and his Mexican counterpart, Alejandro Cortes, persuaded newspapers on both sides of the border to run articles highlighting increased government spending on schools and hospitals in the major cities. However, none of the pieces gave much space to similar, though far more modest, improvements for the thousands of poor indigenous Indians in the southern states of Oaxaca and Guerrero.

Two days before Posadas was to deliver a national televised address on his economic and social reform program, paramilitaries gunned down more than fifty peasant villagers. The media claimed that the paramilitaries were linked to the federal government, but other observers believed they were acting on the orders of the big landowners in the state. This switched the national and international media's focus to the misery of the Mexican Indian population and crippled the government's campaign to present an image of a more caring and effectively governed Mexico. The mass murder in the Chiapas mountain village forced President Posadas to cancel his annual May Day national televised address.

Instead, appalling images of defenseless men shot in the back, pregnant women butchered, and children left orphaned dominated the reporting of CNN and other networks. In the face of what seemed to be an intensified reign of terror throughout Mexico, for the first time, several major Mexican newspapers began to call for the immediate resignation of the president. None of this, of course, helped Carlos Alverez, the anointed successor of Posadas, who was out campaigning and facing increasingly smaller and less enthusiastic crowds.

Reuters reported Hidalgo's scathing comments on the inability of the current government to provide even the minimum assurances of public safety and order. The ruling party angrily denounced Hidalgo's sweeping accusations— but the damage from the massacre quickly translated into the lowest approval rating the party had received during its seventy-year control of the government.

* * *

Navarro and Espinosa were eating dinner in one of the private clubs on the Plaza Ciudadela and enjoying the CNN coverage when Navarro's cell phone rang.

"Yes?" Navarro answered without turning away from the television.

"This is Bolivar . . . I hope I'm not disturbing you."

"Not at all. Arturo and I are at Blanco's watching CNN. I was anticipating your call."

"Yes. We concluded the business. I hope the contract terms meet your expectations. Unless you have further instructions, I will leave in the morning."

"The timing was perfect. I was more than pleased."

"I plan to pick up a few things before going ahead with the next phase of the plan."

"Yes . . . and Bolivar, I am sorry to place this additional burden on you but it is important to that other business."

"I'll take care of it and keep you informed."

Navarro put the cell phone down on the table and picked up his glass of red wine, giving the television his undivided attention.

Espinosa was certain, from hearing parts of the conversation, that "Bolivar" was Juan Ortega—and that Ortega had instigated the Chiapas affair. He wasn't sure about the "other business"; he would find out when, and if, Navarro wanted him to know. As the waiter delivered his second course of *petroleras*—flat corn tortillas filled with black beans, cheese, and green salsa—Espinosa decided that the secret of a long and happy life was to refrain, whenever possible, from being directly involved. It was better for him if Navarro ultimately told him nothing.

CHAPTER 13

Presidential Palace

"When will the drum beat of Chiapas stop?" Mexico's president was looking out through one of the tall windows that reached almost to the high ceiling of his private office in the Presidential Palace. A cascade of oleander and hibiscus tumbled out of large stone planters on the terrace outside but Posadas was blind to the brilliant reds and oranges of the blossoms. The images of bodies swollen in the damp heat of the devastated mountain village haunted him.

Carlos Alverez, the finance minister, Posadas's anointed successor as head of the party and its presidential candidate and Valentin Peña, the defense minister remained silent. Alverez knew how this horror had almost pushed Posadas over the edge. A short man with thinning black hair, nearsighted black eyes magnified by thick glasses with heavy black rims, the president of Mexico did not project a commanding presence. Once he had been eager to fill the shoes of his illustrious and then disgraced predecessor and mentor. Now he wished that Hidalgo were the one dealing with an apparently endless sequence of new and overwhelming problems. Alverez finally spoke up, determined to bring matters to a head.

"Unfortunately, sir, I don't think the issue will go away until some agreement is struck with the Indian communities."

The president's face tightened perceptibly. "But that is impossible, Carlos. You know what they want—formal recognition and creation of autonomous indigenous communities. We would be the first government to cave in to such demands. It could kill us in the elections. Can you imagine how Hidalgo would use this?"

"You couldn't be more right, sir," the defense minister said confidently. "Just give me a little more time and we'll take care of these so-called self-governing rebels."

"No . . . no . . . no," the president groaned. "The heavy-handed police and army actions and expulsion of all the reporters in the area has led to the resignation in protest by the archbishop heading the mediation team. What you propose to do would just make it worse."

"But what can we—?"

Carlos Alverez knew that this was a critical moment; Posadas could still be persuaded to go against the prevailing opinion in the party's leadership. At nearly six feet tall and a well-muscled frame charged by an unusually high energy level, Alverez made a striking contrast to the diminutive Posadas.

"Mr. President, what we have done in the past won't work. We need to take the lead and suggest that we will accept the recommendations of the UN Human Rights Commission. It will buy us time, give us some cover. We don't have to yield; we just have to open negotiations."

While aware that the defense minister would strenuously object to taking this course of action, Posadas decided to hear out Alverez, one of the few members of his cabinet that he trusted and the one he selected to follow him. "Go on, Carlos."

"The UN Human Rights Commission will be here in two days. The chairman, Kobaladze, went through the breakup of the old Soviet Union and established a forthright reputation. He is aware of our dilemma and he can make the rest see that it is not susceptible to a quick resolution. Their goal is clear—develop some middle ground that the government and the Zapatista Rebels representing the villagers can agree to. In my opinion, we have only one choice."

The defense minister jumped to his feet and protested. "Mr. President, we cannot give them a free reign to do what they want. They don't understand or care about a unified, intact Mexico. I strongly urge you to delay their visit until we have cleaned up things down there."

The president stared at his defense minister and then turned away. "Go on, Carlos, with what you were saying."

"We need to present a fresh and creative proposal to the commission. The consensus in the international community is that the indigenous communities have special problems— problems that we have failed to address effectively. We cannot afford to be in a position of simply reacting to the commission and world opinion—we have to agree in advance, on what we are willing to do, how far we can go. That's just what Snyder was trying to tell us when we were in Washington last week to discuss the Chiapas incident."

"I don't like it. I think we're moving too fast," grumbled the defense minister, reluctantly sitting down. "We should not have any dialogue with the rebels until they hand over their weapons. If it were not for the foreign press stirring things up, the whole matter would go away."

The president tried to ignore Peña. "Yes, we can be sure that Snyder, at least, is on our side. We can trust him. What do you have in mind?"

"At a bare minimum, sir, we must strike a careful balance. We have to maintain real control; priority must be given to establishing and maintaining the rule of law, including the disarming of all armed groups. But we must agree—or be seen to agree—to resume the dialogue with the Zapatistas. We should promise, now, to correct injustices and punish human rights violators."

"I see where you are going. If we do it right, it could make it more difficult for the opposition to attack our position, especially if the UN Commission and the United States are with us. Snyder is probably right. It is time to deal with this issue in a new way. If we handle it properly—and I like what you say—we might just be able to shift the momentum from Chiapas to something positive before the elections." The president had turned to look out the window again; the two other men found it difficult to catch what he was saying.

The minister of defense was not sure what he had just heard and could not contain himself. "I'm not sure I agree. We are moving too fast. Why should we meekly accept the recommendations of an outside commission or allow the White House to tell us what to do? We need to keep the pressure on those revolutionary bastards and—"

"Why is that, Peña?" The president had enough and turned on his defense minister. "Alverez is right—we need a new strategy. Read the newspapers. The Zapatistas wear the white hats, and the government wears the black hats. We're running out of time to change that."

The minister of defense remained silent for a moment and then got out of his chair, towering over Posadas.

"How do we know that the separatist movement in the southern states is not CIA orchestrated and funded? We have seen it before and should not ignore the ulterior motive of the United States. It is obvious that certain U.S. companies want access to unexploited mineral resources in the area."

The president stopped pacing and looked directly at the defense minister.

"Come again? What do you mean?"

"Ah . . . ah . . . well, we know what the CIA is capable of and we can't let the Indians sell what doesn't belong to them. The constitution forbids it. We cannot allow it. In addition, I hear other rumors that since the United States relinquished control of the Panama Canal, it is looking at the Isthmus of Tehuantepec."

"That's absurd, Peña. Where do you come up with such stuff. This is sheer paranoia."

The minister looked at the president and tried to mask his contempt. If we don't stop him, he thought, the son of a bitch would give our country away, bit by bit. He is a coward, a weakling. If I had a free hand I would turn the army loose and our troubles with the *Indios* would end.

"Are you with us, Peña?" The president asked, his patience clearly wearing thin. "Keep your damn dogs on a chain, *comprende?*"

The president looked directly at his defense minister and felt a sudden surge of determination. Turning to Alverez, he said, "There is one more thing, Carlos. I think it would be wise if we sent the interior minister to Chiapas to express our concern and try to start the process of reconciliation before the UN Commission arrives."

"Of course, sir. It will send the right signal to the commission. I would be happy to accompany him if you want me to."

"I don't think so, but thank you. I need you to spend time with Kobaladze when he arrives. Do your best to make him understand that we want to do the right thing."

After the meeting ended, the defense minister walked down the wide marble stairs covered with a long runner of deep blue carpeting and punched in a number on his cell and gave some brief orders. "Yes, it will be as you said, sir." He ended the call and impatiently signaled his military aide to bring the car over. There was no other way out, he thought. It must stop here—now.

The two-hour flight on the president's Boeing 737 from Mexico City to Tuxtla Gutierrez gave the interior minister time to review his schedule of visits to the villages of Oaxaca. After a brief stop with the city officials, Fernando Muñoz boarded an army helo for the forty-minute ride to the village of Chiapas where the massacre had taken place. Ten minutes into the flight, the helo disappeared off the radarscope over dense jungle west of the village. A search party took four days to hack their way through the jungle and locate the bodies of the crew and the minister. A subsequent investigation into the cause of the crash revealed that the flow of lubricant to the main gearbox had apparently been interrupted, which in turn had frozen the rotor and sent the copter out of control. It had gone down almost vertically from an altitude of two thousand feet to the ground. Ten days later, the special investigation reported that it was a clear case of sabotage rather than of mechanical failure. Within hours of the report reaching Mexico City, the minister of defense, without offering any supporting evidence, stated on national television that supporters of the Zapatista rebels had engineered the crash.

CHAPTER 14

Moscow

Yuri Kaliniev trailed the listless passengers from Aeroflot's Minsk-to-Moscow morning commuter flight through the dim greenish light of Sheremetyevo Airport. Normally he considered the quarterly conferences a total waste of time. They were largely a means of measuring political reliability. But this trip might prove to be productive.

Before exiting the domestic terminal he stopped off in the men's room and relieved himself in one of the many urinals in a long line against the wall. An elderly woman was listlessly swabbing the floor with a filthy mop. When he left he stopped at one of the battered public telephones. The ones in the more presentable international terminal had been replaced by more modern equipment. These phones were still tied into the faltering network of the old system. Straining to hear against the popping noises on the line, Kaliniev dialed Anatoly Markovitch's number. When a young woman's sleepy voice answered; he identified himself and heard Markovitch come on the line after a long wait.

"I'm free after four."

"Good. Come to my place on Kolinsky. I will be there at six. Did you bring the drawing?"

"Yes. The markings—"

Markovitch stopped him before he could continue.

"At six, then. Don't be late. I have another appointment."

It still amazed Kaliniev that the Ministry of Defense was maintained in such good condition. The walls were gleaming with fresh paint and some of the office furniture was new, polished wood from Finland or Sweden. Lunch was excellent, better than anything he had been served there before; the chicken tasted fresh and the black bread was flavorful and moist, not dried out and hard.

When he walked out through the massive portals with their huge bronze doors, he felt invigorated. Maybe things would get better, he thought. But when he went down into the subway the faces of those around him were still more stoical and resigned than hopeful.

It took him less than twenty minutes to get to the station nearest Markovitch's bar. As he came out of the metro he sidestepped a gaping hole in the sidewalk and made his way through the flood of people heading home. When he arrived in front of the faded yellow stucco facade of what once, long ago, had been a private house later cut up into apartments, Yuri Kaliniev looked carefully at the scrap of paper on which he had scrawled the number and made sure he was in the right place. There was no sign, no name, just a tarnished brass plate with the number 43 incised into it. He brushed aside a faded red curtain inside the door and, peering through the dim light, saw his old friend sitting at a table, with a bottle of whisky, two glasses and some mineral water on it. There were no customers, just a bartender squinting at a copy of *Moscow News* and picking his nose.

Kaliniev gave his old friend a bear hug, slipped out of his heavy army greatcoat and draped it over the back of one of the chairs.

"So, you are a real "biznessman" now!"

Markovitch shrugged and gave him a wan smile. "We are all capitalists, these days. Except for those who still serve the *Rodina* like you, Yuri."

Markovitch had not aged well. The skin on his face was mottled with a fine network of veins and the wrinkled back of his hands were those of a much older man. But his gray suit and blue tie with a fine white pattern, as well as a large gold watch on his wrist, testified to his prosperity. Without asking, Markovitch poured a generous measure of Scotch into both glasses.

"Water?"

"No, that's fine."

It took Kaliniev some time, after the conversation began flowing, to ask his friend who had answered the phone when he called.

"Ah, yes. Ludmilla." Markovitch grinned. "Nothing keeps an old man going like a young wife. You must meet her. Come around and we will have dinner. You will like her. Maybe she will find a friend for you!"

Kaliniev drew a folded piece of paper from the inside pocket of his tunic and slid it across the table. "I don't need new friends. Just an old friend I can trust."

Markovitch put on a pair of wire-rimmed glasses, smoothed the paper out, and stared at it for a long time.

"Yes. What I thought. But God knows how it ended up in your shop. Are you sure you put the markings down right?"

Kaliniev brushed aside the question impatiently. "Don't fuck around with me, Anatoly. What are these things?"

The lights in the bar suddenly came on and a man and two women lurched through the door, took a quick look at Kaliniev and Markovitch, and headed for the bar.

"These are things that could make you a capitalist."

It was well after eleven when Markovitch returned to his bar. Kaliniev was in the back room, sitting in a booth. He had consumed the enormous meal that the barman had put in front of him, belted down a few vodkas, topped off with a Georgian brandy that could have been used to strip paint, before briefly dozing off. What Markovitch had told him, before he left for another appointment, had given him a great deal to think about.

"We had those devices for 'special purposes.' They weren't used a great deal. At least by my directorate. Sometimes we gave them to 'friends.'" By friends Markovitch meant the GRU, military intelligence. "Our friends used them in interesting ways. In many places."

Markovitch slid into the booth opposite Kaliniev. He carried with him a glass of tea in a filigree metal holder, a sugar cube gripped between his teeth. He took his time finishing it and then whispered, "Yuri, there is someone who wants to talk to you . . . the well-dressed foreigner in the last booth."

"About what?" Kaliniev asked. He had sensed that the man was watching him but had shrugged it off.

"I don't know who he is, and he is not Russian, but he has paid me handsomely. He wants to talk about those devices we have been discussing. So, do me a favor and take a couple of minutes to listen to him. What do you have better to do?"

Kaliniev glanced over to where the man was sitting and sized him up as physically fit and in his early forties. He got up as Kaliniev approached and asked him to join him. An open bottle of whisky and two glasses sat on the table.

For almost a minute neither of them spoke. "Okay,

what do you want to see me about?" Kaliniev finally asked looking directly across at the man after lighting a cigarette.

"I apologize, but I must be somewhat discreet," the man replied. Kaliniev quickly placed his accent, although his Russian was understandable. The stranger was dressed in a dark suit; he was not wearing a tie and the two unfastened buttons at the top of his white shirt revealed a thick gold chain snuggled against curly black hair. "My name is Rafael. I think you can help me with a problem."

Rafael had dark, penetrating eyes that focused directly on him. Kaliniev remembered what Markovitch had said and decided to listen.

"A problem with what? And we can speak English." Kaliniev had studied English at the Language School—a drab two-story structure on Granousky Street two blocks from the Kremlin—and wanted to check out Rafael's reaction.

"Thank you. That would be easier. My Russian—as you heard—is barely passable." Rafael poured two glasses of whisky, leaned forward across the table separating them, and lowered his voice. "My associates, who we do not need to identify, are in need of some small portable bombs that we understand are stowed at various arsenals."

Before Kaliniev could react, he went on, in a low, urgent tone. "If such bombs are available, we would transfer a large sum of dollars into a Swiss account with your personal number and code word." Rafael sat back in the booth, lit a small dark cigarillo, and watched Kaliniev.

Years ago, he would have shot someone asking him to do such a thing. Now, he calmly stubbed out his Marlboro in the overflowing ashtray.

"Are you serious? How did you find out?"

Rafael never took his eyes off Kaliniev and it made him uncomfortable.

"Yes, we are very serious. Does two million U.S. dollars

sound like we are serious? And it serves no purpose to discuss how we know about the bombs."

Again Kaliniev attempted to respond but Rafael stopped him by reaching across the table and gripping Kaliniev's arm.

"Because of certain time constraints I must deal with, I established a private account at Credit Suisse in Zurich." He handed Kaliniev a Credit Suisse business card with the distinctive embossed Swiss banking emblem. On the back of the card was a name of a bank officer and a telephone number—a three-digit country code followed by an eleven-digit international phone number.

Rafael lowered his voice and Kaliniev could barely hear him. "The code word to verify that the money is in your account is 'Jehovah' and you should memorize it. When the transfer of the package is complete, you should make a second call, which will then activate the account. The bank will ask you to establish a new code word, only known to you, and the bank will provide a confidential fourteen alphanumeric account number. Once established, only you can access the private account."

Kaliniev stared at the card, trying to take it all in.

"Perhaps I am pushing too fast?"

"No, go ahead," Kaliniev, said. It was as if another, different person was speaking, not him.

"Do we have an understanding, Yuri?"

Rafael again leaned forward and looked Kaliniev straight in the eye.

"When you return to the arsenal on Sunday, you should remove the bomb package to an accessible location without attracting attention. On Tuesday, wait until everyone has departed and then place the package in the trunk of your car. Are we correct in assuming the package contains six small bombs and that it will fit in the trunk?"

"Yes," Kaliniev answered, surprised that Rafael was so well informed about the number of weapons available and approximate size of the package required to contain them. He realized now that Markovitch had known a great deal more about the devices than he had let on. And he wondered how much money his old friend would get for setting up the deal.

"Good. We do not think there will be any problems because you are accustomed to departing from the arsenal after most everyone is gone. When you reach your apartment, park your car in your apartment's lot as usual."

"Damn it!" Kaliniev exclaimed, before catching himself and again lowering his voice. "You've been watching me and I haven't known about it?"

"Yes," Rafael replied calmly. "For a number of days. We need everything to go simply and smoothly. There is no room for error."

Rafael refilled their glasses. "There is one change to your routine on Tuesday night. Instead of parking as you normally do, you should back your car into the same parking place with its front pointing to the street. This will be our signal that all is clear and then we will not have to communicate again. Also Yuri, please leave the trunk unlocked. Sometime during the night, the package will be removed without bothering anyone."

After a pause, Kaliniev cleared his throat and swallowed the whisky in his glass. "Is that all there is?"

"Yes," Rafael reassured him. "You won't hear from us again. I know you are smart enough to forget everything. You might even consider moving to some congenial foreign country with your new wealth. It does not matter to us. We want you to enjoy it."

"You are leaving everything to trust?" Kaliniev persisted.

"Everything will be fine, Yuri."

Rafael got up to leave. "You are a professional, a soldier, and your word is good."

Kaliniev nodded and lit another cigarette. "Leave me a number where I can reach you."

"No. I am sorry." Again, Rafael put his hand on Kaliniev's arm. "I can give you one day to decide. I have already waited too long. I realize that you need to think about it. I will be back tomorrow night. Consider it carefully."

CHAPTER 15

Mexico City

It was after four when Liz Cramer dropped Palmer at the Maria Isabel, one of the more fashionable hotels in the center of Mexico City. Surrounded by mountains, the city—one of the largest urban centers in the world and home to 30 million people—sits in a huge bowl some 7,000 feet above sea level, assuring near-perfect weather almost year-around. However, like Los Angeles, its topography and thousands of automobiles make it a perfect site for trapped smog and inversion layers. Before driving off, Liz leaned over to the window and reminded him that they were scheduled to call on the ambassador at 8:15 on the following morning. "It's like an audience with the Pope. Being on time is essential."

Palmer followed one of the assistant managers of the hotel and a bellhop through the vast marble lobby, its cool surfaces balanced by beautiful carpets and wall hangings. People grouped around small tables set off to one side were having tea. Everything so far seemed normal; he found it difficult to reconcile the swirling, intense life of the sprawling city with the social volcano Andrews had described. When he got to his room, he unpacked and went directly to bed.

Palmer woke up headache-free after some ten hours of sleep. He ordered breakfast from room service and started making mental notes for his first official day in Mexico City. His gray suit looked slightly wrinkled but presentable and he selected a bright blue paisley tie for color. He was counting on the springlike weather to cover his shortfall in clothing until he had enough time to do some shopping.

The embassy was directly across from Chapultepec Park with its 2,000 acres of gardens and lakes and separated by a busy roundabout from the hotel. Instead of cutting through the park, Cole followed the roundabout, enjoying the opportunity to take in the many sidewalk cafes and stores. Tomorrow, he promised himself, he would start jogging in the park early each morning and get back into his SEAL regimen of training.

A tall Marine corporal stopped Palmer and checked his ID. He gave Palmer a sharp salute and directed him to the security office inside the rotunda. After another ID check, the security officer handed Palmer access code cards tied loosely together with a chain. Palmer put the chain over his head, tucking the plastic covered cards inside his suit coat breast pocket.

"Right on time. Good." Cramer led the way toward the ambassador's suite of offices. When they reached the door to the outer office, she stopped and turned around. "The program is five minutes with the ambassador followed by introductions to a few of the senior Foreign Service officers on the staff. If there is time left before lunch, we'll try and see Willie Graham, who runs the operations center."

Liz Cramer had already given Palmer a concise profile of Ambassador Donald Reimann, a political appointee, formerly a banker, and generous contributor to Washburn's campaign. He was a tall, thin somewhat aloof man who found Mexico's political and social complexity often bewildering and not infrequently irritating. He had wanted London but had been persuaded to settle, reluctantly, for Mexico. Palmer wondered what the professional Foreign Service folks thought about that. The bottom line was that Reimann handled the ceremonial side of things quite adroitly. However, he dumped far too much responsibility on his deputy chief of mission and the senior staff, which did not enhance his understanding of the deteriorating situation in Mexico.

The brief meeting with Reimann went much along the lines that Andrews had predicted it would. The ambassador was courteous but hardly effusive. He seemed quite happy to accept, without comment or probing, the cover story that Andrews had concocted to explain Palmer's sudden assignment to the embassy. But Reimann made it clear that he expected to be informed, through his deputy chief of mission, of any substantive conversations Palmer had with officials of the Mexican government.

"I suggest you use Dr. Cramer's car and driver until you get to know the lay of the land around here. As the security people will tell you, taking one of those little VW Beetle taxis scurrying around is not recommended. As you've probably heard, Mexico City has a fairly high level of crime—and a taxi is no protection from it. In fact, many of the cab drivers make their own contribution to it. Since I understand, from Secretary Snyder as well as the national security adviser, that you will be here for a limited time, so I've told Charlie Hinton in the administrative section to arrange a rental car for you. Andrews also told me you know how to take care of yourself—early SEAL background. Still, if I were you, I'd avoid using the cabs and I wouldn't go out on the streets at night, even in the Zona

Rosa, unless it is absolutely necessary. Use a car—even if you've got only three or four blocks to go."

The ambassador stood up, indicating that the brief audience was over. As Palmer got out of his chair, he wondered what Reimann would have said about his determination to start running in the park. He decided it probably wasn't a good idea to mention it.

"I understand you were sent here to do a job but, as I said, I expect you to keep me in the loop. Things are pretty dicey down here and we need to stay on the same page."

With that pointed message, Palmer shook the ambassador's hand, and nodded to make it clear that he understood.

The embassy staff members he met that first morning were reserved but cordial. The type of reception that one expects when thrown into an established organization without any notice, especially when you are from the national security adviser's office. The one thing that Palmer observed was that Liz Cramer was both generally liked and respected. Given her professional background in economics, she was able to help the FSOs in the commercial attaché's office with the endless reports and analyses expected by the Commerce Department, as well as Treasury.

In contrast, the meeting with Willie Graham, a former chief warrant officer in the U.S. Navy and an established genius in the fields of electronics and communications, was a revelation. Graham, who was nearly bald and running to fat—an occupational hazard when you parked yourself in a chair for most of the working day—had a long, bony face. His eyes, which generally were fixed unwaveringly on the person to whom he was speaking, suggested a formidable intelligence. Graham, a contract employee for the State Department, and not an FSO, presided over a surprisingly large and well-equipped operations center. Willy effectively reported to no one but Willy Graham and he had a reputation for suffering fools badly. The result was that few embassy staffers went down to that part of the basement where the ops center was located unless they had a good reason to do so. Cramer watched, as Palmer and Graham sized each other up and quickly developed mutual respect. Graham was not surprised when Palmer alluded to his role in redesigning the Pentagon's National Command Center prior to his retirement from the Navy. Anyone who spent anytime in the Pentagon soon heard about the legendary warrant officer who had no hesitation about pushing the procurement officers to get electronic data processing, electronic countermeasures, and communications black boxes barely off the lab benches of defense contractors. When contractors could not furnish what Graham wanted, he would design the equipment and systems, give them the specs, and make sure they came through for him. If the budget did not cover the item, Graham had it hidden in another department's account. In many cases, the custom-made equipment designed by Willie Graham helped provide America's margin of advantage over the Soviets during the last stages of the Cold War. Someday, Palmer was sure, the whole story of how U.S. technology literally forced the Soviets into bankruptcy trying to keep up, would be told.

Liz Cramer finally had to interrupt the two men. She led Palmer to the cafeteria. They got salads and iced tea, and then found a quiet table away from the dozen or so other people catching a late lunch.

"It's been a fast morning, Liz. I'm glad that I collapsed early last night."

"The afternoon will be slower," said Liz. "I'll show you where your office is and be on my way."

"Wahoo. I didn't mean that my morning wasn't interesting. I had a lot of fun with Willie shooting the breeze and probably got a little carried away," Palmer said apologetically.

"Don't worry about it. I enjoyed watching you and Willie do your thing; in fact, I have seldom seen Willie Graham warm up to someone so quickly. It must be your irresistible charm!" She drained the last of her iced tea and got up.

Palmer let the comment pass and pushed back his chair. "How did Willie end up here? The last I heard in Washington, they were offering him the sun, moon, and stars to keep him on in the Pentagon."

"Well Cole, as the saying goes, *Amor vincit omnia*— 'love conquers all.' About three years ago, Willie married a lovely Mexican woman who worked at their embassy in Washington. She is the only person who can really handle him. Anyway, there was a lot of huffing and puffing from the security folks about the possible compromise of all the compartmented security programs that Willie was cleared for. They weren't happy campers about his marrying a foreign national. The story is that several important folks in DoD and State made calls telling the bloodhounds to back off. Tenita, that's his wife's name, told me that she wanted to stay in Washington but Willie wanted to tweak the security guys and basically said Mexico City or I'm gone."

"Yeah. It figures. Willy is a law unto himself."

Palmer asked Liz Cramer to remain for a few minutes when they arrived at his office in the commercial section. "I have a contact here in Mexico City who is well connected and might be able to help us. We met at the Naval War College in Newport and became good friends. He might be able to help. His name is Luis Vasquez."

Liz was startled. "This is one hell of a coincidence. We just completed a background on him for the secretary of state. He's one cool guy who stays clear of any controversy and political ties—a hard thing to do in Mexico. As I recall, he spent some time heading up the U.S. offices of some Mexican banks in New York and Philadelphia."

"Yeah. That sounds right. He was doing some of that while at Newport."

"How well did you get to know him?

"Well, we were sorta thrown together because we were both interested in the same arcane area of international law. I found out about it when I discovered that he had checked most of the books I needed out of the library. We played a lot of tennis together and I really grew fond on him. You know, someone you'd want on your side if you got into trouble."

"How do you want to play it?"

"I'll give him a call and see if I can cook up some tennis. Then we'll see what develops."

"Sounds good to me. I'll drop off a copy of the background paper on Vasquez, but I don't imagine you'll find anything new in it, from what you told me."

After she left his office, Palmer took a small leather bound black notebook out of his inside coat pocket. He thumbed through it until he found the number he was looking for. It was probably out of date. Well, he thought, if it doesn't work, I'll find out how efficient Mexican telephone information is.

Then another thought stopped him. What did the State Department want from Vasquez?

CHAPTER 16

Washington, D.C.

Dr. Mills scanned the congressional "bluesheet"—a daily
news sheet that highlighted national articles—while waiting to see Senator Flagler. One of the senator's staffers had
circled the news on Promontorio Mountain Repository.
Mills read the digests of the two articles and decided there
was nothing damaging; *Time* and *Newsweek* had already
done their share of that. Fortunately, the flap the articles
had caused in the White House did not directly affect him;
in fact, his unwelcome notoriety actually enhanced his
scheduling priority on the Hill.

As Mills waited, he congratulated himself on creating an
improbable alliance between the major environmental
groups and the nuclear power industry. It strengthened the
position of those in Congress who supported building the
prototype repository in Mexico. The energy industry and
its Washington lobbyists desperately wanted to solve the
growing nuclear waste problem that had capped the development of new nuclear power plants, while the environ-

mentalists wanted to control the potential threat posed by the increasing amount of waste in short-term, inadequate storage. Putting the repository in Mexico solved the problem for both parties, and it would satisfy the strong opposition from the public to constructing a repository in the United States. Mills wondered how Washburn had gotten the new Mexican president to move so quickly to restart construction on the repository after the long delay imposed by former President Hidalgo. He had heard conflicting stories but he had not paid much attention to them. The important thing was that the White House had gotten the program back on track without giving up any operational or security control.

Now, with only seven months to go before the formal opening of the repository, Mills knew that his congressional testimony would be critical. If he overemphasized the risks, Congress might get skittish and the whole thing could come to another embarrassing halt.

As he entered the senator's office, Flagler confirmed his apprehensions.

"Dr. Mills, these risk studies that *Time* and *Newsweek* referred to scare the hell out of me. I'm not sure I want to go on record supporting this project—especially before elections this November," Flagler warned him.

"I understand, Senator. However, the risks, although significant, should not derail the program after all the years of work and hundreds of millions of dollars. I'm not sure if the taxpayers would accept that." Mills paused to let the point sink in. "Besides, I am confident that American ingenuity can solve the problems cited in the CalTech study."

"But can we count on the Mexicans to cooperate ten or twenty years down the road?"

"We don't have a problem there. The president has assurances from the Mexican government that the U.S. will have permanent and complete control."

Mills knew that the White House had boxed Congress in. It was too late to cry wolf after they supported, by a narrow margin, the White House proposal to construct the prototype site in Mexico. It would take a few more days but Mills was confident that he would get what he wanted—a clear acknowledgment of the risks placed in the Congressional Record by those who supported the decision—before he testified.

Mills decided to change the subject before the senator started fretting again.

"What we need to do is persuade the president not to open the repository to all the neighboring countries that see another opportunity for Uncle Sam to take care of their problems. Your influence could make the critical difference, Senator."

"I hear you. However, getting the president to do something after he makes a policy decision is the problem. You know what I mean."

"Yes, but we should hold things off until we get the prototype up and running."

"Okay, Dr. Mills. Let me see what I can do."

When Mills finished briefing the last senator on his list, he was more confident and relaxed about his upcoming testimony. He was torn between remaining in Washington and being on-site to cope with the headaches the White House had caused him by moving up the date of the ceremonial opening of the repository without consulting anyone at the site.

Mills's confidence was justified; the Promontorio Mountain Repository hearings were uneventful. Too many congressmen and senators had fought to keep the nuclear waste out of their respective states and quietly breathed a sigh of relief that the project had found a home in Mexico. The chairperson had put the report on the potential risks in the Congressional Record; members of the committee asked Mills about the opening date of the repository and asked a few other innocuous questions after he testified. The committee cut the hearings short after a mere two days of testimony.

CHAPTER 17

Moscow

After Rafael walked out, Kaliniev waited for ten minutes and left through the back door of the bar. His head was spinning, not just from alcohol but also from what he had just heard. A year, or even a month ago, he would have refused to consider such a thing. He was being asked to break his oath as an officer, to engage in a criminal act.

When Kaliniev stepped outside, he saw there were no waiting taxies. They had all parked in and around Red Square for tomorrow's May Day celebrations. He started walking to the small and inexpensive hotel that he always used. It was fine for Kaliniev. A bed and a washbasin were all that he needed. Markovitch had pressed him to stay at his place and meet the beautiful Ludmilla but he had politely declined.

Before Rafael or whatever his name was had materialized, Markovitch, sensing that Kaliniev was not exactly pleased about being dragged into some murky business, had shrugged and explained apologetically, "Look, this is the real world. Where do you think I got the money to buy this place? The 'entrepreneurs' own a piece of it; they own a piece of me. I do some things for them . . . so, I'm just like a lot of other guys. The word comes, like it's whizzing around the Garden Ring, maybe four months ago, that there is a certain requirement. My . . . er . . . partner comes to me and says, 'Anatoly, you know about such things. We have an eager buyer. You must see what you can do.' "

Markovitch stopped, sighed, and rubbed his nose vigorously with the back of his hand.

"You understand, Yuri—this is not a request, not a 'please do me a favor' sort of thing. So I talk to some of the old gang I know. Go to see Tartikov, he's still on the job, SVR. He says to me, 'Are you out of your fucking mind? Those things don't exist.' He tells me that the United States was aware of the 'suitcase' bombs and some of the people we—stupidly—gave them to. Gave, sold, what's the difference?"

After suitcase bombs were used in the devastating Beirut marine barracks bombing, the U.S. intelligence services— DIA, CIA—put out the word that big rewards would be paid to anyone who had hard information on these bombs—or turned in one in mint condition. A device covered with the special KGB markings like the ones Kaliniev had sketched, looking at the gray boxes in the dim light of the arsenal, and shown to Markovitch.

Tartikov had reminded Markovitch that the new Russian government denied the existence of any terrorist suitcase bombs. When the SVR officer had been stationed "above the line" at the Russian Embassy in Washington, however, he had watched Aleksandr Lebed, former secretary of Boris Yeltsin's security council, tell *Sixty Minutes* that the KGB had developed the suitcase bombs in the 1990s.

"What could make for problems? You report them—

then you have problems, yes?" Markovitch asked. "The people running things now don't want to know. I suspect most of the damn things were dismantled. So I told my partner I'd come up empty. Then suddenly I get your call. These things, you tell me, are sitting next to you. They aren't on any inventory. Nobody knows how they got there; probably no one remembers that they *are* there. So—how can you steal something that doesn't exist?"

By the time Kaliniev covered the three and a half miles to his hotel, he was struggling with his conscience. He had seen the lethal destructive force of even small high explosive bombs. And if they fell into the wrong hands? Who would that be—the wrong hands? Muslim extremists? They could be planning to use the weapons on some target in Israel—or in some corner of the former Soviet Union. Maybe in the United States.

Once inside his room, Kaliniev sat in the single wobbly chair, smoking, and staring at the grimy walls, worn curtains, and a narrow unmade bed with a thin brown blanket pushed to one side. He was convinced that, until now, he was the only one who knew about the bombs. Now Markovitch knew. And Rafael. And probably others.

But he could soon be rich and go somewhere far away, where he would not have to put up with a government that betrayed his country. If he chose not to go ahead, he knew that someone else, somewhere in Russia, would provide the bombs. Others must be sitting in scattered locations, possibly recorded in inventories, possibly not. He lit up another cigarette from the butt of his last one. What did he owe to the new Russia? Mother Russia was dead. It had taken away his family; it had made his life meaningless, empty.

The decision came suddenly, filling him with a powerful sense of relief. He would accept their terms and it would be over and maybe a new life could start.

* * *

The following evening Kaliniev, in gray slacks and a loose-fitting pullover, sat in the same booth in the back of the room, nervously tapping his fingers on the table and smoking. Rafael appeared at exactly the time that he promised and slid quietly into the opposite seat of the booth. Kaliniev noted that Rafael was taller than he remembered, a striking man with slightly exotic features, olive skin, and slicked back hair secured at the nape of his neck. His clothes, from the wool sport coat to the comfortable-looking black loafers, were clearly very expensive.

Markovitch delivered a bottle of whisky and two glasses, and walked away without greeting either man. When Kaliniev started to speak, Rafael raised his hand to stop him and continued to fill the two glasses.

"Yuri, I can see that your conscience is tearing at you. We know you are a professional soldier and please believe me when I say that I share your feelings."

The sincerity of the low and mellifluous voice kept Kaliniev from interrupting.

"The package we need is—how should I say it—is more symbolic. Something to strike out at those who oppress my people. We are aware of the bomb's destructive power and would be foolish to use them indiscriminately. I ask you to believe me. As a soldier, you understand that there are times when one must strike out to be free and independent."

What he heard unsettled Kaliniev. Rafael must mean some type of civil war or another one of those religious conflicts. Over the years, Kaliniev had seen how civil wars, initially driven by deeply held beliefs, noble beliefs, degenerated into cycles of reflexive violence that were endlessly repeated. But what did it matter?

"I have told you all that I can." Rafael paused and lit one of his cigarillos. "We need to close on this deal or end our discussion. I think you know that we will be successful—either with your help or in some other way."

Yuri Kaliniev realized that he had gone too far to turn back.

"Go ahead and give the bank the necessary instructions."

CHAPTER 18

Mexico City

Navarro threw a large towel around his shoulders as he finished his routine laps in the pool. It was a near perfect June day and he was in an unusually good mood after receiving Juan Ortega's phone call from Gdansk. Like Tartikov, Navarro had also watched Aleksandr Lebed, on *Sixty Minutes* some years back. The possibility of actually getting his hands on the small bombs had fascinated him.

As Navarro relaxed alongside the pool, he thought about how different he was from his lieutenant, Juan Ortega. Navarro never felt close to him; part of it may have been an undercurrent of resentment. Ortega's family was prominent and he had enjoyed the benefits of wealth, education, and travel. When he finished university, Ortega moved up easily through both government and corporate positions, using charm or ruthlessness when required.

When he got bored with his job as CFO of a conglomerate that, among other things, procured or manufactured material for Mexico's armed forces, he opened his own consulting firm and only accepted work if it interested him. Navarro leaned back and remembered their initial meetings.

He had been introduced to Ortega in one of the exclusive clubs off Parque Sullivan. After beginning a conversation about Mexico's chances in the World Cup, the two men continued to talk about a variety of subjects over lunch. The casual meetings and lunches continued during the next six months. Ortega knew just who Navarro was; his friends had tried to persuade him to break off his friendship with the leader of La Eme. But there was a part of Ortega that had always wanted to walk on the wild side—and Navarro fascinated him. Here was a man who had sophisticated knowledge of management and finance—and had people killed if that's what it took to solve a "business" problem.

When their friendship had reached the right point, Navarro decided to recruit Ortega.

"Tell me, Juan, how you would go about uniting the competing drug barons in a business arrangement—maybe a cartel?"

Ortega's eyes lit up. It was the type of challenge that excited him—unlimited resources and freedom to create something many would think impossible. After a series of meetings involving lengthy discussions on diversifying the cartel, once it was fully organized, into legitimate business, Ortega accepted the offer to join Navarro.

"Now you have to tell me what you want."

"What I want you have already given me—an intriguing challenge and unlimited rewards. Something I can turn into legitimate businesses one day. As to compensation, I know that I will be treated fairly."

Over the years since, Ortega had done everything Navarro asked but there was that persistent undertone to their relationship, a level of discomfort or uneasiness that continued to bother him. Perhaps it was Ortega's insistence on moving into legitimate businesses. How naive can he be, thought Navarro.

Navarro savored the softness of the robe against his tanned and well-muscled body. He obsession with control ruled everything—including staying in shape. He meticulously followed a disciplined schedule. He did not have time for a wife, family; he had never even considered it. Nothing was allowed to divert him from his audacious but visionary plan to make the cartel the most important organization not only in Mexico but also eventually in the world. At times, he wished that he could delegate more responsibility to his closest associates but he had never learned to trust anyone.

Ortega, thanks to the Russian he had learned while engaged in quietly procuring certain weapons from the crumbling Soviet Union—most of which did not end up in Mexico but were resold, for a handsome profit, to other countries—made an ideal ambassador to Navarro's Russian counterparts. So when Navarro made the decision to move to procure the suitcase bombs, Ortega had reached out to a contact he knew only as "Viktor," a small, dark man who lived in Tbilisi and whose back was bent over in a kind of hump from osteoporosis. In the *mafyia*, Viktor's nickname was "The Poison Dwarf." In the years before his disease crippled him, Viktor had killed over twenty people. Now he had plenty of underlings to do his killing for him. He was not a man you crossed. At first resistant to Ortega's request, he finally and reluctantly agreed to spread the word about what Ortega was looking for, but insisted that his organization have no direct involvement. If someone with access could be found, they would set up a meeting—nothing more.

Once Navarro learned that the bombs could be obtained, he spent over fifty million dollars to pay a fee to the Russians, set up a weapons lab in an abandoned hacienda located a considerable distance from Mexico City, and hired foreign bomb experts to check out and modify the bombs as necessary. To cover his tracks if anything went wrong, he reached out to the al-Qaeda terrorist organization and struck a deal. They had the expertise he needed; and they wanted some of the bombs. Their demolition people would perform the modifications necessary and then return to the Middle East—with two of the bombs.

Three weeks after Ortega's call, Navarro was informed that the Minsk package and bomb experts had arrived at the hacienda. It was July and Navarro reassured himself that there was enough time to repackage the bombs and keep his plan on track. He sent Espinosa to oversee the operation. What Espinosa lacked in finesse was more than compensated for by his unwavering loyalty; he could be trusted to do what Navarro wanted and not allow anyone involved making stupid mistakes or compromising security.

The isolated hacienda with its well-equipped lab was two miles outside the fishing village of Salina Cruz on the Gulf of Tehuantepec, where a rusting Polish registered freighter had anchored. The transfer was made using one of the freighter's small workboats during the night while the village slept. The entire operation took less than an hour. By sunrise, the freighter was well out to sea.

The laboratory facilities inside the hacienda provided everything needed by the technicians. Twenty armed men from Espinosa's Oaxaca drug organization provided security. They kept a careful watch for any strangers arriving at the fishing village or the larger village of Juchitan, twelve miles away. The foreign bomb experts grumbled about the isolation but methodically worked at their tasks, encouraged by the large bonuses payable upon completion of the checkout and repackaging of the bombs. Unfortunately for them, it was a bonus they would not collect. The plan was too important to risk any leaks; they would never leave the hacienda. Nor would the promised bombs be delivered to the al-Qaeda terrorist network.

The reconfiguration of the bombs was technically simple—coupling a small programmed digital timer and semtex explosive triggering device to the bomb. The more difficult problem was to size the bombs as small as possible to fit inside innocuous containers like briefcases and packages wrapped in brown paper, stamped, addressed, and ready to be mailed. A hydroelectric plant, the central terminal of an airport, two government buildings, and an open-air marketplace were the targets for five of the bombs. Navarro allowed only the most experienced bomb technician to work on the sixth bomb: It would be reconfigured to fit within the false bottom of a cylindrical steel container—a container with radioactive warning labels attached.

CHAPTER 19

Mexico City

The American Department of Energy had shipped ten empty steel containers to the Mexican government to use for stowing their nuclear waste from hospitals and research facilities until final permanent storage was available. On arrival at Mexico City's Benito Juarez International Airport, the cargo handlers put the containers with their embossed radioactive warning labels into temporary storage bins. During the late night hours, when the airport activity level had tapered off, airport security personnel on the drug cartel's payroll quietly diverted one of the steel containers and loaded it into a conveniently located panel truck. A two-month investigation failed to recover the container and the authorities on both sides of the border shifted their attention to more immediate problems.

Mexico's temporary low-level nuclear waste stowage facility was located in the old underground chambers of Mexico City's Guadalupe Hospital. Everything was on track—until the unexpected White House decision to make stowage of the Mexican wastes in the repository a prelude to the opening ceremony—and moving forward with the opening date. Shortly after moving up the timetable, the U.S. and Mexican presidents announced that they intended to take part in the opening ceremony.

"That was a big mistake," Navarro said aloud as he drew on his cigar and closed his eyes.

When the Mexican energy minister had designated the Guadalupe Hospital as a nuclear waste storage site in 1974, the abandoned but solidly constructed cellar converted into a storage facility that had formally served as the hospital's morgue. The twenty-five tube-like chambers that extended twelve feet into the rock wall of the large cellar morgue were adequate for the small amount of radioactive waste expected.

Years later, when the major hospitals installed more modern diagnostic imaging equipment that generated radioactive waste, the Energy Ministry, with U.S. technical assistance, redesigned the hospital site to handle the increased waste. A hardened steel lining was put in place of the original wood on the inside of the empty chambers and the thick oak hatch covers exchanged for hermetically sealed stainless steel covers. Technicians installed self-calibrating devices to monitor and record the low-level radiation readings, completing the modernization.

Julio Montoya completed university in May with an accounting major and became one of the growing number of restless college graduates without jobs. Their prospects were bleak, given the faltering economy. He managed to secure what he referred to as his temporary job, working as one of the monitor watches at the Guadalupe Hospital nuclear storage site. He liked the night shift—10 P.M. to 6 A.M.—because he could catch some sleep. But he also did more than sleep down in the quiet darkness.

In between crossword puzzles and televised soccer matches, Julio recorded the monitor readings in the watch-log notebooks and tested the security alarms on the only entrance to the converted morgue. The television monitoring tape was replaced daily with another tape during the morning watch shift after he departed from his watch. On arrival, Julio would complete these tasks and then head for the hospital's cafeteria after locking the door and activating the security alarms.

That's where he first ran into a nurse who had just joined the hospital staff. She wasn't permanent; she was working as a substitute, but hoped, she told Julio, to get a full-time position. Maria Contreras had a spectacular figure with large, firm breasts, long and well-shaped legs and long black hair that, when she took off her uniform cap and let it cascade down, reached well below her shoulders.

The old law of attraction of opposites went to work. Maria loved listening to Julio describe the glamorous goings-on in the discos, bars, stores, and restaurants on the Zocalo. Maria came from a poor, hardworking family who lived near San Miguel de Allende, she told Julio, and had fought her way through school to the point where she could qualify for training in nursing. Julio's world, she told him, was a fantasy for her. And Julio was good-looking.

When she switched to duty on the 8 P.M. to 4 A.M. shift, she was able to slip down to the basement and visit him. The visits grew longer as the weeks passed and their intimacy deepened. So Maria was more than ready when Julio showed her the air mattress he had blown up and placed on the floor in a dark corner well away from the main door.

It was Maria who discovered the unused semi-darkened doctor's lounge. It was a far more romantic venue than the dim, humid basement with its large radiation warning posters and flickering red monitor lights. The two beds in the lounge were narrow, but they were far more comfortable than the air mattress. When they met there for the first time, Julio, who had taken the risk of abandoning his post in order to make love to the most arousing woman he had ever encountered, wasted little time stripping off his clothes and embracing the waiting, warm, nude body of Maria Contreras. There were no preliminaries or unnecessary words.

While they were making love, four men quietly made their way to the cellar area of the hospital from the basement entrance. The double-locked doors of the nuclear waste storage site presented no problems. One of the men punched in a code disarming the alarm system while another substituted a programmed cassette to offset the time lapse for the one removed from the television-monitoring camera. The other two men in the well-drilled team, wearing Mexican Army special protective outfits, entered the large space carrying the bomb-laden container. They proceeded directly to the fourth chamber, removed the outer seal, and opened the outer door. Without difficulty, they removed the container and placed it next to the container carried in by the team. They signaled the other two men not in protective clothing to stand outside the storage room, before opening the seal of the container removed from the chamber. When it was opened, they emptied the low-level waste into the bomb-laden container. One of the men shifted the inventory tag from the original container and placed it on the bomb-laden container. The two men then hoisted the bomb-laden container back inside the opened chamber and resealed it. The team handed the empty container to the two men outside the door and the last man out replaced the original cassette and activated the television monitor, alarm system, and door locks. The entire operation took less than twenty minutes and the team departed in an army truck outside the basement exit.

Julio returned to the storage site, glowing from an unusually vigorous session with Maria—obviously the doctor's lounge was a far better place for their clandestine activity. He sat down, recorded the unchanged readings, and fell asleep with a smile on his face.

When Maria left the hospital that night, she reached behind her locker, pulled out an envelope that had been taped on the back and opened it, quickly counting the five thousand pesos inside it. Maria also had a smile on her face as she put the money in her purse. What a nice bonus, she thought.

Almost everything she had told the infatuated Julio about her background was true. And she was a very competent nurse. The hospital was sorry to see her go when, at the end of the week, she went back to her permanent position—at a small, well-equipped clinic, one reserved for members of Navarro's organization.

Two days later, a convoy consisting of two jeeps and a deuce-and-a half truck arrived at the hospital. It was the army's responsibility to move the containment canisters from Mexico City to the Promontorio repository. Before departure from the Guadalupe Hospital temporary storage site, nuclear waste handlers had sealed the waste-filled containers inside the housing of four specially designed steel canisters.

"Some of these containers are not even full. Why are we breaking our necks to move four of them to that new repository?" One of the waste handlers asked in a muffled voice through the plastic face mask of his protective suit.

"Who cares?" The supervisor, Mariano Ledo, had been called in at the last minute to oversee the handling at the hospital. He had questioned what the rush was all about and his boss curtly told him that the orders were coming direct from the presidential palace. "Our orders are to move four canisters to the repository, so let's get with it and stop bitching. The sooner we get done the sooner we can get out of these outfits."

* * *

Arturo Espinosa was jolted out of sleep by the telephone that stood on a table next to his bed.

"The switch went well?"

"*Si, jefe . . . momentito, por favor.*"

He prodded the woman laying next to him, wrapped only in a sheet, her mouth half open, and her hair slick from the sweat of a strenuous sexual workout with Espinosa.

Cupping one big hand over the phone's handset, he nudged her with his foot until she rolled over and looked at him, bleary-eyed and only half awake.

"Go down to the kitchen and bring me a beer. And don't hurry."

Putting the phone back to his ear, he apologized for the delay.

"What about the technicians?" Navarro asked impatiently.

"Everything at the hacienda has been taken care of . . . including the ragheads. I took care of that personally."

"Okay. What else has to be done?"

"We've got some cleanup . . . a couple of days. I'll leave a few of my guys here to ensure that no one snoops around."

"Well, we've done everything possible. If the bomb is discovered, Hamid swears that everything is untraceable. Even if he screwed up and the damn thing doesn't go off, we'll make sure someone finds out about it. It would still serve our purposes. *Bueno*—at last it's done. Let's meet in Acapulco. September should be perfect now that the tourists are gone. You've earned a few days off."

CHAPTER 20

Acapulco, Mexico

Javier Navarro, Arturo Espinosa, and Juan Ortega finished lunch at the Acapulco beach resort hotel owned by the drug cartel. Espinosa clearly had a monster hangover. He was dressed casually—black slacks and shirt, opened at the throat, and the usual chunky gold chains. Ortega, in contrast, was dressed much more conservatively than the other two; his face was paler, and more refined than those of his swarthy companions. In his early forties and younger than either of them, he seemed to belong to another world, to have fallen from the sky and landed accidentally in the gaudy resort, still crowded with German and French tourists eager to pay too much money to get too much sun.

Espinosa stood and tucked his shirt, bulging over his large belly, into his pants. He wanted to go to his room, close the drapes and sleep. His head hammered so much that he could barely think. He dropped back into his chair and suppressed a groan.

"Will we have any problems with the driver?" Navarro asked abruptly.

"Ah, you mean the guy that hauled the container to the city?"

Navarro nodded impatiently.

"Shit. He is just a poor produce farmer who runs his stuff into Mexico City twice a week. We won't have any problems. The poor bastard didn't even know what he was carrying." Espinosa looked over at Ortega and grimaced while holding a hand to his pounding head.

Ortega felt sorry for him, so he asked Navarro, "If I am not out of line, what plans do we have for the repackaged bombs?"

Navarro did not immediately respond and his piercing eyes hardened for a moment. He decided that he might as well let Ortega know what was going down. After all, the guy had gotten the damn things out of Russia.

"Five of them will be used on soft targets as close to the U.S. border as possible for max effect."

"Why so close to the border? Doesn't that raise the risk?"

Navarro again paused before responding. "There is always a risk, Juan—something that you will have to learn." Navarro never missed an opportunity to demonstrate that Ortega had a lot to learn before they could ever take over his position. "What can the U.S. do . . . invade us? Economic sanctions? That would pull the plug on NAFTA and threaten their investment. The real risk is not having the balls to keep the pressure on. When Congress sees what is happening on their border, the bastards will think some kind of revolution is spreading from Chiapas and look for a way out. We already have some of their non-stop TV commentators playing up the Zapatistas as some kind of Castro revolution on their border."

* * *

Navarro got up, headed for the restroom, and began thinking about the bizarre phone call that had come through just as he was getting ready to leave to meet Arturo and Juan in Acapulco. At first, he was incredulous. He wasn't even sure where the call originated from although he had assumed Washington.

"I have a proposition for you and I think you will want to listen to it."

"What the hell are you talking about? Where did you get this number?"

"Who I am or where I got your number is not important. If you need a name, you can call me Zircon. Now, let me ask the question: How important would it be to have the United States back off from the ruling party?"

Navarro was stunned. His first instinct was to hang up but something stopped him. Was it the polished Castilian accent and self-confidence in the voice on the other end? "Why would I believe that you could do what you say?"

"I figured you would ask. If you want proof, watch the president's speech to the NATO foreign ministers meeting two weeks from this Friday. You will see it on CNN and you'll get your answer."

Navarro did not know what to say. He had been so stunned by the call that all he could manage was to stammer, "Yeah, right. Okay, we'll see what happens on Friday. Then we might talk." Navarro was squeezing the phone trying to picture the man he was dealing with. He felt like telling whoever it was that the real show would take place soon and he didn't need any help to make it happen.

"I'll call again. Nice talking with you."

Navarro returned to the table in a kind of daze and suddenly realized that Ortega was talking to him.

"I hope no one checks them out," Ortega said, referring to the Zapatistas and laughing. "From what I observed, those guys have a hard time figuring out what day it is."

"Who gives a fuck? The U.S. media will stretch anything for a story."

"Where is Hidalgo in all this?" Espinosa wiped the perspiration from his face with a napkin. "Doesn't he fly back to Mexico sometime next week. How far are you going to let him go with his Independent Party?"

"Don't worry about him. He'll be dealt with at the right time."

"What about those so-called political leaders in the PAN opposition party?" Ortega asked. "You haven't mentioned them and they haven't been making much noise lately."

Navarro glanced at Espinosa slyly and slowly unwrapped a cigar before answering Ortega. The Washington call was still on his mind.

"Well, let me just say that they fell into line after their weak-kneed presidential candidate had that accident a couple of weeks ago. We had a meeting of the minds last month. It was funny to watch them eye Chapa, who stood in the back of the room. Anyway, they will follow our advice and join forces with the PRD."

Ortega realized that if the PRD did indeed scrape by and get into office, Navarro could expand the drug cartel and his power without any real opposition from the new government—and then no one could stop him.

Ortega also knew that he was getting more involved in things that went beyond making the cartel more efficient or, more importantly, shifting into legit businesses. This was about taking down a whole country. When Navarro had given him the order to orchestrate Chiapas and find a way to buy the suitcase bombs, he realized that if he did not manage to carry out the order, he would be moved out or possibly even killed. Navarro had said to him, in effect, "Juan, here is how you prove you are worthy of being in the inner circle and my successor." Now, as he looked at Navarro and Espinosa stretched out in the chairs in the sun, like two iguanas on a rock, trickles of sweat ran down his side. For the first time, the enormity of what the cartel leader intended to do had fully hit home. He knew, now, that he needed to find a way out—and somehow remain alive.

Espinosa yawned; his foul breath made Ortega feel sick to his stomach. "How about the other one . . . you know . . . the sixth one?"

"Ah, yes, the special bomb you had transported by that farmer. That will present some interesting problems. We have to be very careful about talking about this. I will tell you now that we are going to get this special bomb inside a place they would never dream of—the Promontorio Mountain Repository in Sonora."

Navarro stopped and enjoyed their startled reaction. His associates found it chilling to watch their relaxed companion turn into the unflinching cruel head of La Eme when he wanted to make a point. It was in the way he looked at you, thought Ortega.

"The problem is that we don't have anyone on the inside of the repository. That is the reason we need some luck to get the bomb inside the repository. At first, I just wanted to explode the damn thing, to show how screwed up the government was taking nuclear waste from the United States and storing it in Mexico. When the government moved up the timetable and decided to make a big deal of the fact that radioactive waste from our country would be the first to be put into the mountain, I was determined to have the bomb ready in time to give some people a big surprise."

Ortega was clearly puzzled.

"But how are you going to detonate the bomb at exactly the right time? This type of ceremony can run late; there could be some kind of last-minute delay."

Navarro's smile faded as he momentarily wondered why Ortega was asking so many questions.

"I really don't give a shit if it goes off an hour before or after the ceremony. We will get the same result. However, I'd love to watch Posadas's expression if it exploded when he was there."

Ortega decided to back off. He was relieved when Espinosa joined in.

"Well, don't get pissed . . . but if it doesn't detonate, what in the hell good will it be?"

Navarro couldn't help smiling at Espinosa.

"If it gets inside the repository and doesn't go off, we will make sure the press finds out it is in there, which will break it all wide open. Everyone will blame Posadas and Alverez for using Mexico as a dump site and the bomb will just be the final straw—because they gave up control of the repository to the United States. But I think it will go off on time. In any event, we can't lose."

CHAPTER 21

U.S. Embassy
Mexico City

Palmer had settled into a daily routine. Despite the ambassador's warning he was up at dawn and running five to seven miles before it got hot. Then he would have a cup of coffee with the marines on the security detail and get the latest embassy scuttlebutt. The marines had their own network and they saw and heard a lot more than people in the embassy realized.

Like Liz Cramer, he had been given an office in the section of the embassy reserved for commercial officers, but unlike her, he devoted no time to working in his cover job. Since the office in "commercial" was not much larger than a broom closed, he gladly relinquished it and spent his time in a cubicle in the secure area where the CIA station was located. He spent most of the morning plowing through classified traffic, which was either addressed specifically to him or included him on a distribution list.

Tom Halligan, the CIA station chief, shared some of the

intel he put into the daily 11 A.M. briefing to Ambassador Reimann and diplomatically asked no more about Palmer's role in operations than he felt he needed to know. Palmer, in turn, knew that Halligan was fully briefed on SKY-HAWK so they had little reason to discuss it. Since Palmer was using a cover slot in commercial, Halligan advised him on how to "live" his cover, a difficult business since Palmer was not actually doing any work in the commercial section. His connection with the NSC and Andrews was both recent and not widely known. Apart from Halligan, Graham, the ambassador, and Liz Cramer, no one on the embassy staff knew about the connection. However, Palmer assumed that staff members were curious about who he was and why he was there—and some were probably using contacts at the State Department to nose around a little. It was easy enough to determine that Palmer "worked on the other side," the term FSOs used in referring to people under State Department cover positions in embassies and consulates. All Foreign Service officers were listed in a restricted publication called, inside the State Department, the "stud book" so it was not hard to figure out who was working undercover positions in an embassy.

"We bury a lot of our people in commercial but we limit their contacts with businesspeople from either the United States or Mexico. The Commerce Department would have a fit if one of our officers strayed from the contact guidelines. But you are a different breed of cat."

Halligan grinned at him and leaned back in his swivel chair. "Langley ordered me to make resources available to you at my discretion. That means no exposure of sources and methods to you—that we keep in the family. But if you want a profile on a national, I can make it available if we have compiled one. You can also use our secure voice and data transmission circuits, if you want. But I hear your pal Willy Graham has patched in a comm line to NSC for you. Just as well—the load of traffic up here is heavy and you might have to get in the queue to send out a cable or get a voice link. Anyhow, Willy has a lot more capacity than we do since he routes all priority classified embassy traffic through the ops center."

They had finally come to a joint decision that Palmer, since he had the personal attention of the national security adviser, could make contacts with Mexican nationals whenever he had good reason to do so.

"I understand you want to get your finger on the pulse of things down here, so no better way than to spend time with the locals in business and government."

"Yeah, but I have to come up with some excuse for meetings outside the embassy. Dr. Cramer suggested that I help commercial out with their monthly economic forecast. Just means following a questionnaire, collecting some data."

"Sounds good." Halligan winked at him. "And you might learn something about economics. I bet Dr. Cramer is a nifty teacher."

On Thursday morning, two days after Posadas had flown to Washington to meet with Washburn in a hastily scheduled meeting following the Chiapas incident, Palmer was reading a long "eyes only" cable from David Andrews giving his account of the meeting and aftermath. Andrews's message was composed in his usual style—terse, burstlike sentences that he employed not just in cable drafting but also in memoranda and annotations. It was a style that irritated those in Washington already predisposed to be critical of the national security adviser's activist role in operational matters. "Cableese"—the traditional form of State Department communications dating back to the days when telegrams or cables were just that—came naturally to Andrews, whose operating style was seldom less than "All ahead full!"

MAY 15. PHOTO OP IN ROSE GARDEN FOL-
LOWED BY PRIVATE MEETING OF POTUS,
PRESMEX, AND SECSTATE. NOT PRESENT BUT
AM RELIABLY INFORMED POTUS STRONGLY
CRITICAL OF MEXGOV LEADERSHIP. WARNED
PRESMEX THAT CONGRESS UNFRIENDLY TO
ADDITIONAL AID PACKAGE. SECSTATE PRE-
VAILED. POTUS WILL MAINTAIN SUPPORT
PRESMEX IN PUBLIC BUT IS CLEARLY WOR-
RIED ABOUT FATE OF FTAA AND MEXTHREAT
TO SECOND TERM. STILL WEDDED TO PRI.
MARRIED IN HASTE. REPENTING AT LEISURE.
ANDREWS.

Palmer shook his head. Working in the NSC, one couldn't
help being aware of the complex relationship between Snyder and Andrews. It was both critical and competitive, and
it seemed to suit both of them. He put the cable in his burn
bag and headed for the ops center. Palmer preferred using
the stairs but stories about certain "suits"—Marine slang
for embassy personnel in coats and ties—who still could
not properly insert their access cards while punching in the
right number code for locks on security doors and accidentally set off alarms had convinced him to avoid making the
same mistake and take the elevator. He figured that the
Marines had better things to do other than reacting to
false alarms.

Willie Graham's perpetual frown changed to a sponta-
neous smile when he saw Palmer fumbling with his access
cards. He hit the OPEN button at the side of his desk and
waved Palmer in. As Palmer entered his office, he watched
Willie carefully siphon coffee into large mugs from a contraption of multiple glass tubes and beakers that resembled
a small distillery more than a coffeemaker. It was a Willie

contraption that produced the best coffee in town. Graham lived on coffee, a liquid diet that kept both his energy level and his impatience index high.

"Got a hot one for you, Cole." Carrying his mug, Palmer followed Graham into one of the glass partitioned rooms—"sanitized" rooms with thick concrete walls and special acoustical soundproofing and electromagnetic shielding—that prevented acoustic and electronic leakage and frustrated electronic eavesdropping.

"So what's going on, Cole? This one came through 'Flash,' you, and Dr. Cramer addressees. The vibes I'm picking up is that you're here on something big." Graham's eyes looked huge peering out of the thick lenses of his wire-rimmed glasses. Palmer had to suppress a smile. Graham had been cleared for part of Palmer's operational role; it was probably time to give him a no-shit briefing.

If Graham could be trusted to design and operate the world's most sophisticated "sigint"—signal-intelligence— equipment, he should know how to handle what he intended to tell him.

He looked at the scrap of printout Graham handed him. SKYHAWK GREENLIGHTED. Originator was listed as NSC/DEP.

"Okay, Willie. I don't have to tell you how paranoid Washington is about sensitive information."

Graham did not respond but nodded his head.

"The spooks have picked up some nasty rumors on possible terrorist bombings before the elections down here. As usual, we do not know much more. We do know, however, that any type of terrorist bombing would panic the country—especially after Chiapas—and possibly end any ruling party's hope of remaining in power."

Graham removed his glasses and rubbed his eyes. "How do we know it's not just some kind of nutcase who is pissed off and shooting off his mouth?"

"I wish that's all it was, Willie. The spooks in their infinite wisdom figure that there is something else going down. The problem is that no one really knows who is doing what down here. Lots of players—La Eme, rebels down south, ruling party, PRD, and Hidalgo's new independent party."

When Graham heard Hidalgo's name, he snapped his head around and stared at Palmer in surprise. "Jesus Christ! I knew that Hidalgo was making noises about getting back in the race but he's too smart to get involved in something like this."

"Well, whoever is pulling the strings down here for the last eighteen months or so has been pretty damn successful."

Graham sat back and was now rubbing his temples with quick circular movements that indicated he was thinking hard and fast.

"Well, I think you're on the wrong track with Hidalgo. My money is on the drug cartel and their left-wing PRD flunkies. If they get into power, Washington will have some real problems. All hell is going to break loose."

Palmer remembered what David Andrews had told him about the involvement of the cartel in a destabilization program, but decided to keep it to himself.

"Um, well I tend to agree with you, Willie. In fact, some folks in Washington believe that the cartel was responsible for the hit on General Swanson as payback for interfering in their business."

"Holy shit! Why don't they pick up some of the Eme leaders and squeeze what they need out of them?"

"I wish we could, Willie. I knew Swanson and he was one of the good guys. We cannot do what we used to be able to do—especially in a foreign country."

Palmer had decided that he would have to fill Graham in on SKYHAWK soon, which meant he had to get him cleared and only Andrews could authorize it. He was looking forward to it—being able to tell Graham that in the very near future the United States and selected Mexican forces were indeed going to squeeze the cartel leaders. Squeeze the life out of them, if he had a say in it.

"Getting back to the rumors about a possible sequence of terrorist incidents down here, Willy, we need to run them to ground and we don't have much time." Palmer knew that Tom Halligan was using every asset he had in place to do just that.

Graham peered at Palmer and asked, a note of suspicion in his voice. "Are they telling you everything?" He caught the surprised look on Palmer's face. "You know the game. The pol and ops people in Washington tell you only part of the info until you force their hand."

Palmer knew that Graham's intuition told him that something like SKYHAWK was going down. It was rare to have someone from the NSC sitting in a cover position in any embassy and doing a clearly operational job. What communications didn't come to Palmer "eyes only" from both State and NSC had NOINFORN and other restrictions all over them.

Palmer decided to play for time. The sooner he could put Graham in the loop the better.

"I've always tried to stay away from that stuff. I'm not inclined to be paranoid and I'm too naive to play those games. 'Need to know,' Willie. That goes for you and me both."

What he did not want to come out was the full story of Cole Palmer's one man crusade against the drug business and how it had driven him to risk his life and his career, not that he had cared much about either one during the past few years. How much had his hatred for traffickers affected his judgment? Would it cause him to screw up things down here? He thought that he had gained control of himself but was not sure. He had a gut feeling that there were more tests ahead before he could rebuild his life.

"Yeah—all I'm saying is you better watch your backside. Your comment about Hidalgo also bothers me."

"I guess from what you say that you know more than I do, Willie."

"Well, I can tell you that there are a lot of high-level and influential people in this country who did not like the way that Hidalgo was run out of town."

"I'm not sure of anything, Willie—even why I'm down here," Palmer said, trying to get back on point. "All I want to do is what I can to head things off down here and get back to my sailboat."

"Hell, you sailors never change," said Graham with a frown. "Okay, consider these factors. The Mexican government blames Chiapas on the Zapatistas. Then other people claim that paramilitary forces in the area were responsible. What is Washington's read on the Chiapas thing?"

Palmer thought it over for a minute: How far could he go on this?

"The thinking is—well one faction in State thinks it was staged by the rebels as an attention-getter. Another one thinks the people who bought and paid for the PRD orchestrated the massacre. But I'm not sure how all that relates to the terrorism rumors. That's why I need your help to figure it out before we run out of time."

They walked back inside Graham's office in the ops center to refill their coffee. Graham took a sip, winced when he found out it was too hot, and turned to Palmer. "You know it's the damnedest thing now that I think about it. A month ago, at one of our informal counterpart meetings, one of their federal agents who is a plant inside the telecom setup down here mentioned some 'possible disturbances' or something like that before the elections. When I tried to follow up, he clamed up. I didn't worry about it at the time because the guy is sorta flaky and not one of the senior people in his agency."

"I think we need to worry about it now," Palmer said. He slid the SKYHAWK message into a machine next to Graham's control console. It would be immediately and completely destroyed. Unlike shredders, which left behind strips of recoverable information and were no longer used by U.S. agencies dealing with classified material, this large gray box, about four feet high and with a letter box–like slit on the top, reduced paper to fine ash.

"Okay. How do you want to play it?"

Palmer paused before answering. If something is going down, the last thing we want to do is to tip our hand too early, he thought, remembering what Andrews had said about protecting SKYHAWK at all costs, especially from nominally "friendly" Mexican intelligence and armed forces personnel.

"Can you trust any of them? Willy, if you do have someone you trust inside that agency—and that is your call—I suggest you find a reason to run down what that guy was talking about."

Palmer looked at his watch and got up to leave the ops center. It was a few minutes before he was to meet Liz Cramer in her "secure" office. He would pass on the word about the go-ahead on SKYHAWK. Now he understood the real reason for the Posadas late-minute visit to Washington—pushing him to clear the way for the operation.

He wondered why all of a sudden he was inventing reasons to see Liz Cramer. Things were edging a bit beyond the boundaries of business and shading into the personal. He had not been involved in a long-term relationship with anyone since Catherine's death. He had an affair with a woman five years younger than he, who he met at a sailing party in Annapolis. She was a successful real estate agent who made a substantial income from handling sales of some of the more expensive homes on the water, which meant very expensive homes. But her active social life, an essential part of her work, was not something Palmer wanted to be involved with, so intimacy had mellowed into friendship. Shortly before he had returned to the West Coast, she had become engaged to a contractor, a man considerably older than Cole and considerably richer.

Liz Cramer had a smile that could light up a room. She was fun to be with and made Palmer feel comfortable and at ease. And she had even managed to convince Palmer, a dedicated tennis player, to join her in taking golf lessons. So far, they had only squeezed in two of them. Where did he see this relationship going? He still could not figure out how interested she was in him as something other than a colleague and friend. He had only known her for a few weeks, after all, he told himself. And was he ready for something that went beyond friendship?

The elevator doors opened and he decided to return to his own office before meeting with Liz. He picked up the phone and dialed Luis Vasquez.

"Luis, Cole Palmer here. I'm in town for a while. Can we get together."

"Good God, Cole, it's great to hear from you. What a nice surprise."

Palmer sensed, only minutes into their conversation, that their friendship remained a warm one. When Luis asked him if would stay at his house, Palmer almost accepted the invitation. Living in a hotel had started to get on his nerves and he felt guilty about the money his room was costing taxpayers back home.

After a few minutes spent exchanging the latest news about their lives, during which Palmer managed to avoid giving a reason for his presence in Mexico City, a tennis game was scheduled at a club Luis belonged to. When Palmer hung up, he found himself feeling conflicted. Luis was indeed a trustworthy and good friend, and Palmer was about to use him as a source. After trying to convince himself that the end justified the means, especially if it stopped people from getting killed, he decided that he had to tell Luis some version of the truth. What that version would be depended a great deal on his calculation of the risks involved. Palmer might be willing to put himself at risk in this operation, as he had in the past, but he did not want to drag Luis Vasquez, or anyone else any deeper into muddy and dangerous waters than he had to.

CHAPTER 22

Mexico City

The tennis was crisp and competitive. Palmer worked harder than Vasquez who was more familiar with the erratic bounce of grass play. After losing the first set, Palmer's legs felt like jelly and he thought he might have to stop. However, after a brief break, he started seeing the ball and it started flying off his racket with a pop. After winning the second set, court time expired and they headed for the locker room spa. Palmer was relieved and exhausted. He tried not to wince in front of the smiling Vasquez as he pushed his limbs into the welcoming steaming Jacuzzi. Palmer hated those pain-free natural athletes who moved effortlessly with a quick easy grace like Vasquez.

The two dressed while talking about how their lives had taken unexpected paths since their Newport days.

"I don't want to push, Cole, but how are you doing? We've never really had the chance to talk since I saw you at the funeral."

"Seeing you there really made a difference to me, Luis. When I got through the thing, I looked around to see if you had a place to stay but couldn't find you."

"I wanted very much to stay . . . to see if I could do anything. However, I figured you needed some time and space. When you sent me updates on what you were doing, I felt a lot better."

"That's a nice way to describe my years of drifting, pal."

"I meant it sincerely. Sometimes it takes a long time, Cole. Whatever you did is not important if you can get along with your life after something like that. I heard that there was a period . . . that you were not like the man I thought I knew."

Luis Vasquez took a sip of mineral water from a tall glass and handed one to Palmer.

"Well, I'm not that proud of some of the things I did, Luis. The hate and revenge demons seemed to take over my life no matter how hard I tried to change things. It almost turned into a one man war on anything associated with drugs until I turned the corner."

"Well, I'm just so pleased to see you again. Your friendship was so important during some tough times for me in Newport and I'll never forget it."

As they were leaving the locker room, Vasquez put his arm around Palmer's shoulders. "I'm so glad, so relieved to have back the Cole whom I knew then."

They headed for the club dinning room. Vasquez was wearing a lightweight blue cashmere sport coat covering an open white button-down shirt, gray wool slacks, and Gucci loafers. Cole was dressed in khaki slacks with a blue denim shirt covered by an off-white Polo tennis sweater. As the headwaiter escorted them to a table, Vasquez was treated with deference and attentiveness. They had hardly sat down when a waiter in a starched white jacket came over to take their order for drinks.

"Well Cole, your tennis is much too good for me and I was lucky to get a set."

Palmer chuckled and rolled his eyes. "I have a feeling you're setting me up for the next time. Anyway, it was just like the good old days at the War College."

They ordered a bottle of Macon and salads. Vasquez offered a brief history of the club and discreetly pointed out some of Mexico's richest and most powerful men sitting at other tables. When he finished, Palmer got to the point. Looking Vasquez in the eye, he said quietly, "As you know, the last time we briefly saw one another, I was working in the national security adviser's office."

"Yes. I briefly met David Andrews at Catherine's funeral."

"That's right. Well, a month after seeing you in Washington last year my parents both died within weeks of each other. I spent most of the last part of the year in California dealing with selling my father's business and executing their wills. I was just starting to think what I was going to do when David asked me to come to Mexico City. I got here in February and have been waiting for the opportunity to call you. We've got a problem that I need your help on."

"Please, how can I help? You don't even have to ask."

Palmer pushed what remained of his salad off to one side and tried to sort out how he was going to tell Vasquez. He decided years ago that the best way was to be straightforward. He told him about the ongoing debates in Washington following the Chiapas massacre and the strong sentiment of Congress against pouring more money into aiding Mexico. And that Hidalgo's intervention could lead to disaster.

Palmer paused and Vasquez swirled some of the golden wine around in his glass, taking time to frame a response.

"Posadas took office a few weeks before the country

plunged into the deepest recession since the 1930s. Social welfare spending stopped, especially in the southern states, where it was needed the most. From that point on, the Chiapas incident was inevitable."

Vasquez again paused and Palmer remained silent. "After Posadas agreed to support certain White House initiatives that had been stalled by former President Hidalgo, the promised $50 billion U.S.-led IMF suddenly materialized to meet loan interest payments and reassure the banks and investors who had again started to pull capital out of Mexico. Since then, the president has tried but the ruling party is mired in corruption; the *mordida*—bribes, payoffs—has reached a point where businesses are paying two different taxes, *blanco* to the government, *negro* to the black economy. That's the one economy that's really working down here—La Eme dominates it and they are cutting off Posadas's *conjones*. Instead of leading, the government has tried to blame Hidalgo for everything and the people are tired of it."

Palmer waited for a moment and asked, "Okay, what needs to happen, Luis?"

Vasquez shook his head slowly, and replied, "*Quien sabe?* But I can assure you that it is essential for the United States to continue to support Posadas. Do not get me wrong. I understand how difficult it is for your president, but the ruling party needs to buy time until the economy comes around. If we can make that happen—and I need to point out that Hidalgo was close to getting it done—I believe that the party will purge itself of at least some of the corrupt members of the leadership and the people will turn against La Eme. But they need to believe the state can uphold the law, and right now, that is by no means certain. So we must all hang on. Unfortunately, there is no easier way."

Palmer hesitated before he asked, "But is there enough

time left for President Posadas to turn things around. Your own papers are saying that his ruling party might be out after some seventy years in power."

"I don't know the answer, Cole. Many things can quickly change in the fifteen months before national elections next July. The United States is the only hope to stabilize the economy and block the radical opposition parties from taking power. If the United States backs down, I am not sure Mexico can recover. So we have some tough issues that must be dealt with today. Washington must understand what it would mean if the ruling party loses in the national elections. We cannot let La Eme take over Mexico. We could be faced with . . . with a civil war. Or a revolution. Fortunately, your secretary of state understands and is our one hope."

Palmer nodded his head indicating he understood the seriousness of the situation.

"The issue will be Congress—and that will be a tough nut to crack after Chiapas. However, I understand and will do everything I can to convey the message."

"Thanks for being so patient, Cole, and I apologize for carrying on so long. Now tell me how I can help you?"

Palmer checked that they were out of range of being overheard and leaned toward Vasquez.

"We have picked up some rumors about possible terrorist actions close to the border. It could be no more than rumors calculated to weaken the resolve of the president and supporters in Congress. On the other hand, if the opposition parties share your view that the United States is the only thing stopping them from gaining power in Mexico, they could be desperate and dangerous. That is the reason I am down here, Luis. I need to get a handle on these rumors and we don't have much time."

Vasquez had already heard through his business and government connections that some kind of disruption was likely before the election, but people were reluctant to say more. La Eme's network of informers was so insidious that even friends were not sure of one another anymore.

"Knowing something of your background, Cole, I guessed that you were here for a special reason. I will do everything possible to help. I will start by telling you that Washington is wrong about Hidalgo. I am a close associate of Hidalgo's campaign strategist—Ramiro Chemor. We attended school together. Later, he was a successful banker and then an effective finance minister in the Hidalgo administration. He insists that Hidalgo was unaware of the corrupt actions of his brother Francisco and others in his administration. Chemor is adamant that the truth will vindicate Hidalgo when everything finally comes out. I put a lot of faith in what Chemor says and I have heard similar strong feelings expressed by other credible leaders both in and out of government. I have to tell you that in my circles most people believe that Hidalgo was betrayed by the White House during his final year in office."

Palmer reminded himself that this was the second time in the last two days that people had told him that Hidalgo had not been personally corrupt. Something was missing— he had to get at the truth about Hidalgo.

"I'm glad you will help, Luis, and I am glad that we can still say what is on our minds—like we used to at War College."

As they walked outside, they scheduled another tennis time and Palmer accepted an invitation to dinner. "You will meet some interesting people who could help us. Maria and I will make sure that you'll have an attractive lady sitting next to you."

"I'm looking forward to dinner—it has been too long since I've seen Maria. As for an attractive lady . . . could I bring a colleague from the embassy?"

They shook hands and Palmer took a taxi back to the hotel to change. As the cab headed to the center of the city, he began to wonder why so many people he had talked to in Mexico viewed Hidalgo positively while Andrews and others so negatively. He remembered Graham's question, "Are you sure they're telling you everything?"

CHAPTER 23

Promontorio Mountain
Sonora, Mexico

Security guards in gray uniforms cleared the truck after checking the driver's papers and his load secured to the bed of the truck. It had been a long, hot, weary drive for Raul Zamora, who had to keep a careful distance back from the lead army jeep. He couldn't remember a September so warm and there had been no stops; Zamora's bladder felt like it was about to burst.

"Follow the security van inside the gate," said one of the security guards as he got inside the truck.

As they proceeded, Zamora noticed a large outer perimeter fence topped with concertina wire and other smaller fences that separated different areas of the repository. Hard to break into this place, Zamora thought. Or get out of it.

"Pull over next to the large hanger building behind the security van."

Zamora stopped behind the van and killed the engine.

When the guard jumped out of the truck, Zamora started to get out too.

"Hey, you—back inside!" the guard shouted, resting one hand on his sidearm.

Zamora scrambled back inside.

"Fuck you guys," he mumbled under his breath as he leaned back in the seat adjusting his side mirror. He watched the portable crane lift his load of four metal canisters on railroad carts that the handlers called transporters. He traced the tracks supporting the transporters as they zigzagged through several buildings before leading away to the mountain. When the transfer was completed, the same surly guard slapped the door, jumped back inside without a word, and told him to follow the escort van.

"Where can I go to the bathroom?" Zamora asked anxiously.

The guard did not answer. He gave a nod to the gate guards, the gates, and the high chain-link barrier slid back. As he jumped out of the truck, he looked back at Zamora.

"That's your problem."

"I don't believe this shit." Zamora put the truck in gear and never looked back.

The test site buildings where the truck had unloaded were copies of the monster hangers designed for the C-5A cargo plane. Inside the structure and alongside the flanks of the transporter tracks were a series of large machines and monitors with oversized digital display counters. Warning signs attached to the machines indicated that they were various types of radioscopic equipment—commonly referred as atom-taggers—X-ray imaging equipment and large radiographic machines. As the individual canisters moved on the tracked transporters, they first passed through a large hydraulic airlock chamber that pumped out pockets of oxygen and replaced it with nonflammable nitrogen. From the airlock chamber, the canisters moved to an imaging station to identify possible minute cracks or fractures. If defect-free, the automated line moved the canister to the next test site where the accumulated radioactive brine was pumped out through one of the canister drain valves into recessed carbon steel holding tanks.

As each canister moved past the various testing stations, digital monitors recorded the radiation level and test results. When final checkout was complete, the transporters moved the radioactive waste canisters to the mountain repository for final preps before permanent stowage.

With the U.S. and Mexican presidents attending the opening of Promontorio Mountain Repository, stowing the Mexican waste became the number one priority. Phil Gunderson, the operations director, felt a twinge of guilt as he picked up the phone.

"Mike, I hate to ruin your weekend but we gotta move some canisters."

"But I thought we decided that Monday was okay to start the job. That should give us a whole week."

"I know—but the phone has been ringing off the hook since then. The wonder bees up North want it done now."

"Okay . . . I understand. I'll get cracking on getting a team together and head in."

"Thanks, Mike, and tell your wife I'm sorry to spoil the weekend."

"Hay . . . we've been through this drill before. I'll keep you posted."

Grissini had been a master sargent in the marines who recently retired after twenty-two years, including the last stages of Vietnam and the more recent Gulf War. Built like a fullback, Grissini was broad at the base and neck, and he had picked up the tag "Chesty" after the famous marine hero, Chesty Puller.

He accepted the job at the repository within two weeks of retirement. His wife had been born and raised in

Guadalajara, so Mexico was as much of a home as any of the places Grissini had been stationed.

The team of four gathered at the final test station to review the results of the Mexican canisters—canisters now stenciled M-0060 through M-0063. The M stood for the Mexican country code and the numerals the number of the canister. The low-level radiation reading of M-0061 was the focus of attention.

"What's the story on 61?" Grissini asked.

Sarah Chan was responsible for the radiation and monitoring devices had anticipated the question. A graduate from William and Mary and Cal-Berkeley with a Ph.D. in nuclear physics, everyone figured Sarah was getting her hands-on training before some upper-management placement in DOE.

"I caught it when it passed station two," responded Chan. "It's not a monitor problem. We got similar readings as it passed four and five."

"So where does that leave us? Do we have a problem?"

"No, I don't think so. Probably a case of having a lower waste concentration."

"And?"

Chan shrugged before answering. "Well, the lower reading of the radioactive brine tends to confirm that we did not have a full waste load on 61."

"Come again? I don't track," pressed Grissini.

"What I mean is that a lower radiation reading could be affected by a lot of things. You know . . . how full the container was packed, and so forth. I checked the records that came with the canisters and, unfortunately, they are incomplete to say the least. As you know, the name of the game was to get the waste processed for the opening ceremony. With only a week to go, I don't think anyone had much time to get ready for it and ensure that all the canisters were full."

Grissini wiped his brow with the bill of his ball cap.

Even with the low reading on M-0061, all canisters fell within the acceptable range of tolerance in weight and radiation levels.

"Yeah . . . right. Maybe we should yank 61 off the line and send it to the contamination shed and let the moon guys open it up and check it out," Grissini said thoughtfully.

Grissini was referring to the personnel inside the C-shed who wore blue protective clothing and spacelike helmets. But members of his team objected to adding on to an already tight schedule when they had come in on the weekend to get the job done.

"Hey! That is what they pay us for—"

"I don't think it's necessary, Mike," said Chan interrupting. "As I mentioned, all the canisters fall within the guidelines. In addition, while we were talking, I switched the low-level radiation monitors at stations four and five to the more sensitive and accurate high-level radiation monitors to see what we really had."

"Okay, what did we get?"

"Well, the needle barely twitched in the lowest radiation quadrant at both stations. Sure, we have a lower level of radiation in M-0061 but it is within acceptable standards. In addition, the lower the radiation the better. We don't need to worry about it."

"Um, well, have you ever seen anything like it before?" Grissini asked, unwilling to let it go.

"Yes," said Chan as she turned to directly face the ex-marine. "As I mentioned, a lot depends on how densely the hospital or research centers packed the container with their low-level waste. In the rush to get the waste to the repository, they probably moved everything they had and M-61 got a short load."

The other team members jumped in and supported Chan, so Grissini signed off on the four Mexican canisters, thinking to himself that he would not be doing this if he were inspecting his marines or their weapons. On the other hand, you cannot run a bunch of civilians like marines, so he told himself to loosen up.

The four Mexican canisters moved from the test site building on the tracked transporters to the repository entrance. The access and exit to the repository were through two tunnels, which comprised the sides of a U-shaped loop that stretched deep into the mountain. The engineers had designed each tunnel with a gradual downward slope that led to the trenchlike final stowage or burial area. The gently sloping tunnels had steel tracks that ran down the center; transporters carrying the waste canisters would move on them. The engineers had divided the burial trench site into two sections. They designated the larger section for the tons of high-level radioactive waste from spent U.S. nuclear fuel and a smaller area for the low-level waste from hospitals and research facilities. This was the area reserved for the four Mexican canisters.

Canister M-0061, with its modified suitcase bomb that was cleverly tucked inside a false bottom of the canister, had cleared all security checks. The possibility of a bomb inside one of the radioactive waste containers was not something envisaged by the engineers who had designed the facility. Once M-0061 had been placed horizontally in one of the shallow trenches, all that remained was the activation of the programmed timer and countdown to terror.

CHAPTER 24

Mexico City

The morning light found its way around the bedroom drapes and Cole Palmer fought with himself to get up. He had spent most of the restless night thinking about David Andrews's late call before going to bed.

The pressure must really be something, Palmer thought, as he walked to the bathroom, noticing that it was only five fifteen. Andrews wanted Cole to come to Washington as soon as possible but couldn't say why on an unsecured line.

An earlier evening call from Luis made him reluctant to leave for Washington. For one thing, he had been looking forward to taking Liz Cramer to Luis and Maria's dinner party. Well, it was a date he intended to keep. As he shaved, Palmer replayed the conversation with Vasquez.

"We're looking forward to seeing you tomorrow night, Cole. By the way, I found you a new tennis racket to replace the one you broke the other day. I'll put it in my car before the dinner and give it to you in case you need it this weekend."

Palmer had not broken his racket. Vasquez was sending a message—something he did not want to discuss over the phone.

Before heading for the embassy, he once more tried on his rented tuxedo and found it adequate. The coat was a little tight over the shoulders. He was fairly sure that in a formal dress Dr. Cramer would show another side of her self—and a bit more of her figure than he had seen previously.

Embassies limit the number of cars and drivers made available to staff, in part because of tight budgets. The administrative officer, however, had allocated a car and driver to Palmer since he was new to the area and needed to learn his way around before driving himself in the lottery of Mexican traffic.

When the driver arrived at Liz Cramer's town house, Palmer saw that the door was partly opened and stepped inside the hallway.

"Hi, Cole. Hmm... you look quite dashing," Liz Cramer said as she came down the stairs. Palmer would have been impressed to know that she had bought a new dress for the occasion. He was certainly impressed with how she filled the dress out. It was a sheath, fitting her slender figure closely and cut fairly low in front to display her ample bosom. Liz had, at the last moment, decided to look for something new. She told herself that she wanted to make a good impression on what she knew would be a fairly elite group of guests. Showing the flag, she thought.

Palmer felt like a tongue-tied adolescent for a moment, and then burst out, "Wow!"

Her striking eyes twinkled with amusement.

"I'm really not sure how to take that, Cole Palmer. However, in your case, I am taking it as a compliment. But have I really been that unnoticeable for the past months?"

"Uh . . . well no . . . not at all," stammered Palmer again trying to recover. "It's just that you look so great I didn't know what to say."

Liz caught her breath as she looked at Palmer. Then she walked over and amazed him by briefly kissing him on the lips. Palmer felt a sharp stirring of desire but before he could recover, she pulled his arm and headed to the car.

Palmer had anticipated a relatively small dinner party but when they entered the house that Luis and Maria shared with his elderly parents and walked up the stairs into the formal reception room overlooking the flower-filled courtyard and fountain, he estimated that nearly a dozen couples were present. He hardly had a chance to look around before Luis and Maria came over to greet them. Maria was almost as tall as her husband and her hair was as dark, almost black, as his. She was eight years younger than Luis and strikingly beautiful, with full, sensual lips and a gleaming smile. Her arms were more muscular than most women, evidence of her three years of rowing in the women's crew at Harvard, a form of exercise she had continued by rowing a single shell. Vasquez had met her in Washington when he was there on business, a few years after he and Palmer had been at the Naval War College together.

Palmer introduced Liz to his hosts and then received a warm embrace from Maria.

Then she turned to Liz. "Luis said you worked at the embassy with Cole. When he said you were a 'Doctor' Cramer I did not anticipate anyone so beautiful."

Taking them both by the arm, she smiled at her husband and said, "I'm going to introduce them to the others. You go back and finish your conversation with Castillo."

They had been seated with Luis and Maria at one of four large round tables in the adjoining dining room and served five courses of complex and subtly flavored Mexican cuisine that most Americans would find in relatively few restaurants in the United States. Maria had the essential skill for any good host of drawing people out and encouraging them to talk about themselves. Palmer noticed that she discreetly avoided asking Liz or him many questions by talking about how she and Vasquez and Palmer had originally met, deftly keeping the focus on herself. An industrialist from Tampico and his lively, petite blond wife saved Maria considerable effort as they rattled on about the yatch her husband had just bought and their recent trip to China.

After dessert, the women retired. The table was cleared of the cloth and, in the English fashion, a decanter of port went around the table after coffee had been served, followed by brandy and Cuban cigars. Palmer's somewhat utilitarian Spanish was strained on social occasions. Fortunately, both men at his table spoke excellent English. After a suitable interval, Luis suggested that they join the ladies.

As the others left the room, Luis placed his hand on Palmer's arm and detained him, leading him out to the balcony that ran around the courtyard.

"I'm sure you gathered that I had some news," as he closed the French doors behind him. "We don't have much time—I have to get back to my guests—so I'll cover it fairly quickly. About four months ago, a friend that runs a helicopter business started ferrying laboratory-type equipment to a secluded hacienda outside the village of San Augustin Loxicha. Supposedly, the equipment was for some agriculture research project. On one trip, my friend picked up three foreigners who had just arrived in Mexico City. He got a quick glance at one of their luggage tags before the man escorting them ripped them off. He is sure the tag said BEI indicating Beirut as the transfer point. They could have flown into there from anywhere—Syria, Iraq, Iran.

Who knows? My friend said that they did not look like scientists but he did not pursue it. They paid up front and the schedule was not demanding."

Palmer attempted to break in but Luis lifted his hand to stop him.

"We have to get back, Cole, or it will be noticed—and we need to get through this."

"Sorry, go ahead."

"On one of the trips about five weeks ago, a summer storm front was passing through the area as he landed at the hacienda. He decided to stay put until it passed and take shelter in one of the buildings. The folks on the ground took exception, forced him back inside the helo, and directed him to leave. My friend is not someone you want to push around and he refused to move until the front passed. What happened next made him question his decision. Armed men in various degrees of uniforms arrived in two jeeps and pointed their rifles at him. Fortunately, the storm was letting up about this same time so he cranked up the helo and lifted off before anything more developed. He put two and two together and decided that it had to be something illegal going on, possibly drug related. That was when he decided to tell someone in the government. Two days later, he received an unexpected fax canceling the contract.

"Before you ask, Cole, I had a contact in the Interior Ministry run down the name of the company that had contracted for the services and discovered it was a suspected front company owned by La Eme."

"But couldn't it be just some drug processing lab or—"

Before Palmer could finish, Maria came out on the balcony and told them that they were the only ones not dancing. As they followed Maria, Vasquez muttered, "I think we can assume it was something more than opium-based or cocaine processing."

* * *

During the drive back to Cramer's town house, Palmer did not say much as he thought about what Luis had said. *Am I missing something here? What does Vasquez think the link might be between the hacienda and the rumors of some kind of terrorism campaign?*

Liz had been watching Palmer stare out the window and finally nudged him. "Am I going to find out about what you and Luis discussed on the patio?"

"Probably best to wait until we get a chance to get to a secure area."

Their eyes met and Liz sat back and nodded.

As the car entered the gated community, she leaned forward and spoke to the driver.

"Thanks. We won't need the car for the rest of the evening." She then turned to Palmer in a voice loud enough for the driver to overhear. "Some of our friends are following us for coffee and we'll find someone to drop you at your hotel."

Palmer was surprised and wondered how he missed hearing anything about guests coming over.

"Who is coming over?" he asked as they entered the town house.

Liz turned around and faced him. She put her arms around his neck and looked at him. "No one is coming over, Cole," she said as she slowly moved one hand across his neck. "I wanted some time alone with you. Does that bother you?"

Palmer put his arms around her waist and she moved close enough for him to feel the warmth of her body. She turned her head up to his and he cupped the back of her neck, giving her a tentative kiss. He stood motionless, dazzled and almost expecting Liz to back away. Instead, she kissed him, hard and insistently. Her tongue played with his and she started moving against him. When his hands started working the zipper at the back of her dress, she backed away, but took his hand and led him up the stairs.

CHAPTER 25

U.S. Embassy
Mexico City

Palmer felt the eyes of the doorman following him as he walked through the lobby of the hotel, his tuxedo creased, his dress shirt rumpled, and his bow tie hanging loosely from his coat pocket. When he got inside the elevator, he told himself that he lucked out. Other than the desk clerk who pretended not to notice, he did not have to exchange good mornings with anyone. Thirty minutes later, showered and dressed in business suit, he cut through the park for the embassy.

After scanning the overnight message traffic, he headed for the ops center. He surprised himself when his access card activated the door on the first try. He made a practice of dropping by the Comm-Center once or twice a week to check on what was happening in the world.

"Cole, what makes you smile in reading all that BS?"

Graham had come across the hall when he saw Cole enter the center.

"Hey, Willie. How goes it? Did you catch this message concerning the laser shot on an obsolete satellite out at White Sands Missile Range?"

"Yeah, some two hundred and sixty miles above the earth according to what it says. What is interesting is the part about the laser selectively shutting down targeted equipment like sensors, avionics, and navigation gear. All that high energy floating around bothers me. It could really raise hell with my equipment."

"You worry too much, Willie."

"Oh yeah," growled Willie. "Gotta go to the ambassador's residence. I'll catch you later."

"What's going on?"

"Nothing except a screwed-up phone scrambler. It's an older unit and it breaks down periodically. Particularly if you don't operate it properly."

"Ah, I can appreciate that. You guys purposely make things so the average person can't operate them," said Palmer smiling. "Listen, when you get back, can you call Dr. Cramer or me? We need to have a talk with you—down here in your spaces."

As Palmer got off the elevator, he bypassed his office and left the embassy. He needed some space to think about last night. He had a new problem. He had to decide if he was ready to make a commitment, as women put it. He wondered if he was ready. But he didn't want to do anything that would impair the relationship with Liz. As he walked, he willed himself to believe that somehow the pieces of his life would come together.

When he returned from his walk, he went directly up to Cramer's office in the secure area. When he got there, Liz was on the phone but broke off the conversation when she saw him in the doorway.

For a few moments, they stared at each other. She was the first to break the silence.

"We should talk. My place, tonight? Don't use the embassy car."

"Okay . . . fine." He had not told her about what Luis had told him last night; there had been other things on his mind. Now he gave her a capsule summary.

"I think we ought to go to Ted Halligan with this—"

"I agree. Unless someone thinks it's a wild goose chase, I think we need to find out what's going on at that hacienda. Halligan has the resources—and it's happening in his backyard, so you're right, he has to know."

Palmer had to fight off the lingering thoughts of last night. He visualized the curve of her breast and her endless legs. And when he thought about how he had fallen asleep nestled close to her, he smiled. And forced himself to get back to the business at hand.

"If it is drugs, we have to go to the DEA and the Mexican liaison people. We do not want to get on the wrong side of the Federales. If something is going down and its drug related, they might already have a lead on it. But we don't know who we can trust and Vasquez probably had a good reason to bypass the Mexican authorities."

Fifteen minutes later, they were in Halligan's office.

"It's not a hell of a lot to go on. If there is some chance of Middle Eastern involvement, I have to pass the word on to the appropriate people at Langley, and they will notify the counter terrorism coordinator at State. This means all kinds of bells and whistles going off. If I read what Cole is saying, we might want to try and find out more before we pass this on officially."

"Could your people check the situation out?" Palmer asked Halligan.

"Hell no! With SKYHAWK ready to launch, we have

been told to avoid any unnecessary Mexican counterpart liaison until further notice. They would have to be notified; we can't do anything unilaterally."

"Well, maybe I have a way to do it."

"How are you going to do that?" Cramer asked.

"Well, I was thinking that some of my Navy SEAL friends could come in handy."

"That could be real risky down here with things being on the knife edge. Would Andrews go along with it?"

"I think so. He has some real pressure on him. He did not elaborate but he made it clear that we needed to come up with something. Anyway, when terrorism is the issue, a lot of the rules go out the window including boundary lines. He could argue that this operation is a prelim to SKYHAWK. I think he could sell that."

Halligan lit his pipe and said, "Speaking of La Eme, I meant to tell you that my friends down the street keep track of some of the top Eme leaders. Let me fill you in on some of the charming cast of characters. First of all, there is their chief hit man; a psychopath named José Chapa. We have just found out that Chapa dropped out of sight for three weeks—a time frame that brackets the period of time in which Swanson was killed last January."

"Holy shit!" Palmer exclaimed. "Some of the FBI and Agency already believe La Eme was involved. They'll jump on that."

Halligan raised his hand. "There is more. The other guy they watch is one Juan Ortega. He helped Navarro, the so-called chief executive officer of the drug cartel, transform La Eme from a bunch of guys who were constantly engaged in turf wars into a modern business organization that controls everything to do with drugs. This guy is as smooth as silk, handsome, and with all the right tickets and connections. Anyhow, word came down here that the Russian Interior Ministry is concerned about why Ortega went to Moscow, and then to Minsk a few months back.

They picked him up on airport arrivals surveillance, lost him when he took the train to Minsk. Now it's not often their domestic intelligence service comes to us for a favor—and they sure as hell will expect one in return. But the real funny thing is that the SVR has considerable contacts on the ground here. Their station is nothing compared to the good old days when they had a huge embassy with a First Directorate and GRU residencies running ops all over Central and South America."

Halligan's pipe had gone out and he relit it with a butane lighter and made a face. "This is my way of giving up cigarettes. My wife doesn't allow it in the house. Anyhow, for their own very good reasons they don't want their guys tramping around and leaving big footprints. Ortega was involved in something, God knows what, that has them riled up."

"I don't get the connection to the hacienda, Russia, and La Eme," Palmer said as he scratched his head. "Am I missing something?"

"And what about Minsk? I knew that the drug cartel moved their drug money around Europe but you don't launder money in Minsk," added Cramer. "It's gotta be something different."

"Don't look to me for answers," Halligan responded. "We're getting a lot of things that don't make any sense. Now you tell me about this hacienda out in the middle of nowhere and La Eme is the possible landlord. While I'm at it, Ortega is a friend of Ramiro Chemor, Hidalgo's right hand man." Halligan paused and looked down at his desk.

"Cole, here's another piece of the puzzle—and you aren't going to like it. There is a third individual in the Ortega-Chemor relationship—Luis Vasquez. They were all together at school and played on the same soccer team."

After Cramer departed for another meeting, Palmer grabbed one of the secure voice handsets and put a call through to Andrews on the direct line. Twenty minutes later, without any interruptions, Palmer had passed all the information he had compiled over the last four days.

"Well, you were right, things are moving too fast for a trip to Washington," Andrews told him, his voice echoing on the line. "From what you told me, I agree that we need to check out that hacienda. We simply don't have anything else. And no one in place to do it."

"Yeah. I wish we had more to go on but we don't."

"On the money trail, tell Liz to contact her friend in Treasury and see what we can find about the front company that rented the helicopter. The other appropriate agencies here will start a parallel investigation. We can put some pressure on the offshore banks if we need to. In addition, I will get the Belarus Country Intelligence Desk—CID folks—working on the Minsk-Ortega connection. A guy like Ortega doesn't visit somewhere like Minsk for the hell of it."

"Okay. As mentioned, I will need some resources for the hacienda. It would probably be best if you call the Special Warfare Command in Coronado. Captain Bill Parrish runs the place and will know what I need if you authorize it. You can trust him to keep the lid on things. He and I go back a long way."

Years ago Bill Parrish and his team were transported on Palmer's destroyer for a special operation to collect intel on the Indian Navy missile test firings on Andaman Island in the Bay of Bengal. A risky night insertion by small boat on the island following the missile tests produced important bits of the missile cone that held the guidance system and other pieces to establish the size and range. When unexpected heavy winds kicked up, Palmer, who had been assigned the responsibility for coordinating the insertion with Parrish, forced the Zodiac through the churning surf line to pick up the stranded SEAL team and avert a potentially disastrous incident. Over the years, Palmer and Parrish continued their friendship.

"I don't want to put you in an Ollie North bind on this one, Cole. I have to run this through a Deputies Committee meeting and get everybody concerned to sign off on it. The agency won't want to be involved, so it's probably going to go down, technically, as a DEA operation. Your suggestion that we make it an add-on to SKYHAWK is a good one."

"I could call Parrish. Give him a heads up and some lead time. Hopefully, he won't ask too many questions."

"I won't bite on that, Cole. This thing doesn't go down until we get the right people to sign off on it. By the way, I am going to go around the ambassador on this one, if Snyder agrees. There just isn't enough time and as long as we're on this secure line I can tell you that some of the ambassador's Mexican staff are suspect. They are under surveillance; we want to keep them in place until we can nail someone for sure."

This stunned Palmer. Nothing, but nothing, was to be done operationally in an ambassador's host country without his being informed. The only reason for it, in very rare circumstances, would be to give him deniability. But he kept his mouth shut.

"Okay. Thanks for the heads-up."

"You do understand that if something goes wrong, we'll all be hanging out so try and keep things under control."

Palmer knew full well that if somebody screwed the pooch, Reimann would be asking for the head of Cole Palmer.

"Roger that. We'll just get a few quick sniffs and be out of there before anyone knows anything."

"I figured you would be with them, Cole. Frankly, I wish I was going with you."

"Hey! We would love that. Can you see the headlines in

GET UP TO 4 FREE BOOKS!

You can have the best fiction delivered to your door for less than what you'd pay in a bookstore or online—only $4.25 a book! Sign up for our book clubs today, and we'll send you **FREE* BOOKS** just for trying it out...**with no obligation to buy, ever!**

LEISURE HORROR BOOK CLUB

With more award-winning horror authors than any other publisher, it's easy to see why CNN.com says "Leisure Books has been leading the way in paperback horror novels." Your shipments will include authors such as RICHARD LAYMON, DOUGLAS CLEGG, JACK KETCHUM, MARY ANN MITCHELL, and many more.

LEISURE THRILLER BOOK CLUB

If you love fast-paced page-turners, you won't want to miss any of the books in Leisure's thriller line. Filled with gripping tension and edge-of-your-seat excitement, these titles feature everything from psychological suspense to legal thrillers to police procedurals and more!

As a book club member you also receive the following special benefits:

- **30% OFF** all orders through our website & telecenter!
- **Exclusive access** to special discounts!
- **Convenient** home delivery and 10 days to return any books you don't want to keep.

There is no minimum number of books to buy, and you may cancel membership at any time. See back to sign up!

*Please include $2.00 for shipping and handling.

YES! ☐

Sign me up for the Leisure Horror Book Club and send my TWO FREE BOOKS! If I choose to stay in the club, I will pay only $8.50* each month, a savings of $5.48!

YES! ☐

Sign me up for the Leisure Thriller Book Club and send my TWO FREE BOOKS! If I choose to stay in the club, I will pay only $8.50* each month, a savings of $5.48!

NAME: _____

ADDRESS: _____

_____

TELEPHONE: _____

E-MAIL: _____

☐ I WANT TO PAY BY CREDIT CARD.

☐ VISA ☐ MasterCard ☐ DISCOVER

ACCOUNT #: _____

EXPIRATION DATE: _____

SIGNATURE: _____

Send this card along with $2.00 shipping & handling for each club you wish to join, to:

**Horror/Thriller Book Clubs
20 Academy Street
Norwalk, CT 06850-4032**

Or fax (must include credit card information!) to: 610.995.9274. You can also sign up online at www.dorchesterpub.com.

*Plus $2.00 for shipping. Offer open to residents of the U.S. and Canada only. Canadian residents please call 1.800.481.9191 for pricing information.

If under 18, a parent or guardian must sign. Terms, prices and conditions subject to change. Subscription subject to acceptance. Dorchester Publishing reserves the right to reject any order or cancel any subscription.

JOIN NOW!

the *Washington Post*? National security adviser caught peeking around Mexican hacienda."

Andrews laughed. "It would sure as hell make me topic number one on the Sunday talk shows. But seriously Cole, I want to know more about what Luis Vasquez knows about Hidalgo. And you can tell him that his message got to the right people in Washington." Andrews did not say that he only delivered a part of Vasquez's message—not the positive part about Hidalgo.

"I will and that will be a big relief to him. What do you make of his connection to Ortega and Chemor?"

"I'm not sure. Let's see what we can find out about the Ortega trip. If I get anything, I will call you. My gut instinct is that there isn't anything to worry about."

"That's my take on it."

"Okay, I'll let you go. You can start planning—but stand by until you get my execute message."

CHAPTER 26

Oaxaca, Mexico

When Palmer returned to his hotel the following morning after running a few miles in the park, he noticed the blinking phone light. The message had come in a few minutes after seven. He dialed the code to hear his message. It was Willy Graham.

"Suggest you come in. We have a Special Delivery letter for you."

Two hours after he had unbuttoned the "eyes only/decode yourself" message from Andrews, which read simply "DOCTOR CAN MAKE HOUSE CALL," Palmer got a call from the duty corporal at Reception. He went downstairs to meet his visitor. It was not difficult to figure out who the man waiting for him was. He fit the profile of the Navy elite SEALs—about a hundred sixty, five-nine, large natural shoulders that angled down to an athletic waistline, tanned, and with short cropped hair. Even in loose-fitting sport clothes, it was obvious that he was in superb shape and he had the quiet aura of calm and self-possession typical of someone who could handle himself in hairy situations. As a young, newly commissioned officer, Palmer had gone through the unyielding SEAL training and learned that SEALs were also smart, decisive, and trained killers.

As Palmer approached, the visitor introduced himself.

"Hi, I'm Lieutenant Commander Jack Tisdale. Captain Parrish sent me down."

"Appreciate you getting here so quickly. Let's find some breakfast."

Palmer led the way to the cafeteria and picked up some coffee and croissants before leading Tisdale to the ops center. One of the watch-standers told Palmer that Graham had left earlier with a bunch of equipment for the marine barracks. Palmer wondered what that was all about and asked if one of the secure cubicles was available. The watch-stander nodded and pointed to one with its door open.

After exchanging a few sea stories about their time in the Special Warfare Command and Bill Parrish, Palmer went straight to the issue that was probably on Tisdale's mind.

"I want to make one thing clear. You're the boss in the field and the one who calls the shots."

Tisdale looked at Palmer and nodded. With that out of the way, Palmer noticed that Tisdale was visibly relieved. He proceeded to give Tisdale an initial brief on the operation. Tisdale interrupted occasionally with questions, all of them to a point and incisive. When Palmer was finished he said, "The bottom line is that we need to find out what's going on down there without raising any ruckus."

"I appreciate what you said about calling the shots in the op-area. It makes things a lot easier especially for my team. Now from what you say about the hacienda, we can handle that part of it. Our cover down here is that we are part of the routine training package for the embassy's Marine Security Force. We do this type of training all over the world so I don't see any questions coming down from the ambassador's staff or any other place—his DCM should get the word within hours. We can billet my team with the marines. I did not know what we were in for but I went ahead and arranged for transportation for the operation. One of my team members, Herb Corr, is checked out on just about anything with wings or rotors."

One of the watch-standers knocked on the door holding a pot of coffee. Palmer and Tisdale walked over, and filled their cups and thanked the young woman.

Palmer produced a map of the area that Luis Vasquez had sent over showing the location of the hacienda and a ranch that belonged to a friend some 40 clicks north of it. Vasquez had attached a note indicating that support facilities, including fuel and accommodations, would be provided with no questions asked. The map also highlighted the closest village, Juchitan, which was about equal distance between the hacienda and the ranch. Tisdale took the map and said that if he could get it enlarged, he could mark it up and use it during his team briefing. They agreed on a 6:40 morning liftoff.

"Great. We don't have any time to waste. Do you have everything you need?

"I think we do. Captain 'P' told us to keep a low profile, so we will stay close to the barracks."

And I'm staying close to the embassy tonight, Palmer thought. My talk with Liz just got put on hold. He reluctantly picked up the phone to call her.

The unmarked UH-1M Huey, painted in faded brown, looked its age. Looks were deceiving, however. It had recently received a complete overhaul with new avionics, engine rotors and blades, and certain airframe modifications. As Palmer jumped inside early the following morning, he did not notice any U.S. insignia, just a registration number on the side. It had been quietly borrowed from the DEA liaison command that kept it at the facility they shared with Mexico's *contra trafficante* forces. Other than the two front seats and several canvas bucket seats aft of the doors, the stripped helo had a metal rack holding comm gear and weapons. On each seat, a clear plastic-covered operational chart with the hacienda and ranch highlighted had been adapted from the area map supplied by Vasquez.

Shortly before scheduled liftoff, two of Tisdale's SEALs, Mike Patton and Peter Fowler, humped their gear into the helicopter and strapped in.

As Herb Corr thrusted off the helo pad and veered nose down to gain speed, Palmer tugged at the crotch of his borrowed cammies, which were just a shade too small. Two hours later, Tisdale, who was sitting in the right front seat, announced that he could see the hacienda through his long-range binoculars. He signaled Herb to head for Point Bravo, identified on the chart as "friendly ranch." As the helo banked to port, Tisdale told Palmer over the intercom that he did not want to get too close to the hacienda, just close enough to determine whether or not they had a helicopter on the ground. As they approached the ranch, Palmer saw that it included several houses, large barnlike buildings and smaller sheds and cottages. The well-maintained fence line covered over 1,300 acres of irrigated grazing land and reminded him of some of the large ranches he had worked on during the summers in Montana. As they made their final approach, someone turned on the helo pad lighting system and they could see a petrol truck and Range Rover heading toward the pad.

Palmer was the first one out and José Iturbide, who identified himself as the ranch manager, warmly greeted him. Iturbide was dressed in a denim shirt and worn blue jeans held up by a thick belt with a large silver buckle. His cowboy boots looked worn but comfortable.

"Good . . . welcome. My English is no good." Iturbide shrugged an apology and lifted his hands.

Palmer moved forward to shake hands with him. "Your English is just fine. Thank you for meeting us."

The manager haltingly explained that the owners of the ranch were in Europe. He had been instructed to render all possible assistance to the "geological survey team." Mike Patton, a petty officer first class gunner's mate, and an assistant SEAL team leader joined Palmer when he saw that there was some problem communicating. As Patton spoke in Spanish, Iturbide looked relieved and smiled. Patton then took over the conversation asking where they should bunkdown and how to get hold of the petrol truck if necessary.

When they finished refueling, Herb Corr gave a thumbs-up and the ranch manager handed the Range Rover keys to Palmer and waved to the others as he departed with the truck driver. The ranch house was about 100 feet from the owner's brick ranch home and had seven bedrooms with shared bathrooms and showers. A large central kitchen was fully equipped and stocked with food and drink. When they finished storing their weapons and special equipment that always accompanied them, Patton and the other team members left to check out the ranch. He returned in forty minutes and reported that things were secure.

"The main house is empty as José reported, boss. The ranch manager plus the truck driver and five other Mexicans are living with their families in the bungalows bordering the property behind the main house. That's it—no other bodies."

"Thanks, Mike." Palmer and Tisdale were going over the map and did not look up. "Let's keep a rotating roving watch on alert anyway."

"Roger that."

* * *

After getting something to eat and resting for a couple of hours, the team lifted off at dusk and headed south to check landing sites about eight or ten clicks from the hacienda. When they reached altitude, Palmer noted that the area was cut off from the rest of Mexico by two mountain ranges that crisscrossed Oaxaca some 250 miles from Mexico City on the Gulf of Tehuantepec.

When they decided on one of the landing sites, it was too dark to chance a hard landing on the rough terrain of undulating sand dunes and broad plains of mesquite and cactus. Hovering over the site, Patton slid down a zip line carrying his automatic weapon and a small canvas bag. A few minutes later, the portable receiver cracked with the word "Go!" Patton had laid down three strobe lights in the form of a triangle. Minutes later, the chopper made a soft landing and the now armed SEALs were out both sides of the helo setting up a perimeter defense. Patton secured the low intensity lights and Herb Corr landed the helo. Toting their equipment, the team started west toward the hacienda. Corr remained to provide security and backup if things went to hell. All team members checked their portable transmitters and receivers before departing.

The rough desert and darkness were not impediments to the superbly trained SEALs and the pace was quick. They moved in silence, followed the natural shadows of the terrain, and seemed impervious to fatigue. It had been a long time since Palmer had been on a SEAL operation and he was thankful that he had resumed his running regime. He noted that each SEAL was comm-linked with a small receiver earpiece and small transmitter hooked to their collars. With the exception of Palmer, all carried Swedish carbine-type semiautomatics, 9mm Sig-Sauers, and belted hunting knives. In addition, each carried a special piece of canvas-covered equipment. Palmer figured the equipment was an assortment of listening devices and heat-sensitive sensors. Other than the boots and cammies borrowed from his marine friends, Palmer carried a standard Colt .45 and night vision goggles.

When they arrived at a point some 600 meters from the hacienda, Tisdale raised his arm and the team took cover where they could find it. Another silent hand signal resulted in a final check of weapons and removal of the protective coverings on the special equipment. Palmer followed Tisdale's tug to the back slope of one of the sandy berms. As he crouched down behind the berm, Tisdale handed him the telescopic binoculars to view the hacienda. The hacienda's outside lights provided a good visual backdrop. Although they could not hear anything from where they were, it was obvious that a lot of activity was taking place.

"What in the hell would be going on at this hour?"

"I haven't the foggiest. We'll know a lot more when Mike and Pete get back," Tisdale whispered.

Palmer turned around to look at the place where Patton and Fowler had been only seconds before. He was surprised that he completely missed seeing or hearing the two SEALs with their black-and-green painted faces take off. *I wouldn't have missed the movement a few years ago,* Palmer chided himself.

Tisdale fiddled with his earpiece and whispered. "If Mike and Pete don't run into any perimeter patrols, they'll get within 150 feet or so of the hacienda."

The night vision goggles turned everything to shades of green with shadows moving around outside the hacienda. Fifty-five minutes later, the two SEALs seemed to materialize out of nowhere. Again, Palmer was unaware of their approach until they flashed their strobe light two or three meters away. Tisdale had heard or seen some movement because he had quickly shifted into a firing position for a few seconds before the brief strobe flash. Without any words and with another hand signal, the team started back. As they approached, Tisdale clicked his transmitter three quick times. Almost instantly, Corr returned with two clicks. The team broke off in different directions to make the final approach to the helo from different quadrants.

After securing their equipment inside the helo, Patton picked up the nod from Tisdale and started his report in a hushed voice.

"Well, there is an armed security force of approximately fifteen that we could see with two old jeeps parked in front of the hacienda."

"I wonder why so many?" Tisdale muttered, concerned.

"I don't know boss. I can tell you that they appear to be a bunch of greenhorns. Pete and I could have taken out most of them."

"But why all the activity around the hacienda at this time of night?"

"Don't know. It looks like everything is coming apart. What doesn't burn goes into a couple of dump trucks parked on the left side of the hacienda."

"Most of the stuff looks like lab equipment and some small machine shop stuff."

Anticipating the question, Patton interrupted Fowler. "Whatever they were using the equipment for, we couldn't tell. We need to get inside the hacienda."

"Was there anything unusual?"

"Well, yes. There is a dug-up trench area on the left side. At first, we didn't notice it until Pete spotted some shovels on the ground next to the trench. When we put our goggles down, we could see that the trench had altered the terrain. My guess is something was recently buried."

"Did you catch anything on the sniffer and listening probes?"

"Not really, boss. We were too far away and the large trash fire screwed up the sniffer. We caught a bunch of stuff on the squawk box—the usual griping about this and that from the guards."

"Could you understand them?"

"C'mon boss. There is nothing I can't understand down here. Anyway, one of the guards was complaining about some foreign types always wanting this or that and looking down at the guards. From what they said, they didn't understand what the foreigners—he called them *barbudos*—were doing there. Another guard said that if the pay weren't so good, he would be out of there. Something was spooking them."

"Anything else?"

"Well, from bits and pieces of conversations, it appears the big boys left the area by helo a couple days ago. Also, one of the guards mentioned something about a produce truck picking up a large canvas-covered container of some sort. He was *muy* pissed off."

"What was that all about?"

"From what I picked up, some of the guards helped the driver and a couple of other people they had not seen before lift the container on the truck. According to the guard, it took several of them to hoist it. He probably remembers it because the two people he had not seen before gave him a ration of shit about not moving fast enough."

"Anything else?"

"Well, the guard did add that the two tough-looking guys they hadn't seen before followed directly behind the truck in a sedan. Let's see, what else. Oh, yeah. The guard that didn't like the *barbudos* said that he hadn't seen them around for a couple days and wanted to know if anyone had seen them leave. It appears that no one did."

Tisdale looked at Palmer and shook his head. "Okay, guys, good work. Let's get out of here."

It was 2:30 in the morning by the time they made their approach to the ranch. After securing their gear, Tisdale and Palmer opened a couple beers, went over the surveillance operation again, and decided there was little benefit and too much risk to return to the hacienda with the security guards around.

"Based on what Mike and Pete told us, I think we missed the boat. However, it is your call, Cole. We go in now and deal with the security or wait until they vacate the place as we discussed."

"I hear you, Jack, but I'm still of the opinion that we can't risk it. I need to talk to my boss before we go on the offensive."

"Okay. What about leaving Mike and Pete here with some of Willie's comm gear? They can keep us cut-in on what is happening." Graham had installed some special comm gear onboard the helo when he found out about the operation.

"I like that . . . but they need to stay clear of any firefight."

"Got it loud and clear. They won't like it but they know what to do."

"Okay. I'll be ready when you want to lift off. Just give a few pounds on the door," Palmer said as he headed for his room with another beer in hand.

Palmer was tired but his mind was in overdrive. The new information did not make sense. He kept asking himself how the hacienda, the foreigners, and the security guards still on duty connected. Then there was the truck—where did it go and with what? Instead of getting some answers, it seemed the complexity of the damn puzzle was increasing. The last thing Palmer remembered before dropping off was that somehow the pieces had to fit together—and soon.

CHAPTER 27

U.S. Embassy
Mexico City

The Huey touched down a little after 8:30 in the morning and Palmer, accompanied by Tisdale, headed to the marine barracks to change. It was after 11:00 before they got through the city's tortuous traffic. When the two men passed through the embassy's security panels, the duty corporal whispered a heads-up to Palmer that the national security adviser "himself," added the corporal for emphasis, was onboard in the ops center.

"How long?"

This question got a quick look from Tisdale as he missed the front end of the corporal's message.

"Sir. The national security adviser's plane landed at 0730 hours. The admin officer provided car and driver, plus marine escort to the ambassador's residence for a 0830 hours call. Corporal Shaw then escorted the national security adviser to the embassy arriving at 0955 hours, sir. Doctor Cramer met the national security adviser and es-

196

corted him to the operations center. The national security adviser has not moved from that location, sir."

The young marine gulped and added, "Our Gunny told us not to discuss the presence of the adviser among ourselves and to keep our mouth shut around embassy personnel, sir."

As Palmer and Tisdale left, the corporal quietly alerted the ops center that they were on their way down. Graham greeted them at the security doors with two mugs of black coffee.

"I figured you might need this."

"Thanks, Willie. The run from the ambassador's to the city was the worst part of the trip. Do we have a problem?" Palmer had figured the worst—the ambassador got wind of the hacienda operation and Andrews came down for damage control.

"Not that I know of, Cole. I think everything is okay."

They followed Graham into the restricted access area and Palmer introduced Jack Tisdale to Andrews, noting that David looked more fatigued than either of them. The Washington power game is taking its toll, Palmer thought, as he slipped over and squeezed Liz's hand.

"Your timing is great, Cole. I just finished some Washington calls when Willie reported that you were on your way."

"You must have left Washington at an ungodly hour?"

"Yeah. We left around five this morning and with the time change, it wasn't so bad. The president is at Camp David and I figured this was a good time to touch base with you."

"No surprises with the ambassador?"

"No, nothing really came up. I gave him a summary of what we are up to in Washington and the meeting with President Posadas. State asked me to meet with Carlos Alverez and convey the president's continuing support of the ruling party. He seemed satisfied."

Palmer took the seat next to Liz vacated by Graham, who went off to talk to his watch-officer.

"Anyway," continued Andrews, "I can get more work done on one of those Air Force planes than I can in a week of interruptions and phone calls at the office. Okay, let's see what you guys turned up."

Palmer pushed away from the table and moved to the other end. "First off, Jack and his team did a great job on short notice. We got in and out without incident. The problem is whatever was going on appears over."

Palmer caught the disappointed look from Andrews after launching into what they observed. "I'd sure like to know what was hauled off in that produce truck and where? Maybe we'll find out more when we revisit but right now I'm more confused than when we started."

The room remained silent for a minute. Andrews broke the silence and asked Liz Cramer to update everyone on what she had found out.

"We had some success with my Treasury contact. They traced two recent large offshore money transfers . . . $2 million from UBS—Union Bank of Switzerland—to a numbered account at Credit-Suisse and $50 million from SBC—Swiss Bank Corporation—to Grupo Financiero Anahuac here in the city. By the way, it is the holding company for the outfit that rented the helicopter."

"The real owners of Anahuac Bank," interrupted Andrews, "are linked to the Juarez drug organization, one of the largest and most powerful of the cartel."

"Isn't there some kind of reporting required for large transactions?" Palmer asked Liz Cramer.

"In the United States, yes. But here banks are supposedly required to submit only quarterly reports on what they call 'suspicious' transactions to the National Banking and Securities Commission. But the commission claims that it can't effectively monitor wire transfers. Anyway, after some veiled threats, I understand NBSC agreed to look into the Anahuac situation. The Treasury folks are not optimistic. They estimate that $300 to $500 billion is laundered worldwide."

"Still," Andrews said in an optimistic tone, "we still got something and the connection will become clearer as we continue. We were also able to make some sense out of some of the other info. The problem is that I don't think you are going to like the picture."

Andrews got up and moved behind his chair, leaning on its back. "Let me start by covering a few things. We could not find anything linking Chapa to General Swanson. All we know, unfortunately, is that it was a professional hit and Chapa was out of Mexico at the time. But the investigation is continuing, focused on this new information."

"Is that the best we can do?"

"I'm afraid so, Cole. Chapa remains a suspect, but without hard evidence, our hands our tied. The Mexican government is playing ball with us on this one. Concerning Ortega, we got lucky. We have a reliable report from an informant"—no one asked about the source and Andrews probably did not know more than he was telling them— "that Ortega was sighted in the former Soviet Republic of Belorusskaja, or Belarus, as it now calls itself. Our contact there is hardwired into the clandestine sales of leftover Soviet weaponry and figured that Ortega was shopping. How he knew about Ortega or his connection to La Eme, I don't know. My guess is that he got a tip from one of his *mafyia* associates. Anyway, he reported that Ortega spent the entire time in Minsk and seldom went out except for meals and a few late nights of bar hopping. He did not visit the banks, consulates, trade ministries, or shop for weapons."

"What the hell? So what was he doing? That doesn't track with anything," interrupted Palmer impatiently. "Are we saying that Ortega spent a week in Minsk and all he did was go to a bar for a drink. That doesn't track. How good is the source?"

Andrews deflected the question and pressed on. "We lost track of Ortega after he left Minsk. Three days later, he returned to Mexico City."

"Am I also missing the message here or where does all this lead us?" Tisdale asked, glancing at Palmer.

"Before answering, Jack, let me give you another interesting piece. When the CID desk folks started inquiring about anything new in or around Minsk, the CIA reported something that didn't make a lot of sense at first. Supposedly, a Russian colonel at the Minsk Weapons Arsenal, some six miles outside the city, recently disappeared and caused a hell of a stir in Moscow. At the same time, the Russian Interior Ministry started asking questions about Ortega through informal contacts with the CIA. Why in the hell they didn't ask the SVR I'm not sure. Anyway, the CIA wasn't sure it meant anything until they started comparing notes with some of the other source information. Strangely enough, the date of the disappearance of the Minsk colonel just happened to coincide with the return date of Ortega from Minsk."

Andrews paused for a moment to see if everyone was following him.

"Now you can see why I wanted to come down here—because I knew we could not track everything over secure voice. Anyway, back to the Minsk Arsenal. We know the arsenal, which is still a Russian responsibility, was loaded with conventional weapons. It used to contain some nuclear tactical weapons, but the CIS republics agreed to return the nuclear weapons to Russia after decoupling the warheads for centralized storage. This was subsidized by the United States to keep these weapons out of the wrong hands—"

Jack Tisdale could not contain himself and interrupted. "Maybe I'm just slow but I don't track the connection to all this. If no nuclear material was involved, why are the

Russians so concerned about one colonel who may have gone AWOL or something?"

"Well, we don't know, Jack, and our Russian friends aren't about to tell us. I gather that it isn't part of the exchange of information they agreed to. As I said, we do know that this Colonel Yuri Kaliniev's disappearance coincides with the time frame of Ortega's visit to Minsk and we think there might be a connection."

Tisdale was tired and frustrated from the long trip and lack of results from the recon of the hacienda. "Okay. Are you implying that Ortega and this Russian colonel cooked up some deal? What kind of deal? Something from the arsenal? How does somebody walk away with a weapon from an arsenal? I don't get it."

"I know it's a stretch," Andrews said patiently. "But there are non-nuclear weapons available that are portable, easy to get hold of, and extremely deadly and you know more about that than I do. With the right help, Ortega could indeed buy and transport some of these weapons to Mexico. Put that together with our intel about a possible series of terrorist incidents down here and you have something worth losing sleep over."

"Didn't I read something a couple of years ago that some portable munitions of extraordinary power, terrorist-type bombs, were unaccounted for in the Soviet Union?" Willie Graham asked. He had a reputation of a prodigious memory—reading everything, categorizing it, and never forgetting it.

"Yes. There were some startling claims by a Russian weapons expert that small but very powerful high-explosive bombs, or suitcase bombs as he called them, were developed by the KGB in the 1980s for terrorist purposes. Everyone tended to discount the report until the Beirut bombing. As Jack probably knows, investigation of the explosion revealed the type of small portable suitcase bombs that the Russian described. A small package with a hell of a punch."

"Have we learned anything more since the Beirut bombing?" Palmer asked.

"Well, from what we have pieced together from some of our contacts who were in the KGB First Directorate before it morphed into the SVR, the suitcase bombs were hurriedly moved out of Moscow during the unexpected 1991 coup to out of the way arsenals in the Ukraine, Kazakstan, and Belarus."

"Okay, let's pursue this line of thinking. Ortega gets his hands on some of these suitcase bombs—but how does he move them?" Palmer asked.

"That's the same question I had so I asked the question to the weapons experts at Los Alamos and they did not think it would be difficult. Remember, the bombs were designed by the KGB for terrorism, if we believe the story, and that translates into something small, portable, and easy to move around."

"Yes, damn right." Tisdale said emphatically. "The couple of times we exercised with training mockups of our small nuclear land mines, we had no problems moving them. Small conventional bombs would be easier."

"I also asked a special group of analysts at the new Anti-Terrorism Center outside Richmond—who are paid to develop various terrorism type scenarios for training purposes—to tell me how they would move the bombs from Minsk. They said that they would move the bombs by truck or van to some nearby seaport like Gdansk."

Liz Cramer was trying to find some flaw in the scenario. "Surely there must be some problems getting bombs across the border."

"I'm not so sure, Liz," Andrews responded. "Since the breakup of the Soviet Union, the borders are essentially porous and checkpoints, customs posts, all the usual control points are staffed with a lot of people who are more than willing to take a bribe, particularly when you consider how small their salaries are. Port controls are spotty at best—and once aboard a merchant ship, it's an easy ride back to Mexico."

Andrews sat back down in his chair; a faint line of beads of sweat had popped out on his forehead despite the air-conditioning blasting away in the ops center to cool the electronics.

"I think we have to assume that Ortega has gotten hold of some of these suitcase bombs. The sixty-four-thousand dollar question is what they intend to do with them and where are they?"

Before Andrews could continue, a marine sergeant knocked while opening the door. It was almost 3:00 in the afternoon.

"Sorry, sir. The ambassador requests the presence of the national security adviser in his office."

Andrews got up and signaled Palmer to join him.

"I hope he hasn't caught some flack on the hacienda, David, although I don't know how he could have," Palmer said as they left the ops center.

"I don't think so. That's probably the least of our worries. If those bombs are in Mexico, then the gloves come off."

CHAPTER 28

U.S. Embassy
Mexico City

As soon as his secretary closed the door behind her, Reimann walked over to Andrews and Palmer and shook hands with them. He steered them over to a low table with comfortable chairs grouped around it. They had barely sat down when the ambassador said, "I just received a most unusual call on my residence line."

He paused and lowered his voice. "The caller identified himself as Victor Hidalgo. At first, I thought it was some kind of crank call, but now I think it was indeed the former president. He was cordial and apologized for disturbing me, but he had some information that had to get to the U.S. government immediately."

Andrews's astonishment was evident. He sat forward in his chair and stared intently at Reimann as he continued.

"He told me that he had some reliable information that a series of terrorist bombings would take place in Mexico during the period between now and the U.S. elections. I pressed him to be more precise but he said he was telling as much as he knew. I considered asking whether or not he had informed the Mexican government but something held me back. When he finished, I assured him that I would pass on his information. Can you believe it? The call really caught me off guard."

"I can understand that, sir. Did he have any specifics—exactly when these bombings might take place, what the targets might be, who was behind it?"

"Yes. He did say that the devices—I think that is what he called them—were brought into Mexico from outside the country. Right before he signed off, he said that Promontorio Mountain could also be a target. That's right around the corner with the advanced opening date of the repository." He stopped and ran his hand through his thinning hair before turning to Andrews. "I'm not sure how they would pull that off. It is supposed to be a highly secure facility. What do you think?"

"I think the information he gave you was reliable. I'm not ready to jump at anything but there are some other factors that make this threat more credible. We have some recent intelligence that some high explosive bombs, similar to those used in the Beirut bombing a few years back, have possibly gotten to Mexico."

"What? That is news to me. Why haven't I been informed?" The ambassador was shocked and angry. "Halligan didn't say anything about this in his morning briefings. What's going on?"

"Mr. Ambassador, the information is new and hasn't been verified," replied Andrews calmly. "The agency is attempting to find out more—we didn't want to act prematurely."

"Why would Hidalgo know about this? Why would he tell us?"

"Those are the two key questions, sir, and I don't have an answer."

"It is my responsibility to inform the secretary of state," the ambassador said firmly. He got up and started to walk over to his desk.

"Mr. Ambassador, the secretary and the president will be briefed on this within a few hours. I'm sure you understand the sensitivity of this information and I ask that you not discuss it—even with your State Department contacts, sir." Andrews needed to make the point as strongly as he could.

The ambassador stared at Andrews coldly.

"Perhaps you don't understand. As chief of the mission here, I am expected to communicate directly with the secretary on a matter of this importance. What happens after that is up to him, as far as I'm concerned."

He sat down behind his desk and put on his reading glasses.

"Please excuse me, gentlemen. I have a cable to draft."

As they walked down the hall, Palmer, obviously rattled, exclaimed in a low voice, "Holy shit. I thought we were never going to get out of there. What's your take on all that?"

"I don't know, Cole, but I need to discuss all this with Snyder and the president. I can only hope that Reimann doesn't discuss this with anyone other than the secretary. I can't afford to be down here when this hits the fan."

"You mean you're flying back?"

"Yes—I need to have a face-to-face with Snyder and the president. Hidalgo just raised the stakes bigtime. We have less time than we thought to put a stop to this madness."

"Okay. What do you want us to do?"

"Well, as starters, how about riding out to the airport with me so we can continue talking? I didn't know how long I was going to stay so the aircrew decided to wait."

"I can do that. What was it that set you off on the Hidalgo message?"

"His mention of Promontorio Mountain got my attention. I will fill you in on our way. I'm worried about the ambassador. We have to keep the Hidalgo call under wraps."

They left directly for the airport in the car that had been assigned to Andrews. Palmer had stopped by the marine guard desk and asked if one of the off-duty marines could drive them, so they could talk freely. Once under way, they spent the next forty minutes going over a game plan—a game plan Palmer knew would change ten times in the next forty-eight hours.

As they turned into the airport, Andrews tore a sheet on which he had jotted some numbers off a yellow legal pad, handed it to Palmer, then stuffed the pad into his briefcase and closed it.

"These are the numbers that you can contact me at any time. Some of these are not secure lines, so if you have a problem, just call me and say it's about 'the suitcase' and I'll call you back on a secure line as quickly as I can."

The embassy car came to a halt when the driver stopped at the security gate leading to a section of the airport reserved for Mexican military and other government operations.

"Give my regards to Liz Cramer. I want you to work closely with her and keep everyone else, I repeat everyone, out of the loop who doesn't have need to know."

Palmer nodded to indicate his understanding. He wondered briefly if he should tell Andrews that he had become very close indeed to Dr. Elizabeth Cramer, but decided that this was not the right time.

The pilot of the Air Force 727 that Andrews had flown down on was completing his walk-around inspection as they pulled up to the plane. Sitting opposite it on the apron was the Navy Learjet that delivered Tisdale and his

SEAL team. Before Andrews boarded, he and Palmer agreed that despite the risks, Hidalgo's call to the ambassador made it clear that the hacienda had to be checked out immediately.

"With the opening of the Promontorio Mountain Repository moved to the first Saturday in October, we don't have many options left, Cole. Time is running out.

"Call me as soon as you know anything, Cole. I don't know what you will find out there. If the Hidalgo info is right, we might have a break. But if Hidalgo is fucking with our heads, the son of a bitch is asking for trouble."

Palmer had never seen Andrews so worked up. He could not repress the thought that Andrews might be worried about the impact this whole situation would have on his own political future. The two men shook hands and Andrews started walking toward the plane.

"Hey, David," Palmer called out. Andrews turned around.

"What if the call is legit? It could provide a way out for the president."

"What are you saying?"

"You've been arguing for the president to distance himself from Posadas. At the very least, it provides a good reason for postponing the formal opening of Promontorio Mountain."

Andrews smiled. "Right. I only wish it were that easy. This Hidalgo business has turned everything upside down. Hidalgo is clever. His call makes him the good guy. If the bombing starts along the Border States right before our November elections, he's warned us. How and why he knows about it is quite another matter. I don't trust the man—he has a major grudge against the United States, and I think he is willing to do anything to regain power."

"I hope someone understands that we're running out of

maneuvering room." Once again, Palmer wondered why Andrews was so hostile toward Hidalgo.

"I'll work the Washington end. You work the hacienda and come up with something that we can use. We need to find the bombs—and the people behind the operation must be stopped."

Andrews looked extremely tired and worried as he boarded the plane.

"Keep in touch," he called out as he disappeared inside the aircraft.

Liz Cramer was one of the few still working in the commercial section when Palmer returned. They decided to seize the chance to talk things over and go out for dinner. "You don't look happy, Cole. Did things go badly with the ambassador? Where is David?"

Palmer told her about the somewhat confrontational meeting with the ambassador and Andrews's return to Washington.

"I guess from what you're saying you believe that Andrews might be wrong about Hidalgo."

"I'm not sure. I don't seem to be able to read him anymore. Part of him seems to be kind of shut down."

"Hmm . . . maybe he's just tired, Cole. With his schedule, I can't blame him."

"Yeah. Perhaps you are right. He is walking into a real mess with this bomb information and I don't envy him. Everyone will be trying to cover their you-know-what."

They stopped at one of the local small restaurants close to the historic heart of the city and across from the famous Metropolitan Cathedral. Before ordering, Palmer pulled out his cell and left a message for Luis Vasquez to call at Liz's place. A light dinner accompanied by a good Mexican cabernet brought some relief to a day full of surprises.

When Liz excused herself, Palmer dialed the marine barracks. Herb Corr answered and said that his boss was at dinner but due to call in within the hour. Palmer told Corr that he wanted to lift off at 0600 hours so the helicopter should be serviced and Iturbide told to expect them.

"Who was that on the phone?" Liz asked as she returned.

Palmer knew he would have to tell her. "I gave a heads-up to the SEAL guys that we need to recheck the hacienda. If we can verify that the bombs were there, Andrews will be in a stronger position to make his case with the president."

Liz stared at Palmer for a moment, then asked. "Why are you going on this operation? You know that there is the possibility of a firefight."

"Um, well, the SEALs will have to deal with that Liz. We need to get inside that hacienda no matter what it takes."

"Yes, but why the 'we,' Cole? Is it really necessary for you to participate in this operation? Tisdale is capable of finding out whatever there is to find out. What's going on with you?"

He momentarily bridled; was she implying that he was, once again, pursuing some sort of private vendetta—and unnecessarily risking his life?

"I need to see it through, Liz. I owe it to the team and Andrews." Cole shifted in his seat and put away his cell in a way that indicated the issue was dead.

When they finished dinner, they drove back to Liz Cramer's town house. There had been little conversation since their hacienda flare-up. Both were lost in their own thoughts.

Palmer sank into the soft cushions of the couch in the living room and closed his eyes. He felt exhausted, physically and emotionally. And he was not prepared to examine his motives for going along with the SEAL team.

Liz started to go back to the kitchen and said, "I'm sure you're getting an early start in the morning. Do you want some decaf—or maybe a drink?"

"Forget the coffee. Come over here. I want to tell you I'm sorry for being my stubborn self but I can't help it."

Liz kissed him lightly on the forehead. "Can you stay?"

Palmer noticed that when she was aroused her eyes became brighter and larger.

"Am I worth getting up for before dawn?"

"We'll talk about that later," answered Liz as she headed upstairs.

CHAPTER 29

The White House

Andrews unbuckled his seat belt as the 727 leveled out at 33,000 feet and walked aft to the state-of-the-art comm suite. One of the radio techs saw him coming and handed him the satellite-linked secure voice handset. The NSC duty officer responded immediately.

"We've had a change in departure dates. We're about fifteen minutes out of Mexico City with a heading to Homeplate."

"I understand, sir. We got a heads-up from the crew. We'll coordinate and have transport standing by."

"Thanks. I just talked with the secretary of state. He asked that we schedule a meeting of principals tomorrow. I know that the president just got back from Camp David, but make it clear that State considers it priority to get a half hour on his schedule. Also, the attendance should be limited to principals. You can quote State directly on that."

"Do you want the principals called now, sir?" The answer was obvious but the duty officer wanted a direct order if he was going to roust a bunch of elephants out of bed.

"Yes," David crisply replied. "And if one of the principals can't make it, we don't want a backup. Do you follow me?"

The duty officer had been around long enough to know that a principals-only stipulation implied that something heavy was going down and that very sensitive issues would be discussed. Whatever was going on, it wasn't ready to be discussed at the Deputies Committee level. He wondered why he was coordinating everything instead of his counterpart at the State Department until he remembered that Snyder had taken most of his office staff to Camp David.

"Yes, sir. I'll get back to you."

Air Force Sergeant Moore announced that dinner would be served in ten minutes and replaced the scotch on the rocks with a fresh one. Andrews was in the lounge area watching the sun disappear while reviewing his meeting with the ambassador.

"Good. I'm starved, Sergeant. Except for a bagel and coffee this morning, I haven't had a chance to eat anything."

"We'll fix that, sir," said Moore. "Did I tell you that I just took a cooking course?" He laughed and added, "Everything you need to know about warming things up in a convection oven!"

Andrews wondered how long it had been since he could relax and laugh; enjoy himself without being constantly aware of the next meeting, the next problem, the next struggle to advance a policy or an initiative. He recalled a recent explosive argument with Brooke after he showed up a couple hours late for a dinner party.

"You have no outside interests; you don't have a life, apart from the sixteen-hour days you put in at work. When we go out, almost always it's to a dinner party or a reception that has something to do with work. We never see our old friends, our real friends. I don't think you even want friends; you just want people who can be useful to you. Or you want to use them."

"Don't pretend you're not a partner in this," he shot back. "You wanted me out of the Navy—fine! You wanted me to go to work for some mind-deadening investment banking operation. But then you decided that Washington might be fun. And you sure as hell loved all the parties, all the crap that comes with making it in this town."

"You just don't get it, do you? I want you, the person I married, the guy who disappeared on me. Thank God, we don't have children. They wouldn't have a full-time father. David, nothing else matters to you. Your career defines you . . . there isn't a private person living inside that role."

Andrews started to protest, but she broke into tears. And he sat there, seemingly unable to walk across the room and put his arms around her. He was becoming good at making someone who loved him cry. He did not mean to, he just could not seem to help it. Despite years of professional accomplishments, he still did not know how to make his marriage work. He realized that he could lose everything dear to him and yet he was willing to put everything on the line. The glittering prize was there for the taking, the job he had wanted, but never dreamed of actually getting, from his earliest days in government.

"But only if Mexico doesn't drag all of us down with it," he mumbled.

Andrews had fallen into a light doze when one of the crew told him he had an incoming. He went directly to the comm suite and picked up the secure voice handset.

"Good evening, sir. The meeting has been set for ten in the West Wing conference room. All principals will be present but the president."

"Dammit!" He caught himself and got back under control. He had to find a way to talk to Washburn before Snyder did. Reimann must have sent the cable before he even got out to the plane, Andrews thought.

"Yes, sir. I . . . I . . . know, but the chief of staff said the president will rework his afternoon schedule and there will be a two o'clock follow-on meeting."

Andrews cautioned himself to slow down. "Okay, good staffing and thanks."

He relaxed. The afternoon meeting might be a better option. "Perhaps, I can press Snyder to play his hand on Hidalgo during the morning meeting before we meet with the president," Andrews muttered to himself.

"What did you say, sir?" The duty radioman looked up from his desk.

"Nothing. Just thinking aloud."

Everyone was on time for the meeting including the vice president. The urgency of the last-minute meeting had gotten everyone's attention. The vice president took the seat at the head of the table. Richard Snyder was sitting quietly to the right of the vice president reading the morning traffic from various embassies. Only minutes after the meeting got under way, although the vice president was the nominal chair, it became clear that Snyder was running it.

After finishing his briefing in which nothing was mentioned about the Hidalgo call, Snyder asked Andrews to amplify any areas that he might have missed. When Andrews finished, Snyder made it obvious that he had more to say. "Let's be very clear on this. Nothing should leave the room or be discussed until the president's briefing this afternoon. The president will have to decide how we deal with the issues in Mexico." The message registered loud and clear.

It did not take long to reach a consensus; it had to be assumed that the bombs had reached Mexico.

"The next thing to worry about," the director of the Central Intelligence Agency warned them, "is what they were doing with these bombs at this hacienda. If they have been extensively repackaged, that could cause some real problems—if they knew what they were doing."

"But why?" The vice president pressed. "Why would they rework the bombs?"

"I don't think we know, sir. We're checking out the hacienda as we speak and we might know something more," Andrews responded.

As soon as he finished, he knew he had made a mistake. Other than Snyder, he had not discussed with anyone the business of sending a SEAL team to the hacienda. There simply had not been time to bring it before a full NSC or deputies meeting.

"Come again? What do you mean checking out the hacienda . . . who authorized it? Who's doing it?" The DCI snapped. The secretary of defense and the FBI director were poised to ask the same questions.

Snyder tapped his pencil on the table to get everyone's attention and to rescue Andrews at the same time. "We need to get back on track. We only have a few minutes left and we need to establish an agenda for the afternoon session."

"I don't see what we can recommend," remarked the secretary of defense. "If the bombs are in-country, I'm not sure what we can do about it."

"Well, one thing is clear. We can't count on the Posadas government to solve this alone—and we're not sure on which side of the border the bombs are targeted." Snyder's flat assertion hung in the air for a moment. Andrews sat there wondering if anyone would openly disagree with the secretary of state.

The president's chief of staff leaned forward. He sat in the row of chairs directly behind the vice president.

"Do we have any idea, really, of who we are dealing with? I think we're missing something here. How should our government react to a possible—I emphasize possible—terrorist situation on our borders? And what is the Mexican government going to do about it? I think we had better be prepared to answer these questions before the afternoon meeting with the president."

"You are right," Snyder admitted, "but the United States has already made it clear that terrorists cannot hide behind international borders. That puts a different face on things."

"It doesn't matter who they are," the director of Central Intelligence said forcefully. "We have to locate these bombs. If I follow the national security adviser's scenario, whoever is behind all this is probably aiming to shut down the government in Mexico City and disrupt the November elections in this country."

"I agree," the FBI director said. "The only sure way of stopping this is to find the suitcase bombs."

The vice president tried to regain control of the meeting. He turned to Snyder.

"Richard, couldn't we somehow establish some contact with the group that is most likely behind this—the Zapatista rebels . . . or whatever they call themselves. We need to buy time until we know something more concrete."

"Mr. Vice President," Snyder always addressed him formally when he wanted to make a point, "we don't want to get out ahead of our Mexican counterparts. We need to proceed cautiously and continue working with our counterparts until we know more. But there is another issue to be discussed before we present this complex problem to the president."

Snyder waited for a few seconds before resuming. "As you know, the president is addressing the NATO ministers on Friday—the day before the opening ceremony of Promontorio Repository. During that address, the president has agreed to include a statement concerning Chiapas and the general situation in Mexico. With this new potential terrorist crisis, we need to get the statement updated and ready to go by this afternoon."

"I thought the president already approved that statement. It's a little late to be changing things." The vice president glanced at Browning but the press secretary shrugged his shoulders and remained silent.

"Yes, you are right, sir, but as the secretary of state mentioned, we now face another crisis—potentially worse than Chiapas. I think what State is saying is that we need to give the president some maneuvering room. If indiscriminate terrorist bombings start along our borders, the president's second-term prospects could be seriously damaged." Andrews surprised himself by coming over so strongly but the opportunity was too great to pass up—especially with Snyder providing the opening.

Snyder shot a quick look at Andrews before responding. "The national security adviser is right. Until we get a handle on these bombs, we need to make sure that the president's statement does not lock-in the administration to a situation in Mexico that we cannot handle."

Browning, with some help from Andrews, had already worked up some suggested changes to the statement. If the president accepted the changes, he would be sending a message; the United States was deeply concerned about the deteriorating Mexican situation and reviewing its policies with respect to the present government. A message that the Mexican Mafia leader was waiting to hear.

Snyder turned to Browning. "When we finish, get that statement over to me. I'll work on it and get it back to you in an hour."

The secretary of state and the national security adviser remained after everyone departed. Andrews was feeling better. His argument for distancing the administration from Posadas would be enormously strengthened if Snyder did not tinker with the message too much.

"Well, how did we do?" Snyder asked, while stretching out his arms and yawning.

"I hope the president will understand the need for a different approach with the new bomb information, sir."

"Yes, we'll see. But this change in signals has to be done delicately. I am more immediately concerned about how the president will react to the information about Hidalgo's call to Ambassador Reimann. I think it might even be a good time if we made direct contact with Hidalgo."

"What! You're not serious . . . you mean cut some kind of deal?" Andrews knew he had come on too strong, but he needed to find out what Snyder was planning.

"Let's not be naive. The president is dead set on a second term and preserving his FTAA legacy. He does not like Hidalgo, but he might change his mind if he sees that the ruling party is finished or threatening his second term. The suitcase bombs could do just that. On the other hand, whoever wins needs the financial support of the United States. That is Washburn's trump card and he will play it with any party, including Hidalgo's, to achieve his goals."

"But, are you saying that the president would dump the ruling party if an accommodation could be reached with Hidalgo?"

"It doesn't have to be that dramatic, David. A lot now depends on whether we can get to the bombs before they start going off. If we do, dumping the ruling party won't be necessary. Perhaps Hidalgo understands this; his call to the ambassador may be intended to kick-start that process. We just don't know."

Snyder's comments surprised Andrews so much that he hardly knew what to say. "But do we want to deal with someone like Hidalgo?"

"You know the president, accommodation is part and parcel of his philosophy—and to his credit, he has been successful. The critical missing piece is that we do not know where Hidalgo is coming from. We cannot let all that past history about Hidalgo blind us to overshadow an opportunity. If suitcase bombs start exploding on our borders, everyone loses. That's why I'm thinking that a meeting with Hidalgo might be productive. I think you—with a little help from your guy Palmer and his contact, Luis Vasquez—could open a back channel for us. In fact, I suggest you do that as a matter of priority. Let me know when you have something set up."

The secretary of state looked away. "I am also intrigued about this Luis Vasquez. He has an interesting background and I understand your friend Cole Palmer thinks the world of him. I'm playing with an idea about how he might be able to help us with Hidalgo."

"Now that you mention it, Cole wants me to meet with him."

"Yes. As I mentioned, I would do that as a matter of priority."

CHAPTER 30

The White House

The cabinet members arrived early for the afternoon meeting. The absence of any morning consensus was particularly frustrating to those accustomed to wielding enormous power and demanding results. It was obvious that they were nervous waiting for the president's reaction to their unproductive morning session. They stole glances at the faces around the table trying to figure out how they would react if confronted by the president. Each cabinet member had his or her own theory on what the president should do. Some felt strongly that the president had tied himself too closely to the ruling party to risk a change in policy now with elections less than a year away. Others felt that he was a captive of his own FTAA initiative and needed the support of Mexico to carry it off. Only two considered that the president needed to have an exit strategy now regardless of the impact on the ruling party or his own policies—to salvage his second-term hopes.

* * *

When the president entered the cabinet room, conversation came to a halt. Michael Kerr cleared his throat and summed up the main points of the morning meeting. His rather perfunctory delivery tipped Andrews off—the vice president had already briefed the president and was simply going through the motions.

"What's all this stuff about suitcase bombs?" The president interrupted before the vice president had mentioned anything about bombs.

The CIA director, Leslie Drummond, pushed back and then removed the glasses that had a tendency to slide partway down his nose. He briefed the president on what the agency knew about the suitcase bombs without adding any opinion.

"What do the Russians say about this?"

"The Russian government won't acknowledge or corroborate the suitcase bombs, sir."

"What I want is an answer," insisted the president testily. "Do they exist or not?"

"Sir, I think that we have to assume the bombs exist," Drummond replied. "Our analysis of the Beirut bombing and information from the Mossad support the existence of these KGB suitcase bombs."

"What do we know about these bombs?"

The secretary of defense had asked Dr. William Finnerman, the director of the Livermore Laboratory and weapons expert, to attend the afternoon session. He was visibly anxious and nervous—a physicist who until recently had been at MIT and was more comfortable in research labs or university classrooms.

"Mr. President, unfortunately we don't know much about this type of small but powerful high explosive bomb. We do know that the bomb used in the Beirut disaster appears to fit the characteristics of what we know about the suitcase bombs. The bottom line is that they can do major damage, sir."

"Okay, I've got that picture," Washburn said. "Now where does all this stuff going on at some hacienda in the middle of nowhere have to do with them?"

Finnerman took a sip of water. "I can only give you an informed guess. If these devices had been in storage for a considerable period, they would have to be checked out. The type of explosive we think would be in them can deteriorate over time if it has been exposed to high humidity or a sudden shift in ambient temperature. And whoever intends to use them would have to check the arming and firing circuits."

"Well, I'm not sure I buy into all these loose ends . . . suitcase bombs . . . Minsk arsenal . . . foreign scientists . . . hacienda . . . and on and on. There are too many unanswered questions. We have to do better than that before we can react."

Snyder was the first to respond to the president's challenge.

"I understand what you are saying, Mr. President, but the possibility that the loose ends do tie together is too great a risk to ignore."

"Okay," the president said, scratching his jaw thoughtfully. "I'm not saying to ignore it but I want facts. What's the worst scenario that we're talking about?"

"The worst scenario is a series of indiscriminate bombings close to border cities to maximize the devastation and press impact right before our elections. Following Chiapas, this action could break the back of the ruling party and have a major impact with the voters."

"How in the hell have we gotten to this point?" the president asked in a tone of perplexity.

"Mr. President, I think we have to assume that whoever is behind what is happening in Mexico knows exactly what they are doing. In my opinion, they have a much larger agenda than making some statement in Chiapas or exploding bombs."

"What are you saying, Richard? Do I hear a recommendation or not?"

"What I am suggesting, Mr. President, is that whoever is calling the shots has a more important goal—to replace the ruling party with their candidate in the Presidential Palace in order to carry out broader goals, and without any interference from the United States."

President Washburn straightened up in his seat before looking away. "It's got to be Hidalgo. The son of a bitch has been biding his time for revenge."

Apparently, the vice president decided that this was the right moment to make his move. He picked up the line of argument that he had advanced that morning.

"I think we need to establish contacts with the PRD and others, on a low-key basis of course. The last poll that I saw had all three parties running even. They need to understand where the United States stands on things."

Before Snyder could respond, the president closed his briefing book and stood up. "I agree. It's dangerous as hell, getting mixed up in the domestic politics, but we've done it before—in Europe after World War Two and God knows for years in Central and South America, so its nothing new. Let's open up channels. Deniable channels."

The president picked up three sheets of paper that had been concealed beneath his briefing book. "I took a quick look at the suggest revisions to my NATO statement. I want to work on it a little, but basically it looks okay. In the interim, I want more information about these suitcase bombs. We need to find some answers before I start making statements or bombs start exploding."

As the president started to leave, he stopped and turned back to Snyder.

"Richard, I'm dead serious. Get some informal contact going with the power brokers down there—without upsetting the ruling party. You know what I mean."

* * *

Andrews followed the secretary of state toward his small White House office. He waited to say anything until they were clear of the other principals.

"May I ask why you did not play the Hidalgo card with the president, sir?"

"I thought about it a lot, David, and decided not to."

Snyder's expression made it clear that he was not going to discuss it further.

"I'd like to move up that meeting with Vasquez."

"I'll jump on it as soon as I get back."

Andrews slumped into the backseat of his car. "Charlie, I'm calling it a day. Take me home."

He sat in the car trying to figure out his next move. The bombings could give the Republicans just what they needed to defeat the president—something that would also end his career and probably his marriage. Fortunately, he had prepared for this worst-case scenario. He had come up with something drastic and, of course, very risky. It had come to him in a burst of inspiration. Was there a way to broker a deal to stop the bombings even if it meant dealing with the devil? Now, all he needed were the right words in the president's speech. And with Richard Snyder buying-in, now was not the time to give up.

"Charlie, cancel my last. Take me back to the West Wing entrance."

He needed to stop by Browning's office. If his last-ditch plan was to work, he had to use Browning as an ally—and take his chances with the secretary of state after the fallout.

CHAPTER 31

Oaxaca, Mexico

It was still dark when Palmer arrived with Liz Cramer at the embassy compound. Jack Tisdale was waiting inside the marine barracks with a set of fatigues and lightweight boots for Palmer.

"We're set. Willie has already checked his equipment with Herb. I touched base with Mike and Pete and they are standing by at the ranch."

"Did Mike and Pete have any news?" Palmer asked, as he sat down on a bench to try on the boots.

"Oh, yeah. It looks as if the security force has taken off."

"What does that translate to?"

"They figure five or six max. We'll know more when we pick them up."

Palmer walked Liz back to her van and kissed her lightly. "We'll be back before you know it," he said while opening the van door for her.

"Okay. I want you to make me a promise."

"What?"

"That you take care of yourself and let Jack and his team do their thing. Don't try to be a hero."

"I promise—and don't worry. I'll keep you posted on Willie's circuit."

When they lifted off it was getting light. Tisdale made a radio check with the embassy's backup marine alert force while Palmer checked in with Willie Graham. Two hours later, when they got within range of the hacienda, Tisdale told Herb Corr to make a quick high altitude pass. He grabbed the Swedish binoculars hanging on the back of his seat.

"I don't see anything moving," reported Jack over the intercom. "Wait a minute. I just picked up movement, right front side of the hacienda. I never would have seen it if the sun had not reflected off something, probably the guy's rifle. There must be a reason they're still hanging around."

As the helicopter approached the ranch, Palmer could see Mike Patton, Pete Fowler, and José Iturbide standing next to the fuel truck. After touchdown, Tisdale briefed his team. The plan was simple and straightforward—take out the security force without setting off any alarms.

"What do you want me to do?"

"We'd love to have your company, Cole, but we work as a team and frankly you would slow us down." Before Palmer could respond, Tisdale continued. "You and Herb will be backup for possible covering fire if things turn to shit. I understand that you know how to handle the MAC-10s."

Palmer nodded, remembering what he promised Liz. He also wondered how Jack Tisdale had found out what weapons he knew how to handle.

Patton and Fowler reported that nothing much had changed since their last report.

"One day we count five, then six. The number looks solid, boss," said Fowler. "I also found a better drop point some four to five clicks from the hacienda. Herb knows where it is."

Before lifting off, the SEALs greased their faces with desert camouflage paint, checked their weapons, and made a quick radio check. When Herb reported that they were approaching the new drop point, Tisdale gave the thumbs down signal and the helo descended rapidly. Seconds after touching down, the SEALs jumped out and headed for a ridgeline some fifty feet away. The helo was back in the air within seconds, turning away to minimize the noise from its engines and rotors.

The three-man team moved quickly within the contours of the rugged landscape and covered over two and a half miles in less than thirty minutes. They took position on the perimeter of the hacienda behind an open storage shed adjacent to the concrete helo pad. The hacienda and a row of small bungalows were about 200 feet directly ahead of them. Tisdale saw that the security guard was still in the same shaded area in front of the hacienda. He pointed his index finger at the guard and the other index finger at Fowler. Jack then signaled Patton to cover the row of bungalows some 165 feet to the left for any guards that might be holed up inside. He followed with a sweep of his arm that he would slip around the backside and work his way inside the hacienda. The three SEALs gave one another a quick eye-check and Jack Tisdale gave a thumbs-up.

The security guard was lazily smoking a cigarette on the portico attached to the hacienda with his AK-47 slung over his shoulder. He did not expect any trouble and had been there for some time, given the number of cigarette butts on the wood deck. The side of the hacienda and shadows of the portico provided good coverage for Pete Fowler. The last noise the guard heard was the hissing noise of blood gushing from his neck. The guard's body jerked involuntarily and then quietly drifted backward as Fowler eased the body underneath the portico. Before taking position behind the side of the hacienda, he cleaned his knife on the guard's shirt.

Tisdale caught the report from Fowler as he moved through large French doors opening to the courtyard. He clicked his transmitter one time to acknowledge. Once inside, he crouched down with his 9mm submachine gun held low and in front of him. He remained stationary as he scanned the surroundings. Right away, he had a problem. The large stairway was in the middle of the hacienda and lead into an upstairs U-shaped hallway that opened above the large main rooms of the hacienda. It was impossible to cover. He was about to signal Patton to join him when he heard some talking from the area left of the main room. As Tisdale eased forward as close to the wall as he could, he guessed that the talking was coming from the kitchen area. As he got closer, the smell of coffee confirmed his suspicions.

When he reached the kitchen entrance, Tisdale rechecked the safety of the machine gun and casually reached down to touch his backup 9mm Sig-Sauer attached to his web waist belt. The two guards froze as Tisdale jumped through the open door. They were sitting at a long wood table covered with dirty dishes. Both dropped their cups, which shattered on the rough tile floor, and dove for their AK-47s leaning against one of the table chairs. No one spoke. The rapid bursts of silenced rounds cut both men down before they could reach their weapons.

After making sure that both guards were dead, Tisdale eased back to the main hallway area and signaled that two guards were down. Before he could finish, gunfire erupted from outside. A security guard, alerted somehow, charged from one of the bungalows toward the hacienda firing wildly as he ran. He never got farther than a few feet when he ran into the killing crossfire from Patton and Fowler.

After receiving Fowler's report, Tisdale mentally counted four down while wondering what had spooked the last guard. Something did not track. What made him make a dash for the hacienda? Tisdale instantly decided that someone must have signaled from inside the hacienda. He spun around in a crouched position to try to cover the upstairs hallway that opened above him. He knew that he was in trouble and he felt a cold tingle run up his spine as he twisted halfway around. The bullet hit the inside of his left forearm and exited out the other side. The force of the bullet knocked Tisdale to the tile floor. His submachine gun was on the floor, some three feet away. His eyes were getting blurry from shock when he noticed movement on the upstairs hallway railing. He had run out of time; a killing shot would follow. He drew in a deep breath and willed himself to roll over as he hosed down the hallway railing area with fire from his backup 9mm Sig-Sauer automatic. One burst ripped through the surprised shooter just as he was about to squeeze off a kill shot from his AK-47.

Tisdale retrieved his submachine gun with his foot and dragged himself to the side of the stairwell, which gave him some protection. When he determined that there was no movement upstairs, he cut off his shirtsleeve and managed to wrap it around the bloody hole, using the handle of his knife to tighten the cloth in a tourniquet to check the flow of blood. Then he clicked his transmitter three times. Pete Fowler was already heading for the hacienda when he heard the three quick clicks indicating trouble.

"Dragon One, what's the situation?" He asked over the radio.

"One shooter down in the upstairs area . . . two down in the kitchen . . . maybe more shooters in upstairs area. I've been hit. I'm in the main hallway by the front entrance. I'll cover your approach from the back of the hacienda."

Fowler entered the hacienda the same way that his team leader had and rolled into the hallway. When he came up, he saw Tisdale propped up against the stairwell.

"Are you okay?"

Tisdale nodded his head and tried to ignore the screaming pain in his arm. "See if you can get upstairs and check things out. I'll cover you as far as I can from here."

Mike Patton reported that all the bungalows were secure and that he was taking a position outside the hacienda to cover any movement in or out. Fowler had already reached the upstairs and confirmed that the shooter was down; there were two holes in the man's chest, so he did not have to waste any time checking that the guard was dead. A few minutes later, Fowler reported the upstairs area secure.

Tisdale directed Patton and Fowler to make another sweep of every building. When they reported all clear, he called in the helo. Corr didn't waste any time; he came in fast and put the helo down directly in front of the hacienda. Palmer had taken off his headset and missed the report that Tisdale had been hit. He was shocked when he saw Patton helping Tisdale from the hacienda. Fragments of adobe wall blown out by the impact of the burst had resulted in multiple lacerations on Tisdale's face and scalp, which had bled profusely and made things appear even worse. Palmer also saw Pete Fowler dragging a number of bodies next to the entrance of the hacienda.

"What the hell happened?" Palmer yelled as he jumped from the helo.

"Not much. Everything is secure. I'm a little pissed off that I missed seeing one of the shooters."

Herb Corr followed with the medical kit and started dressing Tisdale's arm.

"You're lucky," Corr said, "damn lucky." Corr was the trained medical tech among other things on the SEAL team. "It looks pretty clean . . . in and out . . . no bone damage . . . or at least that I can see. I'll finish dressing it and then get some of those splinters out of your face."

The shock was wearing off and Jack Tisdale was speaking rapidly, a common reaction in such high-adrenaline situations.

"Yeah, I sure was lucky. That guy hesitated just enough when I was down. As they say, it is better to be lucky than good sometimes. I'll debrief Palmer while I get my legs back. You can start checking out the lab area so we can get out of here. If there's anyone within miles of this place who didn't hear all this firing then he's deaf."

As soon as he finished his debrief, a somewhat shaky Tisdale led Palmer over to the lab area. The windows had been covered with plywood and fluorescent strip lighting had been hastily installed on the ceiling. There was a hand truck in one corner and three large wood crates, which were empty except for wadded up packing material. A workbench made out of unpainted wood was fixed against one wall and ran the length of the now empty lab room. The workbench had scraps of wiring and electronic parts—resistors, condensers, a couple of small printed circuit boards—scattered over the top, as well as an oscilloscope and a multifunction electrical measurement instrument.

Sloppy cleanup, Palmer thought. He had seen it before—arrogant people make stupid mistakes. Fowler and Patton, moving swiftly, started stuffing everything that looked in any way significant into two large black plastic bags. When Herb Corr came in with the portable explosive monitoring module and, as he passed it over the workbench, it came to life with a noticeable buzz.

"I don't think we need to cart much of this stuff back with us," Corr announced as he switched to a backup monitor to cross-check. "I have plenty of readings to indicate that there are trace residues of the compound we are looking for. Good news and bad news; the bad news is that these bombs start looking like they're for real; the good news is that we were right to hit this place when we did."

"Yeah, you're right about that, Herb," Palmer said. "But we'll take the small electronic stuff that we already picked up. The FBI labs can do wonders with stuff like that."

"What do you want done with the bodies?" Fowler asked.

Tisdale thought for a minute. "Let's look at that dug up area that you saw on our first visit. I wanted to check it out anyhow and if the soil is still fairly loose, it will be easier to dig a grave there."

A hurried search turned up two shovels in a shed at the rear of the main house. Fowler and Patton had barely started digging when the stench of rotting flesh came from the sandy soil. In a few minutes, they uncovered the remains of three bodies.

"Well, I think we know what happened to the foreigners," Pete Fowler said quietly.

Palmer covered his nose with his handkerchief soaked in insect repellent. It wasn't a good idea to breathe in the stuff; but he needed something to cut the horrible smell. Corr reckoned that the condition of the bodies indicated that they had not been there more than two weeks. "Just enough time to get really ripe," he added.

Fowler and Patton stood aside to allow Palmer to examine the bodies. Three men, ages difficult to determine. But all had full beards. So, Palmer thought, here are the *barbudos*.

"Pete, can you bring me that broom I saw on the front porch?"

When Fowler handed it to him, Palmer used the handle as a lever to roll over one body and began brushing dirt off it. He didn't know exactly what he was looking for. The upper part of the man's face had been badly damaged by the exiting round that had been fired into the back of the neck, execution fashion. A very large caliber round. Fighting against his revulsion, Palmer started going through the man's clothing. The pockets of his trousers contained nothing but a few coins and a disposable cigarette lighter. Palmer was not surprised to find no wallets or identifying papers. He was sure it would be the same with the other two.

Squatting on his heels, Palmer looked down at the corpse. He took his flashlight and ran the beam carefully over the body, looking for anything that might give him a clue. Something prompted him to take another look at the white shirt the man was wearing. It had a breast pocket. Palmer gingerly poked his finger into it and felt a piece of folder, thin paper. He carefully extracted it, then unfolded it, and spread it on his knee. The paper was covered on one side with small, beautifully formed calligraphy. Palmer knew enough to recognize it as Arabic script. Possibly a letter.

"Sorry, Mike. We got to get those other two cleaned off so I can search them. Grit your teeth."

Tisdale was sitting on the ground watching, while Corr washed some of the blood off his face.

"Cole, we're wearing out our welcome here. We should bug out pretty soon."

"Give me another ten, Jack. Then we can split."

When Palmer was finished, Corr took photos of the three bodies and the security guards while Patton and Fowler dropped them inside the shallow grave. They hastily rolled the bodies of the security guards into the grave next to the others, shoveled the dirt back on the bodies, and made one more sweep of the hacienda.

It was just over fifteen minutes later when Palmer and the SEAL team climbed into the helicopter. As it rose into the pitch-black night, its nav lights and warning beacon turned off, Palmer made his way up to the front, where a groggy Jack Tisdale was strapped into the right seat.

"I've got four things that give me a bearing on where these guys came from. First, a handwritten letter that—I'm pretty sure—is in Arabic. Second, one of the men had a squashed pack of cigarettes—Egyptian manufacture. The third one had a kind of rosary thing in his pocket—amber beads strung together—I think they call them 'worry beads.' So if you put all this together with the beards, my guess is that all three were observant, probably fundamentalist Muslims, and probably from some of the countries in the Middle East."

"It's obvious they weren't going to let the bastards go home, wherever they came from," Herb Corr shouted over the noise of the engine. "Whoever shot them didn't like them very much judging from the ugly head wounds. I don't know if anyone will be able to get a match on those pictures I took of the faces—or what was left of them."

"Arrogance always gets you in the end. Whoever did these guys stripped them of their ID—but then left the stuff in the pockets. They do a half-assed job of digging a grave, so anybody who stumbles across the place is going to notice it. Bottom line: they screwed up. The forensics people at the FBI will find out a lot from what was carelessly left on the bodies."

Tisdale shifted in his seat, trying to find a more comfortable position for his wounded arm. "It seems clear to me that the bombs from Minsk ended up at the hacienda and the three foreigners were imported to do something with the bombs. But what?"

"Yeah—good question, Jack. And where did they move them and how much time do we have?"

CHAPTER 32

Villa Rosselet

The idea had come toVictor Hidalgo three months before when he watched the CNN coverage of the Mexican president's White House visit following the Chiapas massacre. Hidalgo intuitively sensed a change in Washburn's attitude toward Posadas. Perhaps it was Washburn's body language; he imperceptibly inched away from Posadas, ending up well to one side of the lectern Posadas peered over nervously while delivering his lackluster prepared remarks. For the past year, Hidalgo had been quietly watching the U.S. secretary of state working to hold things together with Mexico and wondered if he would be able to persuade the U.S. president to continue supporting the ruling party.

"I might be reading things wrong," he told himself, "but I think it's time to find out if there is someone in Washington who wants to solve the real problems between Mexico and the United States. Richard Snyder had no part in the betrayal—he might be the one individual who can make a difference. But only if he will listen to me."

Hidalgo waited patiently for the right opportunity. And then his friend Chemor, when he passed on the news about the bombing plot, had handed him just what he needed to get Snyder's attention.

Chemor, who had arrived late the night before, was stunned when Hidalgo told him about his call to Ambassador Reimann.

"*Madre de dios*, Victor. Why did you do this?"

Chemor did not notice that he had upset his glass of juice; it pooled on the glass tabletop and then started to drip on the tiles of the patio.

"You obviously must have considered that the information could be a setup by Navarro?"

"Yes. And of course, that made my decision even harder."

"What if Washington simply ignores the information?"

Hidalgo was fully aware that the call could destroy everything he and Chemor and so many others had worked so hard for, but he could not have lived with himself knowing that he did nothing to stop the bombs and the killing of innocents. He also realized that the bombs could radically destabilize the country. If that happened, Mexico would lose everything. He would not let that happen even if it cost him everything that he had worked for during the past five and a half years.

"I have taken a calculated risk. I believe the information you received and passed on to me is credible for reasons that only I can perhaps understand. If Washington doesn't react and indiscriminate bombing and killing take place, then we all lose—innocent people on both sides of the border, the ruling party, the White House . . . all of us."

"But, sir, with all respect," Chemor protested, "Washburn believes that you are cooperating with Navarro and La Eme. Why should they believe you?"

"My dear and valued friend," Hidalgo said softly, "you know and I know that when Navarro and that other monster Espinosa attended the meeting, I made no commitments to him. What he wanted to believe after the meeting is no concern of mine. But I am concerned if it looks like he will succeed in pushing the PRD into power. I'm not surprised what they are saying in Washington, Ramiro, but we know the truth."

Chemor started rolling his napkin through his fingers. "I would hope that Washington is smart enough to open some form of dialogue with us. Whether we like it or not, some accommodation will be necessary if we are to be successful."

"I know. But we can't control that. We will have to let things play out."

"Did the ambassador ask about your source?"

"No, and of course I would not tell him. Just as I did not ask you."

Had Hidalgo pressed him, Chemor would have revealed that his source was his old schoolmate, Juan Ortega.

When the maid cleared the table, Chemor shifted the conversation back to the political situation in Mexico City. The most important news—that the PAN had announced it was dropping out and forming a coalition with the PRD—did not elicit any response from Hidalgo. Chemor realized that Hidalgo was still thinking about something else.

"Ramiro, now that almost four months have passed since Chiapas, are you still certain that Navarro is directly responsible?"

Chemor picked his words carefully. "Ultimately responsible, yes. But I found out that he used the landowners and the paramilitary to do the actual butchery."

Hidalgo nodded his head and looked away. "Navarro is smart and ruthless. He doesn't give a damn about the poor in our country; he doesn't care if we are teetering on the brink. Chiapas got the result he wanted. I am deeply concerned."

"I know how you feel, but it did indirectly benefit our campaign in the poll numbers."

"Yes, but if we follow that logic, Ramiro, we will be drawn into the gutter with Navarro and his PRD friends. You must be patient. My call to Ambassador Reimann is just another way to get where we need to go."

Hidalgo got up, took a cigar from the humidor on the table, clipped and lit it.

"Cheer up. I am going to take you for dinner at my favorite restaurant in the Alcantara quarters—the Parreirinha de Alfamanea."

Hidalgo had one more surprise in store for his friend. But it could wait until evening.

Chapter 33

U.S. Embassy
Mexico City

The morning after the assault on the hacienda, Palmer arrived at the ops center a few minutes before eight and was happy to see that Liz Cramer was already there.

"Hey, I missed you. But I needed sleep more than I realized."

She did not return his smile.

"In case you haven't heard, Tisdale was flown back to San Diego for surgery at Balboa. They are afraid that there's some nerve damage. It could impair the functioning of his hand. And put an end to his career."

"God, that's terrible. Corr didn't think the wound was all that bad."

"Yes, but he's not a doctor," she said, a note of anger in her voice. "And you aren't supposed to be out in the field getting shot at."

"But I wasn't shot at."

She ignored his protest. "I sent a cable to David Andrews. I told him that I did not think it was appropriate for you to expose yourself to that kind of risk. The two of us are supposed to be running this operation, in addition to calling the shots on SKYHAWK. Neither one of us should be involved in operations in the field."

Palmer felt a surge of anger.

"You could have at least discussed this with me before you sent that cable."

"Sure—and you would have probably talked me out of sending it."

Palmer looked around and lowered his voice.

"Liz, this isn't the time, and certainly not the right place, for this conversation."

Willie Graham came over at that moment and said, "Cole, I've got things set up for a secure call with the national security adviser"

"You're always one step ahead, Willie."

He followed Graham into his office and picked up the green handset on the communications console.

"Hello, David. I am here with Liz. She just told me about the cable she sent you."

"I'll deal with that later. Right now, I want the skinny on what went down. I gather that Tisdale was wounded."

"Yeah. I didn't appreciate how severe the injury was at the time. Anyhow, he got the job done—and very professionally."

"How good are the explosive readings?"

"About as good as you could hope for. Two different portable snifters confirmed them. We can fax in the results if you like?"

Palmer gave Andrews a concise report on how the operation had unfolded, what was found in the lab, the gruesome discovery of the bodies, and the conclusions he had drawn from his examination of their few personal effects.

"We sent all the physical evidence up to the FBI lab by diplomatic courier. I don't know how fast they can move.

I'm particularly interested in what that letter in Arabic said. Maybe it can give us a line on who these technicians were, or at least where they came from."

Palmer heard Andrews take a deep breath and sensed his frustration. "Okay. At least we know what we are looking for. Fax those readings directly to Dr. Finnermann. I will give him a heads-up.

There was a brief burst of static on the line and then Andrews's voice came back in mid-sentence.

". . . car is just about to drop me at the office. Listen, I think I have figured out a way to buy us some time before these things start going off."

"Great—but how exactly do you propose to accomplish that?"

"I'll tell you more later."

The evasiveness he heard in Andrews's voice bothered Palmer, but he decided to let it ride for the moment.

Andrews's transmission broke up again before he said, "I think you will find this interesting. The Russian defense minister notified us that the missing Colonel Kaliniev turned up dead in Christchurch, New Zealand. Shot dead in his hotel room. From sketchy information, it appears that he had arrived only a week before and was negotiating to buy a large sheep ranch. For cash on the barrelhead."

Palmer had expected something like this; Kaliniev was a loose end—and loose ends get tidied up.

"Another piece of the puzzle," he said thoughtfully. "Nothing surprises me anymore and I don't like what I'm thinking. Anyway, before I forget, I will be talking with Luis Vasquez today. Any message?"

"Yes. We need to move up the meeting, on a priority basis."

"What's this all about?"

"Just get it moved up. Synder wants the meeting. So, let him carry the ball on this one. Set it up—fast."

Palmer picked up the coldness in Andrews's voice when he talked about Snyder. *What the hell is going on?* The national security adviser and the secretary of state going their separate ways on something as vital as this made no sense. But he kept his doubts to himself.

"Okay, that shouldn't be too hard."

"Good—let me know ASAP. I will be in the office or they will know where to reach me. Talk later."

Just as Andrews broke the connection and Palmer was about to tell Liz Cramer what had been said during the conversation, Willie Graham came back into his office, and announced, "We may have hit the jackpot!"

"What are you talking about?"

"Remember you asked me to scratch around and see if I could come up with any information from my federal police and intel contacts?"

"Yeah, but I said to keep it low-key."

"Hey, Cole, I barely started talking with my police contact when he said he had been about to call me. I am not sure where his information takes us but—"

"Okay, you have our attention Willie," Palmer said, as he tried to put his concerns about David Andrews out of his mind and find a way to approach Liz.

"Well, it seems that the police were trying to recover a car that had gone over the edge of the highway and crashed into a lake—Lago de Cuitzeo, about sixty-two miles from here near the town of Morleon. Anyway, one of their divers came across what turned out to be a large empty steel container that had nuclear radiation warning labels and an identification plate with Hospital del Guadalupe on it. Guadalupe Hospital is the central stowage site for radioactive waste in Mexico."

"So—where does that take us?" Palmer asked.

"Ask yourself a question: why would a radioactive waste container end up at the bottom of a lake?"

"Come on, Willy. That's what we're waiting to hear."

"Okay. When the police questioned the hospital authorities, all they got was an acknowledgment that the container appeared to be one of several containers supplied by DOE to store low-level waste."

Graham saw that Palmer was getting impatient, so he continued. "It gets more puzzling. The hospital states that they are not missing any containers."

"What? Where in the hell did the thing come from?"

"The police dug around in their records and found out that the initial shipment of waste containers from the United States came up one short after it was unloaded in Mexico over two years ago. There was an investigation but it turned up nothing."

"I know that patience is not one of my virtues, but I don't see any connection."

"Okay, Cole. Early this morning they started interviewing staff members at the hospital who worked in the storage facility. One of the guys who monitors the radiation detection and security systems—they have watch-standers around the clock, largely to appease the U.S. Nuclear Regulatory Agency, but that is a separate story and—"

"C'mon, Willie. Give me the bottom line," Palmer said, trying to figure out how this might be related to the problem at hand.

"Stay with me, Cole." Graham was getting more excited as he went on. "When the police got to one young watch-stander, by the name of Julio Montoya, he gets nervous. His story is that army handlers from the Energy Directorship showed up unexpectedly on his watch and hurriedly removed four of the waste containers two weeks ago for permanent stowage in conjunction with the opening ceremony of Promontorio Mountain."

The mention of Promontorio Mountain really got Palmer's interest.

"Now listen to this. Montoya reported that he noticed

that one of the four containers was out of sequence—I mean three of them had sequential serial numbers but one did not. It puzzled him because he was sure that something had changed but figured some official made the change when he wasn't on watch. He did not think he should report anything because it was no big deal and way above his pay grade to get into, so he signed off on the manifest for the army handlers."

Liz Cramer suddenly broke in. "Willie . . . are you saying that there could have been some kind of swap of containers at the hospital?"

"Yes. It's the only thing that makes sense. And the connection to Promontorio Mountain sounded my inner alarm. Big time. Here's how it could have gone down. The stiffs you found at the hacienda could have repackaged the bombs."

"Yes, and put one in a radioactive waste container," Palmer said, finally convinced that the pieces were falling into place. "Someone then swaps out the bomb-laden container with one of the hospital containers destined for the repository. On the way home, they dump the other container in the lake."

"The only question is how and when," Liz Cramer said thoughtfully.

"We don't have time to figure that out," Palmer said firmly. "I am damn sure the bomb got inside that mountain."

"Okay, but surely someone must check the waste containers before they go into permanent stowage?" Cramer objected.

"I don't think we know what they do out there," Palmer said, "but we sure as hell are going to find out."

Palmer was not able to get through to Andrews for twenty minutes and he was growing increasingly restless and worried by the time his old friend came on the line. Andrews listened to Palmer's report without asking any questions. When he finished, there was a long period of silence on the line. Andrews was obviously trying to see if the pieces fitted together logically.

When he finally spoke, there was no hesitation in his tone. .

"I'm going to get on to DOE right now. How quickly can you get to the repository?"

"Well, the Lear that the SEAL team came down on is available," Palmer replied. He had anticipated the question. "Willie says maybe four hours to the nearest airstrip, in Hermosillo, and then get to the site by road."

"Okay. Go Cole. The opening ceremony is Saturday and if they have programmed the bomb for that event, we have barely three days left. When I call DOE, I'll arrange pickup in Hermosillo."

"Thanks. We are going to need some real breaks to catch up. Time is almost out if they have tied that bomb with the opening ceremony. I'm sure the priority has changed but I want to pass on that Luis Vasquez has opened his whole week to meet with us."

"Great. I will work it, but you're right, the priority just shifted. With Washburn and Posadas scheduled to attend the repository opening ceremony, we have to find a way to get to that bomb. I'm heading to Promontorio tonight."

Andrews told his secretary to hold all calls and closed the door to his office. "Christ . . . why does everything happen at once," he said to himself.

After he factored in the latest information, he stopped pacing and took a cell phone out of the back of the drawer in his desk. The 914 area code and carrier's records were registered to a real estate brokerage in White Plains, New York.

Promontorio Mountain
Mexico

More than six hundred feet below the surface ridge of Promontorio Mountain, M-0061 rested alongside the other three Mexican canisters.

At 12:00 hours on Wednesday, the timer came to life. The digital clock started the seventy-two-hour programmed countdown.

CHAPTER 34

Promontorio Mountain

Hayden Mills was taking a late afternoon nap on the couch in his office when the secure phone rang, jolting him out of his slumber. It was the last sleep he would have for some time to come. He instinctively knew that it was not good news as he lifted the receiver.

After the secretary of the Department of Energy informed him of developments over the past twenty-four hours and told him to expect plenty of company in the next few days, Mills put down the phone and burst out of his office.

His secretary was getting ready to leave for the day.

"Ellen, thank God you're still here! Would you alert the manager at the guest quarters to get rooms ready for at least ten? If he is tight on space, tell him that one of them can use my room. They should be arriving late tonight or Thursday morning. And I would really appreciate it if you would stand by here until further notice. I'm going to the mountain."

It was late in the day when Mills arrived at the security

gates. The waiting guards opened the gate after ensuring no one was accompanying the director and waved the Ford Explorer through while another guard alerted control center that the boss was on his way. The control center building was in a low-rise modern building that stood out from the other hangerlike structures around it where vehicles and equipment were kept. The mountain site for the waste stowage was another four miles beyond the center. As he walked inside, the watch supervisor was waiting.

The supervisor was an experienced senior engineer who had previously worked in a nuclear power plant in the United States, one of six men and one woman who oversaw the twenty-four/seven remote monitoring of the mountain site.

"First off, anything we say will not leave this room. Understand?"

"Yes, sir," the supervisor responded, trying to conceal his surprise at the sudden appearance of his boss after normal working hours.

"We might—and I repeat might—have a problem with the recent Mexican shipment."

"I haven't noticed anything unusual from the Whisky Site where the stuff is located," the supervisor responded.

Mills ignored his comment and asked nervously, "Do you know how many canisters were in the Mexican shipment?"

"Yes, sir. There were four canisters all located in section Whiskey-2."

"What else is in the mountain?" Mills knew the answer but wanted to confirm what he had told the secretary of energy.

"Let's see. Six canisters from Canada . . . one from Panama—next to the Mexican canisters. The three Puerto Rico canisters were buried in Whisky-3 yesterday—Tuesday—right after the Mexican stuff."

Mills took a handkerchief out of his pocket and wiped his forehead and neck.

"We need to bring in the operations director, security and robotics, plus our radiation expert, Dr. Chan, and probably the team leader that processed the Mexican waste."

"You mean you want me to start calling them now, sir?" *Shit! That was a dumb question,* he said to himself.

Mills glared at him. "Right now. And don't get everybody all stirred up. Just tell them we have a problem and I will explain everything when they get here."

In less than an hour, all of those notified gathered in the control center's small cafeteria; it was the only room in the facility large enough for meetings involving a large number of people.

Mills began by stressing the security aspects of what he was about to discuss and the implications if something got out, particularly with the opening ceremony only three days away.

"Unfortunately, we don't have the time to speculate on how probable the scenario is or the technical feasibility of getting a small high explosive bomb inside one of the containers. As far as we are concerned, the bomb is in the repository. Now what we need to do is figure out the options and risks in moving the canisters out of the mountain to a safe area—and before the opening ceremony on Saturday."

He paused to glance at his watch.

"It's a few minutes before six. We will meet again in a couple of hours with some people who will tell us more about the situation, if they get here. Remember—everything stays inside these walls. No outside cell calls period."

Mills retreated to the main control room and called the security desk to confirm that transportation was waiting at the airport. "Yes, I said three vans and I'm not sure when they will arrive. But I want the vans waiting."

* * *

The Navy Learjet landed at Hermosillo an hour ahead of the national security adviser's plane. Palmer and Liz Cramer had just enough time to eat before Andrews arrived and they piled into one of the waiting vans to drive to the mountain. As the vehicle pulled away from the terminal, Andrews pulled a small, slim notebook bound in black leather out of his breast pocket, quickly jotted down a few words and showed Palmer. When Palmer read the message, he looked shocked. As he started to speak, Andrews shook his head and pointed to the driver. Palmer sat back and closed his eyes.

Meanwhile, back at the makeshift conference room, the group broke off into different teams to figure out a recommended course of action. The operations director and principal assistant to Dr. Mills, Phil Gunderson, did not need much time to figure out that there were little or no options. The obvious answer was to remove the four Mexican canisters from the mountain and let the bomb experts take over. Mills left the room while the discussion went forward.

Mike Grissini sat quietly. He was the only nonengineer in the room. When the talking died down, he raised his hand hesitantly as if afraid to interrupt.

"Phil, I don't know if this means anything. But when we processed the Mexican stuff, one of the canisters had a much lower radiation reading. I think it was M-0061."

"You're right! I remember that now that you mention it, Mike," Sarah Chan spoke up. "As I remember, it was lower than the other three but within specs."

"Could a small high-explosive bomb packaged with low-level radioactive waste cause a decrease—or a lower radiation level?" The ops boss asked.

"I guess it could," Chan replied.

Gunderson looked frustrated. "Okay. Let me try it another way. If someone planted a bomb inside one of the containers, is M-0061 a likely candidate?"

"I see where you are going and the answer is yes. If the bomb displaced some of the waste inside the container—or it did not have much waste to begin with—then we could expect a lower reading."

"Okay. Let's move forward and focus on M-0061," Gunderson said, looking around the room to see if everyone agreed.

"We might have narrowed down which container has the bomb but it doesn't make a lot of difference. Why take any chances? Do we know for sure that there are no other bombs? I recommend we move all the canisters if we have time," Doug Terman, the robotics director, suggested.

The discussion came to a halt when Mills came into the room with several people following him. He briefly introduced the national security adviser, Palmer, Dr. Cramer, as well as two weapons experts from Los Alamos, who had flown in on a Department of Energy aircraft. Following the introductions, Mills asked Gunderson to bring them up to date. It was almost midnight.

"Well, once we got over the hump accepting that we could be dealing with a bomb," Gunderson paused for his statement to sink in, "we figured out a couple of things. First, we have a good idea that canister M-0061 holds the bomb and secondly, we know the exact location of it. Now if we're right, what do we do with it? Our consensus is that the best and safest course of action is to move all the Mexican canisters out of the mountain—that is, if we have the time."

"How do we know M-0061 is the one with the bomb?" Mills sounded skeptical.

Grissini, bitterly regretting having not acted on his gut-level feeling that day when the shipment was checked, lowered his head as the ops boss explained his reasoning.

One of the experts from Los Alamos wanted to know

more about the recorded readings and types of monitors used by the inspection team. The discussion quickly turned into a technical argument between Sarah Chan and one of the men from Los Alamos. Mills grew increasingly irritated and put a stop to the disagreement.

"We need to move on. Let's assume we have made the right call on M-0061. I think what I heard you say Phil was that the safest course of action was to remove all the canisters and not take any chances. Is that correct?"

"Yes, sir. That is the way we see it unless we run into problems moving them. You know, we don't have much room inside there. The designers of the emplacement areas did not consider removal of the canisters, once buried. My recommendation is that we focus on M-0061—get it out first and then the rest."

Andrews and Palmer glanced at each other. It was time to disclose the latest information from the FBI that Andrews had received while enroute to Hermosillo—the information that he had jotted down and shown to Palmer. The sister of the foreign engineer, Hamid al Serif, who had worked on the bomb at the hacienda, lived in Saudi Arabia and had written the letter in Arabic to her brother. In his particular line of work, Hamid had become quite well known to those who worried about his handiwork—particularly the FBI and the Anti-Terrorism Group at the State Department.

"Unfortunately, it's not that easy," Andrews said making sure that everyone was paying close attention. "We have to assume that the bomb is activated and into countdown; how much time we have, we don't know. We also have to assume that the bomb has been rigged to explode if moved. In other words, the simple option to move the canisters out of the mountain is not on the table. We now know that at least one of the people who worked on the bomb was a highly sophisticated weapons expert who belongs to a terrorist movement. According to our info, his style of bomb designing—on past bombs—virtually guarantees that it will detonate if moved once armed."

The mood in the room changed as Andrews spoke. The two weapons experts started arguing about the risk associated with an explosion inside the repository and the possibility of the radioactive waste contaminating the groundwater.

Palmer shook his head, frustrated and dismayed by the bickering. Finally, he could not stand it any longer and, after muttering to Andrews, "I need some fresh air," he got up and headed for the exit.

CHAPTER 35

Promontorio Mountain

Liz Cramer waited a few minutes before joining Palmer outside. She put her arm around his waist. The two of them walked slowly through the cool late evening air without saying anything. Then, Cramer broke the silence.

"Are you still angry about my cable?"

Palmer didn't answer for a moment and then said gently, "Liz, I would find it very hard to stay mad at you for long. But, yes—I was kind of pissed off. Mostly that you did it without saying anything to me. Our relationship has been pretty honest and open."

He stopped walking and turned to face her.

"Let's put that little issue aside. It's not important. What is important is that I would feel a whole lot better if you were back in Mexico City, Liz. We really don't know what to expect out here."

"But you told me that Andrews said that some wording he was able to get inserted into the President's NATO Address on Friday might put this thing on hold."

"You're right. But Andrews hasn't told me any more than that. I wish I could believe he's right, but I don't. I can't imagine whoever is behind all this will care at this point. More important, I'm not sure they can do anything about it with the bomb ticking inside the mountain."

Palmer did not mention that he also feared there would be something else—not just the bomb. The opportunity to strike while the presidents of both countries were in the same place was too tempting to pass up. But he said only, "We haven't a clue where the other five bombs are."

They continued walking arm in arm until they reached a wood picnic table and benches set in the middle of a small patch of grass. As they started to sit down and rest, Cramer said, "I understand and I'm sorry to add to your worries but you can forget about me leaving."

Palmer started to speak, but Cramer doggedly continued. "And let me tell you why I felt so strongly about your taking what I think are unjustified risks. I almost said irresponsible behavior, but that wouldn't be fair. Maybe a few years ago, yes. But not now. Still, your role in the assault on the hacienda—it just wasn't a necessary risk."

In the darkness, she could not see the expression on Palmer's face.

"I'm sorry, Cole, but you have to know how I feel. And there is probably some reason for it. After my father died when I was twelve, I was sent away to boarding school. My mother had a child who needed her, but she was absorbed in her own grief and sense of loss—even while she tried to . . . look, Cole, I loved my mother but she shut me out. And my husband thought he was doing me a kindness when he withheld the information about his cancer until it became obvious that he was very sick. The three most crucial emotional attachments in my life, and look what happened—I'm not going to set myself up for another blowout. Maybe you're not ready, either. But I need to feel safe about you."

When Palmer made no reply, she said, with a note of regret in her voice, "If you get run over by a bus or something like that, well that's fate. I can live with that. But if you subject yourself—and that means us—to the kinds of risks you have on past operations, then this is not going to be a story with a happy ending."

While the meeting inside the control center building drifted indecisively along, Andrews made a decision. He would wait until after the president's NATO speech and the president was actually on board Air Force One before making the decision to postpone the opening. That would be late Friday. He had suggested several fallback stories to Jim Browning to cover the need for the president's immediate, unscheduled return to Washington. Browning was very good at his job—improving on the truth when possible, and inventing it when necessary.

The last-minute changes that Andrews had been able to slip into the president's speech to the NATO ministers, which would be delivered before he left Washington for the ceremony, included one sentence that would be a powerful signal to three people—Posadas, Hidalgo, and most importantly, Navarro. Andrews had been convinced, from the moment of Hidalgo's warning came through last week, that Navarro was the one responsible for Chiapas, as well as other incidents that raised the level of crisis. The bombs, Andrews knew, would be the finishing blow. He still could not figure out Hidalgo's real role in this murky business and when it would all start.

Yet despite his uncertainty, he had gone ahead with the riskiest thing he had ever done; the key sentence had been inserted. He realized that it could undermine Snyder, who would regard it as a betrayal if he found out—but it was the only way, he believed, to avert the terrorist bombings. It was his only high ground.

Andrews thought about making one more call—using

the code-name "Zircon" to Navarro after Washburn's speech, to get some sense of reaction. But the follow-up call would be too risky. Still, he would have enjoyed hearing Navarro concede that he had accomplished something that Navarro himself could not do.

The gamble was worth it, Andrews assured himself—it could save a president from defeat. And—no matter what it took—this one bomb in the mountain could not be allowed to explode.

CHAPTER 36

Promontorio Mountain

Inside the mountain repository, the bomb digital clock
clicked at 09:17 Thursday morning.

"Bad news?" Liz Cramer asked, noting the tired frown on
David Andrews's face. Andrews had finally crashed on the
couch for a few hours of sleep in Dr. Mills's office.

"Not in the last ten minutes. But give it time. As the
bard put it, 'When troubles come, they come not as single
spies but in battalions.'"

"Speaking of troubles, I need to give Luis Vasquez a
heads-up on delaying the meeting that was so urgent."

"Sorry, Cole. I forgot. Snyder convinced the president
that we should open a back channel and arrange a meeting
with Hidalgo."

"That should be interesting. By the way, is the president
still coming?"

"The last I heard he was."

"Did you give him the whole picture?"

"Well . . . yes and no. He was adamant that he was not going to change his schedule. All that could change of course once he gets here."

"That must have been an interesting conversation." Palmer was bothered by Andrews's evasiveness; it was another sign that their old ties of trust and friendship were fraying. Perhaps, Palmer thought, Andrews had reached a point in his life where he can't afford to have real friends.

Gunderson walked out of the conference room. Everyone had reassembled after breaking up around two o'clock in the morning.

"Well, we finally reached a consensus that the mountain will contain the explosion and there would be no physical danger to the president if he attends the ceremony."

"I think the three of us ought to get back in there," Andrews said.

When they came back, they discovered that Andrews had been able to deliver on what Palmer had suggested last night. After the bad news sunk in about the likelihood of the bomb exploding if it was moved, Palmer had come up with the idea to have a special Navy Explosive Ordinance Disposal team flown down from the naval base in Coronado. The EOD team had gotten to the repository four hours later.

When they got inside the conference room, they saw that everyone was gathered around the EOD team leader, Lieutenant Bob Fisher. Fisher explained what he and his men did and how the special equipment worked. Palmer watched as Mills, Gunderson, Doug Terman, Fisher, and EOD Senior Chief Woods huddled over a large schematic of the interior of the mountain. The schematic highlighted the waste sites within the emplacement tunnels. It also showed how the transporters followed a gradual descent from the north entrance portal through the sloping tunnel with stops at the connecting emplacement sites where some 7,500 canisters would eventually be stowed.

The EOD team offered a workable but high-risk option. Since the Vietnam War, the U.S. Armed Forces had been developing a capability to disarm weapons by using tiny shaped charges to "decapitate" the weapon. Using X-ray and ultrasound scans, they would locate the various parts of an explosive device, arming and timer mechanisms, wiring of firing circuits, detonator, main charge, and so forth. By properly detonating the small plastic shaped charge placed carefully on the outside of a device, the resulting explosion would directly cut through the firing and arming circuits of the bomb—thus decapitating it. It was not a task for those with delicate nerves and unsteady hands.

"What's going on?" Palmer asked as they joined the group.

"Um, well, we've come up with a couple potential problems," responded Gunderson. "According to Lieutenant Fisher, the X-ray machine might have some problems getting a clear picture through the canister's cover. And we don't know what is inside, or if the bomb is covered with something."

"Okay, what is the other problem?"

"Well, it's tied to the first problem to some extent. Radiation and X-ray pictures don't mix. Radiation fogs the image, degrades the quality depending on how much radioactive leakage there is."

Seeing the discouraged expression on Palmer's face, Fisher attempted to reassure him.

"We never know what kind of imagery we are going to get until we start imaging. Sometimes we get a break . . . find a particular angle and ladder it until we start seeing something. We just have to do it."

At that moment, Andrews gestured to Palmer to come outside the conference room.

"I think I know what's going through your head and I would probably be wasting my time arguing with you but

Liz is worried. When she sent me that cable—well, it's not like her. Obviously, she cares a lot about you. I probably shouldn't have but I gave her a quick dump on your time with the special ops teams while working for me. I thought it might reassure her that you know what you are doing out in the field but now I think it had the opposite effect. I'm sorry . . . well, you and she have to sort all that out."

Palmer pursed his lips and nodded. "Unfortunately, it was my dumb idea to bring in the EOD guys so I figure I'm the one to see it through. I'll have to deal with Liz."

"Okay, but one thing understood. If things look shaky, abort and get the hell out. Beating those odds isn't good. The mountain can absorb it."

Mills, Phil Gunderson, and Sarah Chan were in Chan's small office on a conference call. After answering numerous questions about how the waste was stored, a Livermore radiation expert said they would work the data and call back. Twenty minutes later, he called back and hedged his opinion with an elaborate set of "on the one hand" qualifications. When pressed hard for a clear-cut answer, he reluctantly delivered himself of the opinion that since the repository contained relatively little waste, the standard time-risk ratios were not applicable. The bottom line was that if they controlled the time inside, the radiation risk was low. He also recommended that protective clothing would dampen the risk. When pressed by Chan for a stay time they could work with, the scientist at Livermore, after reminding Chan that he could give her a better answer if he knew more about what was going on at the repository, finally said, "Anything over fifty minutes, the contamination risk would go up geometrically."

When Liz turned a corner in the hall leading to the unisex restroom, she saw Palmer coming her way.

"Hi, I was hoping to find you."

Liz Cramer immediately sensed something. His smile was just a little too bright and his tone had a certain false ring to it.

"When I saw you talking with David, I had the awful feeling that you were getting yourself more involved with this bomb thing."

Palmer desperately tried to find the right words, but was reduced, finally, to blurting out, "Liz, somebody has to go in there with the EOD team and since it's my idea, I need to be the one."

Liz involuntarily stiffened and the words rolled out before she could stop them. "Oh, my God, no, Cole. You can't go. How could you do this to me?"

Liz Cramer slumped against the wall of the corridor. She looked haggard and stunned. Palmer could hardly bear the look in her eyes. He swallowed hard.

"Don't make it harder than it already is."

Liz knew that she had to break away before she did something that she would regret. She wiped her eyes and started to walk away. She stopped and looked around at him.

"No—I take it back. Irresponsible is the right word."

Gunderson, Terman, and Fisher were studying the layout of Whisky-2 where the handlers had positioned the Mexican waste canisters.

"I'm the designated driver for this little tour," Palmer said as he walked over to join them. "I need to get checked out—controls, brakes on the transporter before we go inside the mountain in the morning."

Chief Woods looked over the rims of his glasses and rumbled, "We could definitely use the backup but we can manage."

"I appreciate that, but I wouldn't miss watching you pros do your magic."

"Roger that," Fisher said cheerfully. "If we have to make a quick decision to punch-out, I'd like to have you to back me up."

The go time was set for 11:30 hours in the morning. They had done what they could in the way of preparations and getting some sleep was the most important thing at this point. Andrews and Palmer had a late dinner at the support compound but neither had much to say. Their minds were on what was in store for them in the next twenty-four hours. After they departed for the their assigned rooms, Palmer had looked for Liz Cramer but she wasn't around or answering her phone.

The timer inside the false bottom of canister M-0061 clicked at 09:39 Friday morning.

Preparations continued outside the north portal entrance. Palmer had arrived early to go over the controls of the transporter one more time—realizing it was a way to release some of his nervousness—while Woods and Fisher sorted the equipment they wanted to take. Walkie-talkies were jury-rigged on the two transporters for comms with the site control station adjacent to the entrance. Everything appeared good to go.

"Before you head off, I want you to know that you'll have another backup team," announced Mike Grissini.

"What backup team is that?" Palmer asked.

"The Grissini team. If you get in trouble, I'm on my way."

"You mean some hardheaded marine is going to bail us out," Palmer cried in mock horror. Grissini smiled and nodded his head.

Sarah Chan arrived with a couple of associates carrying red cardboard boxes.

"You are safe inside the mountain for fifty minutes. After that, radiation exposures become unacceptable."

"That's cutting it close," Fisher said. "I'm not sure we can do that."

"I thought you might say that. In that case, they recommended wearing some of this protective clothing I brought down." Chan did not want to start a discussion about how long they could actually stay inside the mountain and shifted back to the protective clothing issue. "We've rigged up some real lightweight stuff and my folks will be disappointed if you don't try them. They've been scrambling to get all this together."

Palmer stepped forward, and pulled on the yellow-layered cotton suit that covered everything but his head and hands. Fisher and Woods slowly put on theirs.

Discussion time had ended. Now it was time to make their run on the bomb.

Andrews and Palmer eased over to the waiting transporter. Grissini waved from one of the other transporters ready to go if needed, some 150 feet behind Palmer. The EOD team was loading on their gear. David Andrews watched them. In his mind, he was replaying the conversation after dinner when Brooke had warned him against exploiting his friend and their friendship. For God's sake, it was his idea, Andrews told himself. But he would have Liz Cramer on his case now. Don't let this one go sour, he prayed silently.

Palmer turned around and looked at the EOD team. "Okay guys, its down and dirty time. Are we all set?"

It was 11:25 hours. The large hydraulic double steel doors slowly opened and the two transporters headed out of the bright floodlights at the portal and into the dark tunnel with only the flicker of dimmed shadows in the distance. Once past the portal entrance, the doors closed behind them creating an ear-popping vacuum. Palmer knew that the ventilation system was adequate, but for a claustrophobic like him, he could not help faintly grasping for air. He focused on breathing—in, out—trying to maintain a rhythm. In past operations, he had always been ready and, in most cases, looking forward to such challenges. Now it was different. He no longer wanted any part of it. As the transporter picked up speed, he closed his eyes and wondered if this were the final challenge—would this rid his life of the demons that tormented him since losing Catherine. Or would it irrevocably alienate Liz Cramer from him.

CHAPTER 37

Promontorio Mountain
Time: Friday 11:50

The shrill beeping of his satellite phone startled Andrews, who was closely following the action from the control station some 150 feet from the portal entrance to the repository. It was his deputy. The news he had for Andrews was devastating.

"Jeffery Boyd just called. They had a bombing in Mexico City, near the Paseo de la Reforma . . . about an hour ago . . . extensive damage and loss of life. Boyd thinks it was one of the suitcase bombs."

The national security adviser felt as if someone had hit him in the stomach with a baseball bat. Why couldn't Navarro hold off until the president's speech? Did Navarro even take him seriously? Or had he ignored him, making the high-stakes risk he had taken futile. And if his operation under the cover name Zircon was ever found out, he was finished. All he could hope for now is that Palmer and the EOD team would be able to disarm the bomb.

When, Andrews wondered, would the other four bombs explode? And where? As to the president's plans, Andrews learned from his deputy that the news of the bombing had made the president even more determined to attend the opening ceremony with Posadas.

He rationalized that he had done everything he could to stop the bombings, even putting his career on the line. At least Washburn would see that there was no other choice—he had to distance himself from Posadas. The NATO minister's speech was only minutes away. After that the White House party—the president, Snyder, and the members of the White House staff—would be flying down to Mexico.

Andrews walked inside the control center and joined the group around the television. CNN announced that the president was due shortly to address the NATO Ministers and that CNN would cover the speech.

"Have we comms with Palmer?"

"Yes. Do you want to talk with him?" Gunderson handed Andrews the handset.

"Cole, this is David. Can you hear me?"

"Loud and clear, David."

Andrews could hear the transporter rolling over the tracks. "Just finished talking with my deputy. The president is definitely attending."

"Shit! I hope you're not counting on any miracles."

The voice circuit distorted Palmer's voice and his speech was breaking up. Andrews decided that it would be pointless to tell him about the bombing. A miracle was exactly what he was praying for; he did not want Palmer or the EOD team distracted. With everything swirling around in his head, he also realized that if something happened, he was responsible. Everything was coming to a head—his marriage, his future—and he was risking the life of his best friend to save his ass.

Andrews looked down at his hand holding the phone handset and with a curious sense of detachment noticed that it was shaking. At that moment, Hayden Mills tapped him on the shoulder.

The president had started his speech.

After a short statement welcoming the NATO ministers, Washburn devoted the bulk of his address to the continuing problems in southeast Europe and reaffirmed the U.S. commitment of troops.

Washburn paused for a moment and then switched to a new topic.

"I am sure that all of you have watched the critical developments in Mexico and the implications of these developments for world democracy and the global economy."

The president became more emotional as he spoke about the determination to do everything possible to come to the aid of its neighbor to the south. Andrews waited for the inevitable "but"—and it came as the president was concluding his speech. It was clear to anyone listening carefully that the White House was reviewing its fundamental position with respect to Posadas and his government. The president tried to balance it with the usual condemnation of those responsible for the massacre in Chiapas and support for the International Commission, while emphasizing the unreserved support and respect for Mexico's sovereignty. Although the president did not mention the bombing, his speech ended with a significantly different version of Andrew's carefully crafted words, a version suggesting that a change in policy was possible, but for the moment, the United States stood in solidarity with Mexico "in its time of trial." Andrews was stunned. It was obvious that Richard Snyder had, at the last minute, convinced Washburn to defer a decision. The United States would watch and wait to see if the situation in Mexico continued to deteriorate.

"Washburn is on the fence," Liz Cramer said, as the CNN anchor began her instant analysis of the president's speech. "Posadas must be desperate to find out what this all means. I'm damned if I do."

"You're right, Liz. The president played it down the middle. He had to be careful not to overplay the problems and trigger a stampede on the Hill. On the other hand, he can't bet the fate of his second term on a situation that he can't control. You can be sure of one thing—this administration is going to be forced to dump Posadas. There's really no option."

Cramer stared at Andrews; it was as if she had really understood, for the first time, what was going on in his mind.

"David, have you ever considered that there are some things that are more important than a second term?"

The digital clock in the site control station showed 12:09 Friday afternoon. The countdown on the bomb clicked to twenty-three hours and fifty-one minutes.

Doug Terman was tracking the transporters using a stopwatch. "You're moving at a pretty good clip. Start cutting speed. I'm worried about that braking system we discussed." Terman had explained that the initial tests of the transporter brakes had failed and the manufacturer was working on a fix but nothing had been retrofitted to the existing transporters. "When you see the U-curve in the tracks, put some muscle to the brakes for the last 900 meters or so to the site."

"Will I be able to tell when we reach the 900 meter mark?"

"I think so. As you probably noticed, we have yellow lights every 300 meters and phosphorescent signs below the lanterns mark the distance."

"Yeah. I see one now just ahead."

* * *

Palmer could feel the transporter picking up additional speed from the sloping tunnel that formed one of the sides of the U-shaped loop through the mountain; the canisters were stored at the bottom of the tunnel. He started easing down on the brakes. Apart from the transporter's low hum as it rolled along the tracks, the tunnel was eerily silent. Palmer, Fisher, and Woods could easily hear one another as their voices echoed in the tunnel. Palmer started applying greater pressure on the brakes, but the transporter was not slowing down. When he felt the transporter suddenly sway into the gradual turn of the through, he was pushing as hard as he could on the braking system. Something was wrong. The transporter was not slowing.

"Whaddya doing?" Woods shouted.

Palmer pulled the brake handle as far as it would go, desperately attempting to slow the transporter. After a series of metallic shrieks, the brake pads started belching smoke as the speed finally dropped. Palmer watched helplessly as they overshot the W-2 burial site. When they finally came to rest, Palmer notified the alarmed control station about their status.

"We overshot and probably blew out the braking system."

"This is what I was afraid of," Terman said, feeling a faint sense of panic. "It's a goddamn design problem. Can the brakes hold the transporter?"

"Yes . . . but we are in the level part of the tunnel trough so it is hard to tell if I have anything left or not. We have the wheels wedged as a precaution."

"Okay. Can you manhandle the equipment back to W-2?"

"Bob thinks so. Cross your fingers. Getting out of here will be a problem."

They had been inside the mountain for twelve minutes when they started lugging the equipment toward W-2.

Liz Cramer had entered the remote control station. She eased over to Sarah Chan. "Do we have a problem?"

Chan had been watching the monitor and checking her watch. She could hear the strain in Cramer's voice.

"We've got some built-in slack in case of problems like this. It's too early to start worrying about it now."

"You'll tell me if there's a problem, right?"

Chan nodded. "Don't worry. If it looks like they are eating up the safety margin, then I'll pull them out of there."

They were breathing hard when they arrived. Fisher and Woods selected what gear they wanted and left the rest outside the emplacement tunnel. Each man wore an orange helmet with a high-intensity halogen lamp fixed to the front, like a miner's lamp.

It was obvious that the team had worked and trained together for a long time. Conversation was kept to a minimum. Palmer felt a growing sense of confidence; these guys might actually pull it off. Bob Fisher was what they called a limited duty officer, or LDO—he had made his way through the enlisted ranks to officer status. A tall, wiry man with a ready smile, he was precise in his movements and focused like a laser beam on the job at hand. Fisher never raised his voice or lost his temper. He had the kind of discipline and self-confidence that was essential for EOD work. If an officer in his position showed any sign of carelessness, or worse, cockiness, the command simply dropped him from the program and returned him to the fleet. He had one overriding concern: Do nothing to jeopardize the safety of those he worked with.

Senior Chief Woods, in contrast to Fisher, was five foot nine inches and built like the proverbial fireplug. According to sea stories that kept the EOD trainees in awe, Woods knew more about explosives than anyone in the command. His expertise had been called upon numerous times in places all over the world. Chief Woods lived in his own world of clarity and absolutes; he was uncompromising when it came to honesty or loyalty. In his line of work, he had to depend on his shipmates and there were no second chances.

Woods started slowly moving his hands over M-0061, gently and slowly as if he were touching something that was alive. Every now and then, he would gently tap it or place his ear to the canister, as if he was listening for something. While he and Fisher talked in low tones, Palmer waited outside the entrance of the emplacement tunnel, ready to assist if called upon.

After a few minutes, Woods handed Fisher the portable MR32 X-ray machine, called "IMAX" by the EOD team. Unable to resist his curiosity, Palmer came into the tunnel to watch.

"Everything look okay, Bob?"

"Uh-huh. No surprises yet except we are behind time. I am a bit worried about getting some decent pictures. We'll just have to wait and see."

"Is there anything I can do to help?" Palmer asked.

"Not much right now. It is time to see what we have inside that canister. The X-rays are picked up on a detector plate and the images are continuously digitized and enhanced. Ah, there we go," he remarked with satisfaction, looking at a glowing green screen on the side of the X-ray machine. "We got a good reading on the anode."

With Woods marking the surface of the canister using a pencil-shaped marker with a white chalklike substance, Fisher started at the bottom, which, he guessed, was the most likely area for the bomb. He had to straddle M-0061 in order to get a shot down from the top because the emplacement tunnel design called for the canisters to be positioned horizontally on the rock floor. The initial set of images was too fuzzy to work with. Fisher then moved alongside M-0061, lying on his back on the tunnel floor.

Following Wood's directions, he tried to find the best angle to get a workable picture. Finally, after a series of frustrating poor images, the outline of something attached to the bottom inside of the canister appeared on the screen.

Woods carefully marked the area. Then Fisher started capturing images from several different angles. Suddenly Woods whispered, "Bingo!" The screen showed the outline of the bomb mechanism, attached to a false bottom of the canister. The area had been divided into two parts separated by some type of thin metal plate. The power source and triggering device took up one side and the larger area held the compact high explosive material and the detonator.

Fisher was dripping with perspiration as he thought through every step. "I think we have enough to attack the damn thing . . . probably from the top . . . above the power source . . . a small linear shape charge. We got a real break. If they had covered the bomb with a heavier gauge metal, we probably wouldn't have seen it clearly enough."

He suddenly froze, watching the screen and holding the scanner rock-steady in his hands.

"Whoever figured out that the bomb couldn't be moved was pretty smart after all. It looks like there are several motion-sensitive devices—something like trembler switches—to trigger the bomb if moved even a fraction of an inch. This package has just gotten a whole lot of respect."

As Bob Fisher started going through a large metal container similar to an ammunition box and containing various shape charges, Palmer tried unsuccessfully to identify the trembler switches in the picture. Suddenly Chief Woods pushed him gently but firmly aside and wired some device to the canister; it terminated in what looked like a stethoscope, which was jammed into his ears.

"Ah shit!" Woods muttered. "This one's alive and the sequencer is on countdown."

Palmer shivered slightly and tried to remain calm; but he had never before been as scared as he was at that second.

"Any way for the chief to tell where the countdown is?"

"No," Fisher said with a grin. "That would take all the fun out of things. The bomb has the advantage until we level the playing field, so to speak, by knocking out its brain."

He had selected several shape charges; each was about four and a half inches tall and two inches in diameter. For years, the EOD had tested and developed the shape charge as a proven technique for obtaining a highly efficient and accurate cut from a directed explosion. Fisher showed Palmer one of them.

"These are really nifty toys. The basic theory is that when the C-4 charge detonates using this attached blasting cap—you can just see it below this groove. The product gases expand omnidirectionally from the charge center. You get a shock wave . . . a tremendous jet formation of energy on the desired point of entry. Once the outside covering is penetrated, the jet passes directly on the target and disables the triggering device before it can explode the bomb. At least that's the theory. If it doesn't work, we get our heads blown off."

Woods started carefully fitting charges to the side of the canister while Fisher captured more X-ray images from different angles. Palmer looked at his watch.

Fisher noticed and asked quietly, "How long have we been in here?"

"Coming up on forty-nine minutes."

At this point Woods decided where he wanted the shape charges placed and chalked a thin line with a rough bullseye directly above the power source of the bomb. "Time to minimize the risk profile," he growled softly.

Fisher grabbed Palmer by the arm and firmly steered him out of the emplacement tunnel.

"This is now a one-man job. If something goes wrong—well, maybe I can figure out what happened and save a few lives. The chief knows what he's doing and there is nobody better at it in the world—so let's leave him to it."

He had barely finished when Woods shouted, "Better get back here—quick!"

Fisher disappeared into the emplacement tunnel and then reemerged and started groping around in a large canvas bag full of tools.

Palmer did not want to bother them but could not contain himself. "What was that all about?"

"Well, it looks like those bastards want to play hardball. We almost missed it—the chief thinks we have a new wrinkle. Something called collapsing circuits. I am getting the uneasy feeling that those foreign bastards are playing for keeps."

"I'm not sure I follow, Bob."

Fisher took a deep breath and squatted on his heels. "Okay. If you go in with a shape charge and knock out what you think is the power source and the collapsing circuit activates a hidden or redundant power source, you don't have any time to do anything about it. The bomb blows up under your feet and you never know what hit you."

Palmer realized that it was crunch time; he needed to understand what was involved if he had to make a decision. He waited while Fisher went back into the emplacement tunnel carrying the canvas bag. When he returned, Palmer asked, "What's the next step?"

"The chief is getting his special tools ready—portable drills, fiber optic scopes. It is something like open-heart surgery but with higher stakes. This is Woods's game and he is the only one who can do it."

"I'm not sure I want to know," Palmer said, "but what does he do after he gets inside the thing with his fiber optic scopes?"

"Well, you react to what you find. If he thinks he can beat it, he starts snipping the right wires trying to stay ahead of the racing collapsing circuits. If he doesn't like the way it looks, we leave the damn thing and get the hell out of here."

Woods was already drilling a hole from the top of the canister to get a peek inside the bomb. When he slipped the thin fiber optic cable into the canister, he shouted, "Clear the entrance!" An instant after his warning a sharp "crack" reverberated from the tunnel.

Fisher rushed inside and returned with Woods, who was wiping blood away from several fragment cuts on his face.

"You all right?"

"Yeah. I'm okay." He was trembling and rubbing his eyes. "Except I almost bought the farm. But I can lick this fucker; we have to get back on it."

"What? Come on . . . We're getting out of here." Palmer figured they had pushed it as far as they dared.

"Wait," Woods said, dabbing at his forehead with a rag and drawing short, steadying breaths. "I saw something right before . . . I can finish it. I just need a minute." He wiped his bloodstained hands on his shirtfront. "The sneaky bastards put a booby trap right above the power source—but on the other side of the internal casing. Thank God that it vented itself through the top part of the canister or we wouldn't be around talking about it."

While Fisher and Palmer watched, the chief cautiously inserted his backup fiber optic scope; the blast had severed the fiber line on the other one. The explosion had ripped a small hole in the end of the canister, fortunately the end opposite and far removed from the bomb. As Woods carefully manipulated the scope, he saw a small connector wrapped around by wires that led to another connector, which was partly covered by another jumble of wiring. The chief kept looking at it trying to figure out how to separate the first group of wires and then outpace the collapsing circuit once he started cutting. After a few more minutes, he had to stop to wipe the sweat rolling off his forehead. Fisher handed him a canteen of water; the chief took a long pull at it and closed his eyes, thinking things through.

Nervous exhaustion was setting in; the chief pressed his hands against his thighs until he was sure he could stop them from shaking.

"Okay, chief. What's your take on it?"

"Well, it's a son of a bitch, no question about it. I have never seen one quite like it before. But I can beat it. They had their little fun and pissed me off. Now it is my turn."

Bob Fisher stepped closer to his teammate.

"There is nothing wrong in pulling chalks and getting out of here on this one. The mountain can deal with the explosion a hell of lot better than we can."

"I hear you, Bob. You know me well enough that I wouldn't try it if I didn't think it would work. I can deal with it."

Fisher did not immediately respond. He took off his helmet and scratched his head.

"Okay, buddy. If you feel you can handle it that's good enough for me. I support going ahead with it, Cole, but it's your call."

Palmer stared at the weary and exhausted Woods. Here it is at last, he said to himself. This time it was different. His demons of hate and revenge that had driven him in similar situations were gone. He closed his eyes and silently pictured Catherine. He stepped closer, looked into Woods's eyes, and put his hand on the chief's shoulder.

"All right, chief . . . let's do it."

Palmer got nervous chills as he said it. Was he subjecting himself and others at what Liz would call an unacceptable risk? Why not get the hell out?

As Woods started to return to M-0061, he stopped and winked at Palmer and Fisher.

"C'mon, guys. Lighten up . . . everything is going to be fine."

Another five minutes passed before Woods raised his right index finger to signal Fisher.

"Okay. The chief has cut the main power source," Fisher whispered.

Woods furiously worked the cutters to stay ahead of the collapsing circuits. Timing was critical. If he cut the wrong lead, he would not have time to sever the other possible power source leads and the ball game would be over. Finally, Woods grinned triumphantly and dropped the cutters. It was over.

They loaded all the equipment they could on the transporter in the few minutes remaining before they began to absorb too much radiation. When they were all on board, Palmer finally responded to the repeated calls from control.

"What happened in there? We heard something and then lost comms for a while?"

"I'll tell you all about it later. We're on our way out."

"Wait . . . what about the bomb? We're going crazy in here." Palmer could hear the anxiety in Phil Gunderson's voice.

"Okay—slow down. Let's just say the bomb couldn't fart if it wanted to."

In the control station, Liz Cramer suddenly felt shaky and had to sit down. Great moment to faint, she thought. Others in the room were cheering at the top of their voices.

Doug Terman was not celebrating. He had been watching the transporter and looking at his stopwatch. He got on the horn to Palmer.

"I hate to bring it up but we have another problem. The

air lock doors are designed to activate hydraulically when your transporter passes over a trip switch in the track—it's meant to keep any contamination from escaping."

Palmer, glancing at the time on his watch asked, "Okay, what's the problem?"

"The problem is that you'll be going too fast without functional brakes for the doors to fully open after you hit the trip switch. In other words, the breakers activate at a point when the transporter is moving at a certain speed. Without brakes, you'll be exceeding that speed."

"What the hell. Can't someone override the switch?"

"That's what we're scrambling to do, Cole. The designers have all this fail-safe stuff because of the radioactive contamination and leakage potential. We have to find a way to beat the system."

"Yeah, and let me know before we start flying toward the exit. We've already had our share of problems."

Seven minutes later, Terman thought he had successfully bypassed the trip switch—but he was horrified to see that the hydraulic system that opened the doors had not kicked in. The control station's floor was strewn with engineering drawings and schematics; Terman and three other engineers were frantically tracing hydraulic lines and arguing about what to do next.

As they started to pick up speed from the slope of the tunnel, Palmer tried to focus on possible options. If the brakes won't slow them down, they would have to jump; that was a poor option given their speed and the rock walls of the tunnel. They also had exceeded the stay time; they had to get the hell out of the mountain. He strained at the braking lever, hoping that he could cut the speed.

Fisher and Woods were hanging on for dear life as Palmer struggled to remain in control; his eyes were fixed on the remaining stretch of tunnel, searching for a gleam of light indicating the doors were opening. After what seemed an endless period of time, the transporter schussed past the tunnel walls, creaking and swaying unsteadily, and the first glimmer of light appeared.

Inside the control station trailer, Doug Terman and Phil Gunderson watched as the transporter raced for the exit. They finally got the system working. One of the engineers had decided at the last minute to bleed off the air from the vacuum pumps sealing the doors. The doors finally started to open when the transporter was approximately three minutes from the exit and fully opened with some thirty-five seconds to spare.

David Andrews had, without being aware of it, balled both hands into fists. "Can we stop the goddamn thing at this speed, Phil?"

"I think so—if it doesn't get airborne. At least the engineer who designed the transporter tracking system had his head screwed on right."

The engineer has built the tracks leading from the exit on a gradual rise to slow a runaway transporter similar to a runaway truck exit on certain highways. As an additional precaution, when they heard that the transporter braking system has some design problems, Terman had ordered his team to build a barrier of soft dirt where the inclined tracks ended.

The transporter shot through the exit and began to sputter and slow on the inclined tracks before plowing into the soft dirt mound where the tracks ended. The dirt exploded and showered the transporter. At first, Palmer did not move. When he heard Bob Fisher calling, he slowly started to get up although he was not sure his legs would work. He saw Fisher and Woods wiping dust from their eyes.

"Now I know why I have never liked roller coasters,"

Fisher said. "Remind me never to ride on one of these things again. Give me a bomb any day!"

Cole Palmer's stopwatch clicked off an elapsed time of one hour and twenty-one minutes.

CHAPTER 38

Mexico City

The day before the opening of the Promontorio Mountain Repository, a series of indiscriminate bombings created unimaginable fear and anxiety in major cities of Mexico. The Posadas government declared a military-enforced curfew in Mexico City, stifling the normal busy life of the city and adding to the crisis atmosphere. In the United States, the Republicans in Congress scheduled immediate hearings on the loan package proposed by Washburn after Posadas's White House visit.

The final bomb was detonated in the Tijuana Central Market on Saturday morning—the same day the presidents of the United States and Mexico attended the repository opening ceremony. It turned the marketplace into a meat grinder; killing many people in the crowded market stalls.

The bombings put the Mexican crisis back on the front pages of every major newspaper around the world—just as reports about the Chiapas massacre had stopped running.

Navarro was pleased. The government's position—that the bombings were intended to disrupt the national elections and not part of some broader revolutionary movement—did little to ease the growing fear and tension in Mexico as rumors spread about possible new terrorist outrages. After the Tijuana bombing, the governor of California closed the San Diego–Tijuana border, adding to the confusion and anxiety on both sides.

Navarro took another drag on his cigar as a political commentator on Mexico's leading news program reported that the left-center PRD and Hidalgo's Independent Parties were now ahead in the most recent presidential poll. Navarro was still wondering who the mysterious Zircon was.

"I wonder what Zircon was thinking when he tried to buy me off. Did the naive bastard really believe that he could tell me what to do? All that talk about being able to control the White House—the sonofabitch didn't know who he was dealing with," Navarro thought, as he sat in his huge living room with its large and gaudy pieces of furniture with gold detailing. "Nothing can stop us—including the fools in Washington. The bomb at Promontorio will force them to drop the ruling party and stop interfering."

CHAPTER 39

Promontorio Mountain
Saturday Morning

José Chapa was not in any hurry and purposely avoided the new highways with their tollbooths and traffic. He enjoyed taking the old roads through the small villages as he headed for the Buenaventura junction. When he reached it, he turned east and followed Highways 10 and 28 until he arrived at a small mining town that had seen better days. The only thing that made Sahuaripa special was its proximity to Promontorio Mountain.

Chapa slowed and turned the rented Toyota sedan in a dusty, poorly cared for park, empty of people and located in the poorest section of town. He lowered the windows and spread his long and powerful arms wide apart, yawning. He looked like any other traveler taking a break from driving on the hot and desolate roads. Through his dark sunglasses, he saw that not a soul was stirring in the heat of the day; an occasional truck passed through the town without stopping.

Chapa checked his watch to the digital dash clock, removed his sunglasses, and picked up a pair of high-powered binoculars, which he focused on the repository site's perimeter, some two miles distant. It was 11:25. He could see the bunting-decked platform where dignitaries and official guests were standing and talking to one another or seated and fanning themselves by waving the program back and forth. Chapa noticed Mexican and U.S. security forces maintaining a cordon around the speaker's platform. Focusing in tight, he could make out the figures of the two presidents, although he was too far away to see their faces. He had seen President Washburn only on television, so he had not realized how tall he was, as he towered over Posadas.

Chapa put his dark sunglasses back on and waited. There was no breeze and the heat was stifling but it did not bother him. Chapa had disciplined himself to withstand every sort of discomfort by devoting his full, intense concentration to the job at hand.

It was almost 12:00. A quick check with the binoculars showed that everyone had taken their seats on the platform. Chapa pulled another cigarette from his shirt pocket, lit it, and leaned back watching the dashboard clock. In moments, he would shift his binoculars on the entrance to the mountain repository. He was not sure what he would see or hear, since the bomb was buried deep in the massive mountain. Chapa was exhausted and simply did not care. He would report whatever he saw and heard when he made his call.

CHAPTER 40

Promontorio Mountain

Earlier on Saturday morning, two hours before the opening ceremony was to begin, Liz Cramer was in her room in the guest quarters, packing her clothes in a small suitcase. She had slept poorly and eaten a hasty, skimpy breakfast. Cole Palmer, Bob Fisher, and Chief Woods had been whisked away from the transporter by Sarah Chan, who took them first to a decontamination facility and then quarantined them, pending tests of skin particles, mucous secretions, blood samples, and other unpalatable measures to determine the degree of cumulative exposure. She also needed to determine if any of them had breathed in traces of some of the most worrisome elements and isotopes, those with long half-life and high carcinogenic potential.

Apart from a phone call from Chan around 11:00 P.M. last night, in which she assured Liz that the preliminary indications were, according to the dosimeters worn by each of the three men, that they had exceeded the limit postulated by the radiation specialist at Los Alamos by only two rads. There was cause for some concern; careful and thorough medical follow-ups would be necessary for at least two years before it could be determined whether or not any of the three had health problems caused by the exposure.

Liz was not in the best of moods when a cheerful David Andrews stopped by, his breath rancid from the endless cups of coffee and cigarettes bummed from Doug Terman. His eyes were glistening with an almost manic excitement.

"Just wanted to say good-bye, Liz. The Mexican government has laid on a helicopter so I'm off to meet the president and Richard Snyder at the airport. I'm very happy about how everything turned out—I know the President will be pleased. If we can just get through this thing smoothly—"

"Oh, I'm sure everything will go just fine," she said, an acid tone in her voice. "You're the hero of the hour, David. Of course, your splendid achievement came at a cost— three good men almost got killed. Chief Woods took me aside and told me that he thought they had bought the farm. But you're lucky, Mr. National Security Adviser. Maybe your luck even rubs off on the people you use and exploit."

"Now just one goddamn minute, Dr. Cramer." Andrews was blushing with anger and his voice trembling. "Each one of those guys was doing a crucial job voluntarily. They knew what the odds were. Bottom line is that they were serving their country, as corny as that might sound."

"No, David," she shot back. "They were serving you— your fucking career, your political ends. I'm no fool. From things I picked up from Cole—and Willy Graham—you had your own secret agenda going in all this. I wonder what Richard Snyder would say if he knew about it. Maybe I should tell him!"

Liz deliberately turned her back on Andrews and slammed the lid of her suitcase shut.

"Liz, wait, you've got to understand—"

"Oh, I understand more than you think. You exploited that broken and dangerous—to himself and others—part of Cole Palmer. He promised me that he wouldn't get involved in this kind of business—and then you did nothing to stop him. How could you, David? With you for a friend, Cole doesn't need any enemies."

Angry tears began to run down her face and she brushed them away with her hand.

"Would you please get the hell out of here? I'm not sticking around to watch your moment of triumph. As soon as I can get back to the embassy, I am going to ask Ted Halligan to move heaven and earth to get me back to Langley on the next plane. You've used me, too. I was supposed to be your back channel. Instead you kept me in the dark, you did an end run around the ambassador, and you've been running a black op without a presidential finding to sanction it. I've had it with you, Mr. Andrews. I want you to get the hell out of my life!"

Andrews was taken aback by the ferocity of her attack but tried to put the best face on the situation. He didn't know how seriously he should take Liz Cramer's threat to tell Snyder whatever she knew. He had to get this genie back into the bottle.

"Liz, a 'finding' is requisite for covert intelligence operations—by your outfit or any of the other intelligence agencies. But NSC works a bit differently. As national security adviser my power is the power given to me by the president. Everything I have done has been sanctioned by him."

Andrews was a smooth, accomplished liar—but he had a strong feeling that Liz Cramer wasn't buying it.

"Look, we can discuss all this later. I have to get to the airport. I think you have badly misunderstood what has been going on during the past two weeks—and I wouldn't believe everything that busybody Graham told you."

"Go get on board that damn helicopter. You don't have

to worry—I probably don't have enough information to make a case against you. Though you never know . . ."

She dropped her suitcase on the floor and put her hands on her hips, giving Andrews a withering glare.

"Let me tell you one thing, mister—you're no Henry Kissinger. When it comes to playing high-stakes games and deviousness, you're not even remotely in his league."

David Andrews had spent forty-five minutes with the president after he arrived at the airport. He also talked with Richard Snyder. The president was elated by the news that the bomb had been safely disabled. In fact, he wanted to go inside the mountain and look at it. Andrews had carefully described the events leading up to the decision to attack the bomb in place—at great risk. He told the president that he was willing to take the risk to protect his reelection hopes.

At that point, Snyder gave him a wry smile and said, "Yes—and protect our jobs, David. A noble effort, indeed. But we all have to bear in mind that sometimes the end does not justify the means."

Washburn seemed puzzled by the tone and content of Snyder's remark. But Andrews felt his heart sink. What did Snyder know? And how long had he known it? He had changed Washburn's speech at the last moment. There was a good chance that everything Andrews had done could be undone.

Washburn, aware of the strained relations between the two men, and baffled as to the cause of it, decided to change the subject.

"David, President Posadas and I have greenlighted SKY-HAWK, as you know. We've seen enough devastation from what the other bombs have done. We intend to stop them. The operation gets under way tomorrow. We will be flying in men and material tonight."

A note of grim determination came into the president's voice.

"I had some time flying down to think over our problems with Mexico. I think you know Richard's position," he said, glancing at the secretary. "I think he is right—we can't dump Posadas. He doesn't deserve it and it's not the right thing to do after what they have been through with these bombings. When the previous administration cut Hidalgo off at the knees, I was thoroughly in agreement. Now I am not so sure."

The president removed his glasses and rubbed his eyes.

"You know, it's not just Mexico that is under attack. The United States is under attack as well. If the CIA is right, the responsibility for this deliberate campaign to destabilize Mexico and topple the ruling party rests with the drug cartel. I'm damned if I am going to stand by and let them get away with it. By God, with SKYHAWK, we can destroy them before they start bombings on our side of the border. And we need Posadas in place to be successful. He's gone way out on a limb to allow a substantial American force to operate in his backyard. Damn few countries—damn few presidents—would stand for that. But he has no choice. Nor do we. We have to hit them hard and fast and let the ruling party take the offensive in the last months before their elections. We can discuss all this later. By the way, I had the DOE order Dr. Mills to go to work on getting M-0061 removed from the repository as soon as possible—and no leaks to the media. We need to see if it leads us back to the other suitcase bombs and the drug cartel."

The opening ceremony of Promontorio Mountain Repository was uneventful and a huge media success by any measure. Ambassador Reimann was beaming with pleasure. All his hard work to keep things on an even keel was paying off. President Posadas was at his best—he deftly characterized the opening of the repository as a symbol of increased cooperation between the United States and Mexico. President Washburn came out with a ringing statement of support for Mexico's government and expressed compassion for the sufferings of the Mexican people, not just from terrorism but also the pall of economic disaster that had fallen over the nation. The ruthless and indiscriminate bombings over the past week simply stiffened the resolve of both nations to strengthen the friendly relations between them. At the conclusion of his speech, he walked over and warmly embraced the Mexican president. The picture of that *abrazo* played on the front pages of every newspaper in Mexico.

Grissini insisted on driving Cole Palmer and Liz Cramer to the airport where the ambassador's aircraft was waiting. They would join Reimann and fly back to Mexico City. When they arrived at Hermosillo, Palmer could see the president and David Andrews boarding Air Force One.

Twenty-five minutes later, they were heading south toward Mexico City. Everyone seemed relaxed but Cole and Liz. They sat next to each other but making conversation was awkward. There were things to be said that could not be discussed in the plane. The past forty-eight hours should have been a defining moment in the relationship between the two—but Palmer knew that he and Liz had possibly gone past the point of no return.

CHAPTER 41

White House

On board Air Force One, Andrews relaxed for the first time in days. He even thought about collapsing in one of the compartments forward where there were beds for VIPs traveling with the president. But he knew he could not sleep. The unsettling exchange with Liz Cramer had his mind working overtime. Maybe later, he thought. I can sort things out with her. I need to tie all these things together before the president comes down from his high and starts asking questions. "Now what have I missed?" Andrews asked himself.

"Sir, there is a SPECAT that just came in," the duty radiomen interrupted. The special category message was brief, scheduling a cabinet morning briefing and a couple of other events for the president. Andrews was not surprised.

Snyder is running with the ball, Andrews thought. I wonder how he will play it. Well, two can play that game and I'm not ready to quit yet.

He started drafting his own message—one that the president would have to see, approve, and release while enroute to Washington. When he finished the first draft, the mess sergeant informed Andrews that dinner was ready and that the president would not be joining him and Snyder. Washburn treasured the time on Air Force One where he could work and think without interruptions.

Andrews was not ready just yet to start fencing with Snyder. He rang for a steward and asked for a meal to be served to him on a tray at his seat.

"Well, you did your magic again sergeant. Great dinner, thank you." He walked aft with his coffee cup to one of the writing tables in the lounge area. Fortunately, he had the lounge all to himself.

"This should help you to sleep, sir." Sergeant Williams placed a snifter of brandy on the corner of the desk. The brandy had an immediate effect, warming and relaxing him. After making a couple of changes in the message, Andrews was satisfied. The message, drafted for the president's release, discussed the significant political impact associated with the successful opening of Promontorio Mountain and the opportunity for the ruling party to take the offensive. It also subtly noted the important role of the national security adviser in preventing a catastrophe at the repository—an event that could have destroyed the ruling party and severely damaged the United States government.

He walked forward to the elaborate comm-center and handed the draft to the president's duty communications officer.

"When the President is up and about, I want this shown to him for his approval, without any delay. Do you follow me?"

The major nodded. "Yes sir. Once the light comes on, I'll submit it to the boss. Once he OKs it, I'll send it out priority."

* * *

Andrews could not believe that he got over four uninterrupted hours of sleep as he woke up at the moment of touchdown at Andrews AFB. When he got home, Brooke was waiting. She was shocked at his appearance. His eyes were puffy and he was obviously under considerable strain.

"It looks like you had a hard week, David. Why don't you take off tomorrow so we can catch up. I have a million things to tell you."

David followed Brooke upstairs. "I wanted to call you, honey. I just seem to get so involved. Anyway, I missed you . . . a lot more than you think. Unfortunately, tomorrow is impossible—although nothing sounds better than spending a day with you. The president has called a cabinet meeting and I need to be there."

"I figured that—and how many times have I heard that before? Each year you seem to get more involved in this or that. We need time, David."

"I know . . . and I promise it will happen. I really do mean it. For the first time in months, I think we have things under control."

"You mean until the next crisis."

"I know, Brooke," said David as he got into bed. "I know what you are saying and I will do something about it. I just need a little more time."

"Time for your work but no time for me. I've heard that before."

After a minute of silence, Brooke turned to see why David had not answered. The next thing she heard was David's heavy breathing. She looked at him and turned off the light.

Andrews had his moment of glory as Washburn opened the cabinet meeting by recounting how ably he had handled the crisis with the bomb at Promontorio Mountain. Richard Snyder gave him a warm, congratulatory smile, but Andrews wondered what was really going on in that powerful and crafty mind.

Andrews, unprepared for the effusiveness of Washburn's praise, gathered his wits about him. "Um . . . well . . . thank you, Mr. President. If you had a chance to see the president's message, the real heroes are folks like Cole Palmer, Jack Tisdale and his SEAL Team, and the EOD Team . . . and all the dedicated people at the repository. What they did took a lot of guts, especially inside the mountain. I feel proud to know them."

Andrews glanced at Richard Snyder but Snyder's expression told him nothing.

As the meeting went forward, it was clear that Washburn fully appreciated what a close run it had been at Promontorio Mountain. An explosion inside the highly controversial repository would be a body blow to his attempt to enhance support for Mexico—and the president knew it.

"Okay. What do we have?"

"Unfortunately, very little at this time. We also need to move carefully, sir." Snyder could see that the president was getting impatient and continued before he got too out front. "Politically, we do not want to acknowledge anything about the bomb at this time. No one knows anything about it except the few committee chairmen and the leadership in Congress—people I felt needed to know."

"But the press will kill us if they find out that we are suppressing the presence of that bomb," the chief of staff protested.

"It is a risk we have to take," Snyder crisply responded. "We need to check out the repository bomb and compare it with what we know about the other five bombs. We can't afford to make a mistake and get out ahead of this."

A spirited discussion followed with the CIA director leading the charge for some type of response against the drug cartel. The president allowed the debate to continue before nodding to Snyder.

Andrews had guessed, correctly, that Snyder would play Operation SKYHAWK as his trump card.

"I think Les has a point, Mr. President. But we should not jump the gun. We are just getting assets positioned for SKYHAWK. I gather that Defense and DEA believe that an initial strike could be made as early as tomorrow."

State paused and took a drink of water. "What I am suggesting is a three-pronged attack. Attack the headquarters of the Mexico City drug cartel leaders; arrest high government and banking officials on the drug cartel payroll; and freeze the assets of banks and offshore institutions that launder the cartel's drug money. If we move quickly with an integrated series of actions, I think the ruling party has enough time to take the high ground before national elections."

Everyone started talking at once. The president shot Andrews a quick look. Snyder had gone way beyond what Andrews had advised the president about the right tempo for SKYHAWK and managing the political fallback on both sides of the border when it became clear how deeply the United States was involved in a domestic situation in another country. These lightening fast, integrated, and simultaneous actions were a new wrinkle.

"Damn it! You're right," Kerr agreed. "It might be the only way the ruling party is going to make it. If they don't, and they get thrown out of power, our problems will just begin." The vice president saw which way the wind was blowing and trimmed his sails accordingly. He was a member of the oversight committee, along with the secretary of defense and the directors of the FBI and CIA, and he wanted to be seen as playing a leadership role.

Leslie Drummond cleared his throat and began to speak. Browning had given Andrews a heads-up; Snyder and the CIA director had worked up something but he did not have time to dig out more information about it.

"We should be able to conclude the first phase of the operation before there is any organized response. Our people are primed and ready." He grimaced and said, sighing, "I wish I could confidently say the same thing about their Mexican counterparts."

"Can we trust them?" The chief of staff asked skeptically.

"All I can say is that we haven't detected any breech of security and we've ridden that horse hard. In addition, we'll have some of our advisors with them at all times."

"The way I see it, Mr. President," said Snyder, wanting to keep the president openly supporting his position, "Operation SKYHAWK can demonstrate that the Mexican president is leading instead of just reacting. It is his last chance to get back in the race."

"What do you think?" The president asked turning to the attorney general.

The attorney general turned to the president. "Well, it's risky of course, sir. President Posadas needs to be prepared to cover his, er, ass—and ours if the whole thing goes to hell in a handbasket."

Snyder, hoping to put an end to the discussion, broke in. "There won't be any guarantees, Harry. However, the consensus is that it is worth the risk." He was hoping that his statement would end the discussion.

The attorney general, however, had a few more remarks to make on the subject. "I want to add that it will be important to document every step of the operation, to make sure that everything is done within the framework of law, both here and in Mexico. We have to be able to withstand intense scrutiny by the media, Congress, the public. To that end, we have federal prosecutors and people who know how to manage the press working with the strike teams. When the time is right, we can release footage of the operation to the television networks. It will pay big dividends when the high-priced cartel lawyers counterattack. It is risky. But if it is done properly, I agree with Richard that there are no options left."

The president looked around the room. He remembered the forceful assertion from the national security adviser that he could not withstand another crisis in Mexico. He also knew that his FTAA initiative could be fatally damaged if the ruling party failed.

"It sounds like you have everybody onboard with this, Richard."

"Forgive me for saying it again, Mr. President, but we really don't have any other options. In addition, a successful operation will go a long way in helping us justify our actions with the Congress."

Snyder saved the comment about Congress for the end and calculated that it would have a positive effect. The president was facing some dissention in his own party on the issue of continuing support for the ruling party. After fifteen minutes of additional questions, the president went around the table and everyone agreed that it was a "go." He ended the meeting by stating that he would personally call President Posadas and remind him of the importance of doing everything possible to keep things quiet until the first stage of the operation was complete.

As he got up to leave, he asked the vice president and secretary of state to accompany him to the Oval Office.

"I want to discuss Hidalgo," Washburn said quietly, taking Snyder by the arm and steering him through the door.

Andrews returned to his office and cancelled all appointments. Then he called his deputy and told him he would not be sitting in on the Deputies Committee meeting at four that afternoon.

It was clear that Snyder still was in charge; and the president had deliberately and publicly excluded him from the meeting. Hidalgo remained a wild card. Andrews desperately needed to find out if there had been any communication between Snyder and the former president of Mexico.

The president had told him in their discussion after the repository's opening that he did not want to rule out any option—including talking with the former Mexican president. Everything seemed to be shifting toward Hidalgo. Andrews knew how fatal it was to be left out when there was a sudden change in foreign policy—and it undermined the position he had been trying to sell to the president. The train was leaving the station—and Andrews was not on it.

CHAPTER 42

Promontorio Mountain

After the baffling absence of any apparent explosion at the repository, a badly worried Chapa had headed for the Hermosillo airport. He was seldom without a contingency plan prepared for situations like this, but he had failed to anticipate what he would do if the bomb was a dud. After he made his call, he would take a different route back to Mexico City following the coast through Guadalajara and think about his next move.

Chapa entered the terminal and headed to the rear of the building where the restrooms and a row of wall-mounted public telephones stood. He had ten minutes before he was supposed to place the call. He was so intent on trying to figure out what to report that he almost missed the movement of several nonuniformed personnel—personnel whom he knew instinctively, were federal agents. He knew they were setting up a security perimeter.

Within a few minutes, they started scurrying around three black limousines that had pulled up at the terminal entrance. Chapa inched closer to the wall phone and pretended to be looking up a telephone number in the tattered directory chained to the wall. Out of the corner of his eye, he recognized President Posadas shaking hands with the U.S. President.

"How in the hell did I miss seeing them when I entered the airport?" he asked himself. Hermosillo was the obvious destination for the president's aircraft. He shook off his momentary depression—he had failed to stay ahead of events and that could be fatal.

As Chapa watched, the two presidents returned to the limousines and headed for their waiting aircraft. He looked at his watch and saw that it was time for his call. Just as he started to dial, he saw a van with Promontorio Mountain Repository panel markings pull in to the departure area. Chapa watched a man and a woman jump out and shake hands with another man wearing an old marine corps baseball cap and a faded denim shirt. Chapa carefully slipped a small camera lying next to his automatic from his battered briefcase and snapped a series of pictures as the man and the woman picked up their bags and headed his way. When they walked past him, they turned and headed for the exit to the area reserved for private aircraft.

"What's the problem, boss?" Espinosa helped himself to some Scotch. He had never seen Navarro look so worried. When the phone on his massive desk rang he snatched it up and snarled, "You're late!"

Chapa's message was short. "No change recorded in the market. I repeat, no change."

Navarro stared at the phone. "Nothing?" He screamed.

Espinosa knew that whatever news his *jefe* was receiving, it probably boded ill for him.

"That is correct."

There was silence on the line before Chapa said slowly, "I will wait your market instructions."

When there was no response, Chapa slowly replaced the phone. He realized how shocked Navarro was. He did not like being the messenger bearing bad news. He walked to the large window across from the phone booth and saw the two people from the repository van getting inside a small jet with U.S. markings. He wondered who they were. He would send the pictures to Navarro. Let him figure it out.

Javier Navarro leaned against his desk for support as he slammed down the receiver. Espinosa watched Navarro's hooded eyes turn cold.

"But why?" He said aloud "It doesn't make sense . . . everything was taken care of."

"What happened, boss?" Espinosa had put down his drink.

"Somebody screwed up. The bomb did not explode. Nothing happened."

"I never trusted those rag heads boss."

"I'm not sure. Something else happened. It doesn't add up."

"I don't know boss, but do we care? The bomb could still go off."

Navarro did not answer and became more agitated. Espinosa did not know what to do.

"No . . . something else is working here. I don't know what it is but I'm going to find out."

Navarro was convinced that someone had crossed him. Espinosa waited until the right moment and departed without saying anything. At this particular moment, he wanted to be as far away from Navarro as possible.

Navarro was so intent trying to figure out what could have happened that he did not even notice Espinosa leaving. He tried to get a handle on the unanswered questions that echoed in his mind. If the United States had somehow discovered the bomb, how would they respond? Could they tie the bomb to the drug cartel? He knew, however, what really worried him. The predators who made up the drug cartel had little tolerance for a botched operation of this magnitude—especially if it resulted in pressure against the drug cartel.

For the first time, Navarro was concerned about his own survival. He had to shift responsibility for the failure.

Navarro sat in his high-backed leather chair thinking throughout the night, drinking coffee and brandy. Finally, at 3:10 in the morning, he found what was bothering him—a possible vulnerability—something that he did not want to acknowledge. Now he had to face the possibility that the United States had somehow deactivated the bomb. In addition, he had to consider that they could trace it back to the Minsk suitcase bombs. From there, the trail would lead to Ortega. As careful as Ortega was, they would find something. Navarro realized that he was spinning out a worst-case scenario but that is what he needed to do. He had a truly life-threatening problem.

Navarro remembered all the questions Ortega had asked in Acapulco. He had passed them off as simple curiosity at the time. Now, he wondered if Ortega had other reasons for asking the questions. He realized where he was heading. Navarro had found an answer that was beguilingly simple. The failure was not his but that of a traitor. He would provide a traitor's head to satisfy the drug barons. He had no misgivings about ordering the execution of his close associate; that was what it would take to survive.

Navarro refilled his glass of brandy and dialed the special number that he used when he needed immediate action. As the phone rang, he tried to convince himself that it would work.

It was a few minutes before six when the phone rang in the small, unpretentious apartment—one of several small places used by Chapa after assignments. They were sparsely furnished but provided everything needed for the brief periods that he used them. The unexpected early call startled Chapa. He was up but did not expect to talk to Navarro so soon following his call yesterday.

"Yes?"

"I am sorry about yesterday and apologize for my abruptness."

"I understand *patron*."

"We have some unexpected and urgent business as a result of your report." Navarro's thick brows moved up and down, as his tone became more urgent.

"Of course. What can I do?"

"Unfortunately, our business associate, Reno, wants out of his contract."

Chapa could not believe what he was hearing. Reno was one of the code words for Juan Ortega, a trusted associate. He shook his head as if to clear his thinking.

"How soon?"

"Immediately."

After a moment, Chapa nodded. "I understand."

"I will provide my reasons for the buy-out when we next get together."

"There is no need. It will be business as usual."

"There are other matters."

"Yes."

"Remember the airport pictures you faxed?"

"Yes. I have copies on the table in front of me."

"The tall man in the leather flight jacket with the woman has made inquiries and needs information. I understand he is associated with the museum. Can you deal with him?"

Museum was a code word for the U.S. Embassy in Mexico City.

"That might pose some problems if I get delayed in meeting with Reno. I might have to use some other associates."

"Yes, I understand. You take care of it."

* * *

Navarro's informant, roused out of bed in the middle of the night, was an employee on the embassy's cleaning staff. After receiving the faxes of the pictures from Navarro, he had made a number of calls, described the man in the pictures, and discovered that Washington had sent Palmer to Mexico City as their antidrug point man. Was he Zircon? He did not have anything solid to suggest that the man in the picture had played a part in the disabling of the repository bomb—other than a gut feeling. If he was the mysterious Zircon—and if the timing were better—he would get rid of Zircon now. He did not like the man or the way he bragged about what he could do. He would take care of him when he least expected it. Zircon or not, Palmer was now a target.

After spending most of the day making inquiries with dozens of contacts that provided information he required, Chapa headed toward the Zona Rosa, a fashionable area of Mexico City. It was time to deal with Ortega—although he was not looking forward to it. Chapa was filled with a growing sense of anxiety; if Navarro could turn on Ortega, whom would he turn on next?

CHAPTER 43

U.S. Embassy
Mexico City

The ambassador's aircraft arrived at the Mexico City Airport annex around midnight. On the ride into the city, Palmer and Liz Cramer had little to say to one another. When the embassy car dropped Liz off at her home, they agreed to meet in the morning.

Palmer skipped the morning run and walked directly to the embassy, cutting through the park. He got a crisp salute from the marine at the security checkpoint and a whispered "Bravo Zulu, sir!" The Navy signal, standing for "well done," meant a great deal to him. The bonds of the service still mattered. A lot. When he reached his office in the secure area, he slowly went through the accumulated and neatly piled correspondence—some had notes on yellow stickies explaining why Halligan's secretary had underlined certain things in cables and memos. He drafted responses to three memos, scribbled a thank-you on the top one, and left them on the secretary's desk to get them typed up. Then he went down to the ops center where Willie Graham was eagerly awaiting him.

"Hello, Willie. Good to see you. Do the marines report my every movement?"

"Just those people who take the basement stairwell and trip the alarm circuit."

"I'm scared of dark and closed spaces like elevators."

"Right—that's not what I heard from your little repository operation. Do you have time to brief me?"

Palmer gave Graham a condensed version of what had taken place. He suspected that Willie had already heard most of it.

"You were damn lucky, Cole."

"You're right about that. It just wasn't the bomb. I thought I had other things to prove. I'm getting too old for this stuff." And, Palmer thought, I have screwed it up with Liz. How could I have been so damn dumb?

"So what happens now?"

"We need to find out if the bomb matches the remains the Mexican authorities collected from the other ones and what we received back channel from the Russians."

"If anyone can do it the FBI lab can. They are good at what they do . . . matching the residue and trace materials to determine the signature characteristics of a bomb. I think we'll find the Minsk-Eme connection."

Palmer shook his head. "I hope so. We need the evidence before we go after them."

"For your information, the national security adviser is with the president and cabinet now."

Palmer looked at Graham with a wry smile. "Do you keep track of everyone, Willie?"

"No, but I try and keep on top of where the players are."

Both men were startled when Liz Cramer suddenly appeared; they had not noticed her entering the ops center.

"What's new?" Liz asked Graham.

After a night's sleep, Liz's deep blue eyes and dazzling smile were a welcomed sight to Palmer. But the smile was bestowed on Graham; her expression was guardedly neutral when she looked at Palmer. He kept watching her and reminding himself how he had made a mess of things. Palmer was always the toughest critic of his own feelings. For the first time since Catherine's death, he wanted to believe that he was free from the dark side of his life. At the same time, something was holding him back. He could not shake the feeling that there was still something out there, threatening his new equilibrium and casting a dark shadow over his future with Liz Cramer—if there was going to be one.

"Not much. I talked with Luis Vasquez a couple of times and he wants to talk with you, Cole. I didn't tell him when we expected you back."

"Thanks. I'm glad you reminded me. I need to talk with him. Anything else?"

"Um, well . . . no, not right now."

For the second time, Palmer caught something strange in Graham's body language. It was in the way Graham looked at him. He told himself to check into it later.

It was almost eleven o'clock when the NSC direct line rang. The watch-stander patched the call through Graham's office. Graham handed the phone to Palmer and started to leave but Palmer motioned him to stay.

"Sorry I took so long getting back, Cole. The meeting with the president went longer than expected. By the way, he asked that I pass along his personal well done to all of you and wants to thank you personally."

"You're on the speaker phone, David, and everyone copied."

"Great. Willie are we synced-in on secure voice?"

"Yes sir. Both ends are locked solid."

Andrews briefed them about the president's meeting and

the decision to go hard and fast with Operation SKY-HAWK. He quickly detailed how the operation had expanded.

"The president wants to know what we found out about the bomb. Anything new?"

"Not yet. I called earlier and the EOD guys were still in the process of getting it moved. They are handling it with a lot of respect."

"Okay. Let me know the minute you hear anything. The lab guys are sure, from what the Mexican authorities sent up, that everything in the five explosions matches up, but they have to check the characteristics against those of the repository bomb. I think we are close to putting this . . . you know . . . the suitcase bombs, Ortega's trip, and money transfers to bed."

"When do things kick off?"

"That's the good news. The president was willing to go forward with the FBI information we had on the bombings. The operation commences tomorrow at midnight, local time."

"Wow! That is a change for Washington."

"Yeah, right. The only thing that could hold things up is some surprise about the repository bomb."

"Well, if I don't hear back from the site in an hour or so, I'll call them."

"Okay. Switching gears, the president wants to keep the operation under tight control. He told President Posadas the same thing when he called him. Surprise will be our greatest asset. The president has a lot at stake here with the Hill and is betting that success with the operation will cover any sins of omission about actions during the past week. Anyway, the secretary of state does not want to disseminate this info—that includes Vasquez or anyone else."

"Roger, but for what it's worth, we need to start trusting somebody down here. Vasquez could be a key player."

"I hear you. State is calling the shots, Cole."

"What do you want us to do?"

"Keep your head down and ears open. That's all I have until we firm up a meeting with Vasquez—and possibly Hidalgo."

Liz Cramer, Graham, and Palmer sat quietly for a few minutes thinking about the conversation with Andrews. One of the ops center watch-standers opened the door and handed Palmer two messages. One was from the ambassador who wanted to see him and the other was a call from Vasquez. Before he left to go upstairs to the ambassador's office, Palmer pulled Liz aside and quietly asked her if they could meet for a late lunch.

Palmer was just about to step into the elevator with Liz when, acting on impulse, he went back to Graham's office. "I need to tell Willie something. You go ahead, Liz.

"Willie? I got the feeling that you didn't tell me everything."

"I figured you caught it so I waited at the door. I don't really know how to say it and the information could be out in left field anyway."

"Just give it to me straight, Willie. I need to see the ambassador."

"Okay. The federal police have finally screwed up the courage to run phone taps on all of Navarro's lines. They informed Halligan this morning that it looks pretty certain that there is a contract out on you. Ted wanted to make sure you got the word—he's out of pocket at the moment."

"Um, what the hell? Why me?" Palmer frowned and scratched at the scab forming on a small cut on his forehead, a souvenir of his head hitting the control panel of the transporter when it plowed to a stop.

"I don't know. That's all they are telling us, Cole."

Palmer did not say anything for a few seconds. He

thought about several reasons why he might be a target but none of them made sense.

"Thanks for not bringing it up with Liz present, Willie. She's been through enough."

"Agree. Let me give you a piece of advice. I've seen these things before. I think it is time for you to get out of Mexico City. Someone else can finish the job."

"I'll think about it—but I'm not going to let those bastards run me out of town."

"I sorta guessed that reaction but for God's sake, stay alert and don't go wandering around alone. Mexico City is dangerous enough for the civilians. I'll keep pushing for what I can find out from my sources."

"Thanks, Willie. Now I have to run and see the ambassador. If Luis Vasquez calls again, tell him I will be back to him within an hour. Also, if the repository calls, find me."

Cole briefed Ambassador Reimann on the latest from Promontorio Mountain and the FBI lab's discoveries while quietly hoping that the ambassador would not ask something he could not discuss—Andrews's murky role in all this business.

"I'm still disappointed that someone decided to keep me in the dark. After all, I was the one who got the warning from Hidalgo."

"Yes sir, I understand. It was probably because Washington had some real doubts about the former president's information."

The ambassador was not satisfied. "Well, I don't know what's happening at State anymore. The president really surprised us with his unexpected comments during his NATO ministers speech. It was only a matter of hours before President Posadas sent for me and it was professionally embarrassing. Thank God we got things back on track at the opening ceremony."

"I understand, sir," Palmer responded, knowing that

there was a good deal he didn't understand. Maybe Ambassador Reimann wasn't the only one being kept in the dark. What was Andrews holding back? He knew there was something—but what?

As Palmer walked down the hallway toward the elevator, he was thinking about how much he disliked the devious little games played in Washington. Andrews, however, was a big cat thoroughly at home in the jungle. He hunted alone; how much he trusted him, what had happened to their friendship because of Andrews's fixation on his goals, was not at all clear to Palmer. As tempting as it was to walk away, Palmer had decided to hang tight with David Andrews and help him where he could. Whatever had happened in the past, trust and loyalty remained sacred to Palmer. It was the only way he knew how to live and retain his sanity in an increasingly insane world.

"You're back. Where shall we go for lunch, Cole? I'm hungry."

"How about the cafeteria?"

Liz stopped and gave him a funny look. "Well, I was hoping for one of those quiet little places off the Zocalo that we keep hearing about. I want some privacy. We have to talk—and I don't want to do it in a room full of embassy personnel."

Palmer briefly debated whether to tell Liz about the news he'd just gotten from Willie Graham—and then realized that it was the worst thing he could do. Equally bad to keep it secret, he thought. If she finds out, one way or the other, I am in serious trouble.

"Well, ah . . . you know, if the repository calls, I should probably be around."

Liz could tell something was bothering him and decided to go along.

"Okay, maybe we'll be lucky and find a table in a quiet corner."

As they walked toward the cafeteria, Palmer found himself thinking of a saying by Samuel Johnson: "When a man is about to be hanged, it concentrates his mind wonderfully."

CHAPTER 44

Mexico City

Operation SKYHAWK commenced with antidrug assault teams using unmarked U.S. Army helicopters and deploying under cover of darkness, to small private airstrips on the outskirts of Mexico City, Guadalajara, Ciudad Juarez, Tijuana, and Monterey. Prepositioned carryalls waited to transport the assault teams to their designated targets.

The assault teams—divided into five elements of fifteen men in each, armed with automatic weapons, and another five elements of ten in backup—raided the drug cartel strongholds and front companies, achieving complete tactical surprise and encountering little or no opposition. An additional force of fifty Mexican and U.S. antidrug officers stormed known drug laboratories and warehouses and seized tons of illegal drugs and large bundles of cash. In Mexico City, special teams of lightly armed officers, federal judicial officials, and reporters from the TV and major radio stations made simultaneous arrests of prominent government officials, bank presidents, and others suspected of tax evasion and money laundering.

Hours before the operation, the federal attorney general in Mexico City sent messages to the chairmen of the Central Bank of Switzerland, the Grand Caymans, and the Bahamas. He requested that they freeze specific numbered accounts—allegedy funded with illegal drug monies—until they could file for formal hearings. The Mexican finance minister and the U.S. treasury secretary made follow-up calls to ensure cooperation and compliance.

The stunning surprise achieved through meticulous organization of coordinated, simultaneous actions resulted in overwhelming success according to reports that started filtering in to the command center set up inside a vacant warehouse on the outskirts of Mexico City. The assault forces arrested four of the six major drug barons without interference. In Mexico City, the early evening news reported that the special teams of law enforcement officers summarily arrested nineteen government, union, and banking officials, swooping down on them at their homes, dinner parties, and in one case, a mistress's apartment.

As planned, lawyers from the offices of the U.S. and Mexican attorney generals accompanied each element of the assault teams to ensure lawful compliance with arrest guidelines. In addition, the teams videotaped each phase of the operation for supportive documentation. The major television networks, on both sides of the border, received unexpected and dramatic videotapes in time for the late evening news programs.

The crushing assault on the drug cartel got enormous coverage across the world. The on-site videotapes highlighted one drug baron, Ernesto Chavez, as drug enforcement agents and officials from the attorney general's office unceremoniously removed him from the Princess Apartments in Acapulco. Another video segment showed an enraged Arturo Espinosa barely subdued while resisting arrest and shouting curses and threats against the government. It offered a chilling look at one of the real but long-hidden faces of the drug empire. The following day, the newspapers and major networks continued with additional and damning coverage. At one point, CNN, ITV, and other international broadcast networks showed the highly paid lawyers who represented members of the drug cartel scurrying into the Justice Building in Mexico City and trying to cover their faces, as ranks of television cameramen and photographers surrounded the entrances to the building.

President Posadas was energized and thrilled by the success of the initial operation and he capitalized on it by making a nationwide TV address, one that was also picked up and broadcast by Spanish-language stations in the United States as well as stations in other Hispanic countries. He explained in forceful terms why he initiated the action and why he employed a special force of officers outside the normal chain of command, and took pains not to embarrass those in the police or federal law enforcement agencies that had not been given a part in the historic operation.

The president surprised his staff by taking questions following his address.

"Were the actions in retaliation to the bombings?"

"Yes. As long as I am in office, Mexico will do what is necessary to protect our citizens and maintain our democratic principles."

"Do we have proof of who is behind the bombings?"

President Washburn had asked Posadas to withhold any information on the bombings—and especially anything about Promontorio Mountain—until they had time to examine the bombings. President Posadas adroitly ducked the question.

"We are unable to be more specific in order not to hamper our ongoing investigation. However, I want to reassure the country and the relatives of those killed and injured that we will not rest until we apprehended those responsible."

Jorge Posadas was starting to enjoy the opportunity to be vigorously presidential after so many months on the defensive. He was a profoundly different man from the one that had quietly toiled and served the ruling party. He was now his own man, not theirs.

"Let me make it very clear. We will not stand by and let the corrupt control Mexico. We will continue to attack the illegal drug organizations and prosecute those corrupted officials who aid and abet them."

The success of Operation SKYHAWK and the favorable response by the public to the president's address generated a growing wave of support for the ruling party in the final months before national elections. In the United States, the major networks carried comprehensive reports and analyses. During White House ceremonies honoring the World Series champions, President Washburn stated that he fully endorsed and applauded the actions in Mexico. In Congress, the Republicans, wisely deciding to go with the flow of public opinion, refrained from criticizing the questionable use of American forces in the operation and a majority of both the House and Senate came together in support of Washburn's program to aid Mexico in its economic and social crisis. Washburn's second term in next month's elections was all but wrapped up.

Following their release on bail pending investigation of tax evasion and illegal drug trafficking, the drug barons demanded a meeting with Navarro. He expected this and had his response prepared. Playing for time, he promised to meet with them in five days, present a plan to fight back against the government's campaign, and double drug profits in the next two years. In addition, Navarro informed the drug barons that a traitor had caused the problems; he would personally deal with that individual.

Ramiro Chemor called Victor Hidalgo from Mexico City as the news of Operation SKYHAWK broke.

"Yes, I have seen some of the CNN coverage. I was about to call you."

"I have to tell you, Victor, that it has been a major triumph for Posadas. Carlos Alvarez and the ruling party have closed the gap in the latest poll."

Hidalgo knew that Chemor was worried about their chances in the election. "I anticipated that, Ramiro. If my call to the U.S. ambassador forced the government to go on the offensive and stop the bombings and lawlessness, it was worth it. In the end, the people of Mexico will make their choice for president."

"I understand but if we want to remain in the race we have to find a way to recapture the momentum. The PRD took a major hit, with the government's attack on the drug cartel. We are the only real opposition to the ruling party."

Chemor sensed that this was not the right time to discuss campaign strategy. He was somewhat cheered up, however, when Hidalgo told him that he would fly to Mexico City in the next few days and get actively involved in the final months of the campaign.

Juan Ortega was one of the targeted individuals who had not been rounded up in the initial sweep. During that evening, he was dining with three of his banker friends at one of the exclusive private clubs for Mexico's business elite. Ortega had attended graduate school in the United States with two of the three guests. Years later, he was instrumental in their promotions to prominent banking positions—positions that ensured quiet cooperation with the drug cartel. No one really understood what Ortega did in his "consulting" business. He maintained a large suite of offices in the financial district and was quite active on the social scene. Few realized that he was a close associate of the Eme leader and accumulated a vast fortune from drug trafficking.

The club manager discreetly passed a message to one of the bankers, Jorge de la Vega, who read it and momentarily seemed to be in a state of shock. He recovered somewhat and asked to be excused. When he returned some minutes later, his face was ashen. He did not sit down.

"Gentlemen, something momentous is happening. There has been a massive wave of arrests of government officials and businessmen throughout the country. The directors of my bank have summoned me to an emergency meeting tonight. I don't know anything more. I suggest each of you call your bank immediately."

The others looked incredulously at de la Vega.

"What in the world do you mean—it's ten o'clock . . . why . . . what happened? What do you mean?"

"Please . . . please. That is all I know. Now, I . . . I must leave.

The banker was clearly on the edge of panic and had to clutch the back of a chair to steady himself.

As the other dinner members started getting up, Ortega pulled de la Vega toward one of the small sitting rooms off the dinning room.

"Oh God," he breathed. "I am so worried, Juan."

"*Por Dios!* Get hold of yourself. What in the hell are you talking about?"

"We have a serious problem."

His voice was quivering as he cringed and wiped his forehead. "Officials from the attorney general's office summoned the senior members of my staff to come to the bank immediately. When they arrived, government auditors were already present and they ordered that certain accounts be frozen."

"What accounts—and how long can they keep them frozen?" Ortega had a pretty good idea what the answer would be.

"It will depend on which countries—I mean, where the accounts were set up. Once frozen, we have to demonstrate that the account is clean. How did they get the special account numbers you established? We change them as directed every month."

"We have a contingency plan for something like this, right?"

Jorge de la Vega hunched his shoulders, as if he were a turtle trying to withdraw into the safety of his shell.

"We do . . . but . . . it's based on advanced notice from someone . . . you know. We shift account numbers and locations electronically. We have done it before. What went wrong? It is not our fault. No one alerted us."

"The bastards can't get away with this."

"What shall I do, Juan? They are arresting people all over the city."

Ortega looked with contempt at Jorge de la Vega as he began to fall apart. He tried to concentrate and remember which of the offshore accounts held the largest assets.

"I need to make some calls," Ortega snapped and brushed his friend aside. He knew that he was in grave danger. The government had a way to keep someone detained before the lawyers cut through the red tape. In his case, it would be a disaster. He could not move the vulnerable accounts to other offshore havens. He tried to understand what was happening. Someone big must have talked. If that were the case, how far would it go, he muttered to himself? He ducked inside one of the empty manager's offices and closed the door. He faced a problem that was more important than protecting the drug cartel assets. Could the government tie him to the bombs?

He quickly realized that the time had come to use his escape hatch. He wiped the sweat off his face and forced himself to calm down and think clearly. He would not make the same mistakes as the bankers; he had an exit strategy. Ortega had always known that someday he might need a way out of his association with La Eme. He had secretly purchased a safe house in a part of the city that was close to the airport. He hoped that it had not been compromised.

Ortega also wondered if Chemor had betrayed him. He had taken a huge personal risk by tipping off his classmate and friend about the bombs and Promontorio Mountain. Had his passing on the information triggered this avalanche of disaster? He had hoped to curry favor with Hidalgo—if he got back into power. He had been sure that Chemor passed the information to Hidalgo. He was gambling that Hidalgo would be his insurance with Navarro.

Now he understood that his hopes had been dashed. Hidalgo was in no position to offer him protection. If Navarro discovered what he had done, he was a dead man. No one could help him except himself.

Ortega caught himself as he started to leave for the front entrance. He had parked his car hours earlier outside the club. It could already be the object of a search by the police in order to determine his whereabouts. So he had no choice but to abandon the vehicle.

Thinking quickly, he casually walked through the kitchen until he found the service entrance at the rear. The cook closing down the kitchen for the night didn't even look at him as he passed. Outside, in the dark alley behind the club, he began to make his way toward the main street. Ortega estimated that he was about eleven miles from his safe house—too far to walk, and the police could trace a taxi. Ortega stopped and turned back when he saw the light from the rear door of the club as it opened. Someone had come outside the same way he had moments before. At first, he thought someone followed him. He watched from the shadows and was relieved to see a busboy go over to a battered motor scooter. Jesus, he thought, that's it!

Ortega walked toward the young man. "Pardon me. Is that your scooter?"

"Yeah. Do you have a problem with it?"

"No problem at all. I would like to buy it from you."

"Are you joking? Someone dressed as you are?"

Ortega did his best to keep his face out of the illumination shed by a light over the service entrance.

"Well, yes. I see your point. However, I need to make some kind of dramatic entrance at my brother's birthday party tomorrow. You know what I mean—a real surprise; maybe drive right over the lawn to the terrace of his house. Look, I will pay you a very fair price."

Ortega guessed that the kid had not seen him in the club or as he exited through the kitchen. He could also tell that the busboy didn't believe a word of it—but was eager to make some fast and untaxable money.

The kid decided to throw out a big number for the eight-year-old scooter to see if the stranger would back off.

"Um . . . ah . . . okay—twenty-five hundred pesos?"

Ortega nodded and pulled out a large wad of currency. He handed the young man two one thousand peso bills and five one hundreds. Still amazed at his luck, the kid gave Ortega a key to the chain that secured the scooter to a standpipe.

As Ortega headed out of the alley on his slightly wobbly scooter, he heard the kid shout.

"How about the ownership papers . . . don't you want me to send them to you? Hey, wait!"

Within a half an hour, Ortega was near the safe house. He abandoned the scooter behind an empty building after discarding the license plate, then walked the remaining six blocks and carefully approached the house, alert for any signs that it was under surveillance. Ortega felt a wave of relief when he opened the front door and stepped inside. He was hot and dirty and he needed to relax. He had formulated a plan and, so far, his instincts had been on the mark. Ortega turned on the news, went straight over to the bar, poured himself a large glass of vodka over ice, and collapsed on the couch.

The midnight news amply demonstrated just how devastating SKYHAWK had been. He needed to make contact with the manager of his bank in Switzerland. Pushing back the sleeve of his shirt, which had a smear of grease on it from the scooter, he looked at his watch and tried to figure out what time it was in Geneva. His Swiss associate, who was deeply involved in the cartel's money laundering operations, could buy him some breathing space and keep La Eme off his back for at least a few days.

It was morning in Switzerland when he got through to Herr Bessler. When he heard what the manager had to tell him, he was crushed.

"All accounts, I repeat all 'special' accounts, have been impounded by the government."

"But surely you were able to move some of it as planned," Ortega stammered as he felt his hands begin to tremble.

"You know that is impossible. We have very strict laws. I can't move anything without specific directions from an account holder. Now it is too late."

When Ortega did not reply, the Swiss banker continued.

"I am very sorry. I will await your instructions."

When Ortega put the phone down, it was slippery from his sweat. He knew that he needed to vanish from the face of the earth—either he would make himself disappear or Navarro would kill him. Navarro would blame him for the loss of hundreds of millions—and that the drug barons would not be satisfied until the necessary execution took place, probably an excruciatingly slow and painful death.

* * *

Ortega kept some eight million dollars in bearer bonds and currency in safe deposit boxes in two London banks; both were rented under false names. He had tested the system several times, using the requisite documents. Crossing the border and flying out of the United States could pose some problems. He decided that after crossing the border, he would fly from a small airport in Texas to Detroit or Milwaukee before the last leg to London. He went to the back bedroom and opened a locked briefcase containing several passports, U.S. and British currency, and other identification papers. He opened the one piece of luggage in the closet to confirm the supply of clothing that he had neatly folded and packed. He figured that he could be in Heathrow Airport by tomorrow evening. As he returned to get his glass of vodka in the main room deep in thought about his trip, he was so horrified to see Chapa standing in the hallway that he could not speak. Chapa did not say anything as he looked at the hopeless, terror-stricken face of his friend and associate.

Ortega's limbs started to quake uncontrollably and his bladder released a burning stream of urine down his leg. He wanted to cry out and tell Chapa that it was all a mistake but he could not force the words from his frozen mouth. Even if Ortega had been able to beg him and provide reasons why he had failed, it would have made no difference because he was already dead in Chapa's mind. With a swift and forceful motion, Chapa dug the stiletto blade into Ortega's stomach and viciously pulled it free before repeating the thrust and hitting his left lung. Ortega collapsed; the last thing he saw before he died was the dark and implacable eyes of the man who killed him.

Chapter 45

Mexico City

When Andrews called Palmer Saturday night to tell him that the president was seriously considering making another trip to Mexico—"to bask, no doubt, in the warm glow of SKYHAWK's success," Andrews remarked sarcastically—he noticed hollowness in his friend's tone. He resisted the temptation to ask Palmer what was eating him, he would see him soon enough and repair any damage done to their friendship during recent weeks.

His late lunch with Liz Cramer, just before all hell broke loose with SKYHAWK, had left Palmer emotionally bereft and full of despair. After wiping a smear of ketchup off the tabletop before she set down her tray, Liz sat down and picked up her fork. Suddenly, before taking a bite of her grilled chicken, she looked at Palmer straight in the eye and announced that she was flying back to Washington as soon as Halligan clears it.

"I'm done here, Cole. And I told David Andrews to go screw himself."

For a moment, Palmer was so stunned that he said nothing. When he recovered, he asked quietly, "Does that mean we are finished, too, Liz?"

She took a sip of iced tea and stared down at her food.

"That largely depends on you, Cole. There's really no point rehashing things. You know how I feel. Please understand—I'm not blaming it all on you. Andrews has a lot to answer for, especially his letting you go into that damn tunnel. But I can't live this way. I need to feel safe— with you, about you."

"Liz, it's all been burned out of me, I swear. The reck-lessness, the hatred. I'm prepared to do whatever it takes to have a life with you—to make you feel safe, to convince you that I care enough about you to never go out on a limb again, not the way I did at the mountain, anyhow."

"What am I hearing, Cole—reservations, conditions, and buts?"

Palmer saw that she had nervously torn off bits of her roll, leaving flakes scattered on her tray. Her voice turned cold and she seemed to be receding from him, putting him into a kind of past tense.

"It's just not acceptable. You made a promise to me and I expected you to keep it. I don't believe you now. I can't . . . I just can't let it ride."

In her agitation, her voice had risen and Palmer noticed people at another table glancing at them curiously.

He reached over the table and tried to take her hand but she drew back and stood up.

"Please. Let's not make it worse." She got up, leaving her food untouched. "I won't be able to stop worrying about you. And I won't stop caring for you. But I'm going to be a tough sell, Cole."

* * *

Andrew's call had given Palmer an excuse to see Liz once more before she left. She might even want to delay her return and watch what would happen in the next few days. But he was quite sure that Andrews was not riding high on her personal popularity index, so that might be a negative. Crossing his fingers, Palmer hurried up to the CIA station and found out that Liz had left word earlier on that Sunday morning that she could be reached at the club that was part of the golf course and town house complex. After signing out an embassy car, he nervously edged into the insane Mexico City traffic.

When he got to the club, he went first to the pool and felt his heart beating rapidly as he saw her come out of the water, beads of water glistening on her one-piece swimsuit that complimented her voluptuous figure and her long, elegant legs. He felt a pang of raw, helpless desire as he watched her.

Then she saw him, shading her eyes with her hand. She sat down on a chair, vigorously toweling her hair and waited as Palmer made his way over to her. He told her about Andrews's imminent visit and she seemed to be anything but pleased by the news.

"What's going on? I didn't expect him back so soon."

"Well, he didn't say why he was coming and I didn't press him."

Palmer looked around and changed the subject; he was desperate to make a connection of some sort with her, to find some way to repair the damage, if he could.

"I'm going to ask David to take me off the case," he announced impulsively, surprising himself because he had made the decision in that instant.

"That is interesting, Cole. Something I will have to see. In the interim, you can give me a ride back to the embassy. I left the van there and I want to drive it home. I'll be right back. I need to take care of some things inside and get dressed." Liz slipped some shorts and a T-shirt over her suit.

* * *

It was almost six o'clock before Andrews joined Palmer and Liz Cramer in the ops center. It had been a week since the opening ceremony of the Promontorio Repository and Andrews appeared refreshed and rested. He briefed them on the next operational phase of SKYHAWK.

"According to what we hear on the TV, the drug barons took a real hit," Palmer said. "Halligan is going to have a complete report ready for the ambassador tomorrow morning."

"I intend to be present at that meeting. I want to suggest that the ambassador order a level-two security alert for the embassy and consular offices."

Palmer was surprised when Liz spoke up.

"Well, I agree with that. The drug barons have a brutal record of retaliation, certain people get eliminated and everyone gets scared off. They could strike back at both Mexico and the United States. Posadas has to stick to his guns, but I just don't know how strong his follow-up will be. The snake is badly wounded but it still has venom to spare."

Liz's comment startled Cole. Had Willy Graham given her some hint of the threat that was hanging over his head?

"You're right, Liz," Andrews said grimly. "That is why I told you to keep your head down for a while around there. Hopefully, we hit them hard enough so they can't immediately counterpunch."

"How about President Posadas? Does he have the balls to prosecute the arrested drug barons and government officials or will he back down as Liz fears?" Palmer asked.

"President Posadas says he'll hang in—but the problem is the judicial system backing him up."

"Sounds like the same old story to me," Liz said. "Mexico has a chronic problem prosecuting drug traffickers who always seem to buy enough political and judicial influence to beat the system."

"Unfortunately, you're right again, Liz. The president must force the prosecutors and judges to do their jobs vigorously—or fire them. It's not going to happen overnight but it is the best we can hope for."

Palmer was inwardly debating whether he should tell Andrews about Willy's info that a contract had been put on him. The real problem was that he was having a hard time believing it himself.

"Well, we better be prepared to stay the course if we're serious about getting anything done," Liz said thoughtfully.

"You sound like Richard Snyder, Liz. There is some good news. SKYHAWK has cleared the deck for the November elections—and substantially reduced the threat to a second term for Washburn. At this point, I think we ought to stand back and not get deeper into the situation down here. Operation SKYHAWK has given the ruling party some needed momentum for the final push before their national elections in July. It is now up to them. President Washburn has to worry about his own reelection; we should not try and push too much more down here."

"What does that mean? From what we have been hearing, Washburn has his second term locked up."

"It means just what it sounds like, Cole," Andrews retorted. "We don't want any new problems—and you never know about elections until the vote is counted. In addition, we can go only so far in dictating policy to the Posadas government."

"How does the secretary of state feel about it?"

This line of questioning openly irritated Andrews. "I'm not sure I really care. In my opinion, Richard Snyder has taken us too far down the road with the ruling party. He believes—sincerely believes—that Mexico is running out of chances to establish real democracy and the United States must hang tight with them—whatever happens."

"How can you disagree with that?"

"I don't disagree with it. When I was in the State Department, I developed many of the policies and initiatives that we are now seeing at work. The issue is simply one of timing and priorities. We need to get President Washburn reelected or we can forget any hope or progress in Mexico. Either the Posadas government goes all the way with SKYHAWK—or they are finished."

Liz looked at Palmer and shook her head, signaling him to drop it.

Palmer caught the signal, paused, and took a deep breath. "Okay, what's the next step? It's got to have something to do with why you are down here?"

Andrews relaxed. "Well, to be frank with you, the president—or more correctly, the secretary of state—wants Vasquez to join President Posadas's cabinet."

"What? At this late date? How do they expect to pull that off?"

Andrews smiled for the first time. "That's where you come in, buddy." Andrews explained that Snyder had persuaded the president that someone with the credibility of Vasquez was the only way to clean up the judicial system before their national elections. "His appointment will also strengthen the ruling party in the eyes of the voters."

"I agree with that although I'm not sure if Luis would agree."

"Anyway, Snyder also convinced the president to come to Mexico City as soon as arrangements can be worked out. The Secret Service will have to fly in all the vehicles, nail down airport security, and cover all the angles so it's going to take some time. But Washburn intends to give Posadas and his party a big boost."

"And you're down here as advance man?" Palmer asked sarcastically.

"C'mon, Cole—give me a break. My task is to convince Vasquez to join the cabinet before the president gets down here."

Liz Cramer was quietly steaming. Andrews was up to his old tricks by pushing Palmer to exploit his friendship with Luis.

"Okay, David," said Palmer somewhat cynically. "I'll give it a shot. But you gotta close the deal—not me."

While Andrews and Liz continued to discuss the problems involved in arranging for Washburn's visit to Mexico, Palmer rang Luis Vasquez at home.

"We have to meet, Luis—as soon as possible."

"Hey, Cole, *que pasa?*"

"It's not something I can discuss on the phone—and we are going to have a third person joining us."

Vasquez decided not to press Palmer further and agreed to meet him and the mysterious other party for lunch the following day at La Valentina, a restaurant frequented by many top executives in Mexico's leading financial institutions. The tables were set far apart; the staff was discreet—and very good at not overhearing patrons' conversations.

After Liz Cramer left for home, Palmer and Andrews had dinner at the Hotel de Cortes. As the minutes and then hours passed, David Andrews seemed to revert to his old self, the man who had formed a strong bond with Palmer during their years in the Navy and not the driven political animal he had turned into during his years in Washington.

Andrews ordered two healthy shots of Cardinal Mendoza, a muscular, dark brown Spanish brandy, after dinner and indulged himself with a cigar. He kept Palmer entertained with a running commentary on what he called, "The Beltway Comedy Hour,"—witty and mordant sketches of the private lives and foibles of people Palmer knew only as names in news stories. Both men forgot the passage of time. Even though people started eating dinner in Mexico City much later than in the United States, they sat there for so long that their waiter began to hover nearby and glance frequently and pointedly at his watch.

When Andrews dropped Palmer off at his hotel, he got out of the car and walked Palmer to the main entrance.

"Cole, I'm sorry you moved back to the bachelor officers quarters, although this place is a lot more comfortable than the real BOQs we stayed in years gone by. I gather you and Liz—"

Palmer was both surprised and resentful that Andrews had broached this painful subject.

"Jesus, David . . . you been having me followed or something?"

Andrews smiled and said apologetically, "Cole, you are kind of naive about some things. An embassy is like a ship; the scuttlebutt goes around pretty quickly. Halligan dropped a hint or two during our phone conversations over the last few weeks."

"I don't want to get into it, David. It's old news, now. Liz is taking the first plane back to Washington."

"Don't give up on me, Cole," said Andrews in hushed tones as he put his arms around his old friend. "I've found out a lot about myself in the past few weeks . . . what really matters to me. I know I am on Liz's shit list—and I deserve to be. In fact, I am on Brooke's shit list, too. I'm going to do everything I can to straighten things out—in both quarters, so to speak."

Palmer noticed that David was trying to hold back from outright crying. He was somewhat embarrassed because he did not know how to react. He finally grinned at Andrews and punched him playfully on the shoulder.

"Hey, don't worry about it. It has been a real roller coaster. We just need to get back to having some fun like we did tonight, David."

"Yes indeed," Andrews responded warmly. "And I promise you one thing: I am going to try to be a better friend. You know that Brooke has accused me of using you—and it is true to some extent. Unfortunately, it comes with the territory, I'm afraid—using and being used, as Brooke put it. Washington rules—not very nice, but that's the way they—well, me—that's the way it plays out. You're smarter than me, Cole. You learned that years ago."

Luis was waiting outside the restaurant as Palmer and Andrews got out of the car the following day. Palmer had not slept well; his bed felt like a cold and lonely place. He had called Liz, got no answer, and wondered if she had left without saying good-bye. He had finally decided that time was needed to patch things up—if they could be. Palmer was also concerned about Andrews. What was going on at home, he wondered? Brooke had cheered her husband on through every phase of his career; but now things had obviously turned sour. And he kept trying to put his finger on what made the relations between Andrews and Richard Snyder so strained.

The manager escorted them to a private table away from the other patrons. During the small talk that accompanied lunch, Andrews was relieved to see that Vasquez and Palmer hit it off, exchanging tall tales about a few wild nights in some of the Thames Street dives in Newport. By the time coffee was served, all three men were sufficiently relaxed—and ready to get down to business.

Palmer got the ball rolling by turning to Andrews and saying, "David, I think Luis would appreciate your take on Operation SKYHAWK and perhaps some Washington feedback."

Fortunately, Andrews's assessment largely matched up with what Luis Vasquez had heard through his excellent contacts in the Mexican government.

"Please forgive me for interrupting but I think the operation had a much greater disruptive impact on the cartel than you are taking credit for David," Vasquez said. "I absolutely agree with the follow-up measures you are recommending to our government."

"Thank you. Your input is exactly what we need, Luis. In fact, we hope you will play a significant role in implementing the necessary measures."

Andrews first emphasized President Washburn's unwavering support for President Posadas, his successor, Carlos Alvarez, and others who were trying to pull Mexico back from the edge of abyss.

"The president is also going to discuss an additional financial aid package during his visit." Andrews knew that would get Vasquez's attention. "Let me add that your valuable input and insights went a long way in making the financial package a reality." David again paused a few seconds to see if there was any reaction. Other than a quick nod of acknowledgment, Vasquez made no response.

Andrews had lathered on the soft soap; now it was time to shave—with a carefully honed straightedge razor. "President Washburn also asked that I personally convey a request from him."

Vasquez sat up straight in his chair and looked at Andrews warily. "What do you ask of me?"

"The president asks that you accept a position in the ruling party's cabinet."

Vasquez took a sip of coffee and set his cup down with a muted click on the saucer.

"I am encouraged by what your president is doing and encouraged that it appears he will win a second term. I am also most flattered by his confidence. I had a good idea that this is what you were leading up to. Carlos Alverez called me last night and sounded me out about taking a position on the cabinet. My answer—that I could probably do more by remaining outside of politics—still stands."

No one spoke for a few moments. Palmer figured it was

his turn, although he and Andrews had not jointly agreed on any strategy to persuade Vasquez.

"I know this may sound trivial, Luis, but sometimes things happen that you cannot control. Look what happened to me? I could have told my old shipmate no when he asked me to come to Washington and then go to work for him in Mexico City. But I would have always wondered if I could have made a difference. You can't control what happens . . . And I wouldn't have met Liz and fallen in love with her." Palmer mentally kicked himself for letting the last admission slip out. Vasquez should not be burdened with details about his personal life.

Vasquez smiled warmly and exclaimed, "What? Are you saying that you and Liz are getting married, Cole?"

"And you never told me anything," Andrews protested, pretending to be surprised.

"Oh, shit. Now I've really opened my big mouth," Palmer muttered. "And put my foot in it—as usual. Luis, it's kind of complicated and I'm not ready to discuss it just now. Sorry."

"You can count on us," Andrews said, winking at Vasquez so Palmer could see it. "We'll keep your secret— we won't tell Liz that you have fallen for her."

They all laughed; the tension that had arisen when Vasquez turned them down drained away.

"Now that Cole has put the real important news on the table, I should try again to clarify my position," Vasquez said earnestly. "I think your president has it right—this is our chance to change things. I certainly want to do what I can—as a citizen. People do not like to hear it but we could end up in the same situation as Colombia: a situation where the drug cartel has made deep inroads into every aspect of government. We were close to it after what we experienced with the bombings."

"I agree," Andrews said. "And the implications are just as serious for the United States. That is why it will take our joint best efforts working together to make the right course changes."

"Please don't take offense, David, but I need to ask the question. Can we count on Washington to stay the course with Mexico if we make the necessary changes?"

"The question needs to be asked, Luis. I think I know where you are coming from. Yes, and President Washburn is sincere. His second-term hopes are on the line with Mexico. I don't know any better way to demonstrate his personal commitment."

Again, Vasquez failed to respond and Palmer decided to take another shot.

"One last word and then I'll be quiet. I remember that you once told me in Newport that Edmund Burke had warned all that is required for the triumph of evil is for good men to do nothing. Your affiliation with President Posadas and Carlos Alvarez might not be the decisive factor that Washburn—and Alverez—think it could be. They both think you have the guts to do what is required to straighten out the shambles in the judiciary system down here. All any of us can do is give our best shot when called upon. Mexico is calling you, Luis."

The three men fell silent while Vasquez framed a response.

"Let me say that I will seriously discuss the proposal with my family. How could I say anything less when you both believe so strongly in my country? And please know that I am very touched and honored to have such friends—friends who have so much confidence in my abilities—although I fear you overestimate them."

Luis signaled the waiter to bring the check. Then he raised his nearly empty wineglass to make a toast: "God bless Cole Palmer, Liz Cramer—and God protect Mexico!"

On their way back to the embassy, the driver passed a note to Palmer. It was a message from Willie Graham. "Please come to the comm center as soon as possible."

When they arrived, Graham and Liz were waiting for them.

Palmer breathed a sigh of relief when he saw Liz. "What's up, Willie?"

"The FBI lab sent out two experts to analyze the repository bomb. They reported a positive match with the composite of the other bombs."

Palmer shivered; he could not help thinking of Luis Vasquez final words: "God protect Mexico." Well, God had certainly been watching out for Cole Palmer that day inside the mountain.

CHAPTER 46

Mexico City

The following day was a scheduling nightmare. Andrews had accepted an invitation from Vasquez to play an early game of tennis at his club. Palmer sat and watched as Andrews kept up a full head of steam on the tricky grass court and split four sets with Vasquez. Neither Palmer nor Andrews had found an appropriate moment to see if Vasquez had changed his mind about the cabinet position—and he did not bring it up.

Palmer and Andrews hurried back to the embassy to meet with Ambassador Reimann. Halligan's report was completed a day later than he had planned, so Andrews, Liz Cramer, and Palmer sat in on the briefing. After Halligan left, Andrews devoted considerable time and effort to smoothing Reimann's ruffled feathers; he was still angry about his not being fully informed on the situation in the mountain. Andrews gave him a detailed brief on the president's tentative schedule and then, in a deft piece of PR, suggested that the ambassador have a private lunch with the president—and the secretary of state if he accompanied Washburn—at the residency, after the meetings with Posadas were concluded.

After wolfing down a club sandwich and a glass of milk, Andrews spent the rest of the afternoon in the ops center, talking over a secure line with his deputy and other members of the NSC staff. Shortly before 5:00, a call came through from Richard Snyder.

"How's the president's schedule coming, sir?" Andrews asked.

"It's pretty firm. Thanks for letting us know what the Mexican government would like on the agenda. Unfortunately, we won't be able to do all the things they want. I'll forward what we have as suggestions for the tentative schedule in the next hour."

"Is the president still planning to be in and out the same day?"

"That's the schedule. The head of the Secret Service is very pleased about that. There is simply not enough time to do more than nail down a security cover at the airport and acceptable traffic control, fly the cars for the motorcade down from Washington, and then arrange en route protection. It also takes a full day for them to check Air Force One at Andrews, get the plane fully serviced and catered. You know the drill. It is one big headache for all concerned."

Andrews asked if the secretary planned to accompany the president but that decision, he was told, had not been made as yet. He was, however, in full agreement with the idea of a private lunch with the ambassador. And then he added a new wrinkle.

"I'm sorry that Vasquez has not relented on the cabinet job. What do you think about inviting him to come to the residence for coffee after the ambassador's lunch? That would give the president a chance to lean on Vasquez—in a friendly way, of course. The president has indicated that he won't take no for an answer. I am glad you are there to keep things on track. Let's get this done!"

"Great. I'll get with Luis and the ambassador and see what I can do."

Andrews had been quite apprehensive when the call came through. Snyder had been cordial and reassuring, however. Andrews knew that if Snyder ever got wind of his ill-advised approach to Navarro—the consequences were too awful to bear thinking about.

Trying to put that worry at the back of his mind, he left a message for Palmer suggesting that they meet at his hotel for dinner at eight.

When Palmer dropped by the ops center, he called upstairs to tell Andrews that dinner at eight would be fine. Before he left, Willie Graham waylaid him at the door.

"Did you mention anything about the threat warning to the national security adviser?"

"I'm going to, Willie. I just haven't had the right opportunity."

"I don't like it, Cole. The more I think about it, you should get out of town."

"I'll keep my guard up," Palmer assured him as he headed for his office to check for calls. It was almost 7:10 when he headed out after exchanging a few words about liberty in Mexico City with the marine guards. He needed to make contact with Liz and find out what her plans were.

It was dark when Palmer started the short walk to his hotel. It was one of those bleak, unseasonably cold nights with intermittent rain; Palmer sneezed and turned up the collar on his raincoat. The evening traffic was thinning out and the streets around the embassy were unusually quiet. He was thinking about what to say to Liz when he called her and whether or not to ask her to join Andrews and him for dinner. He was so deeply immersed in his thoughts that he paid no attention to the black sedan idling off one of the roundabout spokes separating the embassy from the Maria Isabel. When his peripheral vision registered the first glimpse of the shadow bearing down on him, his shock lasted barely a second before he hurled himself toward the safety of the curb. His reaction was not quick enough. The speeding car swerved onto the curb and hit Palmer with a glancing blow. He felt the impact on his right side and the pain exploded in his brain as he forced himself to crawl away from the curb and toward the bright lights of the main entrance to the embassy.

Corporal Bob Hahn was just beginning his scheduled patrol of the perimeter of the embassy grounds. He had noticed Palmer leaving and was about to turn the corner and head to the rear of the building when screech of the car's tires, followed by the resounding *thump* of it bumping over the curb prompted him to turn around. He could not see what happened but instinctively knew that Palmer was somehow involved. He drew his Colt .45 and pushed the alarm on his handheld radio transmitter before running toward where the car had stopped. The sedan had screeched to a halt on the wet pavement some forty to fifty yards from where it jumped the curb. Hahn observed two men, one more heavily built than the other dressed in dark coveralls, jump out holding what appeared to be light-weight machine guns. They were running toward Palmer, who was desperately trying to crawl away.

Palmer heard the car stop; whoever they were, they would be back to finish the job. He blinked his eyes several times and tried to get a clearer picture. He knew that he had to find cover. It took everything he had to drag himself across the curb before dropping on the pavement. He needed to keep moving but the problem was that he could not command his body to do what he wanted.

The rain was now coming down in sheets and the two men covered some thirty feet before they turned and saw

Hahn running toward them. They were surprised and spun around to see if there were others. The pause translated into a fatal mistake of freezing in place.

"Okay . . . I need a good shot because there isn't going to be a second chance," Hahn muttered to himself. He dropped in firing position and emptied his clip before the two men could raise their weapons. Both fell backward on the wet pavement. Hahn slapped a new clip in his automatic and resumed running where the two gunmen went down. It had been a brilliant job of shooting; a .45 was not a terribly accurate weapon at any sort of longer range, but the stopping power of its heavy round was formidable. When he rolled them over with his boot, the wounds to the head of one and the chest of the other confirmed that they would not be bothering anyone ever again.

Unfortunately for the gunmen, Corporal Hahn had been a finalist in the Armed Services pistol competition for the past three years. As a youth in Ogallala, Nebraska, he learned to hit jackrabbits in midair with his .22 caliber pistol as they sprang off their long hind legs in the cornfields of his parent's farm.

Hahn scrambled over and knelt alongside Cole. Three additional marines from the duty security force came running toward them with automatic weapons at the ready. Cole was barely conscious and cursed himself for not being more vigilant. The last thing he remembered was waking up in what he was informed was the emergency room of Mexico City's Hospital del Guadalupe. What a wild coincidence he thought before lapsing into unconsciousness.

When Corporal Hahn first sounded the alarm, the ops center watch captain called and alerted the marine security force. Willie Graham was still in the ops center and monitored the communications from Hahn while directing backup actions. He figured that the marines would alert Andrews who was supposed to be in the ambassador's guest cottage. When Andrews called at 7:30, Graham reported that the situation was under control and Palmer was en route to the hospital. Graham was surprised by the intensity of Andrews's concern; he knew the two men were old friends, but until now he had not fully appreciated how close these two very different men were.

By 8:00, the security director in the administrative office had put the embassy on full alert. The marine barracks emptied out as every man in the detachment rushed to his assigned position. Their gunny had put them through the drill so often that they could have done it in their sleep.

Meanwhile Graham followed his own checklist. The ambassador was notified at the residence; Halligan was reached at home, only three blocks from the embassy. Graham did not know what to do about Liz Cramer. He could not locate her either at home or in her office. She wasn't answering her phone and her message service had been discontinued. But Halligan exercised his spook skills and tracked her down at a dinner party being hosted by Mexico's Trade and Economics minister.

When she took the call from Halligan, she had to hold on to the table on which the phone rested. Her host, Guillermo Lopez Calderon, left the dining room and ran out into the hall of his residence when he heard Liz scream.

"Are you all right? Is there anything that I can do?" He asked anxiously.

"Yes—please. Please get someone to take me to the Hospital del Guadalupe. We had . . . an incident at the embassy." Despite the feelings of panic and desperation churning inside her, she had the presence that came from her years of work with the agency. How the attack on Palmer would be handled involved many complicated factors. Her responsibility was to keep the incident under wraps until the ambassador and Halligan figured out how to handle people from the media and others.

"Guillermo, I'm going to leave my car here. I don't know the way to the hospital very well." This was a lie, but necessary under the circumstances. She knew she was in no condition to drive in any case.

Calderon reached out and steadied her.

"My son José is upstairs. He will drive you, Liz.

When Palmer opened his eyes at 4:00 in the morning, the first thing he saw was Liz sitting next to his bed with her hand on his. He smiled and she started crying.

"Hey, I'm okay, honey." Palmer squeezed her hand.

"I promised myself that I wasn't going to cry and now look at me."

"You look awful darn good to me, darling."

"When can I stop telling you that you're a lucky guy?"

"I know. I owe my marine buddies from what I remember."

"Well, you'll have plenty of time to thank them."

"Umm . . . does that mean you're not checking me out? I'd like to get out of here."

"You're not going anywhere. The doctors want you to remain quiet for a few days to check out the bump on your head and allow the swelling to go down on the right side before they take more X-rays."

Palmer winced as he tried to rise up to protest. He did not try again. His body ached from the impact with the car and his head throbbed from what the doctor described as a mild concussion.

"How long have you been here, Liz?"

"Most of the night as you can probably see from the way I look." Liz's face was pale with no makeup and her eyelids puffy from the lack of sleep. "Ted Halligan and Willie just left. They said they would be back before lunch. God, I've never seen Halligan so angry. He's gone on the warpath; I heard him giving his Mexican liaison sheer hell on the phone."

They went over the details of the last twelve hours and

Liz was pleased that Palmer remembered most of what happened. One of the attending doctors had warned her that there might be a transient short-term memory deficit, whatever that was. Palmer was still hazy about what happened immediately after the car had hit him.

"Well from what you tell me, the fearless Corporal Hahn came down that street like John Wayne with guns blazing."

"That is exactly what people are saying. You may not be aware of it, but the marine detachment consider you one of their own, which is about the best compliment you can get."

When David Andrews, Ted Halligan, and Willie Graham arrived at a little after eleven, Palmer talked Liz into going home and getting some rest. He gave her a weak grin and assured her that he was not going anywhere in the near future.

Willy Graham could see that Liz was on the ragged edge of total exhaustion, emotional and physical.

"Listen, Cole, I'm going to walk Liz out to the main entrance. There's a car and one of the guys from the embassy security waiting for her there. We want her to bed down at the embassy. Ambassador Reimann had ordered all personnel to either stay in the embassy or remain at home. The Federales, as well as the Mexico City police, finally got their ass in gear and have posted guards at as many of the homes of embassy staff as possible."

Liz Cramer was aching to get home and reassure herself with the comfort of familiar surroundings. A cot in the embassy was not what she had in mind. She started to protest but Halligan cut her off.

"Liz, please do what we ask. The ambassador wants you to stay under guard—not at the embassy but at the residence. Both of us think . . . well, you are working directly with Cole and we have to assume the bad guys know that. We are assuming you are a target until we determine otherwise."

After Liz left, Halligan questioned Palmer carefully, trying to get as much information as possible about the attempted assassination. Unfortunately, there was little that Palmer could add to what Halligan already knew.

During the course of Palmer's debriefing, he received calls from Ambassador Reimann and the manager of his hotel, who asked if Palmer wanted anything sent over from the hotel. After that Halligan called in one of the nurses and told her that no more calls should be put through. As the nurse left the room, Palmer saw two grim-faced men standing by the door. He vaguely recognized them from the embassy. One of them had his coat unbuttoned. Palmer could see that he was wearing a holstered automatic pistol.

"Now that Liz is gone, what do we know about the guys who ran me down?"

Before anyone could answer, the phone rang again and David Andrews grabbed it.

"Damn it," he growled, "we said no more calls."

He paused and then blushed. "My apologies, sir."

"I think you want to take this call, Cole."

It was President Washburn on the line. After inquiring into Palmer's condition, he took the opportunity to thank him for the job he did at Promontorio Mountain. He told Cole that he was very disturbed about the attack but that he was not going to change his plans to come to Mexico City.

"We are at war with these people," Washburn said angrily. "I guess you are a casualty, like Pete Swanson. But we are going to make damn sure that there aren't more. I have no doubt that those bastards in the cartel are responsible for the attempt on your life. Well, if they reach out to strike one American citizen, they are striking at our country as well. Something they will dearly regret."

Washburn ended the call by saying that he looked forward to meeting him when he came to Mexico City. "I hope you are out of the hospital when I get down there. I've always agreed with George Orwell—a hospital is a depressing cross between a third-class hotel and a jail. I hate the damn places. Get well, Mr. Palmer. We need you."

Palmer thanked the president for calling and said he would look forward to the visit. He managed to chuckle when he said, "Mr. President, I fully agree with you about hospitals. If they keep me here too long, I'll tell them I have a presidential pardon and go home!"

He handed the phone back to Andrews. Although his head was aching, he managed to smile.

"Damn! That's something, having the president call you. Too bad Liz wasn't here."

Andrews nodded. "By the way, the president made the call all on his own, Cole. Getting back to your question, we know that you were a target and that it was a professional hit. We don't know much about the two characters who came after you. Willy is tracking what his counterparts have found out. Incidentally, not telling anyone about the warning Willie passed on was not a good idea."

Palmer looked over at Graham, who simply shrugged his shoulders.

"I know. I kept putting it off for various reasons. I hope Liz doesn't know."

"What about me? She is going to want to nail my hide to the wall. In any case, you are one lucky guy that Hahn blew those sons of bitches away."

"What can I say, David, other than you are right—of course?"

Palmer suddenly noticed how haggard Andrews looked. The usual cool, composed, and impeccably dressed national security adviser looked like a wreck; his suit was rumpled and he had cut himself shaving.

"Well, we should know something more pretty soon. In the interim, we are going to keep a close watch on Liz so don't worry about that."

"Around the clock," Willie Graham added.

At that moment, Luis Vasquez walked into the room.

"*Amigo*, you tourists should be more careful about wandering around Mexico City in the dark." Luis made an effort to smile, but he was clearly distressed.

"I am ashamed for my country—and horrified about what happened to you. You were right. I can't stand by any longer. David and I are going to step out for a few moments to discuss things. If I join the team there will be one condition," he said, turning to look at Andrews.

"Anything you ask," Andrews responded.

"Liz called me and told me what had happened. She wants the same thing I do. Get Cole out of this—get him out of Mexico."

CHAPTER 47

Mexico City

Andrews followed Vasquez to a deserted doctor's off-duty lounge. Both men would have been grimly amused to know that this was the place where the infatuated Julio had fallen into Navarro's honey-trap.

"I have a couple of concerns about agreeing to serve under Posadas," Vasquez told him. "First, there is a question of timing and how the announcement is handled. I warn you—it will not go down well with some of the elders in the party. Secondly, I need know how Victor Hidalgo fits into your plans."

Andrews was caught off guard; he didn't want to discuss the Hidalgo matter, so he tried to steer the conversation away from it. "What do you mean by the timing question?"

"Well, what I mean is that my appointment to the cabinet might be too late to make a difference. And any value I had as an independent voice would be thrown away."

"Um, well, I follow you, Luis, but I think it is worth the

350

risk. And I'm no good at forecasting what might happen in the future. Hell, I'm not even sure what the weather is going to be like tomorrow. And what is this about Hidalgo?"

"You know it is strange how things seem to come around. Victor Hidalgo has become a serious potential presidential contender following the linkage of the bombings to the drug cartel and their support of the PRD. In fact, today's editorial in the afternoon *Mediodia* states that the PRD is finished. Now, in a perverse turn of things, Hidalgo might be the one who determines whether the ruling party remains in power."

Andrews, trying to figure out what Vasquez was getting at, parried. "How do you arrive at that conclusion?"

"Before I left for the hospital this afternoon, I had a meeting with Ramiro Chemor—Hidalgo's campaign chairman and closest friend—and two of the leading constitutional lawyers who have been advising Hidalgo about how to get around the prohibition against his having another term in office."

Vasquez saw how surprised Andrews was; he obviously did not know about his ties to Hidalgo's people. And Andrews was recalling what Palmer had said about the worrisome links between Vasquez, Chemor, and the mysteriously missing Ortega.

"The meeting was quite enlightening. By the way, back when Hidalgo was in office, Chemor urged me to accept a position in the government."

"Did you seriously consider it?"

"Yes, I did. At that time, we all believed in Victor Hidalgo and his brand of strong leadership. You know . . . standing up to the United States and the people at the IMF. He was clearly moving Mexico in the right direction, although in hindsight perhaps a bit too fast. Anyway, I declined because I was needed in the family business at the time."

"So where is this taking us?"

"Well, Chemor—and others—believe that Hidalgo became a victim of his success so to speak when he threatened to nationalize certain U.S. and other foreign interests in Mexico. Hidalgo sincerely believed that Mexico had to evolve on its own. It was not what certain elements in Washington and in some of America's largest corporations wanted to hear but Hidalgo realized that Mexico would never emerge as a first-world nation unless it could stand on its own two feet. Which meant fundamental social change and rapid economic development."

"Are you implying that there was some kind of conspiracy to get rid of Hidalgo?" Andrews suddenly experienced a flash of paranoia; was Vasquez trying to lead him into a trap? Did Vasquez know about his efforts to undermine Victor Hidalgo and force him into exile? The president was arriving in two days and he needed to know where Vasquez stood.

Luis leaned forward and stared at Andrews before responding. His expression gave nothing away. "I'm not sure we will ever know that for sure, David. According to Chemor, there was never any doubt in Hidalgo's mind that the White House was behind his undoing. It was a cleverly orchestrated campaign. Very clever. Very subtle. Very effective."

"I am not sure that I agree with that Luis, but I understand what you are saying."

Vasquez leaned against the wall and crossed his arms.

"Hidalgo has to share some blame of course, David. However, regardless of the criminal involvement of his brother and certain administration officials, there is no credible evidence that Hidalgo was involved with the drug cartel or participated directly in anything illegal. Yes, he screwed up—perhaps he was too much of a visionary, one who failed to pay proper attention to what some members of his administration were up to while he worked day and night to move Mexico away from the heavy burden of its past. He has paid a very heavy price, not the least of which was the tragic death of his wife, because he struggled to overcome the many wounds inflicted on our country by its tangled history, a bitter history that stretches back to the *conquistadors*. But you Americans aren't very interested in all that, are you? You're mainly interested in our national resources, our cheap labor, what we can do for you. *Es verdad, senor Andrews?*"

Andrews fought the temptation to fire back. He wasn't sure what Luis was trying to do. He cleared his throat. "So why does he want to upset the country by overturning its constitution—by seeking the presidency?"

"Chemor told me that Hidalgo's decision to run was the only way he could return to Mexico and clear his name."

Andrews nodded but did not speak.

"I hope you understand," Vasquez paused to gauge his reaction. "We need to be very direct and open if we are going to accomplish anything." Vasquez had tried to get Andrews to open up, even to the point of antagonizing him.

"I couldn't agree more but I'm not sure where you're leading me, Luis."

"Okay, let me get back to where I was. Following his wife's death, Hidalgo changed from a proud and vigorous president in his early fifties to someone who was obsessed with the betrayal by a weak Jorge Posadas—and those who manipulated Posadas. Hidalgo made two great mistakes: he anointed Posadas as his successor. But those on the inside report that the two never were that close. In fact, one of my associates blames Posadas for most of the allegations against Hidalgo. The second mistake: Posadas was given the responsibility to oversee the daily business of the administration—something like the White House chief of staff—while Hidalgo was working the outside to persuade foreign investors to do business in Mexico."

"Then why did he endorse him as the ruling party's candidate?"

"Well, I can only imagine that Hidalgo figured he could control him and continue to push his initiatives from the traditional party leadership position of a former president. But the insiders underestimated Hidalgo's wide popular support and political skills. He has scared the hell out of his old guard in the ruling party. They had to destroy him. And they had plenty of help from *El Norte*."

David Andrews was now sure that Vasquez knew something, perhaps a great deal, about his role in "Maximilian"—the ironic code name assigned to the operation that toppled Victor Hidalgo. He tried to ignore a growing feeling that he was badly outmatched, that Vasquez was playing him like a fish hooked on a line.

"Getting back to your lunch with Chemor, what did the constitutional lawyers have to say?"

"They said the same thing everyone else has said—short of a revolution it can't be done. And a revolution is hardly a remote possibility, given the state of affairs here."

"What are you saying, Luis? Are we all supposed to stand around and watch it happen?"

"Well, most of my fellow countrymen do not understand what is happening and they are scared. Many still remember the terrible revolution of the 1930s. Far more remember what happened to the economy and our political institutions in the 1980s. They are watching to see what Hidalgo will do."

Finally, Andrews began to think he understood. Vasquez was trying to keep Hidalgo from leading the country into revolution.

"Do you think Washington really understands the implications—the consequences of what was done in the past, the storm that is about to break now?"

"Perhaps more than you think, Luis. What do you think we have been doing the past six years propping up the ruling party . . . not only economic support—the president's credibility is on the line, damn it! Let me make that absolutely clear."

He forced himself to control his voice. "The U.S. government will not support any leftist drug-controlled party or Victor Hidalgo, for that matter. I think you know that I was involved in the White House–Hidalgo conflict—and perhaps we did not handle it as well as we could have. Nevertheless, at the time, it was impossible to do business with him as president for a number of reasons."

Vasquez smiled bitterly and in a mocking tone said, "Oh yes, I am sure all of you had your reasons. But that was then—that was another chapter in this country's painful history. Now the important thing is that we both have the same objective—and that we stop playing games. This is the only reason I agreed to meet with you. I needed to find out where you stood and I think we have reached that point."

Vasquez jammed his hands in the pockets of his pants and looked Andrews in the eye. "Your secretary of state has arranged a meeting for us with Victor Hidalgo in the morning. The meeting was not agreed on until about three hours ago. The only reason I know about it is from a call from Chemor a few minutes before we met. I am sure you have a call waiting from Washington."

"Are you saying that these negotiations have been under way for some time?" Andrews could not believe that he had been so blind. "And Snyder wants me there?"

"Yes. Hidalgo also knows that you will be there, David—and is fully aware of your involvement with the past administration."

"And he still wants to talk with me?"

"Well, let's say that he did not rule it out. You must understand the man. He is interested in saving Mexico. The message I got from Chemor encourages me. I could be wrong of course but I have to believe that Hidalgo will step aside if he clearly understands the threat to his country. I think that is why he risked calling your ambassador about the bombing."

Andrews was still reeling from the news that Snyder had set up the meeting and had apparently persuaded the president that the national security adviser represent the United States. He remembered Washburn walking out of the cabinet meeting and saying to Snyder that the time had come to discuss Hidalgo. Playing for time, he asked, "So where do you stand on the cabinet appointment?"

"I think that it is fairly obvious—I need to accept—and do so before I speak with Hidalgo."

Andrews nodded and extended his hand to Vasquez. "It's the right decision. Thank you for your candor. We make mistakes along the way—I hope they will not stop Hidalgo from doing the right thing. I have a new appreciation of the man."

"Thank you, David. I am happy to hear you say that."

Vasquez turned and started to leave the stuffy, airless room.

"Oh yes. The other condition. I told you—leave Cole Palmer out of this. He had paid enough of a price—like Hidalgo—for the games some people have been playing."

CHAPTER 48

Cuernavaca, Mexico

The meeting with the former president was in the stately Las Mananitas Hotel in Cuernavaca, an hour or so drive outside Mexico City. Victor Hidalgo and Ramiro Chemor were enjoying the warm morning sun on the wide terrace overlooking the lush gardens that scented the air with jasmine and hibiscus. When they saw Luis Vasquez, they stood and embraced him. Hidalgo greeted Andrews in English.

"Please do me the honor of sitting next to me, Señor Andrews. It seems we have much to discuss."

Then with a quick thrust of irony, he added, "Of course there were matters we should have discussed in the days when I was president of Mexico. But, there was a different president in Washington then. Yes, I think the situation is now more . . . ah . . . encouraging, is it not?"

"Indeed, señor Presidente," Andrews replied. "Perhaps this is the time to speak plainly about the problems of the present—and forget those of the past." He did his best to smile and appear relaxed as he sat down in the chair Hidalgo pointed to. But the strain of making polite conversation, much less negotiating, with a man he helped destroy politically made him acutely uncomfortable.

Aware of the discussion between Hidalgo and Andrews, Vasquez quickly took control by offering a graceful tribute to Victor Hidalgo, enumerating the programs and initiatives that had started to move forward during the former president's term.

"I am sure you know there are many, including myself, sir, who strongly believe you are needed to help guide Mexico in the years ahead."

Hidalgo inclined his head gracefully and smiled.

"I'm not sure what 'helping to guide' really means. But I think we are all aware that in the next few weeks our two countries could face a crisis, one from which our country would take many years to recover."

"Doesn't that mean that we have a responsibility to do what is necessary to help our country?" Vasquez said.

It had come to the crunch much sooner than anyone expected, Andrews thought. He watched Hidalgo intently.

Hidalgo took a sip of tea and then said quietly, "Of course. You must understand, Luis, that is exactly why I felt I must play a role in the elections." He had cagily avoided any suggestion that he was prepared to employ extra-constitutional means to regain power.

"I understand, Mr. President. But you and I both know that the country is waiting for some signal . . . some move by you to help lead Mexico out of this crisis and back to the democratic course you set during your term as president."

"What are you suggesting, Luis? What you say sounds a lot like my campaign platform. Why do I have the feeling that you mean something else?"

Luis Vasquez decided that only a blunt approach would put an end to this circling around the point.

"There is no easy way for me to say what I must, Mr. President, and I hope you do not take offense." Vasquez tried to keep his tone firm but avoid being openly confrontational. "What I mean is that for the country's sake, you need to step aside and not place yourself above the constitutional law. We honestly believe that this action is necessary, sir, to save Mexico."

Andrews found himself holding his breath, wondering how Hidalgo would respond to Vasquez's challenge.

Hidalgo raised his head defiantly and his eyes bored into Vasquez.

"I am sure you have given this careful thought, Luis. But you might be overestimating the impact that I have at this point. Yes, there was a time people bought into the reality of moving Mexico into a global economy and we could have accomplished it. I do not know if that time will ever come again in our lifetimes. I worry about it. That was the reason I started my Independent Party. The next president, whoever that might be, must lead the nation rather than just preside over it."

Hidalgo paused for a few seconds as if he was thinking deeply or collecting his thoughts. "Please forgive me for lecturing, Luis. You are one of the few in Mexico who understands what I am saying."

"Thank you, sir, and again I agree with you. But time is running out and the recent indiscriminate bombings, the economic collapse, the violence in the south and elsewhere have paralyzed the nation with fear. We are in the midst of a financial collapse worse than the one in 1983 and 1984, and we could have a political situation similar to the incredible mess in 1985 when the ruling party claimed it had won all of the governorships and a majority in the national Chamber of Deputies and then in 1986 all the chaos and accusations of fraud in the state elections. Your new party and the PRD could, between you, push the PRI out of power, but do you think either party could actually govern?"

Hidalgo suddenly slapped the table with the flat of his

hand, and angrily asked, "Then why do you want me to step aside? Forget the problems with the parties. Is the situation any worse than when we had the entrenched PRI with the PAN as well as the socialist and all the splinter parties trying to challenge it? Perhaps I can best provide that leadership as president if the people of Mexico want me?"

Oh God, Andrews thought, he's really going to do it. He sees himself as the man on the white horse, the savior of the nation.

But Vasquez pressed on relentlessly. "I think you already know that answer, sir. Your intention to seek the presidency threatens the legitimacy of the constitution—at a time of crisis when the people are showing less patience than ever with democratic reforms and established law, especially in the poor southern states. If the high court rules against you and refuses to sanction your candidacy—which under the law they must—the whole election process could blow up under our feet with the left-center PRD and the drug cartel the only real winners."

"Do you really believe that could happen, Luis? The attack on the cartel has cut off the head of the snake—and blocked the money that has been flowing to the PRD."

Vasquez nodded his head emphatically.

"Unfortunately, yes, I do. With all the fear in Mexico today, I am profoundly worried about the possibility of open revolution in the streets if the high court and government move against you. The people of Mexico are waiting to see what you are going to do."

Hidalgo suddenly stood up and pointed an admonishing finger at Vasquez.

"The people of Mexico were waiting for me to release them from economic and social stagnation—and the repeated challenges to our sovereignty by the U.S. and other nongovernment powers."

Andrews started to object but Hidalgo was not prepared to listen to anyone until he had made his point.

"Does the United States think the ruling party is capable of suddenly offering the kind of leadership that will take Mexico forward? Even the PRD shares some of my own thoughts about the ruling party's compromising Mexico's independence."

"Pardon me, Mr. President. May I say something?"

Andrews finally got Hidalgo's attention.

"The last thing in the world President Washburn wants is to trespass on your country's sovereignty and independence. He wants a strong and truly democratic Mexico to emerge from this difficult period. That's why he has done so much to help in the battle against the drug cartel. And it is the reason he wants to create the Free Trade Area of the Americas; it offers priceless opportunity to link Canada, the United States, and Mexico through shared values and economic prosperity."

Hidalgo sat down and forced himself to remain calm.

"There was a time when I would say that the White House had little credibility concerning such matters—but I truly believe your secretary of state has been working tirelessly . . . supporting and helping us establish a more democratic government. I admire him greatly."

Andrews now fully realized how artfully Richard Snyder had backed him into a corner. Either he would stop arguing for the administration to distance itself from Posadas—or, ironically, he would indirectly help Hidalgo. Snyder had not been a part of the "Maximilian" operation in the previous administration that forced Hidalgo out of power and into exile. He had not approved of the move then—and he seemed to have a role in mind for Hidalgo now. But what role? State had apparently concluded months ago that Hidalgo was the key. He alone had the power to tip the balance against the cartel-controlled opposition party from taking over Mexico. So, how did Snyder see the future of Victor Hidalgo?

Andrews realized that he had just lost in a zero-sum

game. For the first time in his life, he felt not only outmaneuvered but also guilty and foolish. He had not been coolly and objectively pursuing a Kissinger-like *realpolitik* strategy. He had become a victim of his own blind ambition to succeed Richard Snyder. And he had used others to further that ambition—his friend Cole Palmer for one. Worse of all, he had been desperate enough to deal with the devil himself in his pathetic attempt to buy off Navarro. Now he had no choice—he would be the one to implement Snyder's policy.

"Yes, you are quite right. Richard Snyder has never been less than a true friend to your country, the proponent of an equal and productive relationship with Mexico. Yes, we made mistakes in the past, grave mistakes. And I deeply regret them. Now Secretary Snyder has persuaded President Washburn to link the success of his own reelection campaign with the fate of your country. I don't know how he could demonstrate his sincerity any stronger."

Before Andrews had left the city with Vasquez, the secretary of state had called him about the meeting with Hidalgo. Richard Snyder instructed him to make the points he just discussed and whatever else he considered appropriate with the former president. For years, Snyder had worked to develop a shared and trusted relationship with Mexico that mirrored the U.S. relationship with Canada. Andrews now understood that this was all that Snyder wanted.

And, as Andrews soon discovered, there was a convergence between the intentions of Snyder and those of Hidalgo.

To those around the table, Hidalgo appeared detached. But a few moments after David Andrews finished, Hidalgo rose up from his chair indicating with his hand for the others to remain seated.

"I am honored that I can be with you and share your thoughts this morning." He possessed that undeniable magnetism that held each of them in silence. "You are right of course concerning what must be done," he said turning to Luis Vasquez. "What happens to our beloved country is the only important matter. It would be unconscionable for me—or any of us—not to act responsibly."

Hidalgo turned to David Andrews and offered his hand.

"When you return to Washington, tell Mr. Snyder that he is as a good poker player as I am. Perhaps I am a bit better at bluffing. It was widely believed that I wanted revenge by regaining power. But few—even those closest to me—knew that all I wanted was to make certain people think that is was my goal—an exile's revenge! Now what I wanted has finally come to pass: we will, together, put Mexico back on the right course. We will help President Posadas to do it. And whomever the Mexican people select to succeed him."

Hidalgo put his hand on Vasquez's arm.

"Of course I am willing to do what you ask, Luis. And I need to tell you that my dear friend, Ramiro, has been pushing me in the same direction." He looked over at Chemor. "In return Ramiro—and you also, Luis—I ask of you what you have asked of me. You must both do what you can to help the current administration—and be prepared to serve in the one that follows."

CHAPTER 49

Taos, New Mexico

José Chapa had survived by thinking ahead all of his life. So when SKYHAWK ripped into the cartel like a buzz saw and drove Navarro into hiding, Chapa was prepared. He had watched as Navarro became more and more powerful—and made more and more enemies. Chapa knew in his bones that sooner rather than later Navarro would become a victim of his success, and José Chapa was determined not to go down with him. Five years ago, after several scouting trips to various locations in the United States, he decided that he would make his disappearing place in the Taos, New Mexico, area. He had constructed a new identity—Juan Galindo, born in Amarillo, Texas— and bought a small stone house at the end of an unpaved, private road. He established a checking account with a local bank and quietly made two or three short visits each year to establish his residence. Nobody—he hoped—knew about his escape hatch. He had no family or network of friends to leave behind in Mexico. José Chapa traveled light and he traveled alone.

As part of his contingency planning, some years back, Chapa had hired a graduate student from the university in Mexico City to give him English lessons. He also took a correspondence course in accounting. He accumulated a small fortune that he invested conservatively in CDs in various banks and stocks bought through brokerage firms in Taos, Santa Fe, and Albuquerque.

He sat on the tiny side porch of his house drinking a glass of *pulque* and watching the warm wind gently rustle through the cottonwoods. He'd seen enough television; for four days CNN ran coverage almost around the clock, as did MSN—the video footage of SKYHAWK arrests was irresistible infotainment. He couldn't shake thinking about Juan Ortega.

Madre de Dios, he thought. How did the bastard get back to the house?

CHAPTER 50

Mexico City

When, three days ago, Chapa had killed Ortega, he slowly removed a pair of latex gloves while glancing at the television. The morning news coverage of last night's drug raids was unrelenting. He lit a cigarette and wondered if Navarro realized that it was the end—and possibly his death sentence.

Chapa crushed his half-finished cigarette in the kitchen sink and washed it down the drain before wrapping Ortega with the large black plastic bag of the type used by contractors to dispose of rubbish from building sites. Pulling the ghastly bundle by Ortega's plastic shrouded feet, he dragged the body through the kitchen and into the attached garage. He was not in any hurry and moving quickly only made for mistakes. It took all his strength to lift the body inside the rear of the van that he had backed into the garage. Chapa was breathing hard and he took some deep breaths as he opened the windows to let in as much air as possible. Poor Ortega would soon be getting ripe.

As Chapa returned to the living room, he noticed the opened briefcase on the end of the couch. Passports, driver licenses, social security cards, foreign currency, and other identification papers were neatly stacked and secured inside a leather folder along with some other papers. He paged through an address book that Ortega had filled with coded names and numbers. When Chapa recognized his own coded name and number, he figured that there might be something useful in the book and reminded himself to check it out later. There were two entries that were underlined and coded but with fewer letters and numbers—perhaps safe deposit information—or numbered offshore accounts? He thought about it for a few moments, and then threw the book inside the briefcase and closed it.

Chapa took another beer from the refrigerator and started a systematic search of every room. He stuffed anything that contained identifying material into another large plastic contractor's bag and threw it in the van.

It was now almost 4:00 and the early morning news repeated what he had seen earlier. Chapa had urged planning for a contingency like this one but Navarro and the others had brushed him off. He was just muscle; let the big brains worry about such details. They said that they had too many important people on the payroll for anyone to launch a surprise attack successfully.

"Look at them! Scrambling around trying to hide their faces and buy their way out with their stupid lawyers," Chapa growled.

He closed his eyes and tried to relax. It was too early to leave and invite unwanted attention. As he always did, he started retracing the steps he had taken since his call from Navarro. Everything was tracking except the question of how Ortega got to the house. Chapa searched the area for Ortega's car or some rental vehicle without success after he killed him.

"He must have taken a taxi to some point and then walked the rest of the way," Chapa muttered. Shit, what difference did it make? Still, it was a loose end and Chapa wanted every detail in place.

He would dump Ortega's body in a forgotten part of the old dump at Santa Catarina, one he had used on two other occasions. From there, he would drive to the border at Ciudad Juarez, abandon the van, which had been rented under a fictitious name, and cross over at El Paso using his Galindo identification.

Chapa left the safe house for the last time at 7:00 like so many other sleepy commuters. He stopped at a petrol station just outside the city to top off the van. When he was finished, he drove the van around to the side of the station where a pay phone was standing.

It was 7:35 A.M. when he reached Navarro at the emergency number.

"Yes."

Chapa was relieved when Navarro answered. He was worried that the authorities arrested him like so many of the others. But his hiding place apparently had been secure. Since Navarro was using a cell phone, Chapa couldn't tell where he was located. Just as well. He didn't want or need to know.

"The business arrangement has been finalized."

"Thank you, my friend. I know that it was a difficult transaction."

"It was business."

"And the other piece of business?"

"I have no report as yet. I had to use outside business contacts because I was not sure how much time it would take to locate our client."

"What do you make of the news?" Navarro obviously wanted to know if Chapa had received any information from the members of the cartel—the ones who had not yet been found and arrested.

"I am afraid it is not good. The network is down and I recommend that you consider alternative plans."

What Chapa recommended was not unexpected but still hit Navarro hard. He admired Chapa's ability to insulate himself from any emotions or twinges of conscience and simply do what was necessary.

"I know, you are right. Will I be able to reach you on the usual numbers?"

"No. They are no longer operative. I will contact you."

"Do you have the number for . . . Arcturus?"

Chapa had guessed that Navarro would make the decision to move to Rio de Janeiro and the code word Arcturus confirmed it. It was the only option left.

"Yes, I have the number and location. When will you be exercising the option?"

"Immediately, my friend . . . but I want you to know that I will be back." Chapa could hear Navarro breathing hard. "I'm not going to stand in front of those clowns and beg. They are making a big mistake and I'll see them in hell." Navarro blustered.

Chapa did not know what to do. He listened as Navarro swore to personally destroy the drug barons and strike back at the governments of Mexico and the United States.

"There are more suitcases for sale. This is not over—it is only the beginning!"

It is really sad, Chapa thought. I wonder who will get him first. Espinosa's guys probably. After all those years of sucking up and taking shit from Navarro, Espinosa really hated him. No matter where Navarro tried to hide, one of his enemies would find him. It was time to end this pointless conversation.

"I will stay in contact, *patron*," Chapa promised and hung up the phone. He knew that he would never be in contact with Navarro again—at least not on this side of heaven or hell.

CHAPTER 51

Mexico City

The view from the big office on the seventh floor of the somewhat charmless building that houses the Department of State is perhaps not as good as that from the Hill or the White House balcony, but, as Richard Snyder thought, staring out the window, on a clear day you can see America's foreign policy. David Andrews sat in an uncomfortable Windsor chair, one of many antiques that gave the higher floors of the building a Colonial Williamsburg ambience.

"The president was very pleased with the last Mexico visit, David. He appreciates all that you did to set the stage for a very successful meeting. I'm glad you got on so well with Hidalgo. Though I'm not surprised. Both of you are very pragmatic men."

Andrews shifted uneasily in his chair. For God's sake, Richard, he thought, stop rubbing Novocain on the blade. Just stick it in me, plunge it in to the hilt, and get it over with!

Snyder sat down, faced Andrews, picking up a carafe of water, and poured himself a glass of water.

"Time for my afternoon pill." He reached into the pocket of his suit coat, took out a beautiful snuffbox, popped open the lid, and selected a small blue capsule. He swallowed it and washed it down.

"Blood pressure," he explained. "A certain magazine article once described me as 'bloodless' but my doctor could tell the writer otherwise."

Snyder picked up an unlabeled manila folder and handed it to Andrews.

"As you already know, President Posadas has appointed Chemor to head up the vacant Ministry of the Interior. His predecessor had that helicopter accident in Chiapas. And Luis Vasquez will be cleaning out the somewhat dusty corridors of the Mexican judicial system. But I can now inform you that President Washburn will nominate Victor Hidalgo to the prestigious position of director general of the Free Trade Association of the Americas. Of course, we will need the Congress and the other countries to support this most important nomination. Here is a copy of the release. It's being distributed now so that it will hit the morning papers."

Andrews opened the folder and glanced at the release.

"Does this mean that Hidalgo—"

Snyder anticipated his question.

"If he steps aside and shifts his supporters to the ruling party, I think Carlos Alverez has a real chance. But it is a big 'if.'"

Andrews dropped the folder on the table.

"Hidalgo told me that he was a bit better at bluffing in a poker game. Well, sir, that may be so, but you sure as hell are pretty good at it. Tell me—you guessed that Hidalgo wouldn't go all the way."

Snyder smiled and slowly shook his head.

"No, David, it wasn't a guess. It was a careful and very worrisome calculation. My view of Hidalgo was always that he might be a pain in the ass for us, but his job was to do the best he could for his country. That meant—and I was pretty confident—that he would not, as you put it, 'go all the way.' He cared more about his country than he did about power. Yes, he was bitter about what this country did to him. But he would never have let that stand in the way of using his real power—the power of his conviction. I don't know much about poker. Never played it. But I do play chess. So does Victor Hidalgo. We were playing a blind game: I could not see his board; he couldn't see mine. I could only anticipate what move he would make in response to one of mine. And not know for sure if he actually had made the move."

Andrews could not keep the bitterness out of his voice.

"So are we talking about a draw—or what?"

Snyder took off his glasses and pinched the bridge of his nose before responding.

"We are talking about when the games have to stop, David. I'm sure you understand what I mean."

Andrews felt a wave of humiliation wash over him and started to get to his feet.

Snyder held his hand up and said gently, "David, we aren't quite finished yet. There's no guarantee of a happy ending. Not here. Not in Mexico City. But some time ago—when I took this gamble on Hidalgo—I told the president that, for personal reasons, I did not feel I would be able to serve in the second term of his administration. I took it upon myself to suggest that he consider you for this position. Now let me explain why I made the recommendation. I should start by saying that I always had a high estimate of your capabilities. But in recent months, I became convinced that you had learned, through painful personal experience, when the game stops—and real life begins."

CHAPTER 52

Greenwich, Connecticut

"Are you sure this is the right exit?" Liz asked.

Palmer reached into the inside breast pocket of his blazer and handed her a piece of paper on which he had jotted down the directions Andrews had given him.

"He said the next one after Arch Street. But double check."

They turned off the interstate onto the exit ramp. Palmer was driving cautiously. He had not been behind the wheel of a car for a few weeks. The injury to his hip made it difficult to sit but the physical therapist assured him that the daily exercises she had given him would assist the healing process and that the discomfort would gradually go away.

"So why do you think Brooke invited us to stay with her for a weekend?"

Liz did not answer his question immediately because she was trying to read his handwriting.

"Okay—turn right at the bottom of the ramp."

She looked at Palmer and smiled. "I think she and David

want us to be around and help ease some of the strain. It isn't a formal separation. My guess is that neither one of them want things to go any further. We are going to be sort of a buffer, I imagine. As far as I know, it is the first time they've been together since Brooke took over her parent's summer home."

Palmer had picked her up at Kennedy Airport in a rental car. It had taken her longer than she thought to wind up the sale of her house. Mexico's bureaucracy moved at a leisurely pace; the paperwork involved in conveyance of the title to the buyers had been unbelievable. But thanks to Alverez and the PRI getting their act together, the economy was stabilizing somewhat and she had been able to get a decent price.

"Turn right at the second light," she ordered.

Palmer winced as a stab of pain shot through his hip when he made the turn. He drew in a deep breath and tried to relax.

"You're going to like Bloomington, Cole. And being a 'faculty wife' isn't a bad thing. Of course, if you finish your thesis and get your doctorate then I think you are a shoo-in for that assistant professorship. Then it will be Dr. Cramer and Dr. Palmer."

Palmer swore under his breath as a blue Volvo station wagon cut him off. Then he glanced at Liz.

"There's not a lot of water out there in Indiana. Pretty far from the ocean," he said and grinned.

Liz Cramer smiled back at him fondly.

"Yes, indeed. I think it will be good for you to be land-locked for a while. Like the poem goes—if I remember it right, 'Home is the sailor from the sea/And the hunter home from the hill.' "

VICKI STIEFEL

THE DEAD STONE

It starts with a mysterious phone call, summoning homicide counselor Tally Whyte back to the hometown she thought she'd left far behind her. Almost as soon as she arrives, Tally hears that a young woman she knew as a child has been found ritualistically murdered and mutilated.

The deeper Tally probes into the bizarre murder, the more chilling it becomes. Each glimpse into the killer's dark mind only unnerves Tally more. Despite frustrating secrets and silences, Tally suspects she's getting close to the truth, but perhaps she's getting too close for her own good. As each new body is found, Tally has to wonder…will she be next?

VENGEANCE

BRIAN PINKERTON

How far would you go for justice? Rob and Beth are very much in love. He has just proposed to her, but she won't live to see the wedding. Instead, Beth is intentionally sideswiped by an angry driver and knocked off her bike—to her death. Rob witnesses the whole thing, but he can only stand by as the driver gets off with a slap on the wrist.

Rob is devastated. He becomes obsessed with making Beth's killer pay. Then, one day, a strange man approaches Rob. He offers Rob the justice he's been seeking. He tells Rob about "The Circle," a small group of people with one thing in common: They all want revenge for something. But Rob will learn only too late that there is a catch....